Praise for *The Light of Eidon*,
the first book of
LEGENDS OF THE GUARDIAN-KING

Karen Hancock builds a realistic world of nobles and barbarians, Romanesque arena games and a supernatural battle between good and evil. With Hancock's latest, inspiration fantasy continues to come into its own.
—*Romantic Times* TOP PICK (4½ stars)

The Light of Eidon is a worthy addition to my fantasy collection in every way. . . . By making religious pursuit one of the driving elements of the main character's life, she has made it possible to introduce serious discussion of religion within a perfectly logical progression of the story. I was kept as off-kilter as Abramm for much of the story, wondering what really was true and what was not. . . . Christian fantasy is back. I look forward to the next volume of LEGENDS OF THE GUARDIAN-KING with great expectations. Highly recommended.
—Tim Frankovich, *www.christianfictionreview.com*

In the tradition of J.R.R. Tolkien and C.S. Lewis, Karen Hancock has created an exciting allegorical fantasy. . . . Hancock's writing, often eerie and suspenseful, is rich in sights, smells and sounds. . . . The allegories for atonement and salvation are fresh and insightful. . . . *The Light of Eidon* is so well done it should attract new readers to the genre.
—*Christian Retailing* Spotlight Review

The Light of Eidon has the heart of J.R.R. Tolkien, the flare of Terry Brooks, the adventure of Tom Clancy, and the sense of destiny of the Star Wars saga. . . . *The Light of Eidon* speaks to anyone who has faced a seemingly hopeless situation, where God feels the universe away, and those who do evil seem to have all the control. Hancock has a fresh approach to the age-old question: "Where is God when evil prevails?"
—Randi Durham, *Teknofischzone* (*teknofisch.com*)

Books by Karen Hancock

Arena

LEGENDS OF THE GUARDIAN-KING
The Light of Eidon
The Shadow Within

LEGENDS OF THE GUARDIAN-KING

KAREN HANCOCK

THE
SHADOW
WITHIN

BETHANYHOUSE
MINNEAPOLIS, MINNESOTA

The Shadow Within
Copyright © 2004
Karen Hancock

Cover illustration by Bill Graff
Cover design by Lookout Design Group, Inc.

Published by Bethany House Publishers
11400 Hampshire Avenue South
Bloomington, Minnesota 55438
www.bethanyhouse.com

Bethany House Publishers is a Division of
Baker Book House Company, Grand Rapids, Michigan.

Printed in the United States of America

Library of Congress Cataloging-in-Publication Data

Hancock, Karen.
    The shadow within / by Karen Hancock.
        p.   cm. —(Legends of the guardian-king)
    ISBN 0-7642-2795-5 (pbk.)
    1. Kings and rulers—Fiction. 2. Sibling rivalry—Fiction. 3. Brothers—Fiction.
I. Title   II. Series: Hancock, Karen. Legends of the guardian-king.
    PS3608.A698S53   2004
    813'.6—dc22
                                                                    2004002024

KAREN HANCOCK graduated in 1975 from the University of Arizona with bachelor's degrees in biology and wildlife biology. Along with writing, she is a semi-professional watercolorist and has exhibited her work in a number of national juried shows. She and her family reside in Arizona.

For discussion and further information, Karen invites you to visit her Web site at *www.kmhancock.com*.

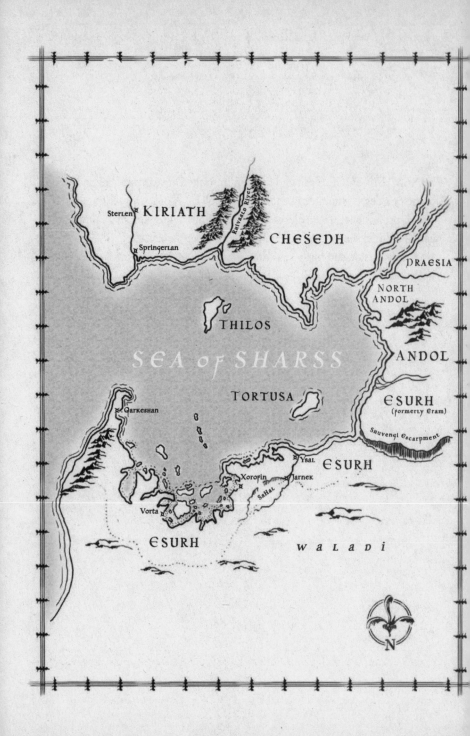

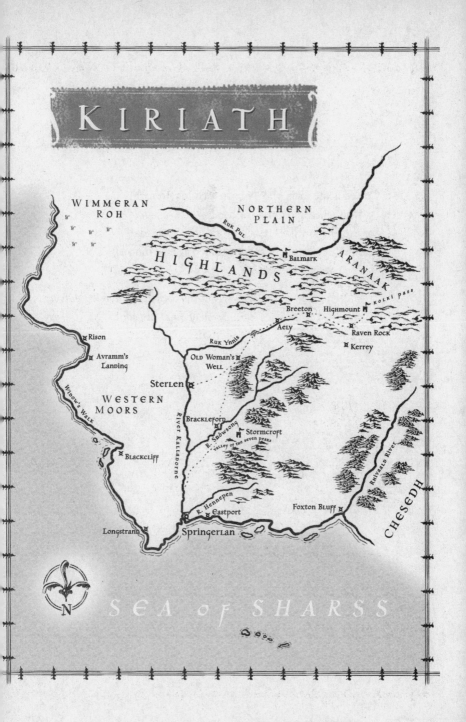

Cursed is the man who looks to man for strength,
    who relies upon his own hand.
For the Shadow lives in all; not one has escaped.
And in it, every man's hand is turned against himself,
    even against his own life.

—From the *Second Word of Revelation*
Scroll of Saint Elspeth

HOMECOMING

PART ONE

1

His senses keyed as tightly as if he'd just stepped back into an Esurhite arena, Abramm Kalladorne stood on *Wanderer*'s quarterdeck with his two liegemen, nervously scanning the leaden waters of Kalladorne Bay. As the white cliffs guarding the bay's mouth slid silently astern, he wondered if the other men's stomachs had just done the same little twist his own had. Probably.

It was one thing to boast of slaying sea monsters and sharing fabulous rewards in the warm, smoky haven of a Qarkeshan tavern, quite another to sail alone past a gaggle of crudely made warning buoys into the quiet, empty waters of what had once been the busiest harbor in Kiriath. Off the port gunwale, a broken mast listed in the spray-plumed rocks at the base of the western headland. With shredded canvas still fluttering from its yardarm, it stood in silent memorial to all the vessels lost to the monster since spring—six of them fully rigged merchantmen weighing over five hundred tons. Large, strong, stable ships.

Back in Qarkeshan's own busy international harbor, *Wanderer* had seemed large and strong herself. Crafted of oak and iron, she floated at just over four hundred ton, with three stout masts and a complement of square-rigged sails now bellying handsomely before the breeze. Plenty strong and safe she'd looked in Qarkeshan.

Suddenly she had grown small and frail and pitifully inadequate. Suddenly Abramm could not imagine how he had thought her anything but, how he had ever let himself get talked into this harebrained scheme. To think that he and his companions could sail into this bay, brazen as gulls, knowing nothing about their adversary, and strike it dead when all who'd come before them had failed, was not only arrogant but incredibly stupid. And even if he and his companions did not mean to use conventional weapons, it was still stupid. Especially considering that the weapon they *did* mean to use could get them all lynched for heresy.

Tendrils of hair, teased free of the warrior's knot on his neck, lashed annoyingly about his face as he glanced down at *Wanderer*'s waist and fore-deck, where every man had turned out, ready for action. Crewmen lined the gunwales, balanced on the bowsprit, and clung to the rigging. Weathered faces with keen eyes searched the gray swells for the telltale ripple, the rock-like hump briefly breaking the surface, the quick breaching grope of a fleshy tentacle, as fat around as one of *Wanderer*'s masts. . . .

They would use the four boats stowed between the two forward masts to engage the kraggin once it was spotted—two eight-man whale hunters and two twenty-man longboats. They also had harpoon guns, axes and spears aplenty, two extra masts, and a crew of one hundred fifty crazies—experi-enced, die-hard adventurers who relished the challenge of facing a creature no one else could slay. And of divvying up the not insubstantial reward money when it was over.

Assuming anyone remained alive to divvy . . .

This is insane, Abramm thought. *Dorsaddi bravado has pushed me into this, and nothing more. It's far too late in the day. At the least we should heel out and go around to Stillwater Cove for the night. Get our bearings. Learn something about this monster . . . where it's been seen, where it hasn't, how often it feeds, what its habits are. . . .*

But just as he was about to give the order to retreat, his liegeman spoke at his side. "It's shadowspawn, all right. Can you feel that aura? About as strong a warding as any I've ever encountered. Griiswurmlike, but not griis-wurm."

Abramm glanced at him, chagrined to realize that was exactly what it was. The all-too-familiar doubts and second thoughts might be his own, but the rising intensity of his anxiety and resistance to proceeding came from outside himself, part of the defensive aura generated by the monster they sought. Abramm's red-bearded, freckle-faced liegeman, oath-made as of last night, raised a brow in unspoken amusement. "Don't feel bad, my lord. I was about to suggest we turn back myself."

Trap Meridon had always read Abramm's thoughts with uncanny ease. It was one of the things that had made them such good partners in Esurh's gladiatorial games—and now made Meridon the invaluable retainer and liege-man he had become. Like Abramm, he had kept the Esurhite beard and warrior's knot, and the loose trousers, tunic, and ochre-hued overrobe of Dor-saddi custom. So had his brother Philip, Abramm's other liegeman, standing now on Trap's offside, squinting across the bay. Both, also like Abramm, wore the deep swarthiness of weeks at sea.

"It must be awfully big," Philip said quietly.

Abramm exchanged a glance with Trap and knew they were all thinking the same thing: Would the three of them alone be strong enough to do the job?

"Do you suppose it senses us?" Philip asked. He stood as tall as Trap now, though leaner and lankier. Strands of curly auburn hair blew across the sparse silken gold of his young beard as he frowned at the sea and gray sky.

"Most likely," his brother replied, bringing up the telescope to examine something off the starboard bow. "Which, unfortunately, may only drive it away."

The ship's captain—Abramm's old friend Kinlock—stepped from where he had been conferring with the helmsmen to join them by the railing. "We'll be taking her up the west side o' the main channel, sir," he said to Abramm with a bob of his head he evidently intended as a covert salute. "Unless you have objections. Wind's stiffer there, and the beast is said to prefer the deeper waters."

"I leave it to your discretion, Captain," Abramm said.

"Aye, Your—er, sir." He gave another little nodding salute, gestured an okay at the helm, and strode across the deck to disappear down the compan-ionway.

Of the crew, only Kinlock knew who Abramm really was, though all were intrigued by the contradictions in his person—a tall, bearded, blue-eyed blond in faded Dorsaddi robes and trousers, who wore his hair tied in the warrior's knot of Esurhite tradition and, for those alert enough to notice, bore a trio of tiny holes along the outer margin of his left ear, silent testimony of combat honor rings no longer worn. He was a northerner who spoke the Esurhites' Tahg as fluently as any native and came to them with a ship and a challenge and a promise of riches beyond imagining.

Ten thousand sovereigns and more if they killed the kraggin that had shut down Kalladorne Bay. The captain would get the largest share, of course, his mates after him, and on down the line, with even the lowest-ranking sailor standing to make himself a tidy profit.

Alone of them Abramm would take no cut.

He had come out of duty. These were *his* people this monster was killing, *his* people who were losing their livelihoods because of it. And where once he would have left it all in bitterness for his brother Gillard to mishandle— he who had wanted rulership so badly he was willing to kill and betray for it—now Abramm found his heart changed. Yes, Gillard might deserve the headaches and burdens of the crown he had snatched, but did the people he misruled?

"These disasters are entirely your fault, you know," Abramm's friend Shemm, king of the Dorsaddi, had told him bluntly back in Esurh. *"What do you expect but that a land and its people suffer when their rightful king has deserted them?"*

Because, of course, Abramm *was* their rightful king, and they both knew it. Even if Kiriath did not.

Thus, after two years of slavery to the Esurhites, and four more spent living among the Dorsaddi in their rugged canyonland fastness, the SaHal, Abramm had come home. Reluctantly, to be sure, for he still had no idea how to go about claiming this inheritance of his, least of all from a brother who'd as soon kill him as look at him. It could well ignite a civil war that would be the fish that sunk the ship for Kiriath. Then what good would his return be?

But, believing it was Eidon who'd sent him, that this was, in fact, the destiny Eidon had prepared for him, Abramm had to believe Eidon would make him a way. Slaying this kraggin might be the first step.

And if, instead, the beast slew him, well, then he wouldn't have to worry about the other. Right now that looked like a very real possibility, for if he had no idea how to go about claiming his inheritance, he had even less of a plan for how they were going to kill the beast, nothing beyond the vaguely shaped hope that it was indeed the shadowspawn legend made of it. If so, and they could provoke it to engage with them, they hoped to use Eidon's Light to slay it.

Unfortunately, Trap was the only one of them who had killed spawn larger than a dog and the only one of them who could throw any significant amount of Light. Philip had only mastered the thinnest threads, and those at close range, while Abramm still required direct contact to release the Light at all. Their only chance was for all three of them to get a spear into the beast, then let loose with the Light all at the same moment.

Just contemplating the logistics of arriving at that moment made Abramm's thoughts snarl and his head hurt. They'd had little choice but to take it one step at a time, the first being to get back to Kiriath and Kalladorne Bay. The second, now facing them, would be to draw the kraggin from its deep-channel lair, a task complicated by the fact that their very presence could well drive it deeper into hiding.

Abramm scowled at the gray tableau of sea and sky, doubt intensifying the ever-rising desire to turn back. Doggedly he held his tongue and continued to search, the hair dancing around his face and the breeze tugging at beard and robe.

"Huh," Trap grunted. "What do you make of that?" He pointed to a distant shape off the starboard bow, and Abramm brought up his own glass.

"Looks like a whaler," he said, squinting at the battered, poorly rigged two-master silhouetted against the lavender haze of the bay's distant end. A likely candidate for monster hunting, it stood at anchor, most of its sails reefed, with only a bit of jib set to keep it stable.

"Yes. But what's that to starboard of it?"

Abramm shifted the glass, his loose sleeves stuttering in the wind. The second vessel was harder to see. Long, low to the water, and white, it looked like—

"A barge?" *What the plague is a barge doing that far out in the bay?* He shifted his stance for more stability and squinted harder, perceiving now the tiny white manforms that encircled what appeared to be a burning, broken-off mast at its midst. Had the vessel already been attacked? No . . .

The chill that rippled up the backs of his arms had nothing to do with the cool of the breeze. "Khrell's Fire!" he muttered. "What incredibly bad timing."

"It *is* Guardians, then," said Trap.

"Guardians!" Philip cried. "What are *they* doing out here?" He snatched the spyglass from his brother to have his own look.

"Probably trying to drive the kraggin away with their Holy Flames," Abramm replied.

"But, my lord," the youth protested, "won't the Flames just draw it to them? I mean, if the beast really is spawn?"

"It might," Abramm agreed gloomily.

Philip missed entirely the significance of Abramm's tone. "Well, then we've got our bait right there!" He looked from Trap to Abramm, his enthusiasm fading into confusion. "Didn't you just say it wouldn't come up for us?"

"Aye," said Abramm. "But I can't see how a flock of Guardians as witnesses to what we do will bring anything but trouble."

Philip's expression turned grave. He glanced across the water toward the dark blot that was whaler and barge, and Abramm could see his mind working. Tales circulating in Qarkeshan—many told firsthand—had painted a grim picture of the religious persecutions going on in Kiriath at present. After—if—Abramm and his liegemen slew this monster, and if it was clear they'd used Terstan power to do it, he had hoped their fellow crewmen would be well enough disposed toward them not to make trouble. That would never happen with a pack of Guardians in their midst, shrilling hysterical condemnations at the merest hint of "evil Terstan magicks."

Still, Philip was right—this *was* a perfect opportunity to engage the kraggin.

By now Captain Kinlock had been alerted to the presence of barge and whaler and came to ask if Abramm wanted to pay them a visit. Shortly *Wanderer*'s bow was angling east of its former track. The ship rose and fell in long graceful swoops, her hull creaking and groaning around them as she made her way up the bay. Water slapped the hull as a small jib sail forward flapped a rapid staccato and the breeze played a high sweet song through the rigging. Out on the bay nothing moved save a distant trio of pelicans, skimming low over the waves near the western shore.

Anxiety corkscrewed in Abramm's belly, igniting a restlessness that made standing still an agony of suspense and self-discipline. Again and again, he was swept with the premonition of imminent disaster, followed by the nearly irresistible compulsion to call off the affair and run for port in Springerlan, the royal city now visible as a sprawling patchwork at the bay's end.

"It's getting right strong," Trap said quietly beside him.

"Right strong, indeed." Even the fading feyna scar that still marked his left wrist had begun to tingle.

They could see the shapes of whaler and barge with naked eye now, and in the gathering gloom of late afternoon could even pick out the crimson flame dancing on the Guardians' brazier. If the wind held, maybe—

"There!" one of the men in the rigging cried, pointing across the water. "Surface wake, moving fast. About ten degrees to port."

Other men echoed the sighting as Abramm snapped open the spyglass again and trained it left, off the port bow. Magnified waves against the dark backdrop of the distant shore filled the field of view. He was sweeping the scope back and forth, seeking the swell when someone else cried, "It's breached! Khrell's Fire! Look at the size of it!"

Abandoning the glass, Abramm scanned the waters with his bare eye, heart pounding in his throat.

"Ope—there it goes, down again, heading straight for the barge."

"What was it?" another man cried.

"Cursed big. Dark and rough, like it had barnacles on it."

"Whale, maybe?"

"Not with those tentacles pumping after it."

Kinlock was already bellowing for the flagman to signal warning to the whaler and barge, for the spears and harpoons to be broken out and the hunting boats readied for launch. Back on the barge, clear and sharp in the round field of Abramm's spyglass, no one seemed to have noticed anything, though a flurry of activity had erupted on the whaler.

"There it is! Still to port, making straight for the barge."

This time Abramm lowered the scope, climbed onto the bollard adjacent the portside railing, and saw it—a massive mound of water, rising and falling in powerful lunges across the bay's gray surface, heading, as the sailor had said, for the same destination as *Wanderer*.

"Merciful Laevion!" someone exclaimed from up in the mizzenmast rigging behind them. "Look at it *go!*"

It appeared to stand as high as *Wanderer*'s top deck, and encompassed as much volume. Once he'd marked it, Abramm found it easily with the glass, tracking it as it moved. Beneath the water's surface sheen, he picked out the dark bulk of the creature's body, laced with jagged, flickering lines of brilliant yellow-green and eye-searing blue. He scanned backward from it over the water's strangely curdled surface to the end of those flickering lines of light, estimating its length. By now his heart hammered at his breastbone and his stomach knotted with dread. The thing was *huge* and moving significantly faster than *Wanderer*.

Snapping his scope back to the leading edge of the mound, he tracked forward of it now, over a league of calm gray swells before he found the barge—much too close. Its white-robed figures still marched obliviously around their pan of flames, but by now the other men aboard, those clad in the blue tunics of royal armsmen, lined the railing, swords and spears a'ready.

"The whalers have launched their first smallboat," Trap said.

If Abramm's will could have powered her, *Wanderer* would have flown across the water. Guardians or not, they were his folk, and it *infuriated* him to see this thing bearing down upon them, to feel the evil at its core, the dark, destructive lust to own and utterly devour. . . .

Half a league from its target, the mound subsided, leaving a remnant of itself to roll on across the bay, losing amplitude until it vanished in the water's normal rise and fall. The Guardians continued to march and the men at the railings to watch as the hunting boat reached the midway point between barge and whaler. Its harpooneer stood now at the bow, searching the depths. Behind it, the whaler's second hunting boat dropped into the water and its crew scrambled down to man her.

Those aboard *Wanderer* held their breath and prayed for speed.

Abramm had the harpooneer in his spyglass when the man recoiled and brought his harpoon to bear on something just before his bow. Then he vanished in an eruption of water and foam. Abramm gave up the scope again for the naked eye, but the hunting boat was gone, lost in a frenzy of churning waves, foam, and writhing gray tentacles laced with blue lightning. One arched against the sky, mind-boggling in its length and breadth, and slapped down on the barge with a dreadful rending crack attended by a chorus of screams and shouts. The vessel's bow leaped skyward, then fell back and was swallowed by the turbulence.

The whaler, its masts gyrating wildly on the stormy seas, had heeled round in an attempt to close with the kraggin. Already it had fired one harpoon, and now it loosed a second as another dark tentacle reared out of the waves and coiled round the top of the whaler's mainmast. Rocking the ship like a child's toy, it yanked down, snapping the four-foot-wide timber like a twig, yardarms shattering, canvas and rigging ripping free.

More tentacles shot out of the churning water, sweeping men off the decks of both vessels. The second small hunting boat had long since vanished as another arm tore down the whaler's foremast with a crash. A horrible booming squeal followed close in its wake as the barge's ailing front half wrenched free of its stern and disappeared under the waves.

Abramm watched in helpless fury, gripping the gunwale with one hand, the spyglass with the other, desperate to close the gap and seeing it wouldn't happen in time. They would lose both ships, and the monster, as well, and he could do nothing to stop it.

Then, as swiftly as it had begun, the attack ceased. The tentacles released both barge and whaler, and the beast sank back into the depths, leaving a field of foam-flecked flotsam and dying waves for *Wanderer* to sail into, far too late. A cluster of keening Guardians clung to the barge's rapidly sinking end section while most of their unfortunate fellows thrashed—or floated limply— in the roiling waters around them. Kinlock ordered *Wanderer*'s longboats dispatched to pick up the survivors, and the hands leaped to obey. But once the two vessels had been dropped into the water, all activity stopped. To a man the crew stood frozen, looking down at the boats, at one another, at the ruined barge and dismasted whaler barely afloat amidst the flotsam of their floggings. Even Kinlock held silence.

Abramm could feel their fear, a thick, stifling mantle crawling across his flesh and squeezing the air from his lungs. These were tough, courageous men, used to incredible danger, but between the power of the kraggin's aura and the horror of what they'd just witnessed, they'd reached the end of their resources. He glanced at Trap. His liegeman saw the decision in his eyes, started to protest, but already Abramm was swinging round the companion-way turnpost and thumping down to the ship's waist.

If I've got it wrong, my Lord Eidon, he prayed grimly, *please head me off now.*

He reached the gunwale unimpeded, men stepping aside to allow him passage, one of them taking his overrobe as he shrugged out of it. Two rope ladders already dangled over the side above the still-empty longboats.

"Hand me down some of those spears," he called as he hitched a leg over the gunwale. "And a harpoon or two, as well."

"Ye can't row and spear at the same time, my lord," Kinlock protested.

"No, but then I probably won't have to." Abramm swung the other leg over to catch a foothold on the rope rungs. "And it's better than standing on deck with this flock of quivering *yelaki.*"

He started down the ladder. By the time he'd jumped into the boat and got his balance, Philip was halfway down the side after him, while Trap was commandeering the other vessel. Philip landed between the thwarts, Abramm steadying him as the boat lurched, and for a moment their eyes locked. Abramm had a flash of memory—the lantern-lit stern cabin last night, an impromptu liege-giving ceremony, this young man on one knee before him, reciting the ancient oath of fealty all Kiriathans gave to their king. Now here he was, ready to make good on that oath, maybe even to die doing it. And hardly more than a boy.

Nausea swirled in Abramm's gut, a sudden sickening realization that it was his own action and need that placed Philip in jeopardy. But then the youth grinned at him with the sense of immortality that belonged only to the young and said, "Eidon has made us a way, Sire!"

Abramm forced a smile back. "Indeed he has, Phil. Now let's do our best to make good on it."

Releasing the youth, he reached to snag the bundle of spears descending toward them, then saw that his parting words to the crew had borne the fruit he'd hoped: seven seamen now came scrambling down *Wanderer*'s hull to take up oars in the two boats. Thus they set out to round up the survivors, undermanned, underequipped, and praying fervently the kraggin did not return until they were done.

2

While Trap swept round to starboard, gathering up those who had been lost when the barge's front end went down, Abramm steered directly for its stern, pausing to fish out survivors on the way and putting those who were able to the oars. It was a gruesome journey paddling past floating bits of barge and whaler, of canvas and rope and oar, of bodies broken and bloodied and still. With twilight moving in, the wind had died away, and now the water gleamed like polished pewter, tendrils of mist coiling from its placid surface. A few tiny lights winked out of the gloom clotted now at the base of the headlands, while at the bay's end, Springerlan was a cascade of stars sprinkled along the shore's dark flank.

Abramm focused on guiding his boat through the wreckage. A snag, a fouling of the oars, even a collision would waste precious moments. The kraggin would return soon—he could sense it in the depths now, as he knew it could sense him—and the last thing he wanted was to fight it with these fanatical holy men at his shoulder.

Though the aura-producing shadowspawn typically avoided Terstans, they would fight if pressed to defend themselves or their kills. And the disabled whaler and barge could now reasonably be classed as kills. The kraggin had already taken a few prizes when it went down, drawing them one after the other toward the wide, beaklike mandibles at the midst of its tentacles, and chewing. . . .

Abramm grunted and shook the image from his head. Where had *that* come from?

Up close the barge was much larger than it appeared from afar. Ten

Guardians clung to its slowly sinking stern, most of them waist-deep in water. Together they held aloft a flattened bronze orb two feet in diameter—a traveling brazier for the Mataio's Holy Flames, which they'd managed to keep alive in all the chaos. Scanning the group as he guided the boat alongside, Abramm gave thanks when he recognized none. Though he knew himself to look a very different man from the youth who had sought Eidon in the Flames until six years ago, someone who'd known him well might see the truth regardless.

He secured the tiller and, with the nearside oarsmen, helped the first of the bedraggled Guardians—a withered horror of a man for whom this present disaster was obviously not his first—into the boat. The left side of his face and neck had been seared into a mask of waxy scar tissue, with no ear, no brow, no eye, and nothing but a slit for lips. Only a scattering of coarse gray hair sprouted from the puckered scalp, his waist-length pigtail drawn predominantly from the hair on the unscathed right side of his head. As Abramm helped him over the side, he felt the hard claw of a hand twisted with scar tissue, the tough, ropy feel of an arm likewise damaged. His one good eye was the worst, though, burning with madness and latent anger, as if it had somehow absorbed the fire that had scarred him.

The Guardian spared Abramm neither glance nor word of thanks, releasing his clawlike grip and swaying to starboard to settle on the first thwart, facing astern. In a voice as rough as a barnacle-covered reef, he demanded they return to *Wanderer* at once, as if the rest of them existed only as instruments of his will. Alone pure among the unworthies that made up the bulk of mankind, he could spare no time for pleasantries—not when he had the work of Eidon before him.

Grimacing to think he'd been like that once, Abramm turned his attention to helping the next man aboard.

"We must continue our supplications before the creature is able to renew its strength!" the disfigured Guardian declared to no one in particular. His mad eye roved the quieting sea as he gripped his knees and muttered to himself. "Cursed Terstans! They have brought this on us. They and that woolwit of a king who wouldn't see the truth if it fell on him. They should all be hanged! No. Burned. Made to renounce their heresies or burned!" He laughed softly.

From the corner of his eye, Abramm saw Philip, helping men in at the bow, glance his way. The oarsmen all faced away from him, so he couldn't read their reactions, but he saw a couple of the rescued armsmen exchange eye-rolling gazes.

Once the last of the survivors was aboard, the oarsmen pushed off from the barge, powering the overloaded vessel about in a creaking of oarlocks.

For a moment Abramm floated in the darkness far below, digesting his prize and savoring the comforting pressure of the depths, his limbs drifting loosely before him in an uneven corona of sparkling blue light.

"We must hurry, I say!" croaked the mad Mataian from afar. "Why aren't we under way?"

"We are under way, Master Rhiad," said one of his subordinates, jerking Abramm violently back to the here and now.

Rhiad?! Abramm gripped the tiller hard and, after one reflexive glance at the scarred man sitting knee to knee with him, tore his stare away and fought to keep his face expressionless. Surely this creature was not the Rhiad he had known, the Rhiad he had last seen four years ago in that ancient cistern in the SaHal, threatening to kill Abramm's sister if he would not drink the man's sedating potion. *That* Rhiad had been young, dark-haired, and handsome.

And yet—Abramm stole another glance—was there was not something familiar in the shape of his unruined eye, the whorl in his hairline above his forehead, that lilt of a sneer at the lip?

Fire and Torment! It is him! But what in Eidon's wide world has happened to him? Had the etherworld corridor Rhiad himself had opened in that cistern done this? Abramm had been unconscious when Carissa shoved the Mataian into it, but she said there'd been an explosion, and the Terstan talisman she'd worn unheeding in her belt showed signs afterward of having conducted the Light.

Abramm's gaze came back to the ruined face, horror—and pity—hitting him hard.

Suddenly the dark, fiery eye snapped up to fix upon him. "Don't you know it's rude to stare, boy?"

Abramm averted his gaze, feeling the blood leave his face. It was the first time Rhiad had actually looked at him, and unlike the others, Rhiad *had* seen him since he'd left six years ago. . . . But if Rhiad recognized him, he said nothing, his attention once more on the sea and the beast he'd come to ward.

Abramm returned to his steering just in time to avoid one of the whaler's masts as it floated under the water's surface in a mass of rigging. As it was, the lead portside oar got snarled in that rigging, and they wasted precious moments working free while Rhiad chastised them bitterly.

In the depths below, the beast drifted in suffocating darkness, peering up at a pale distant glow, its blue-shot limbs floating in an ever-widening circle. Its hunger, weeks in the making, remained unblunted by the meager prizes it had consumed. It needed more. And the enemy that had stolen its kill was much smaller than it had first thought. . . .

Abramm shuddered and blinked at the Guardian on the thwart directly across from him. The man was asking him something, but Abramm couldn't hear him, feeling strangely weak and suddenly very small, a bit of frail flotsam on the sea's vast surface, a tiny morsel to be plucked from this bench and pulled toward those grinding, clattering black beaks—

With a gasp he tore free of the kraggin's spell, shaking his head to clear it. Nausea churned in his gut, and sweat greased his palm, shaking on the tiller. He drew a deep, slow breath, fighting panic. He knew the images invading his mind were part of the creature's defenses, but it was as if the aura had switched on all the fear reflexes of his flesh and he could not turn them off. He could, however, stem the influx of doubts and images it ignited. Thus he set himself not to think about the coming struggle and the beast drifting in the murk below, with eyes big as dinner plates—bright crimson rings encircling pupils of dark red-brown.

No! He would not think of that. Nor of Rhiad, gazing blankly over Abramm's shoulder and muttering curses on all who wore the shield. He would think of the tiller in his hand, the angle needed to steer the bow through the bobbing, rolling beams and planks and pieces of yardarm and canvas—and far too many bodies. He would plan what they would do once they returned to *Wanderer* and off-loaded these Guardians.

Dusk was settling in, foggy veils drifting over the water between them and the sparkle that was Springerlan. Ahead, crewmen lined *Wanderer*'s railings, calling for them to hurry. Trap had already come alongside her hull to debark his passengers, the healthy ones scrambling up the rope ladder, the injured lifted to the deck via canvas stretcher.

Oarblades flashing in single coordinated sweeps, Abramm's longboat surged forward. His legs shook now, along with his hands, and he told himself it was only because they were wet and cold.

He knew the Light could slay this beast. He just didn't know if *he* could keep the channel open long enough, or open it at the right time, or open it at all. He remembered those last moments in Jarnek too well—when the resurrected Beltha'adi had faced him, mouth opening to deliver the last fatal blow while Abramm found himself bereft of the power that moments before had allowed him to slay the greatest warrior of the southern lands. It had been the Light of others that had saved him that day.

Yes, he knew much more of it all now, but he also knew of the Shadow that dwelt within him, straining to choke out the Light. A Shadow that, if he let it, would disrupt his concentration and open his guard to every illusion the kraggin's aura threw at him. It wasn't Eidon or his Light Abramm doubted; it was himself.

In the depths below, the kraggin's long powerful limbs, having drifted downward from its head, sparked yellow-green and stiffened. Then they snapped together in a mighty contraction that sent it arrowing headfirst for the surface.

Across from Abramm, Rhiad hissed. "It comes! Where are the Flames? They must go up first!"

As the sense of imminent attack closed in, Abramm urged the oarsmen to hurry. By the time they finally swung alongside *Wanderer*'s hull, the pressure was nearly unbearable. He secured the tiller and leaped up before the boat had even stopped moving, shouting for *Wanderer*'s crewmen to lower the stretcher and man the harpoon guns. From the corner of his eye, he saw Rhiad lurch upright, muttering fiercely as he staggered forward, falling on oarsmen and fellow Guardians alike. Into the very first stretcher he placed the closed brazier of Flames and ordered it pulled aloft. Then, without waiting for anyone's permission or aid, he climbed onto the longboat's gunwale and scrambled up the rope ladder, ordering his subordinates to follow. Glancing at Abramm like nervous sheep, the other Guardians arose and, rather than helping with the transport of the injured, clambered awkwardly up the ladder after him. Abramm let them go without comment, hoping it didn't cost someone's life.

Trap steered his boat away from *Wanderer* into the open, his voice carrying over the water as he directed his men to break out the spears and see to the harpoon gun on the bow. Meanwhile, aided by several of the royal armsmen, Abramm worked swiftly to get the first casualty strapped into the stretcher and swinging slowly up to *Wanderer*'s deck. Once the second man was also on his way, he gestured at the bundled spears on his own boat and directed his companions to break them out.

They looked at him in horror. One of them, a lean, compact fellow with a bruise already purpling his cheekbone, voiced their shared protest. "They'll just get in the way, sir. And if the beast is comin' back, what good will they do anyway? Like sticking broomstraws in a Basani bull. 'Twill just make him mad."

The man stood amidship straddling a thwart, lifting his palms persuasively. He wore a dark goatee and had thinning, shoulder-length dark hair now plastered wetly to his skull. His blue jacket had been torn away entirely, his white blouse clinging to a well-muscled torso. He looked to be in his early thirties, and from his mien, Abramm judged him commander of the group assigned to guard the barge.

"What's your name, armsman?" Abramm demanded brusquely.

"Lieutenant Shale Channon, sir. Of His Majesty's Royal Guard."

"Well, Lieutenant, would you rather face it with nothing at all? Because the old man's right—it's coming. In fact, I'd say it's practically on us."

Lieutenant Channon blanched as Abramm bent to follow his own orders, seeing as no one else was. The man hesitated, then bent to help him as from above another stretcher came flopping down. Swiftly the other men in the boat transferred their injured comrade into its confines as Abramm tugged free several of the spears. He'd just handed off two of them when the sense of the kraggin's presence tightened hard around his chest.

"Abramm!" Trap's urgent cry brought him around to the sight of a dark-mottled shape floating at the surface a quarter-stone's-throw away. Barely had he registered it, when a huge spade-headed tentacle burst from the water and reached for *Wanderer*, washing him in a choking, eye-watering ammoniac stench. Instants later, a second arm shot out of the water and coiled around his longboat. One of the men immediately started hacking at it with the ax as behind them Trap's harpoon gun banged.

Bellowing at the man to belay the chopping, Abramm grabbed the spear, then windmilled wildly as the boat rolled, spilling all of them into the sea. He came up sputtering in a turmoil of churning waves and foam, still holding the spear. A third tentacle now angled out of the water with the others, passing over top of where the longboat had been, to disappear over *Wanderer*'s gunwale. Though Abramm couldn't see her masts, from the rain of wood and canvas, he could guess what was happening.

His own boat, still intact, floated upside down ahead of him. Lieutenant Channon had already pulled himself atop its keel and shortly Abramm had joined him. Having secured his own spear by stuffing it into his breeches,

Channon seized a floating oar and paddled toward another armsman bobbing on their right. Shortly the three of them sat atop the heaving boat, their combined weight pressing it just under the water as they worked to keep their balance and row free of the destruction raining down past *Wanderer*'s hull. Not far away, Trap was pulling Philip from the water. He had already rescued one of the other men from Abramm's boat and held a spear of his own.

A booming crack preceded the squeal of *Wanderer*'s main mast going down. Moments later it crashed into the water where Abramm had just been unloading his boat. Another tentacle burst out of the sea before them, lashing up toward *Wanderer*'s deck, and at Abramm's command, the men paddled over to a rubbery limb, bigger round than all of them put together and smelling like a privy. Drawing his knees up under him, Abramm passed his oar back to the third man, then glanced over his shoulder. Trap and Phil had used the harpoon's rope to pull themselves over to the creature's body floating near the surface. Both men watched Abramm, awaiting his signal. He nodded, then stood, and with everything he had, plunged the spear into the kraggin's heavy arm.

Truly it was less effective than sticking broomstraws in a Basani bull. The thing didn't even flinch. Beside him, Channon plunged his own spear through the beast's thick hide, its milky phosphorescent blood streaming into the dark waters. Abramm felt the darkness rise up the shaft in his hands, and the Shadow stirred within him in response, like to like, pressing him to let it in, filling his mind with a keen, terrified awareness of his own frailty. Frantically he turned his thoughts to Eidon, and the Light flared out of him, shooting down the shaft in a blaze that lit the gloomy twilight like a rocket's glare.

So much for hoping his efforts would be unobtrusive.

The Light's opalescence gilded the world around him—the spear, the tentacle, the waves, and the man beside him. The shield blazed like a lighthouse beacon from his chest, and even the shaft of Channon's spear glowed with it. But at least the kraggin finally reacted, jerking its limb downward with such force it nearly ripped the spear from Abramm's grip. He managed to hold on as Channon flew off into the distance—or rather, it was Abramm who was flying, holding on with all his might as the tentacle flailed—dusky sky, dark waters, foam, the fractured lace of *Wanderer*'s pummeled rigging, the water again, coming up fast now.

He gulped air a moment before he smacked the surface, his grip nearly jarred loose again. Yet still the fire burned in him, and still he kept his mind on the image he needed: Light pumping into a beast that had never known Light before, that could not know it without wilting before it. Its penetrating wail threatened to split his head as he was dragged down and down.

It occurred to him that if he didn't let go, he'd be pulled too far to make his way back up in time. Even so, it was hard to make his fingers release the wooden shaft. But he did, the action tumbling him through sudden, utter darkness. When he finally stopped, he had no idea which way was up. That distant greenish light was undoubtedly the kraggin. All the rest was darkness. And already his lungs strained for air.

He let out a bit of breath and, from the bubbles spewing past his cheek and ear, determined his course to the surface. It took another act of will to follow that course, though, because he was so disoriented it felt entirely wrong. Finally, his chest burning, his vision flashing, and his arms flailing like leaden lumps, he burst into the cold clean air and gasped in desperate delight. It was only as his breathing eased and the sparks faded that he realized the ringing in his ears had given way to cheering.

And here was Trap, asking what had happened as he reached over the edge of the rescue boat. "Did it have hold of you?"

"No," Abramm gasped. "I had hold of *it*. Why?" He grabbed Trap's arm but found himself too weak to help as the man hauled him halfway over the gunwale.

"Because you were down there far too long," Trap said.

Abramm swiveled his trembling legs into the boat and sat upright, still panting. "I wanted to make sure it was dead."

The other men on the boat, Shale Channon among them, were staring at him with very odd expressions. Not quite as if he were a spawn of the kraggin, but certainly as if he'd grown tentacles. He glanced down at himself to be sure, and saw that his tunic had suffered in its contact with the monster's rough hide. His left sleeve was torn off, revealing a well-developed bicep scraped raw around the red dragon brand he'd received from his Esurhite masters. At least the shield on his chest was still covered, though after the display he'd put on, he couldn't think why that mattered.

Trap shoved his own overrobe into Abramm's hands. "To keep you warm," he said, for the benefit of the men watching. Then he sniffed and made a face. "You smell awful, sir!"

"Well, it was bleeding and spewing all over the place," Abramm said, shrugging into the garment and noting that Channon was still staring at him.

Ignoring the man, Abramm offered to take the tiller so Trap could help with the rescuing, and they got under way. They picked up as many of the survivors as they could fit into the boat, ferried them to *Wanderer*, then went out for more. It was as they waited for this second load to disembark that Channon finally spoke.

Freed from rowing, he'd been stealing glances at Abramm since they'd stopped, brown eyes flicking from Abramm's chest to his face to his chest again. He more than anyone must have seen the power that had shot down the shaft of Abramm's spear, and felt it, too, since it had leaped into the shaft of his own. He had to have guessed the truth by now.

The lieutenant turned more fully toward him, and said, "He called you Abramm."

Which were not at all the words Abramm had expected him to say. "What?"

"Your friend there." Channon gestured toward the bow, where Trap was helping the last of their passengers mount the rope ladder. "When the monster surfaced, he called you Abramm. To get your attention."

By now, though he had spoken quietly, Channon had the attention of every man aboard, Trap included. And though the latter sought to appear only casually interested, Abramm saw the dismay in his eyes at the realization of his slip.

Abramm returned his glance to Channon. "Yes. I believe he did."

The lieutenant held his gaze for a few breaths, then nodded and turned away. The others frowned at him, understanding the cryptic exchange no more than Abramm had. But then the armsman sitting at the port oar on the next thwart, a crusty old soldier in the Royal Guard's blue jacket who'd also been staring at Abramm off and on, now exclaimed into the silence, "Pox an' plagues! That's why he's seemed so familiar! It's Prince Abramm, come back to claim his crown!"

If Abramm had received his companions' attention before, now he was all but impaled by it. Mouths gaped and eyes widened, and for a long, long moment only the slap of the water and the creak of *Wanderer*'s hull filled the silence.

Then someone said, "Comes back, and on his first day does what Gillard's failed to do for six months running!"

"Not afraid to beard the beast in its den, either!"

"Killed it with his own hands—now *there's* a king like we had in the old days."

Trap turned away, a smile tugging at his lips, as Abramm felt the blood rush to his face and a wild discomfort writhe in his middle. "We don't know for certain the beast is dead," he said sharply. "And I most certainly did not do this alone."

They looked away, accepting the rebuke in token, though their covert exchanges of half smiles and knowing looks said otherwise. It irked him, but arguing further would only make him look stupid.

They rowed another circuit of the waters, found only two more men alive, and were returning when an outcry arose from *Wanderer's* deck. As they came around her bow, they saw the men leaning out over the gunwale, point-ing and exclaiming in excitement. The kraggin had returned, floating limply amidst the flotsam it had created. Its tubular body, pale now in death, gleamed in the light of *Wanderer's* lanterns, twelve lifeless tentacles splayed around it like a woman's long plaits of hair.

"Well," Channon said smugly, "I guess we can be certain it's dead now, Your Highness."

A cheer went up, resounding off water and wood and fog-shrouded sky. Channon grinned at Abramm, an uncannily accurate reproduction of the expression Trap wore, while Philip clearly fought to maintain his manly dig-nity against an exuberance that threatened to set him bouncing like a little boy. After they had come alongside and transferred their shivering cargo up to the main deck, Channon soberly requested of Abramm that he and his men be allowed to board next. "So you'll have a proper welcome, sir."

And here was that familiar sense of events sweeping Abramm along, quite out of his control. There was no answer to Channon's question but yes, not if he truly meant to take the next step he'd envisioned for himself once the kraggin was dead.

As the men climbed the rope ladder, their laughter and soft voices drifted down to him, warming his face.

"Did you see him go under. . . ?"

". . . wanted to make sure it was dead, he says. . . ."

"I wouldn't believe it if I hadn't seen it. . . ."

Well, my Lord Eidon, I see you've made a way for me. As usual. Not at all my way, I might add, because I have no idea how it will play out. It would be nice now and then if you could give me some sort of itinerary. . . .

Abramm could almost feel the laughter of his Sovereign. *But you wouldn't need to trust me if I did that, my boy.*

The last man disappeared over the top, and now it was Abramm's turn. It was only as he started the climb that he realized somewhere in all that flailing he'd pulled something in his left shoulder. At least it worked well enough to get him up the ladder and over the gunwale into the pocket of sudden silence that awaited on deck. Two lines of armsmen in tattered uniforms flanked the gateway at stiff attention in honor of his arrival. The crew looked on curiously from deck and rigging, and Captain Kinlock stood with Trap at the gauntlet's end, grinning broadly. Beside him hunched the crooked form of Master Rhiad, and one look at his ruined face and wild eye told Abramm things would not go as smoothly as he had hoped.

He had a sudden sickening flashback to the blaze of white he'd let loose when he'd driven the spear into the kraggin. Men engaged in the struggle with the beast and those tossed about up on the ship might well have missed that flash. But even if Rhiad had not physically seen it, he surely would have felt it, would have known what it was—and therefore could now guess the most important change Abramm had undergone in Esurh.

Channon, standing straight and stiff at the gunwale, announced Abramm's royal name in a loud voice, and the idle chatter of the crewmen on the periphery cut off. Abramm walked the line with as much dignity as he could muster, feeling unspeakably odd. It seemed wrong that he would be doing this, almost silly—as if he were playing king and would shortly be found out.

Before he'd even reached Captain Kinlock, however, Rhiad lurched forward, good eye flashing. "Abramm, is it?" he croaked, limping toward him. "Come back to claim the crown, they say."

"Hello, Rhiad," Abramm said as the man drew up in front of him. "I'm surprised you didn't recognize me earlier."

By the look of confusion that flashed across the ruined face, Abramm knew the man hadn't recognized him yet. Had the trauma that ruined his body also affected his memory? Or was he just pretending? Abramm, of all people, knew how very good he could be at that.

Whatever the explanation, Rhiad set the uncertainty aside and drove on with his mission. "Many have sought to kill this beast," he said. "Sought and failed. Yet you come in knowing nothing of it and on your first engagement kill it outright! I would ask how that was accomplished, sir, for it is not an outcome expected from the mere power of men."

" 'Twas the power and mercy of Eidon," Abramm said.

Rhiad's one eye narrowed. " 'Twas power all right. Whether it was Eidon's is another matter." He glared at Abramm triumphantly. "I demand that you remove your tunic and show us your bare chest."

Abramm slammed down his sudden panic and made himself stand calmly, quietly, eyeing the holy man as if he'd asked if Abramm would like to take tea with him. He let his gaze flick over the sailors and armsmen who crowded the decks and rigging around him, ragged, exhausted men, riveted by the sudden conflict playing out before them. The sailors would have little understanding or real interest in any of it, but the armsmen, Abramm sensed, were very much involved—and already leaning toward him in their sympathies. With a slight smile, he met the Master Guardian's half-mad gaze, lifted his chin, and said, "I'd rather not, thank you."

The dark eye bulged. "Then I must assume—"

"That I am your rightful king," Abramm interrupted. "And that you have no business demanding any such thing of me."

"You *dare* to refuse the command of a servant of the Holy One!"

"It is by the Holy One's power that I hold the office I do. An office whose authority, if I recall correctly, supersedes that of your own in matters like these. It is *you*, sir, who has been overbold this day. Given the circumstances, I will ignore it. But if you overstep again, you *will* regret it."

Silence closed upon his words, filled with the creaking and dripping and groaning of the injured ship, but not a word from the men who rode her, and not a word from the man who had sought to dress Abramm down. A man who looked as if he might burst with the effort of restraining himself.

Abramm nodded. "You understand me, then. Good. Now we have work to do. You can either help us or retire to your prayers and meditations somewhere out of the way."

He turned to Kinlock. "I want to haul the carcass into the harbor by dawn. So everyone can see the beast is really dead. Can we do that?"

"We can and we will, Sire," the captain said, grinning again. His bellowed commands dispersed the crowd like a stick in an anthill. As men raced to attend to their various tasks, Abramm turned to find Trap favoring him with a half smile that was almost paternal.

"Well done, my lord," he murmured. "Well done, indeed."

3

Simon Kalladorne, Duke of Waverlan, Grand Marshall of the Armies of Kiriath, and uncle to the king, stood at the south balustrade of his private balcony, staring into the dark, woolly night. With a thick fog blotting out all sign of the dock and shipyards lying directly below him, he had no hope of detecting anything as far out in the bay as the kraggin's two dismasted victims had been when twilight dropped its curtain on their struggle. Likely there was nothing to see anyway, the two vessels long since reduced to flotsam by the monster's massive tentacles. It was well after eleven o'clock now, and there'd been no victory rockets fired from out on the bay, and no word from the shore watchers beyond reports of bodies and wreckage washed up by the tide.

He sighed and drew his woolen cloak more snugly about himself, the chill seeping into his aged bones. His hip ached where the sword had cut into it forty years ago, a dull pain reaching into the small of his back and down the front of his thigh. He should go in. There was nothing to see out here, nothing that would bring him any more assurance than he already had.

The boats were surely gone, all three of them—the Mataian barge, the whaler that had pulled it out to deep water, and the Andolen trademaster that had foolishly come to their rescue. Or had perhaps come for the kraggin all along, hoping to claim the ten-thousand-sovereign prize Gillard had offered for the monster's carcass. Why else would any ship sail into Kalladorne Bay these days? Whatever her reason, the trademaster had paid for it with her life. And so had the Mataians, their ploy to gain favor and power in the realm defeated, for now. They would try again, but tonight Simon could relax, and mourn the men who were lost. . . .

Wingbeats whispered in the mists coiling overhead, and he glanced upward uneasily. The nights were not safe these days. Especially not a night like this. The kraggin was not the only creature of the Veil to have moved into the realm of late, and only fools pretended otherwise. With a sigh, he turned from the balustrade.

The glass panes rattled in his study door as he closed it behind him and headed for the sideboard to pour himself a brandy. Despite the conclusions of logic, he knew he wouldn't truly relax until he looked on the gray choppy water tomorrow and saw the litter of wood and fabric and rope that had once been vessels full of men. Even then the guilt would remain.

The liquor gurgled pleasantly out of its carafe, its pungent aroma burning his nostrils. Not since his wartime days had he felt an ambivalence of this intensity, hope and fear at odds even as they were the same. For the monster out there absolutely needed to be killed. It had shut down Kalladorne Bay for over six months, devastating the local economy. And since Springerlan was the largest port in Kiriath, accounting for nearly half her population, that translated into a significant amount of hardship and suffering. Suffering that would continue to escalate until the kraggin was removed.

Unless the Guardians did the removing. Then the suffering would merely change form and venue.

He replaced the glass stopper with a clink and shoved the carafe back into line with the others, sniffing the brandy with a frown. *Guardians of the Realm, indeed!* Even the name they chose for themselves was arrogant! To think they alone knew what was best for everyone else, particularly in matters so personal as the spiritual, was not simply galling, it was terrifying. He'd lived this day dreading they would succeed in their effort to deliver the realm from the kraggin.

"A spawn of evil sent by Eidon to judge us!" High Father Bonafil had declared when the barge was launched this morning. Visions of the demands they would make should they succeed haunted Simon still: a place on the royal council, a chapel in the palace, stringent enforcement of their Laity Laws upon the Court, including mandatory observance of Mataian rituals, bans on religious observances not to their liking, their vicious Gadrielite heretic hunters given more leeway than ever. . . . It was a road of increasing tyranny and oppression that would lead all the way to that unholy purge Mataian fanatics were already braying about.

The dread, justified as he considered it to be, nevertheless fueled a powerful self-reproach, for his fears were only fears, while the kraggin was real, and so was the suffering it inflicted. To want that to go on, for any reason, was unconscionable. And it wasn't as if there had been no opportunity for others to act. Gillard had done nothing for all these six months, after all, still waiting, he said, for the development of an experimental harpoon with an exploding tip. *"No need to risk men and ships until we know we can kill it,"* he maintained. Meanwhile, the height of the trading season slipped away as more and more lives were ruined.

Absently he reached for a wilted rose blossom fallen from the flower arrangement at the sideboard's end, catching himself just in time. With a muttered oath, he impaled the bloom with his dagger, uncaring that the blade point drove into the sideboard's polished wood. It was by now one of many such point marks.

Immediately the staffid uncurled from its disguised position, reverting to its normal tricolor of blue, gray, and black. Suppressing a shudder of revulsion, he drew the point free of the wood, the staffid's legs rippling wildly, its multisegmented carapace arching back and forth as it tried to free itself. The cursed things had invaded around the time the kraggin had taken up residence in the bay and were everywhere, disguising themselves as fallen flowers, wadded papers, balls of lint or string, rocks, jewelry, even morsels of food. They were disgusting and annoying, their bites producing itchy red welts that lasted weeks. People had taken to hanging swags of onions near their doors and windows to ward them, but the plague would take him before Simon stooped to that!

"Blasted vermin!" he muttered, casting the creature into the fire. It writhed frantically as the flames consumed it, flaring a harsh, bright blue amidst the gold and amber, and he watched it die with perverse satisfaction. Would that all his troubles could be so easily dispatched!

Snatching up his drink, he collapsed in the overstuffed chair before the hearth as the birdcage clock on the mantel struck the hour in tinny, chiming beats. Midnight already. No rockets. No word. The ships were dead.

So why did he feel this sense of growing doom? And how could Gillard be so oblivious to it? Even after the Mataians' almost-success today, the young king had waved off Simon's concern with that annoying, limp-wristed gesture of disdain he'd recently acquired. Sipping his brandy with an amused smile, he'd even suggested the Mataio was right, that it *was* all the Terstans' fault and a purge wouldn't be so bad. His three little lordlings, without whom he never went anywhere, had laughed, but Simon was long past being intimidated by ignorant young louts. He told Gillard sternly that if he did not get serious about the responsibilities of his station, he could very well lose it. To which Gillard had only huffed. *"And who's going to take it from me? You, Uncle?"*

Which his louts thought even funnier than his earlier remark. They'd gone off to the gaming tables after that, singing and laughing as if twenty good men had not died today, as if a monster didn't still prowl the bay outside their windows and there were no religious fanatics drooling to seize control of the realm.

The brandy's warm fire chased down Simon's gullet, driving away the chill he'd gained from being outside but doing little to alleviate the chill that gripped his heart. He stared gloomily at the life-sized portrait of his grandfather, Ravelin Kalladorne, glowering down at him from above the mantel. Tall and lean and blond with the dark Kalladorne brows and hawkish nose, Ravelin was a man's man, the last real warrior-king in Kiriath. He'd worn his blond hair short, with a close-trimmed beard edging mouth and jaw. No courtly frippery for him—he'd been painted in his hunting leathers astride his favorite stallion, a huge, ill-tempered bay that had terrified Simon as a boy. Those were the days of the Chesedhan wars, and Ravelin was a strong, decisive leader, ruthless, stern, courageous to a fault.

But even Ravelin would not be able to put things to right these days. His personality and methods were for another time, another generation. No, the only one who could do anything was Gillard. But Simon was cursed if he could figure out how to motivate the lad anymore. Dropping his chin onto his chest, he inhaled the brandy's aroma and thought that if he were a praying man, he'd ask that something be sent to startle the boy awake before it was too late.

He didn't remember getting into bed, but the window-rattling booms of what he first thought was cannon fire awakened him there. When it was not repeated, he deemed it his imagination and slipped back into slumber, only to be assaulted anew by his manservant's shrill voice and a blinding light. As he rose up on his elbows, groaning and cursing, the servant, Edwin, turned from where he'd flung wide the velvet draperies to reveal the first glimpse of sun Kiriath had seen in two months.

"My lord Simon!" the man repeated, far too loudly. "They've slain the monster! They're bringing it right into port! Come and see the size of it!"

At first Simon couldn't think what he was talking about, so intrusive was the light and the pain jabbing his skull. His stomach felt queasy, too, and his mouth tasted like the inside of a horse trough. *Did I drink that much brandy last night?*

"My lord?"

What had Edwin said? *"They've slain the monster."*

It all connected in a flash and Simon leaped out of bed, staggered badly, and caught himself on the bed table before he fell. There followed an irritating moment of waiting for his head to settle, but finally he was at the window, fighting the pain from squinting into the bright morning light.

The fog had not yet surrendered fully to the day, a ragged train of gray puffs sailing across the sky and shredding low over the water. The bay stretched southward in a great blue swath, on which two of the many tall-ships stranded in Springerlan now sailed halfway to the distant gold-crowned headlands that marked the verge of open sea. So desperate were they to begin recouping their losses, the tallships' captains hadn't even stayed for the celebration.

And celebration there was.

The harbor teemed with boats as it had not for six months. Mostly small to medium sized, their masts and bows fluttered with the brightly colored pennants reserved for festival days, and they raced about at great speed, a swirling crowd of attendants for the battered Andolen trademaster and her equally battered whaling companion, now limping into port. In the night the trademaster's crew had juryrigged a new main mast and replaced or stitched up enough of her torn rigging and sails to get her under way. But even with the bright, stiff wind—unfortunately a land breeze she had to tack into—and the advantage of most of her sails, she still needed the help of the five smaller vessels arrayed before her, towlines taut as they pulled her into port. It was not her injuries that slowed her, however, but the carcass she dragged behind her, a creature half again as long as she was.

Hangover nearly eclipsed by his sudden, keen interest, Simon hurried from the bedchamber into his study, snatched up his spyglass, and stepped into the cool morning breeze on the balcony, uncaring that all the world might see a grizzled old soldier in his bedgown. He strode to the balustrade, snapped open the scope, and fixed it upon the monster trailing in the trademaster's wake. Dark-mottled, rough-surfaced, it shone wetly in the sun, having a long tubular body with a flangelike tail from which the trademaster's towline was fixed. From its other end a fan of long arms trailed through the waves, some dark, some gleaming pearl white, a few of them twice the length of the rest of it combined.

Some of the boats had come in close, and a few braver souls poked it with gaffs and spears. As he lowered the telescope to view the whole scene again, a puff of smoke erupted near the dock to his left and a rocket shrilled skyward, exploding in a burst of sparklers, its boom making him wince again. Two more followed, and he heard the distant cheers of the men on the docks and in the boats while those on the trademaster—he had the scope up again—waved from rail and rigging. He aimed the glass at the bow, picked out white painted letters spelling *Wanderer*, then swept the telescope sternward along the gunwale. At once he came to a cluster of white-tunicked men carrying a flattened oval of bronze and swore aloud.

Guardians. Their barge was gone—he'd seen the kraggin's tentacles cleave and sink it himself—but somehow they'd survived. Looked like they had their pan of flames, as well. *Plagues! They'll take all the credit sure as they're standing there.*

He continued his survey, stopping again when he came to a group of men in the tattered blue remnants of royal armsman uniforms standing near the boarding portal in the mangled gunwale. Several of the white-garbed Mataians stood among them, conversing with the man who appeared to be the trademaster's captain. One of the group, a tall, bearded blond, snagged Simon's eyes with a sense of the familiar, but then he spied the spare form and goateed face of his friend and one time protégé, Lieutenant Shale Channon, commander of the royal armsmen sent as escort, and joy superseded idle curiosity.

It was short-lived, itself superseded by the realization that no matter how greatly the royal armsmen had figured in the kraggin's defeat, the Mataians would claim it was only because of the protective power of their Flames.

He snapped the scope shut and strode back through the study to the bedchamber, Edwin following him in. "Has the king been told?" Simon asked, throwing off his bedgown and pulling on the breeches Edwin handed him.

"They're rousing him now, my lord."

But the king had still not emerged from his apartments by the time Simon reached the main foyer, and since his own horse had been brought around, he decided not to wait. The quicker someone of rank gained control of the situation, the better.

The Avenue of the Keep thronged with people, and the closer he and his men drew to the dock, the heavier grew the traffic. As they fought their way through the congestion, he spied a cadre of Laine Harrady's men afoot and hurrying back to the palace. Seeing Simon, one of them hailed him. "Have ye heard the news, my lord duke!?"

"O' course 'e has," Simon's master armsman, Gerard, growled at him. "Why d'ye think he's come?"

Simon gave the man a casual salute and pressed on, the crowd nearly shoulder to shoulder, even several streets back from the action. The Avenue ended in a square, brick-paved plaza overlooking the docks. From there the street turned sharply left and sloped down to the wharf proper. It was the first clear view Simon had had of the harbor, now directly below him, since he'd left his balcony. Already there were as many people here as had gathered to watch the Guardians set out yesterday. Striped tents and awnings of every hue floated over the multitude. Spectators lined warehouse roofs, hung out of windows, perched on barrels and hogsheads, and swarmed the masts and gunwales of all neighboring ships.

The frantic swirling of maritime traffic he'd noted earlier had ceased, vessels floating gunwale to gunwale along a narrow gauntlet formed between the Andolen trademaster and an empty berth on the royal dock. Every eye watched the longboat now threading that gauntlet to a chorus of thunderous cheering. Smartly painted in red and white with gold gilding its gunwales, it was none other than the launch reserved for royalty, broken out to honor the commanders of those who had killed the kraggin. Even with his naked eye, Simon could pick out the blue shoulders of the royal armsmen sitting among those in the boat, a great deal more of them than of the men in white. Which was odd. A glance back at the battered trademaster assured him most of the Guardians remained inexplicably on board.

A new uneasiness, whose source he could not identify, blew through him.

His good friend, Ethan Laramor, earl of the border fiefdom of Highmount, sat astride his brown horse near the brick retaining wall, and knowing his master well, Gerard carved a path through the spectators in that direction. Ethan, come south for the annual meeting of the Table of Lords, should be happy at least. The kraggin's depredations had seriously hampered his efforts to gain the military and financial help he sought to stand against an increasingly aggressive barbarian presence along Kiriath's northern borders. With the kraggin prowling the bay right in front of them, no one wanted to think about vague rumblings in the north. Now, perhaps, they would.

Except Ethan wasn't cheering. Instead he had his spyglass out and trained upon the royal launch. With his gaunt, pockmarked face, straight strawy hair, and lanky frame, Laramor had a crude, homespun look, intensified by languid gray eyes and the gold ring of Borderer lordship dangling in his right ear. A barbaric custom, people said behind his back, but then the Borderers *were* only a step away from barbarians themselves. Beneath the bumpkin's exterior, however, lurked an excellent swordsman, a horseman of renown, and an archer whose aim with the longbow was unrivaled in all the realm. Beyond that, Ethan Laramor had one of the most brilliant minds Simon had ever known when it came to waging war, both on the battlefield and off.

As Simon pulled up beside him, Laramor glanced aside, then lowered the glass with a grimace. "So. You've heard the news, then?"

Simon responded with a frown of his own. "Of course. The monster's dead, and we can all rejoice as our pious deliverers seek to steal the credit."

Laramor's frown deepened. "I meant the news about Abramm."

Simon stared at him, struggling to put the name into some kind of context and failing. Abramm was dead. Gone. Abducted six years ago after failing the Mataian test of the Flames and sold into a life of slavery he could not possibly have survived. What news of Abramm could be relevant? Perplexed, he shook his head. "News about Abramm?"

"He's here. Now." Ethan gestured with his chin at the *Wanderer*. "He's the one commissioned that boat. They're saying *he* killed the monster. And that he's come back to claim the Crown. The Mataians are already hailing him as their Guardian-King."

Simon could not have been more stunned had Ethan slapped him in the face.

"He's just coming ashore in the king's launch down there," Laramor went on. "You can clearly see it's him with the glass."

He offered his spyglass to Simon, who continued to stare dumbly at him, cold now from his head to his feet. He saw again in his mind's eye the tall, bearded blond he'd noted earlier on *Wanderer*'s deck. The one that had seemed familiar. *Abramm?*

It can't be.

But somehow, even before Simon had the telescope focused on the man, he knew that it was, and the knowing turned his heart to icy stone. The boy had debarked and was now walking slowly up the dock, preceded and followed by the royal armsmen in their tattered uniforms—now Simon understood why they had come and the Guardians had stayed. And that older, birdlike Mataian at his side was on the Mataians' High Council. Perhaps the two flanking them were, as well. Indeed, it likely would've been High Father Bonafil himself, if the stick wasn't too holy to walk himself down to the docks through that press of unrighteous humanity. No doubt he watched from somewhere safe, farther back. Simon lowered the scope to scan the surroundings and saw at once the white canopy trimmed in red, set up just down the main road in a small outswelling that served as overlook.

The people through whom Abramm walked—thankfully Simon recognized few of Springerlan's upper crust among them—grinned and cheered, some reaching out to touch him as he passed, an indignity he allowed. Occasionally he even stopped to speak to them and clasp their hands as if they were not commoners at all, but fellow highbloods. Even from a distance Simon saw that they loved him.

The boy moved stiffly, as if in pain, his height, his dark, level brows, deep-set eyes, and narrow aristocratic features bearing the unmistakable stamp of the Kalladorne bloodline. A bloodline whose heritage he had once mocked with his pacifist Mataian robes and that long womanly hair tied now into a queue at his nape. The weakest, sickliest, most cowardly of King Meren's sons, the one who had shamed the family by joining the Holy Brethren, then shamed them more by failing the final test of his Novitiate, the one everyone believed—and secretly hoped—was dead and forever forgotten, now stood before them, very much alive.

"If you're not careful, Sire, you could lose the Crown."

"And who's going to take it from me? You, Uncle?"

A stream of muttered blasphemies tumbled from Simon's lips. *Fire and Torment! Pox and plagues! How in all creation could this have happened?*

He lowered the glass, telescoping it shut with trembling hands. *If I go down there to meet him, I'll have to ride with him. And if I ride with him, it'll be thought I support him.*

Simon drew a deep breath, nausea clenching his middle. What to do? What to do? He eyed the white-and-red canopy again, gray-mantled holy men clustered in its shadow, glanced again at Abramm just as the boy lifted his gaze to look right at Simon. Decision crystallized. Tight-lipped, Simon hauled his horse around, plunging heedlessly through the crowd until he broke free of it. Then he kicked the beast to a canter, racing back up the Avenue of the Keep to the palace.

Come to claim the Crown, indeed! What does he know of being king? A scholar, a religious boy, and now a former slave? It's madness.

His horse was lathered and blowing hard when Simon pulled up to the palace's main entrance and vaulted to the ground. Throwing the reins at the waiting footman, he took the steps two at a time, breathlessly asking the steward at the top if the king had left for the dock yet.

"No, my lord," the steward stammered. "They've only just found him. He spent last night with Lady Amelia. She's a new one. No one even thought to look for him in her—" The steward broke off and backed a pace as Simon realized he was sputtering blasphemies again.

4

When Abramm looked up and saw his uncle Simon sitting his big bay horse atop the ramp, his heart lurched with hope. But barely had he focused on the man when he saw him stiffen with that all-too-familiar hostility. Then he was handing off the telescope to his companion and wheeling his horse around, flying back to the palace and Gillard.

Disappointment curdled in Abramm's middle, feeding the anxiety that had nagged him all morning. He suspected exhaustion was to blame—he hadn't slept in over thirty-six hours, the last fourteen of which he'd spent engaged in some of the hardest, heaviest work he'd done since his days in Katahn's galley ships. They'd passed the night patching *Wanderer* together enough to catch the wind again, and even then the kraggin's weight required towlines. So this morning most everyone, him included, had taken a turn at the towboat oars.

Now his legs trembled, his back ached, his palms were blistered, and his hands were stiff and sore from too much pulling. He was getting a headache, too, and his stomach had become seriously uneasy thanks to the sharp, ammoniac stench of the kraggin permeating his clothes and hair and beard— even his skin. With all his extra clothing lost when the monster had splintered the stern cabin, he'd had nothing to change into, and the smell hadn't seemed so bad out on the water. Ashore and in this crowd, however, it was strong enough to choke. Ahead, the people lining the dock wrinkled their noses as it first hit them, frowning, glancing at their neighbors, then realizing what it was and returning to their cheering. At least he was not the only one the kraggin had anointed with its stench. And no one could accuse him of not having been involved.

With Lieutenant Channon and two of his armsmen pressing a path through the crowd, Abramm walked a gauntlet of grateful citizens, his old discipler, Brother Belmir, beside him. He would have preferred it be Trap, but they'd agreed that was out of the question, given that Trap had supposedly been executed six years ago. Belmir had changed little. His gray guardian's braid was whiter, his back more crooked, his face more wrinkled, but overall he was still the same bespectacled, birdlike man Abramm remembered. Except for the fact he was *Master* Belmir now, recently promoted to High Father Bonafil's council of spiritual advisors. He and his two aides had been there to greet Abramm when he disembarked from the king's launch, their warm, excited manner not what he'd expected after Rhiad had gone ashore earlier to present his suspicions to his superiors. Evidently they viewed him as mad as the royal armsmen did. Either that or they realized that in accusing Abramm they'd also have to admit it was Terstan power that slew the monster and not their precious Flames. In which case he figured they would not have shown up at all.

He walked slowly, as much because he was tired as because he honestly wanted to clasp the hands held out to him and look into the eyes of those whom he would rule, see the pain and relief and gratitude and know that what had been risked and sacrificed was worth it.

"You've saved our lives."

"My children will eat now."

"We owe you everything."

Many a tearstained face presented itself, and it must have been fatigue that made his throat keep closing up. These were not highborn nobles, but commoners—freemen, merchants, and sailors—and he was humbled by their response to him.

The nobles, thankfully, had not turned out yet. Stiff with exhaustion, ragged, dirty, and stinking of sweat and sea and kraggin, Abramm could not have presented a less regal impression if he'd tried. The commoners might not mind, but the nobles would be aghast. And in light of what he hoped to do in the coming days, he wanted nothing so much as to get to the palace and a bath as soon as possible.

That would deliver him from Belmir, too. After the Guardian's initial greeting, when puzzlement mingled with an apparently genuine pleasure at their reunion, the man had said little, walking at Abramm's side in a quiet display of Mataian support. That Abramm allowed it, hinted as well, unfortunately, that the Mataio had Abramm's.

Working his way up the dock, Abramm had been clasping hands and receiving thanks without much thought beyond satisfaction at this validation of his choice to return. But when his gaze caught on a small golden shield glittering between the open neck edges of a man's fine leather jerkin, a mark supernaturally burnished into the man's flesh, he stopped in his tracks. His gaze flicked up to the man's face—pale, age wrinkled, with dark bushy brows overshadowing shrewd brown eyes and bristly salt-and-pepper hair cut short in defiance of current fashion.

The man stuck out his hand. "Everitt Kesrin, Your Grace. Owner of the Westland Shipping Company. You have saved the livelihoods of myself and all whom I employ, and for that you have my thanks."

At his side stood a plain young woman, her fawn-colored hair hastily caught into a pair of Chesedhan-style braids, her wide blue-gray eyes fastened upon Abramm as if he were Alaric the Second reborn. She was not the only one to stare, though the others in the suddenly silent crowd had perhaps different reasons. As Abramm regarded the offered hand, a squall of conflicting thoughts blew through his mind—the realization of what this man was doing, the understanding that Abramm's own action would be marked and replayed for days to come, the fear of where that would lead, the purpose of his return. . . .

He hesitated only an instant, then clasped the man's hand firmly, a scribe's hand he judged it, soft as his own had once been. "It is my privilege to serve," he said quietly, holding the merchant's gaze. "And my pleasure to know you."

He started onward, but Belmir lingered behind. "Freeman Kesrin," he said dryly. "Bold as ever, I see."

Kesrin was executing a short bow as Abramm turned back to observe. "Why should I not be bold, Master Belmir, when I stand enfolded in Eidon's Light? Though I fail to see boldness in my actions today. Am I not allowed to express my thanks to our celebrated deliverer like everyone else?"

"As you make sure he knows exactly what you are when he accepts that thanks. Don't think your motives are not obvious, Freeman."

No more than yours, Master Belmir, thought Abramm.

Kesrin only shrugged. "I find no fault in my motives. We have long been free in this land to pursue whatever faith we choose. I hope that will not change with the coming of our new . . . king?" His dark eyes shifted back to Abramm, one bushy brow lifting, and Abramm was seized with the desire to conjure a kelistar in front of them all. *That* would certainly be an action noted by the crowd. And Gillard. And the Table of Lords.

He put away the crazy bravado and said, "You have nothing to fear from me, Freeman. I have every intention of enforcing the freedoms Kiriathans have long guarded."

"Even if Eidon's law says otherwise?"

"I have always understood that *is* Eidon's law." He glanced at Belmir. "That, in fact, it was this very freedom which allowed the Matiao itself to survive two hundred years ago when it was but a tiny gathering of eccentric cultists."

Belmir frowned over his spectacles. As he drew breath to speak, however, some intuition of the need to maintain royal decorum spurred Abramm to end it. Nodding to the Terstan merchant and the starstruck girl at his side, he strode forward to acknowledge the next person in line. In his wake he heard Kesrin say, "Master Belmir, are you *sure* this is your Guardian-King?"

Guardian-King? Abramm's stride faltered. Was *that* why Belmir was here? Because they had decided—Eidon alone knew why—Abramm was their Guardian-King? The thought made his incipient nausea lurch. No wonder Simon had raced away and Everitt Kesrin had come out to bait him.

Belmir ignored Kesrin's jibe, returning to his post at Abramm's side, smiling and lifting his hand to the crowd as if nothing untoward had happened. But after a moment Abramm leaned down toward him and said quietly, "I must tell you sir, that if you believe I am your Guardian-King, you are gravely mistaken."

Belmir flicked him a smile. "You killed the kraggin, my son. You have to be him."

"Brother Rhiad did not share your assessment."

"Rhiad sees Terstans around every corner. He means well, but all know he is unbalanced. It's clear the power he sensed was not in you, but in the kraggin as it fought for its life against the Flames."

Abramm smiled and waved, chilled by the mingle of truth and falsehood in the Guardian's words and not knowing how to counteract it without saying everything.

"He had hoped to have the victory over it himself," Belmir went on, "and was not pleased when Eidon favored you instead. Still, we all see it for what it is: Eidon's Chosen returning to take up the Crown that has awaited him since he left."

"But that is not possible," Abramm said.

"Why?"

"Because I no longer hold with Mataian teachings."

"You may have strayed from the fold, my son, but you'll be back."

"I assure you, I will not."

Belmir smiled benignly over his spectacles. "Eidon's hand is upon you. You cannot help it."

From suspected heretic to the Mataio's prophesied Guardian-King in but a few hours. Incredible. It was the ultimate irony that Abramm would use his Terstan power to kill the kraggin—in a blundering, uncontrolled, appallingly visible burst—and have it viewed as proof of Eidon's anointing. If it were not so galling, and if he were not teetering on the edge of being found out, his bid for the crown ruined before it began, it might have been humorous.

Ahead, where the pier met the main dock, the Mataians had erected a red-and-white awning above an overlook from the street ramping down to dock level. Several benches had been brought down, upon which were seated what appeared to be the High Father of all the Mataio and his chief aides. Abramm didn't suppose he could ignore the High Father of one of the major faiths of his land, particularly in light of what he'd just said about respecting his people's religious freedom. Fortunately he also saw, standing on the dock below the holy men, the horses he'd asked Lieutenant Channon to procure for him and his armsmen. If he had to meet with High Father Bonafil, at least he would do it eye to eye.

He knew his fatigue was all too obvious when Channon offered to help him mount—he refused, of course. No self-respecting Dorsaddi accepted help in mounting. It was bad enough he had to use the stirrup to climb aboard rather than simply swinging into the saddle, but he could barely move his left shoulder and his back was ominously twitchy. Well, only a little longer and he'd have some privacy in which to attend to both his person and his hurts.

As Abramm reined his horse over to address the men sitting on the overlook, he saw that Belmir had rejoined his holy brethren and was whispering something into the High Father's ear. Abramm recognized none of the others. He only knew the High Father's name because Channon had told him earlier that Saeral had died of a heart attack four years ago and Bonafil succeeded him. The new High Father was the typically handsome, placid-faced sort that ascended to his station, with mild blue eyes and soft lips. His auburn hair, liberally sprinkled with gray, frizzed now with age above the long braid. As befitted his station, he wore no rank cords, a sign, the Mandates said of his extreme humility. At his throat—as at the throats of all Guardians—gleamed the red amulet of the Holy Flames, said to carry the very spark of Eidon himself. It was an amulet Abramm had once longed for with a passion that was painful, an amulet that now reminded him chillingly of those worn by the evil priests of Esurh's Khrell. Right down to the dim, fluttering glow lurking within each one of them. Not the spark of Eidon at all, but something else entirely. And he wondered as his gaze stopped on Bonafil—was this Saeral in a new body?

The breeze rushed around Abramm and over the waiting holy men, widening their eyes, wrinkling their noses, and inciting a startled exchange of glances. A couple of them even coughed slightly, and one man sneezed.

Bonafil kept his nose-wrinkling to a minimum, remarking in a gentle voice, "Sweet Fires, man. That is quite a stench." No one else in all this crowd could have spoken such even to the crown prince, let alone the man who could be king by week's end.

"You'll forgive me, then," Abramm said, "if I hasten on to the palace, where I may indulge in the bath we all agree is needed."

"I'll only take a moment, Your Highness." Silence once more enfolded them as Bonafil's blue eyes moved down Abramm's form and up again. "Is that a *weapon* you wear on your hip, my son?"

"It is, in fact, an Andolen rapier, Father."

The High Father received this information without reaction, studying Abramm's robes and hands and face. He wrinkled his nose again, then looked across the crowd and the docked ships to *Wanderer*, forced by her deep draft to anchor farther out in the harbor, while at his side, Belmir smiled with calm assurance. Bonafil's gaze returned to Abramm. "Are you indeed responsible for the monster's death, then?"

"I and the men with me, yes."

" 'Tis a remarkable feat you have accomplished, then."

" 'Twas by the power and mercy of Eidon."

Light flickered in Bonafil's eyes and simultaneously in the amulet at his throat, raising the hairs on Abramm's nape. "And now you come to claim the Crown."

Not Saeral. Abramm thought. *Another.*

"You will need Eidon's help, I think," remarked Bonafil.

"I will indeed, Father."

Again the silence and the thoughtful regard. Then Bonafil nodded as if Abramm had passed some unspoken test. "You will have the Brotherhood's full support."

And here it was: the moment to speak or keep silent. Abramm spoke: "I appreciate your generosity, sir, but as I told Master Belmir, I no longer hold with Mataian teachings."

Bonafil nodded. "Nevertheless, you have our support."

It was on the tip of Abramm's tongue to declare he neither wanted nor needed their support when suddenly he understood. No one knew he had become the White Pretender, or that he had spent the last four years as the close friend, confidant, and advisor to King Shemm of the Dorsaddi. High Father Bonafil no doubt saw him as a simple scribe fresh out of slavery and easily manipulated. This was a bid for power. Abramm could probably offer any insult short of revealing the shield on his chest, and Bonafil would bear it.

"I fear I will disappoint you in the end," Abramm said finally, glancing at Channon. His lieutenant had been waiting for that sign and now turned to give *Wanderer* a casual salute. On deck, Captain Kinlock should have them centered in his spyglass and—yes. Here came the flash that showed he had received the signal.

Abramm turned back to Bonafil, pulling the thick queue of his hair over one shoulder and drawing up the hood of his robe. He lifted a hand in casual salute of his own. "Good day, sir."

Bonafil's soft mouth dropped open as Abramm pulled his horse back and around. It was a borderline breach of etiquette and a calculated risk, but as heir to the throne he was justified in not waiting for dismissal. It was also a clear indication that he had turned from Mataian persuasions.

Before anyone could protest, though, a mighty squeal of wood and metal erupted from out on the bay, drawing the throng's attention. Abramm glanced again over his shoulder as the kraggin's corpse was hauled from the water by cranes set up aboard both *Wanderer* and the whaler that had accompanied her. As the great gray-and-ivory carcass slithered upright into view, the crowd exclaimed in muted susurration. Among them only one kept his attention on Abramm: a figure in Guardian gray standing at the junction of pier and dock, a man whose ruined face and barren scalp only accentuated the fire of hatred burning in his one good eye.

Have you remembered me yet? Abramm thought at him. With a shudder of foreboding he settled himself forward in the saddle, urging his horse after Channon's. Leaving the now-distracted crowd, they trotted into the back ways of Portside, which Channon's men had earlier cleared of spectators, and rode on toward the palace.

5

They rode through the Portside sector and into the hilly city beyond, where a busy service road switchbacked up the steep face of the long escarpment from whose seaward-most point the palace overlooked the bay. Pedestrians and delivery wagon drivers automatically made way for the detachment of Royal Guard as it headed for the southern service gate, eyeing the cloaked figure it escorted with interest. If they guessed who he was, Abramm did not know, for he was paying little attention.

His headache and nausea had worsened dramatically, his middle cramping so violently at one point it doubled him over. With that, it dawned on him that this wasn't just a case of jitters or a bad smell or not having eaten. Nor was the increasing weakness and throbbing pain in his left arm the result of physical exertion or injury. All were the unmistakable signs of spore sickness.

At first he couldn't think how he'd been exposed, until he remembered he'd been swimming in the kraggin's blood. Diluted by seawater, the spore's initial effects would be unnoticeable, increasing gradually over time as they multiplied within him. Cursed—or blessed?—with unusual sensitivity to the stuff, he'd be dog-sick by the end of the day unless he initiated a purge first. But a purge would not only cocoon his body in an aura of Terstan Light—hardly a spectacle he wanted just anyone to see right now—it would also require several hours to complete. He'd have to find a place where he'd be sure no one would stumble onto him. And with no one but Lieutenant Channon available to guard him, he wished yet again that he hadn't sent Trap away. Well, no help for that now. At least in the course of the night's events,

Channon had shown himself an honorable man, a fellow Terstan and already devoted to Abramm's cause.

Passing through the gate without incident, they threaded their way through the congested alleys between the palace service buildings and came at last to the backside of the west wing, its three stories of windows gleaming in the morning light. A trio of blue-jacketed armsmen stood at the small side door through which Abramm had chosen to enter. Dismounting stiffly, he had to lean against the horse and wait for the dizziness to pass before handing off the reins and stepping forward to greet a worried-looking Channon and a tall elderly man he recognized as his own father's Grand Chamberlain, Lord Robert Haldon.

Haldon had changed little in the fourteen years since Abramm had last seen him. Although he was not the giant perceived by a twelve-year-old, he was still big—as tall and broad of shoulder as Abramm. His hands were huge, and his craggy face, with its beak of a nose and jutting chin, was more seamed than ever. Clad in a dark gray doublet with puffy sleeves and those horrible ballooning breeches, he wore his wiry white hair long now and tied at the nape with a black ribbon. Abramm recalled him as a quiet, competent man, so solemn he often seemed stern, especially to the king's sons. Yet for all his imposing bulk he had been kind and respectful of Abramm when others had not.

Now he wore a tense, suspicious look that faded into flatness as Abramm stopped in front of him. "Prince Abramm!" he whispered thickly. "It really is you!"

"Hello, Haldon," Abramm said with a wry smile. "Good to see you again."

Haldon bowed low. "Welcome home, Your Highness."

The guards at the door had stiffened when Haldon greeted Abramm, and Abramm felt their attention fix upon him, though nothing in their mien changed outwardly.

"We have had to put you in the Ivory Apartments," Haldon said. "With the Council of the Realm set to meet tomorrow, the peers have been arriving all week, and I'm afraid we're overcrowded. If you are willing to wait, it would not take long to vacate something more appropriate."

"The Ivory Apartments will be fine."

Haldon looked relieved. "Very good, sir. If you'll come with me?"

As they trod the empty, gleaming corridors, Abramm could only thank Eidon he'd had Channon arrange for his quartering discreetly. Wishing to choose his own time and place for meeting Gillard and the court, he had counted it better not be seen at all than as a weary, bedraggled waif, stinking of kraggin. It never dawned on him he'd have to worry about spore sickness, too. Which was why, when they reached the Ivory Apartments on the second floor of this west wing, he was profoundly displeased to find three noblemen awaiting him.

One was a complete fop, decked out in salmon-colored doublet and breeches trimmed with copious amounts of lace. A wig of golden curls cascaded to the middle of his back, and he carried a beribboned walking stick. The very sight of him raised Abramm's hackles, for he represented all that the Esurhites had mocked in Kiriathan character, an embarrassment Abramm had spent two years fighting to overcome.

The second man, clad in black and brown, wore his own lank brown hair long around a sallow, pockmarked face. Spectacles obscured his eyes, but he looked vaguely familiar.

The third member of the trio was as different from the first two as they were from each other. His gray doublet stretched tightly over a bony frame, its only adornment a tongue of red flame embroidered onto the left breast. Also eschewing the false curls of current fashion, he wore his graying hair queued back from his face like Haldon. His eyes were too small, his nose too round, and his mouth too wide, and he held himself as stiffly upright as if a poker had been rammed up his spine.

All three looked surprised at Abramm's appearance, their eyes flicking up and down his torn and stained clothing, catching on the sword, the bloody hands, the beard. He actually saw the smell hit them, all three recoiling in unison.

The foppish one choked out a faint, "Oh my," and yanked a lace-edged kerchief from his sleeve. Covering his fleshy nose and mouth, he coughed delicately into the cloth, then forced himself to pull it away. "They said that beast had an odor," he said in a strangled voice. "I fear they did not exaggerate."

"I am on my way to address the problem now," Abramm assured him, trying to ignore the pounding in his head.

"Far be it from me to detain you, then." The man backed a step and coughed into his kerchief again. "I only wished to welcome you, sir, and to offer my thanks for ridding us of the monster. Also, I have considerable expertise in matters of wardrobe and cultural affairs, should you have need of counsel."

"And you are?"

The dandy froze in the act of bowing, then straightened. His blue eyes watered. "Temas Darnley, Your Highness. Earl of Bathport." He patted his lips with his kerchief, then straightened his spine. "I shall detain you no longer, sir, and look forward to making your acquaintance at the Table this evening."

And with that he fled, leaving Abramm to address his sudden puzzlement to his two remaining visitors. "The Table is meeting *tonight?*"

"They've called a special session in your honor," said the bespectacled one. He bowed a formal greeting. "Byron Blackwell, Highness. Speaker of the Table of Lords."

Tonight? Plagues! Will I even have enough time to complete a purge? It didn't matter. As another spasm of nausea wrenched through him, he realized he was fast reaching the point where it would either be a purge or days of fevered delirium.

Blackwell was eyeing him sharply. "Perhaps you remember me from years ago?"

"Count Blackwell's son. Yes. I remember." Blackwell's father, Henry, had been a favorite of Abramm's own sire, and Blackwell himself a friend of Abramm's eldest brother. Abramm had been too young at the time to remember much about him save that he'd been a quiet youth with a penchant for reading.

Abramm glanced at the third man, the one in the gray doublet with the tongue of flame who was now bowing stiffly.

"Darak Prittleman, Highness. Lord of Lathby, First Secretary of the Nunn, Headman in the Laity Order of Gadriel, and humble servant of Tersius in the Flames." His voice was dry, nasal, and overly precise. "I, too, wish to offer my welcome and thanks, and to express my joy that at last we shall have a king of Eidon's choosing to deliver this realm from the evil overtaking it."

Abramm stared at him, rankled by this recitation—he'd heard rumors of this new order of Gadriel back in Qarkeshan—and bereft of an appropriate response.

Once again the kraggin's ammoniac musk delivered him. Prittleman had been quietly turning green, and now he straightened abruptly. "I, too, offer my assistance should you require it, sir, but will impose upon you no longer. Eidon's Light be with you."

And with you would have been Abramm's correct response. But he said nothing, and after a moment Prittleman beat a hasty retreat.

"It wasn't so bad out on the water," Abramm murmured apologetically.

Blackwell smiled. "I have sinus trouble, my lord. It doesn't seem that bad to me."

"Ah." Abramm didn't quite manage to keep the dismay out of his tone. The pounding in his head was growing louder.

The son of Count Blackwell, presumably Count Blackwell himself by now, regarded him speculatively. "Are you feeling all right, sir?"

"I've had better days."

"I'll not keep you, then." But he lingered nonetheless. "They say you were actually on the water with the beast. That you stabbed it with a spear."

"I did," Abramm said. "Which is why I smell as bad as I do and why I am so looking forward to a bath."

Blackwell still did not take his cue. "They say you used the power of Eidon to slay it."

In an instant, Abramm's growing frustration transmuted to full wariness. "They are saying that, yes."

Blackwell's spectacles magnified his brown eyes. "And did you?"

"I and three others stabbed it with spears, but as I told High Father Bonafil, it was by the power and mercy of Eidon that we succeeded."

The brown eyes studied him shrewdly. "A politic answer, my lord. Perhaps you are not so naïve as we've been led to believe." He waited as if he expected a response. When Abramm merely stared at him, he went on. "I, too, offer you my support, sir, in whatever capacity you desire it. I have little liking for your brother, and frankly I'll be delighted to see you take the Crown from him. He has never really risen to its demands." Blackwell paused. "But you realize he *will* fight you."

Abramm met his gaze for a long moment, seeking through the haze of his discomfort and fatigue to grasp the man's mettle, to gain the knowledge only time and familiarity would bring. Was this friend or foe?

When again he did not answer, Byron Blackwell nodded once, then bowed and departed, leaving Abramm at long last alone with his chamberlain and Lieutenant Channon, his silent shadow. It was the chamberlain who caught his attention, however, for he should have left long ago.

Realization dawned. "You are not Grand Chamberlain anymore."

"No, sir. The king—er . . . uh, prince-regent brought his own man when he came to the throne."

"The more fortunate for me, it seems."

Haldon inclined his head. "I hope you will pardon the lack of atten-dants—with such short notice we've had a time finding any of suitable rank—but your bath has been prepared. If you'll come this way?"

Inside the bedchamber a handful of body servants waited before the open door of a tile-walled side closet where stood the steaming bath. As much as Abramm had yearned for this earlier, he wondered now if he had the stamina to see it through. What he really wanted was to be shown the bed and left alone so he could . . . what was it he needed to do?

"Are you in pain, sir?"

Haldon's voice shattered his train of thought. "What? Oh. Yes. I do have something of a headache." He unfastened the harness that held his two blades, rapier and dagger, and handed them over to one of the servants, as another took the Dorsaddi overrobe from his shoulders. *There was something I was supposed to do here. Something important. . . . Plagues, that pounding is so loud. . . . They must be doing renovations, making more room for all the arriving peers.*

No. Wait. That's not right.

One of the servants gestured him into the provided chair. As a young valet knelt to remove his stiff, salt-crusted Dorsaddi boots, Abramm surveyed the circle of men surrounding him, and it dawned on him that if he continued to submit to their ministries they would find the mark upon his chest—

He sprang out of the chair, scattering the servants like startled sparrows. "That will be all, thank you. I am accustomed to seeing to my own needs." He motioned toward the door. "You may go. I will call when I need you. Lieutenant, post your guard outside the bedchamber."

Channon nodded and stepped out, but the attendants stared at him in astonishment.

"Your Highness—" Haldon began.

"Go!" Abramm barked, gesturing again at the door.

At Haldon's nod, the others, looking puzzled and hurt to a man, put down the various articles of bathing and clothing they held. When they were all out and the door closed behind them, Abramm sagged against it and let out his breath.

As the tension bled out of him, the sickness he had been holding at bay refused to be ignored any longer and he found the chamber pot just in time. Afterward, as he rinsed his mouth with water to chase away the taste, he noted his hands—chapped and blistered from the rough work he had put them through last night, and also blotched with red welts, a sign of low-grade exposure to spawn spore.

Spawn spore . . . I have to do a purge! His head pounded and his ears buzzed and fatigue pulled at him. *Right now!*

He staggered toward the bed, mentally pressing his way through the fog in his brain to focus on the Light within him, a tiny flicker in a great sea of darkness. He touched it and clung. The buzzing increased, accompanied by the cold blue sensation of the spore coursing through his veins. Fire flamed up his left arm, and his thoughts shifted. The pain was terrible. He might burn his arm. What if there was too much spore? He was so inexperienced, so weak. Maybe he should wait for Trap.

Grimly he resisted the mental distractions, turning his thoughts back to the Light and the One who gave it. The buzzing intensified, making his teeth rattle as it swelled up in him like a cloud of angry bees. His grip on the Light quailed, flickered, faded. . . . He groped again, cried out for help—

And then something snapped. Shards of color exploded through his inner vision as the white burst through his flesh, searing away everything else. And the purge began.

6

Abramm was still at the dock when Simon passed through the vast King's Court on his way to the royal apartments, pushing through the crowd of courtiers as if he were the vanguard of an advancing battle line. Pummeled by questions and suggestions and the offensive perfumes of the more dandified of his peers, he left in his wake scowls and wounded egos, and any number of broken fences he'd be weeks mending.

By the time he limped up the broad staircase at the court's far end to cross the parquet-floored Upper Court and Gallery, his initial fury had submerged itself to a calmer, if no more courteous, state. Thus, when he finally burst into the antechamber of the royal apartments and pushed past the Grand Chamberlain into the sitting room, he had himself under a measure of control. Finding the lofty, blue-carpeted sitting room empty, he followed the murmur of voices through the book-lined privy chamber and study into the blue-and-gold royal bedchamber where the king was just finishing his dressing.

To Simon's surprise, except for the servants, only the diminutive Ives attended the king this morning, the other members of Gillard's trio of merry men presumably still recovering from their night of excess. Or maybe they'd gone down to the docks to have a look at the new arrival. In any case, it was a refreshing change.

Gillard gave him a nod. "Ah, my lord uncle, the duke. Good morning, sir."

In the four years since he had ascended the throne, Gillard had changed much. The constant association with fawning courtiers had worked its inevitable influence, and lately the boy had become almost as much of a dandy as the court's Lord of Fashion, Temas Darnley. Today he wore the ballooning, slash-cut breeches that were the latest rage with white hose and a billowy-sleeved doublet of violet satin brocade trimmed with gold piping and amethyst. A cravat of white lace frothed at his throat, and more peeked from under his cuffs. Rubies and sapphires glittered on his fingers, in the lace at his throat, and off the gold circlet on his head. In deference to feminine persuasion, he had grown his white-blond hair into a thick, shiny mane that curled to his shoulders. He went clean-shaven for the same reason, displaying the slender jagged scar on his chin that was his trophy from the first realm-wide fencing championship he had ever won. Though his appearance was not to Simon's taste, the old duke knew it was admired by all the court ladies and emulated by many of the men.

"Come to accompany me to the docks, have you, Uncle?" Gillard asked, turning to the full-length mirror beside him.

"I've already been down and back, Your Majesty," Simon said brusquely. "And I strongly suggest you forgo that trip just now. It will not help your cause."

Gillard froze in the act of straightening the ruffles at the end of his sleeve, glancing at Simon by way of the mirror. When the latter said nothing, Gillard dropped his gaze and finished with his ruffle, his expression closed and blank. Finally he turned to face his uncle. "So. You've seen him, then."

No need to say who he meant. There was but one "him" of significance at the moment. "Only from a distance, Sire. I thought it best to confront him while standing at your side."

Gillard nodded. "Let us go down, then, and confront him."

"You'd be better doing that here in the palace, sir."

His nephew raised a pale brow. "All these months you've harped at me about giving the people the impression I don't care, and now that I'm ready to share in their jubilation, you tell me to stay home? What impression will that give?"

"One of a man who understands the graveness of his situation."

Gillard turned back to his reflection, fiddling with the lace at his throat. "So Abramm's come back? What's that to me?"

There was that denial again, that façade of maddening indifference. Simon held his temper and grated out, "They're saying he killed the kraggin, boy! With his own hand!"

"That's ridiculous. You know how tales fly at times like these."

"True or not, the point is, many *do* believe it, and they're lauding him as a hero. I just now heard someone say he stabbed the monster with his own spear, then held on so fiercely it pulled him under! Ridiculous, yes, but they love it! They *want* to believe it. If you go down there, he'll have the high ground, and all the people's pleasure, and you'll be the man who did nothing."

Gillard's frown deepened into a scowl. "There was nothing I could've done except get people killed. It would have been stupid—"

"Gillard, your *brother* killed the monster. With a spear apparently. If he could do it, *you* certainly could've. You didn't even try."

Gillard absently tugged and pushed at the lace. "Did you talk to Channon, or any of the other men? Find out what really happened out there?"

"They were escorting him off the launch. I'd have had to wade through the crowd to get to them."

"What of the Mataians? I saw them on the ship when it came in. I thought surely *they'd* claim victory."

"They have." Simon scowled. "They're saying Abramm is their prophesied Guardian-King."

Gillard's face paled. "But . . . didn't he run from the Flames? Physically attack High Father Saeral?"

"I only know what Laramor told me. And what I saw with my own eyes. He was met at the dock by a bevy of high-ranking Mataians, including Bonafil himself."

Gillard stared at him again through the mirror's reflection. Then he spat out a blasphemy and whirled to pace the length of the bedchamber. "He'll never get it," he growled. "He's unfit!"

"He may well get it."

"*NO!* The crown is *mine!*" Gillard paced to the window and back, then stopped to glare at him. "So he killed the kraggin? Even if it's true, in a week everyone will be back at their lives, the monster no longer a concern. In a month no one will care who killed it."

"Sire, you don't *have* a month. The Table meets tonight."

It was as if Gillard didn't hear him. He paced back and forth at the room's end, completing many circuits before he stopped again and declared, "We'll just have to persuade them otherwise." He barked a laugh. "Fire and Torment! This is *Abramm* we're talking about. How hard can that be?!"

As he returned to his pacing, Simon's heart leaped with a feeble hope.

Yes, it *was* Abramm, wasn't it? And when he came before the Table tonight, everyone would see the weakness in him, the timidity, the uncertainty. Despite his words, Simon knew the boy hadn't killed that monster. After years on the battlefield, he knew how such things happened, and so did many of the lords who served on the Table with him. The real heroes were all too often the little men, subordinates who had no choice but to forfeit credit to their superiors.

Channon and his men had most likely killed the thing together. But since Abramm had commissioned the boat, *he* would get the glory. The lords would understand that.

But just because he didn't kill the kraggin doesn't make him unfit to wear the crown.

Over by the bed, Ives cleared his throat and said nervously, "Well, *I* heard that old Master Rhiad accused him of being a Terstan right after he killed the thing. Demanded he bare his chest, and he refused."

Both men turned to face him. "Refused?" Gillard asked.

"It's what I heard."

"Pox and plagues!" Gillard exclaimed, looking at Simon. "Do you suppose my holy little brother could have come back to us a wearing the mark of heresy? Now *that* would solve everything! After what Raynen put us through, no one in their right mind will support another Terstan on the throne."

Simon huffed his exasperation, feeling his hangover headache again. "Didn't you hear me, Gillard?" he said. "*Mataians* came out to escort him from the launch. High Father Bonafil was on hand to welcome him. They're calling him their Guardian-King. They'd never do that if he really wore a shield."

Gillard scowled at him. "Why did Abramm refuse, then?"

"He's crown prince. It's an impertinent and insulting demand. I'd have refused it myself. As would you."

They fell silent, each to his own contemplation, until a tap at the door preceded Gillard's Grand Chamberlain with news of Abramm's arrival at the palace.

"Why wasn't I informed when he reached the front gates?" Gillard demanded angrily. "I gave specific orders that if he came before—"

"He arrived by way of a side entrance, sir. Made some kind of secret arrangements with old Haldon, who put him up in the Ivory Apartments." The Grand Chamberlain paused. "He smells fearsome bad. They say it's on account of him swimming in the kraggin's blood. Did you hear he stuck his spear into it and hung on so tightly it pulled him under? They thought for a time he might have drowned."

"Would that he had," Gillard muttered.

"I beg your pardon, sir?"

"Nothing. Where is Lieutenant Channon?"

"With Prince Abramm, sir."

"Tell him I want his report as soon as he is able."

"Yes, sir."

Gillard scowled at the man's departing back and, once the door closed, exploded into blasphemies. "They'll *never* put him on the throne! He's a weak-willed pigeon. A naïve holy-boy who's spent the last six years sweeping some Esurhite's floor. What does he know about ruling a realm?"

"Surely the Table will see that," Ives said.

"They'll see it," said Simon, "but so long as he's of age, and sound of mind and body, they'll have to approve his claim. And competent advisors can make up for any deficiencies of experience and training."

"Sound of mind!" Gillard exclaimed, whirling from the window where he'd momentarily stopped. "That's it!"

His companions looked at him blankly.

"Whatever the Mataio's intentions in this, the fact is, six years ago *they* said he fled the Flames and attacked the High Father in madness. And really, who wouldn't question the sanity of a man who'll commission an entire ship to bait a known ship killer in its den?" He stopped at the sideboard to inspect the assortment of biscuits, sweet twistbreads, and fruit that had been laid out by the servants. "Or seeks to claim a throne when he has no idea how to rule."

He selected a long double twist and nodded when one of the servants offered to pour him a cup of coffee from the heavy clay pitcher sitting nearby.

Simon frowned at him. "Madness is not a thing one proves just off the bowstring."

"Thus we'll petition the Table to grant an extension to my regency," Gillard said. "To be sure he's really sane. And to provide time for him to be prepared to rule."

He sampled the twistbread, then settled into an overstuffed chair near the sideboard and crossed his legs. "We can also mention the undesirability of having to finance two coronation ceremonies should he prove unfit. And the extended turmoil of changing cabinet members and power structures in the court . . . to say nothing of the nightmare of having another mad king."

Simon frowned at him, surprised. It was a sound argument, one that just might succeed. Before he could say anything further, however, loud familiar laughter echoing in the sitting chamber heralded the arrival of the other two members of Gillard's trio of merry men, Matheson and Moorcock. They'd just come from watching Abramm's arrival at the docks.

"Mataian through and through," Matheson declared. "I wonder if they haven't kept him hidden away 'til now just waiting for a moment like this."

"They're saying he smelled pretty bad," said Ives.

"You didn't think we'd get *that* close, did you?" Matheson protested.

With Gillard's attention abducted by his favorites, Simon slipped away, annoyed as always by their superficial chatter, but far more hopeful than he'd been when he entered. True, the Mataio would surely support its Guardian-King, and its influence at court was not insignificant. The Lower Table of elected representatives also had substantial power, and after what had happened today, he knew where *their* favor would lie. But though they would certainly be in attendance to watch the vote, the Lower Table had no say in approving Abramm's claim. That would be left to the Table of Lords, and the Lords could be persuaded to look beyond one day's heroics to more practical matters.

It seemed he had a bit of work to do today.

—————

The arena lay dark and silent. Arrayed in the white beribboned doublet and ballooning breeches of the Pretender, Abramm stood at the center of the sandy expanse and waited. In the dark sweep of the amphitheater's tiered seating, the crowd waited as well, tense with anticipation.

Movement whispered beside him, and a hot burst of energy surged through him. He restrained it, waiting.

A sigh, a hiss of breath. Close now. Then something touched his arm, and he whirled toward it, shocked to find he had no blade. A backlit figure loomed before him, crying out as his fingers closed round its throat. "Your Highness!"

Another man called out, too. "Your Highness, no! Please!"

Why are they calling me "Your Highness"? Why are they speaking Kiriathan and not the Tahg?

The arena vanished, replaced by the luxurious bedchamber in which he had fallen asleep, the shadow figures transforming into dark-liveried servants. He had one of them by the throat, backed up against the bedpost—old Haldon himself, in fact.

Abramm released the man at once, horrified and embarrassed. "I beg your pardon, Haldon. I was dreaming."

The white-haired chamberlain slid off the bedpost and backed away, stopping as he bumped into his smaller companion. He rubbed his bruised throat with one large hand, straightened his doublet with the other, both men staring at Abramm as if, at the slightest provocation, he might attack again.

"Are you all right?" Abramm asked.

"Yes, Highness." Haldon's voice rasped.

"Are you sure?" Abramm swung his legs out from under him and stood, causing both servants to flinch back a step before holding their ground. Haldon pulled his hand from his throat and straightened his shoulders.

"Plagues, Haldon!" Abramm cried. "I *am* sorry. I swear I meant you no harm."

"It's quite all right, sir," Haldon said stiffly. "I understand." But wariness lingered in his eyes.

Explanation lay on the tip of Abramm's tongue. But explaining would raise more questions than it answered. Already they must be thinking how the Abramm they had once known would no more have attacked a man than flown. Not only would it have violated his most rigidly held standards, but he would have been incapable of pulling it off. And he had obviously been more than capable.

Well, the less made of it, the sooner it would recede into the haze of lost memory. He put the matter from his mind and rubbed his eyes. In the other room, a clock chimed four times. He had slept longer than he had expected, but at least the spore fever was gone.

"Lieutenant Channon said we could come in," Haldon said, his professional dispassion returning. "We made a lot of noise—building up the fire, refreshing the bath—but you slept through it as if you were dead."

"It's been a long two days."

"I should say." He uttered the words without expression, and his eerie neutrality sparked another possibility in Abramm's mind, a possibility that made his stomach knot into a hard ball. Had they seen the cocoon of Terstan Light on him?

Haldon was speaking again: "The Table of Lords will convene at eight this evening, sir. I'll send in a hot-topper for your bath. There are also several suits of properly sized clothing in the wardrobe. I trust you will find something to your taste." He hesitated. "Are you sure you wish no assistance?"

"I'm sure. But I will need the services of a barber. And after that, a second bath, I think."

The manservant bowed. "Very good, sir."

"Oh, and tell Lieutenant Channon he is free to conduct things as he wills."

"Yes, sir."

As Haldon left, Abramm turned toward the bathchamber, where the doorway framed an enameled, claw-legged tub standing on a platform amid white tile. Steam swirled lazily off the water, likely herbal scented, though all he could smell was kraggin.

His stiffness largely gone, thanks to the purge's rejuvenating effects, he pulled off the one boot he still wore, followed by trousers and tunic, and piled them all by the outer door. Then he found his dagger and cut off the long tail of his hair just above the thong that held it, tossing it onto the pile, as well. No point struggling to wash the stink out of it when he'd already determined it would not be part of the image he meant to create for himself.

He fully expected Gillard to lobby the Table for an extension of his own regency so Abramm could be prepared to rule. Somehow Abramm had to convince them all he was not so unprepared as they believed. Unfortunately, his experience as advisor to the Dorsaddi king would count for nothing here, at best, and at worst, could bring him ridicule and disdain. Gillard would be first to stand in that line, he guessed, with Uncle Simon right behind him. And if he feared the lords might disbelieve the tale of his exploits among the Dorsaddi, how much more that they would scoff at the notion he'd been the White Pretender? Especially since the Pretender's exploits had been so embellished and exaggerated even in Qarkeshan, they were unbelievable all on their own. Just a mention of it last night had provoked rolled eyes and sardonic comments among his armsmen.

So if he was unable to cite any of his real accomplishments, that left him with appearances and first impressions, which his time in Esurh had shown him were powerful tools, at least for the short run. He wanted something that would jolt the lords free of their preconceptions and inspire in them at least a moderate confidence that he could do the job—given the appropriate counselors, of course. Something as far from what he had been as Brother

Eldrin—and "little Abramm"—as he could get. Something to hearken back to the days when kings were men of action more than words.

He was about to step into the bath when a knock sounded on the outer bedchamber door, causing the shieldmark, glittering in plain view on his chest, to suddenly burn in his awareness. He snatched up the thick cotton robe hanging on the wall beside the tub and was overlapping its front edges around him when an adolescent boy peeked into the tiled chamber.

"I gave you no leave of entrance!" Abramm snapped, fear of discovery lending harshness to his voice.

The boy blanched and withdrew from sight. "Forgive me, Highness. I . . . I . . ."

"What do you want?"

"I've brought extra towels, sir. And a top-off of hot water for the bath." The youth, dressed in the white shirt and dark britches of his status, his brown hair queued at his nape, moved back into the doorway, revealing the stacked towels and steaming pitcher he carried.

Annoyed mostly by his own overreaction, Abramm made a conscious effort to ease his black expression. "Very well," he said.

After the boy had laid the towels on a sideboard by the tub and added the pitcher's contents to the bathwater, Abramm instructed him to take the clothes and hair by the door and see them burned.

"And tell Master Haldon I should like to eat when I've finished with my preparations."

"Yes, sir."

"What's your name, lad?"

"Jared, sir."

"Very well, Jared. Once you've seen to the clothes, you're to station yourself outside this bathchamber door and let no one open it without my say."

The page drew himself up proudly. "Yes, Your Highness!"

Abramm sighed as the door closed. Obviously, keeping his mark secret from all would be impractical. He was neither slave nor Guardian any longer, and a king must have servants. To deny them would only awaken the very suspicions he wished to allay.

I'll have to find a few I can trust. Men who won't go running to Gillard—or the Mataio—the first chance they get.

Laying the robe close at hand, he eased into the tub and exhaled in delight. The hot springs at Jarnek had given him a taste for baths, and in these last seven weeks he had missed them sorely. This water was nearly hot enough to burn and felt wonderful. Submerging himself to his chin, he sighed again.

Part of him could hardly believe he was here, still free, still in contention for the Crown. It seemed a miracle he had come this far, and yet, he felt as if he trod a knife-edge of disaster. It took but a slight shift of perspective for all his plans of convincing the lords to accept him over Gillard on image alone to look ridiculously naïve. These were men seasoned in the ways of politics and rule, many of them antagonistic and suspicious, most of them having more years of experience than Abramm had even lived. It would take such a little thing to ruin it all. A loss of poise, a breech of protocol, some heedless remark, and it could all come tearing apart. Even assuming the plan would do anything more than make them laugh in the first place. That was the worst part—imagining their laughter.

Little Abramm? King of Kiriath?

For a moment it was as if a great hand squeezed round him, pressing out his breath, replacing it with a snake pit of writhing doubts. How could he possibly think this would work? He had nothing to bring to them. He was nothing. Yes, he had gained experience with the Dorsaddi in Esurh, but Esurh was not Kiriath, and he was a fool to think it had prepared him. A fool to have come here at all, knowing how things were. As Blackwell said earlier, Gillard would fight him, smashing his shield of imagery and projected confidence into rubble.

You should never have come back . . . you'll only make trouble . . . men will die because of you.

He gripped the tub sides and stopped the tumbling thoughts. He was here now and could only go forward. Doubts would not help him—and was not Eidon the one who'd brought him here? Would He not see him through this?

Resolutely refusing to contemplate further all the ways he might fail, all the very real weaknesses he had, he turned back toward the Light, and in that moment it seemed that something left him. Some subtle finger of presence.

He sat upright in a rush of trickling water, his nape hairs rising, his heart pounding hard against his ribcage. A wave of hot prickles rushed over his skin as he wondered—was that a rhu'ema's touch? He couldn't be sure. It had been so subtle, so delicate, hardly even there. Yet Trap had warned him such attacks would come, just last night aboard the crippled *Wanderer.*

"Your biggest enemies will be the ones you cannot see," his liegeman had said.

"Not flesh and bone, but powers of air and shadow. Once you start to walk into your destiny, the opposition becomes intense. Spore, spawn, and rhu'ema themselves—they'll come after you from every quarter. And while High Father Saeral may be dead, you know the rhu'ema that controlled him is not. He'll seek to control you again, and as well as he knows you, don't think he'll have a hard time of it."

If Saeral was not in Bonafil, he was probably in some influential palace courtier. One of the three noblemen he'd met earlier, for instance. Of them, Blackwell, as Speaker of the Table, was the only one who should have been there, Abramm having instructed Channon to inform him discreetly. The other two, the fop and the prig, had not been invited. And though he could think of numerous benign reasons for their presence, including the ones they'd given, he purposed to watch them carefully.

There would be spawn to look out for, as well—staffid, feyna, nightsprols. Staffid especially. He'd watched them come after the Dorsaddi king, Shemm, relentlessly. And Channon had already told him of the staffid infestation the palace had endured this summer. Indeed, he had noted for himself the bowls of onions sitting on hall tables as Haldon had led him to these apartments. There was even one in the bedchamber outside this bath closet.

Every successful attack would deliver new spore, activate the old, and provide a window in which the rhu'ema could work, tainting and twisting his thoughts. Shemm, under constant attack, had grown proficient at zapping them from afar, a Lightskill Abramm had not yet mastered and must. Soon. Meantime he'd better keep his guard up.

When the water had cooled he took up soap and brush from the tub-side table, scrubbing and rinsing himself repeatedly in his efforts to expunge the kraggin's odor. He had just come up from a dunking when something long and gray and fringed slithered over the edge of the tub and into the water with him.

With an oath he flew out of the bath, slipped on the wet tile, windmilled to catch his balance, then leaped aside as another of the multilegged things slithered toward him from under the tub. It was a huge species of staffid, a fact he realized even as his bare foot smashed down upon the segmented carapace. Light flowed out of him on contact, frying it. He stomped another, smacked a third with the scrub brush as it came up the side of the tub. After that he lost count, for they seemed to be everywhere. He dodged and danced around the tub, slipping and sliding on the wet tile as he stomped and smacked them to death. *Where the plague are they coming from?*

It was inevitable one would get him, and ironically it was the first he had seen, the one that had joined him in his bath. It came up out of the water and wriggled over the tub's edge, dropping straight to the floor and landing atop his foot, where it wrapped itself instantly around his instep. With a shout of annoyance, he yanked it off before it could bite, only to have it twist in his palm and clamp around his fist. A bright pain stung the back of one knuckle, followed instantly by a flow of white fire down his arm and into the staffid, loosening its grip. The thing writhed in brief agony, multilegs fluttering. Then it flared blue and went limp.

He flung it to the floor with the others, glanced around warily to be sure it was the last, and froze as his eyes fell upon Jared and Haldon standing in the doorway, staring at him in slack-jawed astonishment.

7

The tub itself, standing hip-high between them, afforded Abramm a measure of modesty, but did nothing to hide the golden shield on his chest. Jared stared at it, transfixed, while Haldon took one look and immediately turned away, stopping the servants now coming up behind him and herding them back out the bedchamber door.

Abramm heard him assure them it was only staffid, heard the door shut and the latch click. Only then did his mind, stunned by the sudden discovery, churn back into action. His robe lay on the other side of the tub, soaking in a puddle of water. Not that it mattered now. Feigning calm, he turned, took one of the towels from the sideboard and wrapped it around his waist.

About that time Haldon returned, stopping in the doorway behind Jared, who still had not closed his mouth. As before, the chamberlain's gaze riveted upon the shieldmark. After a moment, it flicked to the red dragon rampant branded into Abramm's left arm, then to the scars that laced his torso. *"True trophies of a warrior's successes,"* his former master had called those scars. Haldon's eyes catalogued every one before moving on to the dead staffid littering the floor. When his gaze finally returned to Abramm's, he looked pale and shaken.

"Look at all the staffid," Jared murmured. "They're *huge*! And there's so *many* of them. . . ." He lifted his wide eyes to Abramm. "And you killed them all yourself, my lord!"

And not one without my having to touch it first, Abramm thought morosely. He counted eleven of them and wondered again where they had come from. Staffid were self-propagated, either free roamers or cultivated and delivered to a specific target by an agent. In daylight the free roamers might roll into any number of disguises designed to be picked up and brought into the house, unrolling in the night to seek out warm flesh. Others took on the form of jewelry—bracelets, rings, and armbands—and exerted a subtle compulsion over the finder to put them on, sometimes without even knowing it. They fed on blood, injecting their victim with a tiny amount of sense-dulling spore so they would not be felt. Staffid spore was among the most benign. Injected in minute amounts, it produced no negative symptons for weeks.

These particular staffid were not, however, free roamers. They had come after him aggressively, their spore atypically strong. Someone had cultivated them especially for him, hoping no doubt to break down his resistance to deception.

"Who's had access to this chamber?" Abramm asked, scanning the tiled floor for the remains of the membrane pouch that had held them. Quiescent as long as their target was not nearby, they could have been left here for hours, awakening to chew through only when he'd come close enough.

Haldon frowned. "Since you sent us all out, no one save Smyth, me, and the boy here."

"And before I arrived?" He stepped back to look under the tub, then bent closer. Sure enough, shreds of a translucent blue-gray membrane floated in the puddled water near the claw foot farthest from the door.

"Before that," Haldon said, "we were getting ready. . . . There were probably close to fifty people, and no one really watching for anything suspicious. At least nothing like this." Coming around the tub to see what Abramm had found, he bent down to pick up the membrane. It dangled, dripping, from his large, bony fingers, shimmering in the light. "Do you know what this is, sir?"

"It's part of the pouch the staffid came in."

Something in Haldon's expression made Abramm think the man already knew that. He draped it over the tubside with a grimace and wiped his fingers on one of the towels. "Sir," he said finally, "I do not believe this is something your brother orchestrated. You have other enemies here." His eyes darted to the shieldmark on Abramm's chest and away, as if it made him uncomfortable to look at it.

"Yes," said Abramm.

Jared was staring at the mark again, as well, his expression jolting Abramm's thoughts from questions about the staffid to a greater concern.

Feeling his attention, the boy's eyes flicked up to his own, then down to the floor, his face growing white as the tile.

Abramm sighed. "You understand, Jared, that what you have seen here is not information you are free to spread around. That if it does spread, I will know the source."

"Yes, my lord. But—" He stifled his words, looked pleadingly at Haldon, then at the floor again.

Abramm raised a questioning brow to the chamberlain.

"Sire, the rumor that you wear a shield is all over Springerlan. Everyone knows what Master Rhiad accused."

"Nevertheless, this gives neither of you leave to confirm it. If you do, I will know."

Jared drew breath to speak and again stopped himself before the words came out.

"You have something to say, Jared?" Abramm asked.

"Only that . . . sir, it goes against the code of honor for a valet to reveal such information. I would never do such a thing."

"At least not knowingly."

"Maybe it would be best to send him away, sir," Haldon suggested, his tone carefully neutral. "To one of the border fortresses. Archer's Vale, maybe. Or Highmount Holding."

Jared's eyes went wide.

Abramm frowned. "Exile him for accidentally learning something I'd prefer he not know?"

"What he knows could ruin you," Haldon said quietly.

Abramm turned to the boy. "What do you think, Jared? Can you hold your tongue, or would you rather be somewhere distant where it won't matter what you say?"

"I swear to you on my life, Sire, I will say nothing."

Something in his tone, in the solemnity of his mien reminded Abramm of Philip Meridon, hopefully already in Sterlen with his parents by now. Philip would say it the same way. And he would mean it. Abramm sensed that Jared meant it, too. He regarded the boy long and hard before releasing a low breath and nodding. "Very well, Jared. I accept your oath and your service."

"You can start by gathering up these staffid and throwing them into the fire," Haldon said.

"Yes, sir."

His first bath completed by default, Abramm slipped on the plain white shirt and black breeches Haldon brought to him, then followed the chamberlain into the dressing chamber to select the clothes he would wear this evening. Once the older man reached the wardrobe, however, he merely stood there, staring at the closed door. The expression of severe neutrality he had worn throughout the interview with Jared had given way to one of increasing dismay. Now he turned from the wardrobe's dark bulk and lifted a hand.

Abramm gaped as a kelistar bloomed on his large fingers. Completely taken aback, he was a moment finding his tongue. "Thank you for showing me this, Haldon. I am . . . more pleased—and relieved—than you can know."

But that only increased the pain in the old man's face. Flicking out the orb, he said, "To my shame, sir, I must confess that I *have* broken the honor of a valet." He hesitated. "When you attacked me, I thought it proof you were . . . compromised. I am afraid I . . . passed that conclusion on." He dropped both hands to his sides.

"You thought I was controlled by rhu'ema?"

"It was widely known among us they intended that for you six years ago. It seemed the only explanation. You were so strong and quick. You nearly killed me! That is not something a simple scribe could've done." His eyes flicked back to Abramm's chest, hidden now by the shirt. "But then you weren't a scribe, were you?"

"I was for a time. Who did you tell?"

"Only Beeson. Your chef. But he will tell others. Already has, I'm sure."

"Terstans?"

Haldon nodded. "I'll tell him I was wrong, of course. But for many, I fear, it will not matter. They'll just think I've fallen to your deceptive abilities."

It hadn't occurred to Abramm that the men he'd assumed would be his allies might reckon him possessed, and he thought himself an idiot now for the oversight. Had he not on his last arrival at Springerlan been kidnapped by Terstans who believed he was to be the Mataio's puppet king? Why would they think differently now when the Mataio itself was openly claiming exactly that?

Haldon looked more miserable than ever, but he kept his chin up and fixed his gaze on something beyond Abramm's right shoulder. "I am disgraced, sir," he whispered, white hair shining in a halo around his craggy face. "*I* am the one who ought to go to Highmount Holding."

"That is true," said Abramm. And Haldon slowly paled. Abramm let him squirm a moment, then relented. "Nevertheless, I know you for a faithful man, Haldon, and I trust you'll not make the same mistake again."

"Never, sir." Haldon still had not met his gaze.

"Besides, it will hardly be to my advantage to send you away now you've learned my secret, only to have to begin anew with someone else. Although frankly I'm beginning to wonder if this subterfuge is really worth it. I hadn't counted on having to win over my allies as well as my enemies. Maybe I should just come clean of it at the start and see what happens."

Haldon's head jerked up in alarm. "Tonight, sir?"

"Why not? I've already been openly accused."

The chamberlain shook his head. "If you declare it, sir, they will never accept you. It is not good to be a Terstan these days. In the last month alone, two high lords were ruined for it, their titles stripped, their holdings seized. The month before another disappeared without a trace. We suspect the Gadrielites took him. He probably died from their attempts to drive the evil out of him."

Abramm frowned. "I had heard of this new order of heretic hunters back in Qarkeshan—breaking into people's homes and hauling them off—but I believed the tales exaggerated. Assault? Kidnapping? Outright robbery? The authorities allow such things?"

"Civil authorities have no jurisdiction in Mataian matters, sir. And heresy is a Mataian matter."

"But everyone who is not a Mataian is a heretic, so—"

"Only Terstans are considered such right now. And because it's only Terstans, those who might otherwise object look the other way." He hesitated, then added quietly, "King Raynen's last days frightened a lot of people. Even those of us who wear the shield. The Mataio has used that fear to its advantage."

The chamberlain started to open the wardrobe doors, then motioned for Jared to draw the drapes on the tall windows ranged along the western wall. As the scent of dust tickled Abramm's nostrils and the room flickered into dimness, he said, "Tell me about Ray, Haldon. All I've heard is that he went completely mad of the sarotis and threw himself off Graymeer's Point."

Haldon grimaced. "It was seeing Captain Meridon executed that started it, I think. Many say Meridon was set up, that the accusations against him were but a deceit to remove him from the king's circle. Especially after the—well, whatever it was that happened with you."

"When I fled the Mataio, you mean."

"Aye."

Abramm said no more, though Haldon clearly hoped he would. When he held silence, the chamberlain sighed and returned to his own story.

"After that night your brother was never the same. He met assassins in his bedchamber, saw evil spirits behind the draperies, heard voices whispering from the balcony. He turned out all his personal servants, convinced we were spies. He even suspected the birds." Haldon snorted softly. "The drapes and doors and windows had to be closed at all times. He took to slinking around the palace, using the secret passages to spy on those he suspected of spying on him. His hair and beard grew long, his teeth green. He never changed his clothes, never bathed, and often we heard him screaming or cackling afar in those passages he haunted."

He fell silent, lost in recollection while Abramm entertained memories of his own. Raynen had seen their father murdered, knew of Gillard's aspirations for the throne and of Saeral's evil plans involving Abramm himself. He was, in fact, the man responsible for opening Abramm's own eyes to the matter—and who, then, let Gillard sell Abramm into slavery and Trap along with him, betraying them both to save himself.

Guilt could cripple a man—so could fear. In combination they were toxic. Worse, they smothered the Light and so allowed the sarotis to grow.

"He was bent and crippled at the end," Haldon continued. "The curd filled his eyes and dribbled down his face, drying on clothing that had grown ragged and filthy. His decisions became completely illogical and inappropriate. The Table had to remove him. They locked him up in the Chancellor's Tower—for his own safety—but the next day he escaped and slipped off to Graymeer's."

They fell into silence again. After a moment Abramm said, "And no one wants a repeat."

"No, sir. If you reveal your shield tonight, aside from Eidon working a miracle on your behalf, I've no doubt the lords will remove you permanently from the succession and immediately transform Gillard's regent status to full sovereignty."

Abramm regarded him soberly, chilled by the realization that what he said was probably true. "Then I shall not reveal it." He gestured at the wardrobe. "Shall we get on with this?"

"Of course, sir." Haldon pulled open the door, revealing a row of garments sewn of velvet, satin, fine wool, and brocade. There were doublets and cloaks and shirts and trousers, all bedecked with ruffles and lace and ribbons and jewels.

Abramm stared at them in a blank-minded surprise that swiftly turned to revulsion and then an inexplicable rising fury. Haldon riffled through them and pulled out a wine-colored doublet spangled with rubies and fluttering ribbons. "How about this one, sir? I think—"

"No."

Haldon put the garment back, pulled out another, this one deep blue and equally laden with frippery. "Then, how about—"

"I'll not wear any of these."

Haldon frowned at him. "Highness, I assure you, all were selected with an eye to current fashion."

Abramm had no doubt of that, but to him they were straight out of a Game Master's playbook, far too close to what he'd worn as the White Pretender. "I don't care if they are," he said firmly. "I'm not wearing them."

Haldon drew back, brows flying up in surprise.

Abramm ignored him. "Either find me something more conservative, or bring the tailor in to alter one of these. It doesn't matter which, but I'm not going anywhere dressed like a lace-maker's rack. And I'm *surely* not wearing those ridiculous-looking breeches."

Haldon swallowed his surprise "I'll see to it at once, sir."

"You can also start preparing that second bath." Abramm could still smell the kraggin on himself and was beginning to fear he might be living with this odor for days. "And what of the barber? Is he here yet?"

"Yes, sir. I'll send him in."

8

The Council Hall, where the Table of Lords met, presided over the Mall of Civil Government on the shelf of land halfway between the top of the great escarpment that formed the city's eastern boundary and the river at its heart. Feeling confident and upbeat after a day of successful lobbying, Simon rode down in his friend Ethan Laramor's coach, and not even Laramor's unrelenting pessimism could dim his good spirits.

Finding the Hall's front court already clogged with arriving coaches, they drove around to the side and entered through a corridor leading directly onto the Upper Table's crowded central floor. Tobacco smoke hung thickly above the velvet- and satin-clad dignitaries, who, bewigged and otherwise, clustered in knots of animated conversation, their voices echoing in a riot of sound beneath the chamber's magnificent hammer-beamed ceiling. Beyond and below them the Lower Table with its ranked rows of long bench seats was also filling rapidly, as were the curved tiers of the audience galleries overlooking it.

It had been an eventful day, with the biggest event yet to come, and Simon could hear the excitement in the men's voices, see it in their faces. His own efforts fueled by a raft of conflicting rumors, the question of Abramm's fitness to rule was now foremost on everyone's mind.

A broad-chested, beefy-faced lord in burgundy velvet, sleeves slashed with black silk, hailed them as they emerged onto the Floor, drawing them into his circle of conversation. Laine Harrady was a longtime friend and ally, an old war brother and one of Gillard's staunchest supporters. Age had thickened already thick features, enlarging ears and nose as it had robbed him of teeth and hair—Simon had not seen him without his brown, black-ribboned queue wig in at least a decade.

Now Harrady clapped Simon's shoulder and smiled broadly, his mouth full of large ivory false teeth. "What a day this has been, eh, old friend?" he boomed. "Who would have thought we'd ever be here considering little *Abramm's* claim to the throne? The queen's pious pacifist? The little boy who wouldn't stand up to a mouse if it challenged him? Now he seeks to rule us all." He waggled heavy brows. "'Ne'er a fancy queerer than the fortune life delivers,' eh?"

"Indeed," said Simon, eyeing the other lords in attendance and automatically taking the roll.

Harrady leaned closer. "Is it true about his having specifically requested your boy Channon as personal bodyguard? And Channon going along with it?"

Simon scowled, feeling a renewed twinge of the astonishment and dismay he'd felt when he'd first learned of that arrangement. "Apparently so, though I haven't had a chance to talk to him yet."

Channon had spent most of the afternoon on guard in the Ivory Apartments, while Abramm allegedly napped, and retired immediately afterward to his own quarters to bathe, since he'd been on the water with the prince and smelled almost as bad himself.

"I heard he was sick all afternoon," said one of the other men. "Abramm, I mean."

"I heard that, too," said a third, "and also that he flew into a fury when one of the valets took his cloak and drove out all the servants, then demolished the suite in his rage."

"I heard he attacked Haldon himself," said Harrady with a grin. "Slammed him up against the bedpost, clear off his feet—if you can believe that."

"If you can believe that, you'll believe anything," Simon said dryly. It was an occupational hazard of palace living—courtiers' tongues swelled the most insignificant of events into monstrous scandal. He almost felt sorry for the lad. But the silly boy *could* have spent the afternoon cultivating the nobility and proving the rumormongers wrong instead of sleeping in his rooms.

"Yes, but *I* actually spoke to an armsman who saw him arrive," said the first man, "and *he* said the prince was pale and sweating. Looking as if he might collapse. He may not even come tonight."

"Don't we wish!" said Simon. Abramm always had been sickly, so it wasn't impossible, and if he didn't show, after all the talk today, the regency extension would pass without question.

"He'll be here," Laramor growled. "His Mataian friends will make sure of it."

Simon followed the direction of his friend's gaze to the Lower Table, where a handful of gray-mantled Guardians stood at the head of the center aisle, conversing with their lay allies. Not surprisingly, chief among them was Darak Prittleman with his hatchetlike profile, tightly queued hair, and familiar gray doublet. The man either never changed his clothes or had a wardrobe full of the same design, for Simon could not recall having seen him dressed otherwise in years, no matter what the occasion.

"Been scurrying about like a roach in a flour mill," Laramor had said of him earlier over dinner, *"calling in every debt, exerting every pressure to influence the others. And that snake of his, Skurlek, has leaned hard on at least three men that I know of."*

Simon's eye roved along the front row to the opposite end where sat the Terstan contingent, headed by Everitt Kesrin. Unlike the Mataians, the Terstans affected quiet sobriety. They could not be any happier about the prospect of Abramm's claim than Simon—a thought as surprising as it was amusing. Who would have imagined he'd ever find a point of agreement with Terstans of any stripe, especially after Raynen?

"Well, whether Abramm shows or not," Harrady was saying, "it won't matter." He clicked his forward-slipping false teeth back into place and pulled a pipe from his breast pocket. "When both brothers stand before us, side by side, even Abramm's supporters will see he's not king material. And I don't believe *any* of us want a puppet on the throne. The Gadrielites would get ever bolder, and just think what a Mataian-governed court would be like. All those straight-stick Laity rules? No one will give up their fun for that. Especially when the next thing they'll be demanding is money and land." He shook the pipe at them for emphasis. "I'm betting we'll be out of here before the half hour. Which reminds me—we've set up a high-stakes game for this evening. I won't ask you, Ethan"—he glanced at Laramor with a wry grin—"knowing how you feel about that sort of thing, but what about it, Simon?"

Simon shook his head. "I'm with Ethan, Laine. Gambling's not my forte."

Harrady clucked in good-natured disapproval. "Your loss, my friend, your loss."

"That's exactly what it would be if I went: my loss."

Harrady guffawed and clapped his shoulder. "Well, if you change your mind, you're welcome."

Simon moved off from him, Laramor in his wake, the two stopping to chat with friends and allies, mingling their way toward their seats in the far gallery. Every man Simon spoke with assured him he had no intention of accepting Abramm's claim the first time around, even those he'd thought would be more lenient. Abramm might have killed the kraggin, but no one believed that qualified him to rule the realm. From all signs, the extension looked certain to pass.

Still, a niggle of foreboding would not let him go. Long years on the battlefield had taught him the seeming ease with which victory could twist itself to defeat within one's very grasp. Despite all the assurances, there was no way of knowing how things would go until it was over. Thus he found himself growing increasingly tense the closer he got to taking his seat.

He was almost relieved when Byron Blackwell pled indecision and refused to say how he'd vote.

"I'm not opposed to the idea of an extension," Blackwell said, "just unconvinced Gillard will seriously work to prepare him. He's made it clear what he thinks of Abramm, after all." He frowned as his gaze fixed on something across the room. "What is *he* doing here?"

Down in the Lower Table, at the back of the chamber, stood a pale-robed figure whose half-bald head gleamed against the darkened entrance corridor at his back. Rhiad.

"He probably intends to make his ridiculous accusation again," Blackwell predicted. "With more supporters this time. Well, we'll see about that." Excusing himself, he went at once to the guard at the gate in the railed partition separating the Upper and Lower Tables. But the guard had barely left his post when Rhiad vanished into the corridor from whence he'd come. Simon continued on his way, hoping the attention had scared him away and there'd be no unseemly outbursts tonight.

As head of the Shar contingent, Simon sat in the first chair of the first tier on the west side of the floor, thus delivered from having to climb the narrow stair more than a few steps. He settled gratefully into his seat, glad to be off the sore hip that was troubling him more than usual tonight, thanks to spending all day on his feet. Harrady soon settled beside him, and shortly thereafter, the first bell for order clanged across the chamber, triggering a general exodus from the floor, Shar lords moving to one side of the dais, Nunn to the other. The offsides of both galleries held those not affiliated with either party, among them the border lords, now filing up the stairs at the end of the Shar Gallery. They favored leather jerkins and trousers, spurning what they called the womanish fripperies of current court favor, though a few sported the gold earrings of clan lordship. Their faces were closed, and they did not speak to the other lords, hardly taking account of their presence. The other lords in turn regarded the Borderers with cultured disdain.

Ethan couldn't predict which way they would vote. Many still nursed resentment at Gillard's mishandling of Rennalf of Balmark's grievances regarding Carissa's desertion six years ago—essentially he'd faulted the border lord for not controlling his own wife. Rennalf himself was conspicuous by his absence tonight, as were his closest allies. The remainder, while not allied with him, still feared the clanlord's capacity for retaliation should they favor Gillard. Unfortunately for them, Abramm's Mataian ties made him an even less attractive option, worsened by the fact that he was a weak and clumsy youth, ignorant in the ways of war. For a people who had only recently stopped determining their leaders through trial by combat, these were serious deficiencies.

As hall servants went round extinguishing the lamps along the side walls, a line of royal guardsmen strode in to position themselves against the back wall and the Council Lawreaders, black robed and white wigged, filed into the box on the Nunn side of the dais's central stair. Once they were settled, the second bell rang and Byron Blackwell arose. At ten minutes to the hour he called the Table to order and launched into his opening readings while in the darkened Lower Table the audience continued to rustle. In fact, instead of waning as Blackwell droned on, the rustling increased to a rolling susurration that spread to the Upper Table, where it finally clarified into a hissing of drawn breaths and whispered oaths. The Lord Speaker looked up from his reading in surprise and fell silent, staring along with those in the Nunn Gallery beyond him, toward the Lower Table. Puzzled, Simon turned, and when his eyes fell upon the object of their interest, he heard his own breath hiss against his teeth. For a moment he thought it was Ravelin Kalladorne himself, come back from the dead.

"Eidon over all!" Harrady whispered beside him. "Is that *Abramm?*"

Simon had no answer for him. It *was* Abramm, but never in his wildest dreams had he imagined the boy could undergo such a transformation.

He stood in the partition opening at the edge of the Upper Table floor, spotlighted by the main chandelier. With his blond hair shorn to a traditional soldier's crop and his beard trimmed close in the old style of the Kalladorne kings, the hawkishness of his bloodline was now startlingly evident. He wore black close-fitting breeches, knee-high boots, and one of those newfangled jackets of black-and-gold brocade, its simple cut accentuating the lean line of his hips and the surprising broadness of shoulders and chest. A cravat of smooth black silk swelled at his throat and except for the signet ring on his right hand and the sapphire clasp that fastened his cloak, he wore no jewels. The four golden chains of his princely rank looped across his chest comprised his most elaborate adornment.

Yet the very lack of ostentation worked to his advantage, for it served to direct the focus to the man himself, and amazingly, he bore that focus well.

Abramm addressed the Lord Speaker: "I request permission to address the Table, sir." His voice was deep and strong, a boy's voice no longer, and it carried an odd foreign lilt.

Blackwell was staring at him openmouthed, his spectacles reflecting white disks. He took a moment to recover himself, then nodded. "By all means, Your Highness." He gestured to the dais.

Abramm crossed the floor in brisk, purposeful strides. Gone was the timid mien of the past; with his straight-backed carriage, his head held high, and his black cloak billowing behind him, he cut an undeniably impressive figure. On the second step from the top, he stopped and turned to face the Table, and Simon's eyes nearly fell out of his head. *He's wearing a* rapier!

"I am Abramm Alaric Kesrin Galbrath Kalladorne," Abramm declared in a ringing voice, resting a hand on that rapier hilt with casual familiarity. "I am the fifth son of His Majesty, King Meren and, by reason of the reinstatement granted me by His Majesty, the late King Raynen, direct heir to the throne of Kiriath. Is this not so, Master Greenway?"

The Keeper of the Vault of Documents arose from the Lawreader's booth. "It is so, Highness."

"Then in light of my heritage and the laws of succession, I lay claim to the throne of Kiriath. What say you, Council of the Realm? Do you accept?"

Silence fell upon the Table, and Simon realized that everyone else was as taken aback as he. This man who laid his claim before them was not what any of them had expected. Simon could almost believe this Abramm *had* stabbed the kraggin with a spear and ridden it to the bottom of the sea.

He felt an unexpected surge of feeling. Whether respect or pride or approval—or all three—he did not know. Could Abramm finally have come into his own? Was he at last going to act like the Kalladorne he was?

But he had watched this boy grow up, watched him fail and flounder and flee, watched him renounce his heritage and devote eight years of his life to pacifism and holiness in part because he could not live up to the demands expected of one of his bloodline. Could he have changed that much, even in six years?

He heard a rustling, a chair's creak, then Ethan Laramor's voice rang out: "I do not contest the claim, but I would point out that His Highness, Prince Abramm, has been away from the realm for some time, and that prior to his departure his training was not designed to prepare him to rule." He stood ten chairs down the row from Simon, at the head of the Borderers' section, his expression grimmer than ever. "I move, therefore, that the Council extend the regency of Prince Gillard for at least six months so that Prince Abramm can be prepared to meet his responsibilities."

"I second the motion!" cried Michael Ives, jumping up from his seat midway between Simon and Laramor and several tiers up.

Abramm addressed the Council Lawreaders: "Is it not true that regencies are legally justified only when a monarch is absent, incapacitated, or not of legal age?"

The chief of the Council Lawreaders stood. "It is, Your Highness."

"Since I am none of these, I fail to see the logic of your esteemed peer's contention."

"You could be judged incapacitated on account of lack of preparation," said Ethan.

"Perhaps," Abramm replied. "But the intent of this law is clear enough, and I believe laws are meant to be obeyed in accordance with their obvious meaning, not twisted to serve those in power."

He turned his attention to the general assembly, and again Simon felt that flicker of grudging approval. Somewhere along the way, the lad had found his poise. "May I remind you, gentlemen," Abramm said, "that I was born a king's son. And while I admit I am not an expert in all fields, what man is? That is why a king has advisors. That is why he delegates authority. Many of my ancestors came to the throne with little more than I come to you. Alaric the Second was sixteen when crowned, and the people bemoaned his inexperience. Yet he went on to become one of Kiriath's greatest rulers."

"You, however, are not Alaric the Second."

All eyes shifted toward this new voice, whose owner stood now at the foot of the Shar Gallery, closest to the Lower Table, having just come onto the floor through the side door tucked into the paneled wall. Decked in gold satin doublet and blousing breeches encrusted with rubies and gold embroidery, he seemed to glow of his own light, more magnificent than Simon had ever seen him. The epitome of royal majesty—some would say excess—Gillard's brilliance easily eclipsed Abramm's subtler statement of strength and sober-mindedness.

After a moment of hesitation, the herald called out: "His Royal Highness, Gillard Simon Galbrath Aarol Kalladorne."

"Hail King Gillard!" Michael Ives cried boldly.

Traditionally, everyone in the chamber should have stood, for the Crown had not yet passed from Gillard. But tonight the lines of loyalty were too tangled. Although Simon himself stood, and heard behind him the telltale rustling and creaking as some of his peers followed suit, their number was startlingly low. In the Nunn Gallery across the Table from him, not one man among them left his seat.

Abramm's advent in this startling new guise had thrown them all off stride, challenging everything they thought they knew about him.

Even now as Gillard locked gazes with him, Abramm did not lose that unexpected poise, matching, perhaps for the first time in his life, his younger brother stare for stare. A world of unspoken communication seemed to pass between them, Gillard oddly defiant, Abramm hard-jawed and resolute. In the end, it was Gillard who looked away and Abramm who spoke first.

"You are right, brother," he said in that deep, oddly accented voice of his. "I am not Alaric the Second. I am *Abramm* the Second. And *I* have killed the kraggin."

A torrent of sound burst from the Lower Table, the men there on their feet and cheering. Simon could hardly believe what he had just witnessed: Abramm not only talking back to Gillard but taunting him. Right where it hurt the most.

Gillard went white-faced with fury, as the crowd's uproar momentarily precluded speech. When it quieted, his voice came low and trembling. "Killed the kraggin, maybe. But you risked the lives of all the men you hired to help you. A madman's gamble, I'd call it. It makes me wonder all the more . . ." He looked at the Lawreaders. "Isn't it true there's never been a man who failed the Test of the Flames and kept his sanity?"

"Not that we have on record, Si—er—Your Highness."

"Madness would certainly be considered incapacitating," Lord Michael declared.

Abramm turned a sharp gaze on Ives. "Do I appear a madman to you, Lord Michael? Do I appear incapacitated?"

To Simon's amazement Ives wilted beneath Abramm's regard. "No, Your Highness, you do not."

"Madness is not always readily seen," Gillard said.

Abramm wheeled on him. "In that case, how may we be assured you are not mad yourself, brother?"

"*I* did not run from the Flames."

"Nor did I!" Abramm snapped. "I merely changed my mind about taking my final vows. A decision not all were happy with."

"Then why did the Mataians *say* you ran?"

"You'll have to ask them." Abramm nodded to the contingent of Mataians standing front and center in the Lower Table. To a man they stared at him as if they could not believe their eyes.

"So why did you not come to Raynen? Why did you simply disappear?"

Abramm's face became very hard, almost frighteningly cold. "Because I was waylaid and sold into slavery, *brother.*"

Gillard lifted his chin, lips twitching, and they locked gazes. It was Gillard who finally disengaged, shrugging and then walking along the front of the Shar Gallery toward the dais where Abramm stood. "Well, even if we can't prove madness in a matter of moments, I submit to you that Prince Abramm remains ill-prepared to rule. I would not be here if I did not deem this lack to be of vital import.

"What does he know of the situation along our borders? Do you honestly believe *he* will be able to deal with the northern raiders that have recently plagued us? What do you think *he* will do about the Terstan problem?" He paused to rake the Council with his gaze. "My brother promises to make use of his advisors, but how will he know when a man is providing good counsel or bad? Speaking truth or lies?"

"How would you know yourself?" Abramm demanded. "How does any man know? But I *can* tell you one thing—*I* would never have allowed that monster to prowl our bay for six months while trade stood still and our people lost their livelihoods!" His voice had lowered, almost grating with the emotion in it. "You stand on very unstable ground to argue competence with me, brother!"

A second outburst erupted from the Lower Table, deep-throated bellows, cheers, stomps, whistles, and clear and crisp over all of it, cries of "Hail, King Abramm."

It clearly rattled Gillard. Simon had never seen him so pale, so completely beside himself. Normally he would already have begun breaking things in the outventing of his rage. Now he could only stand there and hold it all in.

Abramm raised a hand for quiet. "You all wonder, was I enslaved? Yes. How did I survive it? By Eidon's hand alone, just as it is by His hand I have returned to claim what He decreed was mine before the dawn of time: the throne of Kiriath. I ask you again, my fellow peers and lords of the realm: Do you accept my claim—without extension of the regency—or not?"

His words died into a silence so profound, Simon could hear Harrady breathing beside him. There was a creak, a thud, and then a new voice burst upon them, a harsh, rasping croak erupting from the pale-robed man standing at the head of the Lower Table's left side aisle. A man with a ruined face and barren scalp and eyes ablaze with hatred.

"How dare you speak of Eidon!" he shrieked. "You who by your very presence profane his name and power. I know the dark magic you used to slay the kraggin." Rhiad pointed an accusatory finger at Abramm. "I remember you now! And what you did to me in the cistern. And I accuse you, sir, before these witnesses, of wearing the mark of heresy. Bare your chest and prove me wrong!"

The shrill words rasped into silence, where it seemed men no longer even breathed, all eyes flicking between Abramm and the mad Mataian.

Then Gillard's voice purred. "I should like to see that, as well."

"Fine," said Abramm, and again there was that hard-jawed look of resolution, almost defiant now. He began to unfasten the buttons at the top of his doublet as a susurration of astonishment swept both Tables. Simon shifted uncomfortably, embarrassed and increasingly indignant that such a thing was being allowed. Abramm was the crown prince, after all.

Abramm's fingers had worked down to the buttons over his heart when Blackwell stopped it. "No, Your Highness, please! That will not be necessary. Your action is proof enough, and we all know this man is mad. Guards, remove him!"

Having already moved quietly up the aisle behind the Mataian, the guards seized him on the instant. He did not go easily.

From then on the affair devolved into a surreal nightmare, made all the worse for Simon because he wasn't even sure what his own feelings were in the matter. Part of him admitted that Abramm had taken them all by storm, that he'd done exactly what he'd needed to do tonight, with a finesse no neophyte could have mustered. He deserved a chance to prove himself.

The other part—the greater, stronger part—was horrified, crushed with the conviction that his worst fears were coming to pass, that the realm was crumbling before his very eyes. Everything he held dear, everything that had ever meant anything to him, the land and people for which he'd given his entire life, about to be gobbled up by the pious puppet masters who pulled Abramm's strings.

Splintered images were all he'd ever recall of the remainder of that night. The endless calling of the vote, the final, dreadful tally favoring Abramm, seventy-six to twenty-six. The thunderous applause that greeted it. Gillard standing stunned and blank-eyed on the side, Ethan lurking behind him with a death's-head expression. And all too soon, Blackwell at the top of the dais, with Abramm kneeling before him, intoning the oath of kings in his strong, accented voice. And then the circlet of rule was gleaming on his brow as he stood to face his subjects.

Abramm Alaric Kesrin Galbrath Kalladorne, thirty-sixth king of Kiriath.

SHIELD

AND

DRAGON

PART TWO

9

At the far northeast corner of Kiriath, on the same night the Table approved Abramm's claim to the crown, a gale swept down from the high peaks of the Aranaak Mountains, the first after weeks of cold, windless days and flat, gray skies. It whistled down the barren narrows of Kolki Pass and around the crumbling fortress standing guard at its mouth. Invisible fingers tore at the keep's roof tiles and shutters, rustled through bushes turned brittle with autumn, and rasped the dead vines against the stone. In centuries past, old Highmount Fortress had stood as a formidable barrier against marauders from the north, but it had been long since danger stalked the pass, and the fortress, seriously damaged in its last and greatest battle, had been abandoned to its successor, built farther down the mountain among the trees. When people spoke of Highmount Holding these days, they meant the new one, no fortress at all, but merely the manor of Lord Ethan Laramor and the village that attended it.

The Mataio had converted one of the old fortress's outlying signal towers into a watch, and for a while—until they abandoned it—it was the farthest inhabited structure up the pass. Meanwhile old Highmount fell into ruin, its gates sundered, its walls battered and crumbling, its tower roofs stove in. A handful of villagers remained, descendents of those who had known it in its prime, along with the pigeons, mice, and foxes who called it home.

It was last spring that the reclusive and eccentric Lady Louisa, recently returned to Kiriath from abroad, had leased it from Laramor. Moving in with two score of retainers and laborers, she had immediately begun renovations. Though much of the place remained in ruins, six months later its guard walls were whole again, its main gates strong and solid, and its modest, four-story keep stout against the storm.

Now the wind rattled the shutters outside the sole window of the lady's spacious bedchamber on the keep's fourth floor. Its fingers slipped beneath the heavy woolen drapes drawn shut before them and whispered across the wooden floor to chill the feet of the lady herself. Seated at the battered, paint-chipped vanity, she brushed her hip-length blond hair with mindless, mechanical strokes and reproached herself for feeling bitter and melancholy when she should be rejoicing over the happiness of her beloved retainer and his bride. Bursts of laughter and the wheedle of instruments pierced the vagaries of the wind's moaning, drawing her attention to the party still going on in the Great Room below. The bride and groom had long since retired to their own chambers, and the lady had lingered only until she could no longer pretend to joy, then escaped to her dark, drafty, and very empty chambers.

Her Esurhite maid, Peri, had turned back her bed, banked the fire, helped her into her nightclothes, and would have stayed to brush her rippling curls had not the lady sent her away. Peri had gone reluctantly, sensing her mistress was even more melancholy than usual but helpless to do anything but obey.

Outside, the wind howled with increasing force, gusting ice crystals against the shutters.

"You're a wretch," the lady whispered to the narrow, aristocratic face staring back at her from the vanity's mirror. "A petty, jealous, miserable wretch."

And yet, no matter how she berated herself for it, she could not stop feeling abandoned. Yes, she knew it was ridiculous to expect that Cooper's position as her retainer would preclude for him a man's normal interests. But he had been her guardian ever since she could remember, and a bachelor all that time, so she had assumed he would continue as such. Had, in fact, relied upon it.

He had been at her side through all the trials of her life—her brother Abramm joining the Mataio, her failed marriage to Rennalf of Balmark, her disastrous trip to the southland . . . the aimless travels afterward. Travels which were supposed to have brought fulfillment, but only intensified her sense of worthlessness and alienation. In the end, she'd come home, desperate for the language and culture she'd grown up in, even if she did have to hide up here in Highmount, pretending to be someone she was not.

Cooper had been the one constant in her miserable life. So when he had told her he wished to marry the widow Elayne, she was stunned. Only today, at the wedding itself, had it finally sunk in that he had transferred his affections to someone else, and that she, Carissa Louise Marielle Amelia Kalladorne Balmark, would never again be the sole object of his care and attention.

Seeing them go off together tonight, tiny, dark-haired Elayne tucked under Cooper's strong arm, all smiles and hugs and golden hopes, it had hit her with a scope and finality that had overwhelmed. She was alone. Starkly and utterly alone, with no hopes of that changing, forced to live here on the fringes of the land her family had ruled for centuries, hiding behind a name that was not hers for fear her outraged husband would find her and force her back to him. There'd be no one to stop him if he did, certainly not Gillard.

Her vision blurred with tears, and a sharp pain stabbed her throat. The methodical brushing slowed, then ceased altogether, her hand dropping to her lap. This was like Abramm all over again. She swallowed and blinked, and the tears slid down her cheeks. Never would she forget that day in Jarnek when she had watched him practice the sword with Captain Meridon, shocked at how good he was, how wonderfully he moved, how strong and sure and fluid. She'd wanted so badly for him to come home with her, to put Gillard in his place, and repay Rennalf for his humiliations, to show them all how wrong they'd been about him.

But he wouldn't do it. Whatever his old life had been, whatever it could offer him in the future—even the promise of a kingship—he'd turned his back on it for the sake of that hideous shield he'd let be burned into his chest. Not even for Carissa would he bend. Standing in that practice room staring up at him, she'd felt as if she no longer knew him. As if a stranger had taken over her brother's body, hiding the real Abramm away from her until she, too, surrendered to the power behind the shield.

Devastated, she'd left without him and for four years had nursed something very close to hatred for him. And outright loathing for the shield that had taken him from her. If time had softened the edge of her bitterness toward him, it had only intensified what she felt for that shield. All the more when she had learned what it had done to Raynen.

Perversely her gaze dropped to the small gray pebble she still wore round her neck. The pebble Philip Meridon had given her in Jarnek. The one that was supposed to ward off the staffid for her. The one, she knew now, that had burned the shield into Abramm's chest when she was trapped inside that cistern with him, believing there wasn't a Terstan for miles. She'd brought it to him herself, completely unknowing, and the thought still sickened her.

It lay low upon her breastbone, a perfect orb of pearlescent gray suspended on a golden chain, glowing softly against the white linen of her undergown. She did not know why she kept it after the heartbreak it had brought her. Because it truly did work against the staffid? Because it was, in its own strange way, her last connection with the brother she had loved more than anyone in the world? Because, in some part of her soul there lived the irrational desire to find what he had found in it, even though she knew it was impossible?

And it *was* impossible. That was the worst part.

Shortly before she'd left Abramm, in hopes of breeching the gulf that had opened between them, she had actually tried to take it. Even knowing it would cripple her, drive her mad, and make her despised in Kiriathan society, she had set her will and closed her hand upon it, waiting with clenched eyes, gritted teeth, and fluttering heart for the hated power to sear through her and claim her soul forever. But nothing had happened. No power had stirred in her. No voice had spoken. The stone had remained only a stone, cool and hard in her fist. Her flesh had remained unmarked, and she remained . . . outside. Denied, even by Eidon himself.

But how absurd to expect otherwise from someone who did not exist.

So why do you still wear his orb?

She stared into her own eyes and began to weep again—tears of bitterness and frustration and the deep aching need for someone somewhere to care whether she lived or died. Once the torrent was loosed, it could not be called back until it ran its course. Outside the storm blustered and raged, driving snow against the shutters, which banged and rattled under its fury, obscuring the sound of her weeping to all but herself. In time the sobs subsided and she regained herself, sniffing and snuffling with her head on folded arms and her eyes closed as she listened to the wind. Presently she heard footsteps, quick on the stair, slowing as they approached her door. A light tap preceded its creaking open. Peri peeked around its edge. Seeing Carissa was awake, she slid into the room and pressed the door shut behind her. Her glance flicked over her lady's tearstained face and reddened eyes, and her brow creased. But all she said was, "We have visitors, ma'am."

"Another pack of refugees?" Carissa turned back to the vanity for a kerchief to wipe her face. She recalled now what she'd heard only dimly through her turmoil—the dogs barking, voices in the wind, the boom of the fortress's main gates closing. Visitors arrived often in the night, an occurrence she'd learned long ago to ignore, seeing as it didn't concern her.

She found it ironic that of all the places she could have settled, she'd chosen one of the main rest stops on the underground smuggling route by which Kiriathan Terstans escaped the rising persecutions. Nearly all the holding's original inhabitants were part of it. Had she known, she'd never have agreed to lease the place, but Laramor had said nothing. He probably didn't know. Fortunately the smugglers themselves were as happy to have Carissa look the other way as she was to do so.

"Not Terstans, my lady," Peri said with a dip that begged forgiveness for what she knew would be unwelcome news. "Northmen. Very tall. One of them a great lord."

Carissa laid the kerchief on the vanity and arose. "Lord Ethan?" He'd gone to Springerlan for the meeting of the Table of Lords and shouldn't be back for weeks.

Peri bobbed again. "I don't think so, my lady, but they all look the same to me."

Even if Ethan's back, Carissa thought, *what would he be doing here now, in this storm? Surely he'd have sent someone over rather than come himself.*

She strode to the clothes chest for her cloak, and Peri had just helped settle it over her shoulders when Hogart, Cooper's second in charge, stuck his head in. "My lady," he said quietly, "riders have come seeking succor from the storm."

"I am coming to greet them now."

"I took the liberty of telling them you weren't well and had retired for the night."

Carissa stopped midway to the door, frowning at him, and he answered her unvoiced question: "Lord Rennalf leads them, my lady."

It was as if a horse had kicked her in the chest. She stared at him, unable to breathe, feeling the blood drain out of her face. *Rennalf! How did he learn I was here? We have been so careful.* And then, *I've got to leave!*

Her thoughts were apparently obvious to Hogart, who along with Cooper, understood the ramifications of Rennalf's presence and now raised his hands reassuringly. "No, my lady, I don't think he knows. It seems he is here only to escape the storm."

"And did not go to the manor instead?"

Hogart kept the expression of his surprise subdued. "He would never go to the manor, my lady."

Of course. She knew that very well. It was the reason she'd approached Laramor for succor in the first place. He and Rennalf had nearly come to blood feud in their antagonism. But with Ethan in Springerlan right now, Rennalf's appearance at his manor for any reason would be construed by clan law as both insult and challenge. In fact, Rennalf's being on Laramor lands at all in its clanlord's absence was seriously suspect.

"Have you told Cooper?"

Again Hogart looked surprised. "No, my lady. Lord Rennalf said not to disturb you, that he and his men would be off at first light. I thought, seeing as it's Master's wedding night—" He stopped. "Should I tell him anyway?"

She thought for a moment, struggling for calm. If Rennalf truly meant to leave at first light, he would be gone before Cooper was even awake. And as Hogard had pointed out, it *was* Coop's wedding night.

"No," she said finally. "We'll tell him in the morning. Keep an eye on them though. They're not to be roaming about, and I'd very much like to know what they are doing so far afield of their own lands."

"We'll see to it, my lady."

The night that followed was a long one. Carissa tossed restlessly in her big bed, weighed down by her elk-hide cover. Even with Peri back in her regular place before the bedchamber's hearth, the lady could not find sleep. Every random boom and thump startled her from slumber, mistaken as the heavy footfalls of her husband coming to reclaim her. Once awakened, she listened intently to the wind, assuring herself it was diminishing as she waited hopefully for the barking of the dogs, the horses clattering in the yard, and the gate creaking open and booming shut. But all she heard was the wind and the snow ticking against the shutters until she dozed off and started the cycle again. When morning finally came and the storm had not diminished at all, she knew she had a long day ahead of her.

Resigned to the fact that she would have to greet her guests or rouse unwanted curiosity, she set about selecting an appropriate veil. "Lady Louise" often went veiled, a habit picked up in Esurh and now part of her reputation for eccentricity. It amused her that the garment she had most hated during all her time in the south had become so useful here in Kiriath. For this occasion she selected the heaviest house veil she owned, a dark blue silk laced with sprays of white vines. She was holding it before her face to see how well it hid her features when Cooper came stomping in, Hogart in his wake.

She'd always thought Felmen Cooper a handsome man, tall and strong and leanly muscled. Now in his late forties, his swarthy face was well weathered, but he remained in excellent physical condition, age and his experiences in Esurh having imparted a new sense of command to his presence. The last four years had seen his short-cropped hair turn completely to gray, only the spiked Thilosian-style goatee retaining any of its former dark.

"Rennalf is here," he said quietly.

"Yes." She handed the veil to Peri.

"Why didn't you tell me last night?" he demanded.

"It was your wedding night, Coop," Carissa said as Peri swirled the veil over her head. "We figured he'd be gone by morning, and what could you do anyway? He'll recognize you the moment he sees you." She turned back to the mirror and lowered the veil over her face, Peri pulling and twitching at its folds.

His frown deepened. "What are you doing with that?"

"I am the lady of the manor. I'm going down to greet him."

"And you think he won't recognize your voice? Won't demand to see your face?" Cooper had braced his hands on his hips. "He'll take you, lass. You know he will. If for no other reason than to prove that he can."

"What would you have me do, then?" she demanded, her voice high-pitched with tension. "Go down unveiled and remove all doubt? Or stay up here and arouse his curiosity further than it must already be aroused?"

He gestured at her maid. "Let Peri go."

The girl blanched and turned a terrified look toward Carissa, who was already seriously considering the idea. Peri's accent would add weight to the deception. She'd have only to give greeting before pleading illness. . . . If only she wasn't so obviously a servant. Her posture, her mien, and especially her terror would give her away.

"I'll do it" came a voice from the now-open door. Cooper's new wife, Elayne, stepped into the room. "I've watched you, mistress. I know how it's done."

Since Elayne was already head of the household staff and accustomed to greeting the lords who occasionally came through, she was an eminently appropriate choice. Hogart would take over Cooper's position, while Cooper himself retired to the background as a kitchen drudge, chopping wood and hauling water.

Thus it was decided, leaving Carissa to stew in isolated ignorance. Too restless for needlework and too distracted to read, she spent the morning pacing before the hearth, battling impatience and curiosity. It had been six years since she'd left her husband. Had time changed him as much as it had her? As much as it had Cooper? When she had married Rennalf he was a strong and handsome borderman, mysterious, powerful, and immensely attractive. Perhaps some of that remained. Perhaps his own trials—she'd heard he'd lost his beloved bastard son two years ago—had softened him. It was an absurd hope, one she knew was nothing more than wishful thinking. Everything she'd heard of him told her he'd only grown more hardened and bitter. He blamed Raynen for Carissa's disappearance and later had insulted Gillard and been insulted in turn. He had no love for the House of Kalladorne, his former wife least of all.

She'd be a fool to risk discovery simply to satisfy idle curiosity.

There was the other matter, as well, though—the question of what he was doing here. Would the servants know what to listen for? Would they recognize the crucial words of revelation when they came? Would they miss what Carissa might not?

She fought temptation for most of the day—aided by Cooper's adamant rejection of the slightest suggestion she go down. But at last she could stand it no longer. "I'm only taking a little walk," she told Peri late that afternoon as she donned a servant girl's undertunic, cotte, and baggy wool leggings. "Just to get out of the room for a while." She stripped off her rings, tied a kerchief around her braided hair and slipped a misshapen woolen sweater over the lot, then went down the back way to the stables. There she checked on the horses and dogs, looked in on the goats that were being milked, and offered to take one of the filled pails back to the kitchen.

The milkmaid waved permission, pleasing Carissa by the fact that she had no idea who had come in to ask. Cooper, of course, recognized her the moment she walked through the door, scowling at her furiously as he dumped an armload of wood beside the kitchen hearth. Maya, the cook, struggled to hide a smile and suggested Carissa wipe up the spills near the Great Room doorway lest anyone coming through slip and fall. Despite Cooper's glares, Carissa picked up a rag and dropped to hands and knees just inside the doorway. She did an extremely thorough job, which was remarkable considering she paid no attention to what she was doing.

"Lady Louisa" sat knitting in one of the four large tree-limb chairs arranged before the hearth, shrouded in her blue veil. Her six visitors ignored her entirely, conversing quietly around the big table. Big, tall men, typical of their lineage, they wore leather and wool, with shaggy beards and long blond hair caught up in various modes.

Rennalf of Balmark presided at the table's head, his back to the fire, face to the kitchen. Tallest and broadest of the lot, his rugged countenance was more weathered than she recalled, his crow's feet deeper, the squint of his eyes more pronounced. He wore his frizzy blond hair long and loose, brushed back from his forehead at the crown but caught at the temples into thick, dangling braids that framed his bearded face. It was the beard that betrayed his age, white now at the sides where once it had been all golden brown.

What startled her most, though, were not the signs of age but the hardness in his manner, an intensification of the aura of superiority he'd always carried—and something more. Some indefinable sense of power that raised the hairs on her nape and made her think of men she had seen in Esurh. Though perhaps that was only because of the green-stoned amulet he wore at his throat. Nested in a silver setting, half hidden by his beard and hair and high-collared tunic, it was not readily noticeable, yet her eyes flew to it as to light on a dark night. It was not a piece she recognized.

The men's voices were deep and heavily accented with the northerner dialect, so it was hard to discern their words above the racket Cooper was making with the kitchen fire and Maya's pounding of the bread. They spoke of seasons and fordings, of meetings and agreements, of others unnamed who were important to them, but through it all her conviction mounted that they were up to nothing good.

Maya called her from the doorway then, pressing a rolling pin into her hands and gesturing at the dough on the counter. About that time young Rolf came bursting through the front door into the Great Room. "News from Springerlan," he cried, waving one of the small canisters worn by homing pigeons. "Whitewing's brought back news from Springerlan! And it's got the royal seal on it!" He stopped, taken aback by the realization that they had guests and he shouldn't have been shouting the news. He scanned the room, spied Carissa standing in the kitchen doorway and, in his discombobulation, started toward her.

Elayne called him sharply from her chair: "Rolf, I'm over here."

He whirled and hurried to her, the kitchen help now crowding around Carissa at the doorway. Elayne pried open the canister, then extracted the tiny tube of paper inside. Unrolling it, she stepped closer to the fire to read the tiny missive and seemed to turn to stone.

"Well, woman!" Rennalf cried at length. "Do na keep us in suspense. What news?"

She looked up, her gaze going not to Rennalf, but to Cooper standing just inside the door. "Prince Abramm's come home," she said faintly. "He's in Springerlan now. He's killed the kraggin and means to take the throne."

A loud crack exploded in the ensuing silence as the rolling pin hit the wooden floor, dropped from Carissa's suddenly nerveless fingers. Every face in the room whipped round to look at her and she cringed. Luckily Rennalf only glanced her way long enough to confirm the source of the sound as a servant's clumsiness before returning his attention to Elayne.

"Abramm," he said. "He who took religious vows and vanished six years past?"

"Yes, my lord. Some say he was kidnapped and sold into slavery."

"And now he's back." Rennalf arched his brows at his companions and settled back in his chair. "T' take the Crown, you say?"

"Yes, sir."

"Is that all it says, lady? Let me see."

Elayne frowned her disapproval but relinquished the message without argument.

"I wonder how he killed it," said one of the northmen.

"B'sure he's only taking the credit," Rennalf replied. "So he can get the Crown. Our friend Gillard will na like this."

They exchanged sly, unpleasant looks.

"The gods smile on us today, m'friends," Rennalf said. He looked around, skewering the gaggle of servants eavesdropping from the kitchen doorway. His men did likewise a half breath later, their combined glares sending the fortress menials scurrying back to their work. All except Carissa, held immobile by a state of shock so profound her mind had washed blank.

Elayne, grasping her mistress's condition at once, intruded upon the men's conversation to ask in what way their gods had smiled, and by that impertinence drew their startled eyes off Carissa. Rennalf told her to mind her own business, whereupon she begged his forgiveness and left, even as Maya tugged Carissa back into the kitchen.

Her last image was of Rennalf's second, Ulgar, red haired and coarse featured, swiveling his head around for another look at her, his small eyes bright and shrewd with blooming suspicion. Regaining her wits by the kneading counter, she had almost convinced herself she had imagined that look of dawning recognition when Cooper seized her arm and steered her toward the back door. "Go back to your room at once, my lady," he said, stopping to swath her in cloak and scarf and shove a basket in her hand. "Go round to the henhouse as if to check the eggs, then come up by the north stair."

The screech of a chair stuttering across the wooden floor in the Great Room stilled the protest on her lips and spurred her outside into the wind-driven snow. She'd just reached the outbuilding that served as stable, sty, and henhouse, when the kitchen door squealed open in her wake. Hurriedly she ducked into the stable, ran past the rows of stalls, then down a side aisle and out the rear door. Praying Ulgar would not immediately guess she was fleeing, she dashed up the open stair, then slogged and slid through the foot of snow that had already accumulated on the wallwalk. Afraid to look back—her tracks would be clear in the snow—she hurried around the walkway, along-side the cliff against which the compound was built, to a door in the keep's top floor. Cringing at the shriek of its hinges, she pulled it shut after her and barred it.

Cooper waited in her room, white-faced and grim. "I think he's only sus-picious, my lady," he said as she rushed past him and threw open her clothes chest. "I didn't dare try to stop him."

"You did right." She pulled out a heavy woolen skirt and draped it over the edge of the chest, then shrugged out of the servant's tunic she wore.

"Here, my lady!" Cooper protested. "What are you doing?"

"Give these clothes to one of the girls," she said, pulling the skirt up under her cotte as he turned his back to shield his eyes. "Tell her to say she was meeting a boy or something. I'm sure Elayne can figure something out." She stripped out of cotte and tunic, replacing them with a woolen undertunic.

"What do you mean to do, lass?"

"I'm going up the pass to the old watchtower the Mataians converted." She layered an oversized leather jerkin atop the woolen tunic. "It's windtight, fairly clean, the chimney's working. I think there's even wood there."

"You can't go up there, my lady. The place is haunted!"

"Nervous superstition, nothing more. I'll only be there a few days, but you'll need to send someone with food."

"It's an evil place. I've seen the ghost myself. You can't go there."

She pulled a heavy overcloak from the chest, then stood to face him, regarding him bemusedly. "Ghost, Cooper?"

He stiffened his spine. "It wasn't a man, my lady, I can tell you that."

"Well, whatever it was, it's better than Rennalf right now, and I'll be staying only until he's gone." When he would have protested further, she said, "What are you going to do? You've already admitted we can't stop him."

Someone started pounding on the wallwalk door. "I've got to go," she said.

"There is another place you could hide. A better place."

Carissa flipped the cowl of her cloak over her head. "With your Terstan friends?"

"It's warm, dry, and well stocked. And you wouldn't have to be alone."

She closed her eyes and sighed. A perfect haven, she had no doubt. Except for the company. But then, both Cooper and Elayne wore shields. She'd known it for a long time, just didn't like admitting it. Half her servants wore them, too.

The pounding intensified and Elayne rushed into the room, eyes wide. "They're trying to break down the door, Felmen!"

Felmen Cooper stared evenly at his longtime ward.

"Very well," Carissa said. "Take me where you will."

10

In the late afternoon of his first full day as the new king of Kiriath, Abramm Kalladorne went riding in his royal preserve. A passionate horseman since youth, he'd spent much of the last seven weeks at sea longing for a good hard ride in open country. Now, as king, he not only had his pick of a stable full of fine horseflesh but a hundred acres of forest and field through which to ride.

Riding helped him relax and think, and after his triumph at the Table last night, and the uncertain results of his first official day as king—plus the celebratory burning of the kraggin's corpse slated for this evening—he had much to think about. He'd won the Crown, yes. But could he keep it? Things had changed so radically and so fast, and he'd met so many people in such a short time, that already last night seemed like it had happened months ago. He needed to get away for a while, gain some perspective on what had been accomplished and what still lay before him. An afternoon ride, with only his armsmen for escort, was just the thing to clear his head.

Shale Channon, promoted today to Captain of Abramm's Royal Guard, did not agree. Stretching north and east from the formal palace grounds, the royal preserve was bounded along its western border by the sheer-walled rim of the Keharnen Rise and by an impenetrable hedge everywhere else. It was a wild land, populated only by the royal foresters—a prime spot for an ambush, by men *or* spawn. Abramm was not about to live his life hiding in the wardrobe for fear of spawn attacks, however, and as for the men, though he knew he had enemies aplenty, he doubted they could orchestrate anything in time to take advantage of an unplanned ride whose route not even Abramm himself had decided.

Channon was not mollified. Nothing about this venture made him happy. Not the destination, not Abramm's limitation of the escort, not the late hour—not even the horse Abramm chose to ride. Especially the horse, a feisty two-year-old dapple-gray stallion named Warbanner, whom everyone from the head groom to Channon himself warned Abramm off. *"He'll take you on a wild ride and dump you in a bramble bush somewhere,"* the groom had predicted. *"We'll be lucky to find you with nothing but bruises and wounded pride."* Which only stiffened Abramm's resolve to have *this* horse.

As they set off across the formal grounds, young Warbanner prancing and tossing his head, Channon rode as close as the colt's ill temper allowed, positioning himself and his five men to cut off any attempts at bolting. Abramm hid his amusement and let the man alone. He and Warbanner had already reached an understanding as to who was in control, and as soon as they cleared the formal grounds and entered the preserve itself, he loosened the rein and nudged the young horse's sides. It took only a nudge—Warbanner's speed change was explosive, and his prodigious stride soon left Channon and the others in his dust.

Keeping a light hand on the reins, Abramm crouched over the animal's neck, exulting in the wind on his face, the clatter of hooves on the hard-packed, dirt road, the golden glory of the grasslands flying past, and the exhilarating sense of *freedom*. He let the colt slow on his own, savoring the smell and feel of the horse as he reveled in the scenery. Copses of hickory and oak, leaves just starting to turn, stood interspersed amid a rolling expanse of grassland, all ashimmer in the afternoon light. By the time his escort finally caught up again—dust-cloaked, windblown, and breathing hard—he felt himself renewed already.

As overhead a few gulls wheeled on the updrafts, their raucous cries sounding grace notes alongside the jingle of the horses' tack and the *thud-clop* of their hooves, Abramm turned his mind to the day's events. This morning he'd delivered his first official address to the combined Upper and Lower Tables. Recalling Shemm's advice to speak from the heart and get to the point, he'd told them of Esurh.

How he'd seen the shipyards at Qasok and Usul, and the armies of the Black Moon and the new Supreme Commander, heir to the slain Beltha'adi.

"*I have watched their Games and listened to their boastings of Destiny,*" he'd said. "*The Taking of Springerlan, The Rending of the Northland, The Surrender of the King of Kiriath—those are the names of their Game-tales. They mock us as a race of womanish comfort-seekers without the backbone to fight, worthy only to be conquered. And conquer us they will if we do not prepare.*"

The force of his conviction must have come through, because when he had finished, his listeners sat in stricken silence, staring at him with pale faces. He gave them only a moment to digest it all before outlining what he meant to do: first, to increase the numbers in both army and navy to allow adequate patrolling of the borders and, second, to repair and rebuild the realm's crumbling fortresses—starting with the one at the mouth of Kalladorne Bay, whose languishing had left the very heart of Kiriath open to attack. Yes, a tax would be required to fund all this, and though the projects would provide jobs and business opportunities for those suffering from the effects of the kraggin's blockade, that wouldn't preclude the fact that sacrifices would be required. Starting with Abramm himself. To conserve needed funds, the lavishness and number of palace entertainments would be sharply reduced, and all work on palace additions would be suspended. Furthermore, ambassadors to both Thilos and Chesedh would soon receive authorization to proceed with alliance negotiations—even though the Chesedhans had insisted the only way they'd ally with Kiriath was on condition of a royal marriage.

When he was finished, Abramm summoned Simon Kalladorne, Grand Marshall of his army, and Walter Hamilton, Grand Admiral of his navy, to a private meeting, instructing each to prepare for him a report of the status of their respective forces. While Hamilton displayed an open enthusiasm for Abramm's plan, Simon had been merely professional, according the new king all the deference protocol demanded, but not one flicker of genuine approval. Which Abramm could not deny was bitterly disappointing, though the number of lords who approached him afterward eager to echo Hamilton's endorsement was something of a balm. Byron Blackwell was so enthusiastic, in fact, he had offered to serve as royal secretary until Abramm could appoint someone to the position permanently.

Overall it went well, Abramm admitted. *I just have to give Uncle Simon time.* It was unrealistic, after all, to suppose that a changed appearance and a few well-delivered words would revise opinions held for over twenty years. But it was still difficult to take.

As they followed the road into a fragrant grove of oak, hickory, and evergreen, Abramm's armsmen closed ranks around him, nervously eyeing the close-growing trees. Since human ambushers were highly unlikely to strike this early in the ride, Abramm concluded it must be spawn they feared. Feyna could be deadly in sufficient numbers, after all, as the attack on Abramm's own father fourteen year ago had shown. That that attack had come in the deep forest on a dark and cloudy night—not a clear afternoon in a sun-dappled grove of trees—might have given them comfort, he supposed, had they not believed themselves to be guarding a man who was helpless to defend himself. But maybe that was just as well, for their paranoia freed him to turn his thoughts to the very issues he'd come out here to consider.

Like selecting a cabinet of advisors. And getting the Terstans to quit fighting him—a score of them had been arrested for rioting just last night, in fact. Though he'd questioned them personally this afternoon in hopes of demonstrating he was not their enemy, they had responded with sullen silence, forcing him to cast them into his dungeons. Then there were the Gadrielites to be dealt with, and— But no, he had to take things one at a time or he'd never accomplish anything. And right now he had his cabinet to consider.

Emerging from the shadowed copse into brightness again, he watched his growing escort of sea gulls circle overhead in hopes of a picnicker's handout and thought of the men he had met. Though he'd learned much about Blackwell today, he still didn't trust the man. Arik Foxton, Lord of Summerall, had presented himself as a possible ally after Abramm's address. Rich, athletic, conservative, and quietly sensible, Foxton might be a good choice. The border lord Ethan Laramor had a quick mind and a sense of hard-won man-savvy, but something about him set Abramm on edge. Even apart from his undisguised and undiminished hostility. Then there was—

You must try to win your brother.

His thought flow stopped. Where had *that* come from?

Shrugging mentally, he went on. Laramor had a good grasp of the border situation, though he seemed completely unconcerned about the Esurhites and—

You need to win your brother.

He frowned. That was a ridiculous notion, as distasteful as it was impossible. Why was he even thinking it?

But the third time it intruded, he gave up in exasperation and confronted it. *Try to win my brother? I'd rather throw him in my dungeons!* In fact, last night, seeing him for the first time in years, he'd wanted to do a great deal more than that. Everything he loathed about Gillard had manifested itself in that Council Hall. Even now his sly, baiting words made Abramm's blood boil. *"So why did you not come to Raynen? Why did you simply disappear?"* he'd asked oh-so-innocently, secure in the knowledge that without two witnesses Abramm could bring no accusation against him. *"I sold you into slavery,"* he'd seemed to say, *"and there's not a thing you can do about it!"*

Abramm had wanted to fly across the chamber floor and strangle him on the spot. *Nothing I can do about it? Well, we'll see—*

You must forgive him, Abramm.

And again his inner monologue halted. That thought wasn't from him. *Forgive him, my Lord?* He felt vaguely ill.

My son has paid his debt, and I have forgotten his transgressions. How is it then that you dare to remember them?

Abramm knew the Words very well—could cite that passage by sector and line, in fact—but right now could not care less. Outrage smoldered in him as a dozen memories of that fateful night in Southdock tumbled through his mind. The feel of the net dropping over his head; the narrow, fishy-smelling room; Gillard throwing back his cowl to reveal himself so Abramm would know exactly who was doing this to him.

It is not so easy for me to forget, my Lord. He—

Is a very unhappy young man who is confused and deceived—

And arrogant and selfish and egotistical and just plain mean.

And you, of course, are never any of these things, since you are perfect.

Abramm scowled at the sea gulls swooping and wheeling against a cloud-streaked sky.

Lord, you know I know I am far from perfect.

You need to forgive him, Abramm.

But— Abramm ground his teeth together as a hundred more rationalizations sought to flood his mind. But how could he refuse the One who had bought his very soul? *All right, my Lord. I forgive him, but for your sake and only by my will.* A sick, horrified feeling churned in his stomach.

You must try to work with him.

Work *with him?! Never! Not after what he did!*

And what was it he did, my son? I seem to have forgotten.

Abramm exhaled his frustration. I will *forgive him, Eidon. But I can't work with him. He's insufferable and he hates me.*

You need to offer your hand in peace.

He'll only slap it away.

You must offer it anyway. As I offered mine to you, though you slapped it away many times, were no less insufferable, and hated me even more than he hates you.

He could never argue with Eidon. When would he learn that? Somehow he always ended up like this—without a leg to stand on, feeling foolish and chagrinned, face-to-face again with his own worthlessness.

I will offer him peace, my Lord. Though it's certain to be rebuffed, and I'll only look the fool . . .

But Eidon, he knew, cared nothing for how Abramm looked to others, and thus he shouldn't, either. After that he was left to consider his cabinet selections uninterrupted, and before long it was time to turn back. Angling southwest off the track, he put Warbanner to an easy canter, and soon they reached the wide, hard-packed road edging the Keharnen Rise. Springerlan sprawled below them in a golden haze of smoke and mist bisected by the barge-clogged river, gleaming like molten gold in the sun's lowering rays. Beyond loomed the western headland, shrouded in purple shadow as it stretched southward to form the bay. At its farthest seaward end, old Gray-meer's Fortress was just visible as a jagged upthrust against the darkening blue haze of the sea.

They had ridden along the rim only a few minutes when the drum of approaching hooves brought them all around. To Abramm's surprise it was Byron Blackwell who cantered up to join them, his lifeless brown curls tied back for the ride under a wide-brimmed hat. Looking bemused behind his spectacles, he pulled his horse to a stop and dropped the king a truncated bow. "Your Majesty."

"I certainly didn't expect to meet you out here, Blackwell," Abramm responded.

"It's been a full day, sir. A hard ride in the preserve always clears my head."

"I didn't know you were a horseman."

"A passion we share, I'm guessing." He eyed Warbanner significantly. "Not too many can ride that colt."

Abramm acknowledged the compliment with a nod, sensing it was genuine. At his invitation, the man joined him, and they continued south along the road, the palace a distant gleam behind the trees and hills ahead. Beside them the gulls wheeled in a salmon-tinted sky, winging at eye level with them across the sheer cliffs.

"I must confess," Blackwell said as they rode, "that this meeting is not *entirely* by coincidence. When I saw the gulls circling, I hoped it was you."

"Did you."

"I've had something on my mind since last night, sir, but I wasn't sure how to approach you with it."

Abramm encouraged him with a glance.

"I fear I should not have stopped you from baring your chest to the Table. Better would have been to have let you settle the matter then and there." He paused. "You might want to find a way to be seen bare-chested in the next day or so. Perhaps invite guests for early tea and wear your blouse unfastened. Or take a morning stroll around the lake. The more people who see the truth, the sooner you'll be free of the accusations."

Abramm received the advice soberly.

"You do see my point, don't you, sir? If you do nothing, the question will only fester, and already its—"

"I see your point." Abramm gazed over the valley to his right, watching the light change as the sun slipped behind the headland, turning the clouds to dramatic fiery slashes in a salmon-run-to-pale-blue sky.

"I know it's distasteful," Blackwell added after a moment. "It's just that poor Raynen's fate is so much on everyone's mind again." He shook his head. "There's not been such a dramatic case of Terstan madness in a long time. I'll tell you plainly it horrified even those among us who wear the shield themselves."

Those among us? Are you trying to tell me something, Count? "I'm surprised you allowed him to reign that long," Abramm commented blandly.

"We'd have removed him sooner, but Gillard refused to accept the Crown in his stead."

"Gillard?!" *He's willing to sell me to the night ships to get me out of the way, yet wouldn't remove Ray when he was obviously incompetent?*

Blackwell shrugged again. "They say he loved your brother very much."

He doubted Blackwell had any idea how much that statement cut to his heart.

After a few moments, the count added quietly, "It should be done soon, sir. Time is crucial in these matters and—" He stopped, his eyes flicking to Abramm sharply. "I'm assuming, of course, the accusation has no merit. . . ."

Abramm cocked a brow at him. "Are you asking me if I wear a shield, Count Blackwell?"

At once the man averted his gaze, red-faced. "No, sir. Of course not. I just . . ."

"I appreciate your advice, Count. For now, though, I think I shall take one last run."

And so, with the sea breeze in his face, tainted even here by the ammonia of the kraggin, Abramm nudged Warbanner into an easy rolling canter. But it wasn't nearly as pleasurable as it had been earlier, for Gillard weighed on his thoughts now, and some part of him held Blackwell responsible.

Even so, he couldn't deny Blackwell *had* pretty much single-handedly saved his bid for the Crown last night. He'd learned today that the man had become count only four years ago, after his father died in a hunting accident. Elected speaker of the Table of Lords a year later, he was generally characterized as a political middle-of-the-roader with a conservative bent and a low profile. *"One of those men no one notices much—until they end up Speaker of the Table,"* Lord Foxton had confided with a grin during their private meeting this morning. *"I don't know him well, sir, but he seems a good man and a hard worker, and most everyone likes him. And he's served on a goodly number of committees."*

They slowed again some ways farther on, eyeing uneasily the great cloud of gulls boiling up from the road where it bent out of sight into a copse of trees. Channon said he didn't like the looks of it, and though he didn't much like the idea of taking to the hollows either—not at dusk with all the spawn they had these days—he thought it the better risk. "But we mustn't dally," he warned.

Thus they descended the forested hillside at a trot as the world turned ruddy around them, the fiery streaks overhead fading slowly to pink. Already the scent of damp grass mingled with whiffs of pine and hickory in the still air, and with the squirrels gone to their holes, the only sounds were those of the riders themselves. They started across a meadow cloaked in purple twilight, the gulls swooping and diving above the trees to the right. Whatever had caught their attention, Abramm's party was going to miss it.

Then, halfway across the swale, Abramm's nape tingled with the sense of imminent attack, triggering an instinctive, hard-won set of reactions. Dropping onto Warbanner's neck he kicked the animal forward just as a flight of arrows burst from the hickories to the right. By then he was off the road and galloping over the hummocks in an arc headed round toward his attackers' position. Another horse followed close behind. He thought at first it was Channon, until he heard his captain bellowing from much farther away for some to "Get them!" and others to "Cover the king!"

Then Abramm was among the trees himself, engulfed in the deepening twilight. He checked Banner and, as the horse slid to a stop, groped for the sling that wasn't there, settling instead for his sword. As it hissed from its scabbard, he sat rigidly, scanning the gloom-cloaked foliage and tree trunks, suddenly aware that he wore not one piece of body armor.

The other horseman caught up then—it was Blackwell, his eyes wide in a pale face as he clung to the saddle, reins flapping uselessly, his horse, unguided, having instinctively followed Warbanner. As the count came even with Abramm, the sudden prickly awareness of shadowspawn washed over him, setting his old wrist scar tingling. At the same moment, air stirred above and behind, and he wheeled Banner to face it, glimpsing black wings, a long beak, a glowing blue-white eye. His rapier flashed, white light shimmering down its length as it sliced the feyna in half and flicked back to decapitate another, Banner shying and squealing all the while. Two more came at him, then three, as he slashed and stabbed with one hand and fought to control Banner with the other.

A cry drew his attention to Blackwell, unhorsed in the chaos and caught in a bramble bush, one arm trapped beneath him, a ring of blue eyes shining in the darkness around him. Abramm urged Banner forward, but the horse refused, snorting and swerving away. With an oath Abramm leaped off him, reaching the count just as the spawn attacked. Slashing and thrusting with his rapier in one hand and a stout branch in the other, he drove them off, Eidon's Light flowing effortlessly out of him.

Then it was over. He stood, weapons raised, breathing heavily, waiting to be sure they were gone, before turning to Blackwell, still caught in the thicket and staring at Abramm with wide, startled eyes. Dead feyna littered the ground and dangled in the brambles around him. *Well, I guess he knows the truth about my shield now,* Abramm reflected wryly.

A distant crashing brought him around with the sinking realization that Warbanner had fled. He turned a full circuit, intense irritation washing over him. He knew better than to drop the reins of so young a horse under such conditions. What was he thinking? Nothing. Nothing but how to stop the feyna.

Banner wouldn't stop until he was back at the barn, and afterward, when Abramm came riding in on someone else's horse, all the grooms could smirk and smile I-told-you-so's. *Well, it's only what you deserve for being so stupid.* Grimacing, he tossed the branch aside, sheathed the rapier, and turned to pull Blackwell from the brambles.

"Are you hurt, sir?" he asked as the man straightened on his own two feet and brushed his clothing.

"A bit bruised, but I'll do." Blackwell had recovered his poise, meeting Abramm's eyes evenly and thanking him for his assistance. "My own sword was caught under me. If you hadn't acted so quickly—" He shuddered.

Abramm returned his gaze unflinchingly, wondering irrationally if by some incredible happenstance he hadn't noticed the Light. Before he could broach the subject, however, they were interrupted by the crash of horses trampling the underbrush accompanied by low, harsh cries. Abramm stepped forward, instinctively positioning himself between Blackwell and the direction of the sounds, his hand once more on his rapier as he wondered whether it would be best to stand and fight or seek cover before they were discovered.

Then Channon burst into view, his relief at finding Abramm palpable. "Eidon lives!" he murmured, swinging down off his horse. "Are you all right, Sire?"

"We're fine," Abramm said, irritated all over again by Banner's loss. At least Blackwell had lost his mount, as well, though since he *had* fallen off, it wasn't much consolation. "Did you catch any of them?"

"No, sir. They only loosed the one volley before they fled."

"Anyone hurt?"

"One man was grazed, nothing serious." His eyes had gone to the feyna carcasses lying about them, and a new grimness came into his face. "You must get back to the palace, sir."

"Yes, but I'm afraid I've lost Warbanner."

"You can ride my horse." Channon handed his mount over to Abramm, who swung easily into the saddle, then offered Blackwell a hand up behind him.

As they headed back to the road, the count said quietly in Abramm's ear, "I'm afraid I have to retract my earlier advice."

Abramm glanced over his shoulder. "Oh?"

"I have recently come to believe that your going bare-chested about the palace would not be a good idea after all."

Abramm turned to see him better and found Blackwell's expression as benign and unconcerned as his tone had been. For a moment they shared the glance, then simultaneously broke into laughter.

11

Not long after Abramm had left on his ride, Simon Kalladorne settled on the audience benches of the fencing practice room at Laine Harrady's estate, watching Gillard chase his fencing partner around the floor as if the man were Abramm himself. The crown prince fought in breeches, hose and fencing slippers, his white-blond hair queued at his nape and his muscular chest gleaming with sweat. The afternoon sun slanted through the west windows in a golden haze, marking the polished wood floor into hard-edged sections of dark and yellow gold, and flashing off the sprays of sweat that occasionally erupted from the combatants. The swords met in a constant but irregular clinking, underlain by the thud and slide of the men's feet and the grunting rasp of their breathing.

For all the effort and fury, though, it was no contest at all. Gillard was merely working out his problems.

It had been a difficult day. The former prince-regent had gotten falling-down drunk last night and said unfortunate things. He'd slept it off at Harrady's while servants moved his belongings out of the royal residence and into the same wing Simon himself occupied. As crown prince, Gillard could have had suites nearer the king but had loudly declared to the messenger last night that he would not live cheek by jowl with a coward and thief. He had risen late this morning, so badly hung over he had elected to stay at Harrady's, refusing to talk to anyone, not even his merry men. In fact, Simon had not been invited to observe this match, nor had Gillard yet acknowledged his presence.

Simon had spent the day interviewing the men who'd been aboard

Wanderer, those on the dock when Abramm had come ashore, and even Brother Belmir at the Holy Keep. What he learned had left him more unsettled than ever.

Wanderer's Captain Kinlock affirmed that Abramm was very much involved in the slaying of the kraggin, adding that, when they had first arrived on the scene and his own men had hesitated, it was Abramm who'd taken the lead. *"Shamed the others into going,"* Kinlock said. *"Though from the fire in his eye, I swear he'd have done it alone if he had to."* Of the handful of men who'd actually seen Abramm spear the monster, Simon had only spoken with Shale Channon. It was an awkward and uncommunicative meeting for mentor and former student both, but Channon had solemnly sworn that Abramm had not only speared the beast, he had indeed ridden the spear into the deep.

Simon remained unconvinced. He knew how the distorting lens of panic could lengthen time and exaggerate mundane actions. Likely Abramm *had* stabbed the kraggin, was pulled off balance by its reaction, and simply fell from the overturned boat Channon said they'd been standing on. With the waves and the flotsam and the gathering gloom, it was easy to understand why the rescue boat might have taken some time to find him.

Still, even without the embellishment of the heroic spear ride, the tale was sobering, and Simon had to give the boy credit for his courage. *And face it, old man, for getting the job done. The monster's dead, and they lost only two of their original crew. And you can't say he's done badly since then, either.*

That speech he'd delivered to the combined Tables this morning had been a shocker. Never in Simon's wildest dreams would he have expected to hear such words from "Little Abramm," nor the compelling force of conviction with which they'd been uttered. Simon himself had been warning of the Esurhite threat for years with little result, waved off by men caught up in the pleasantries of court life, who laughed at the idea of "those barbarians" defeating Kiriathan forces. Suddenly they weren't laughing anymore. *"Womanish comfort-seekers without the backbone to fight"*? Abramm had certainly chosen the best words to startle and provoke.

And his plan of preparation? Except for the part about a Chesedhan alliance, Simon had been clamoring for those things for years. Though Raynen had sympathized, he was constantly distracted by his personal problems and his fear of losing the throne, and Gillard had been caught up like his peers in the innumerable amusements of his court. Now suddenly they had a king on the throne who, by word and manner at least, seemed not only able but seriously committed to addressing the problem. Even in meeting privately with him, Simon had been impressed, for Abramm was direct, firm, and very clear about what he wanted and when he wanted it: a comprehensive report—"*with numbers as solid as you can make them*"—on the state of Kiriath's military defenses to be presented to him verbally and with full documentation in one week.

Admiral Hamilton had been overwhelmed, unable to contain his approval, slavering and wagging like a dog. And though Simon had held on to his professional demeanor for the meeting, even he had left the royal audience chamber reeling. Could their new king be sincere? Or was it all an act?

Whatever it was, it was working. And with the burning of the kraggin and the celebration surrounding it tonight, including a reception at the palace for which hundreds of invitations had gone out—presumably the last of its kind for some time—Abramm's popularity would only increase.

Simon frowned, his gaze drawn back to the gasping, flailing figures circling the floor below him, their swords jabbing and flicking about each other. He didn't want to like Abramm. Didn't want to approve him. It made him feel like a traitor. And yet, after the way the boy had handled the Table last night and the way he was conducting himself today, Simon couldn't deny that glimmers of both had crept into his heart.

On the other hand, he thought, *there's still the matter of his Mataian loyalties. You mustn't forget that.* It *had* been Guardians he'd been so quick and brave to rescue. And if he had shown an unexpected mercy to the Southdock Terstans who had rioted over his ascension last night, he'd hardly been lenient with them, either, sending all ten of them to his dungeons for a week. Moreover, Master Belmir had expressed not the slightest concern that Abramm's professed loss of faith was permanent and predicted Abramm would soon be back in the fold. When Simon asked how he was so sure, he'd smiled and said, "*Because he is the Guardian-King, my friend. And Eidon has shown us that, beyond all shadow of doubt.*"

The words had chilled him. Not because he believed Eidon had shown them anything—that was just one of the ploys religious fanatics used when they wanted to win their point—but because it testified of the fact that the Mataio was still very much a part of this picture. And frankly, knowing how Abramm had always been a sucker for that religious nonsense, he would not be surprised if the boy did revert to his old ways.

One of the swords abruptly took flight, arcing through the air to clatter on the floor under the window. The two fencers stood face-to-face, gasping, only Gillard still armed. His opponent regarded him with obvious pleading, and at length the prince relented, allowing the man to limp wearily to the sidelines. As servants scurried out to provide towels and take away the swords, Simon stood. Stepping carefully down the tiered benches, he joined Gillard on the floor, where, for the first time since Simon had arrived, his nephew looked at him.

"We need to talk, Gillard."

The white-blond brows flew up. "What? No 'how are you?' No 'and what did you do today, my nephew?'"

"I can see you are not well, and I know what you did today," Simon snapped. "You should have come to the Table."

"Why? So I could lose my lunch watching all my courtiers fawn over him?" Gillard swiped the towel once more across his chest, then tossed it aside and strode for the dressing chamber just off the practice floor.

"It was an open affront," said Simon, limping after him.

"I was ill. Besides, Harrady told me about his speech and that nonsense about us being conquered by the Esurhites." Inside the dressing chamber he kicked off the fencing slippers, then bent to peel off hose and breeches. "As if a horde of savages in rowboats could defeat our navy!" He shook his head, muttering, "I cannot *believe* they voted to accept his claim!"

Leaving breeches and hose strewn across the tiled floor for the servants to gather, Gillard made for the waiting bath. He eased himself into the steaming water until he was submerged to his chin, then closed his eyes and sighed with satisfaction.

Simon leaned against the doorjamb, arms folded across his chest, frown tightening his forehead. "And yet they did accept it," he said quietly. "Whether we like it or not. And unless Abramm drops dead, or begins to show signs of madness, or really *is* a Terstan, I don't see much chance of anyone forcing him to abdicate. You can't go on openly insulting him."

Gillard opened one eye and tilted his head back to look up at Simon. "You don't really think he'd call me on it, do you?"

"If he has any backbone at all, he'll have to."

"Well, we both know he doesn't."

Simon felt his frown deepen. "Last night's Table might indicate otherwise."

Gillard snorted and sagged back into the water. "Last night's Table just

THE SHADOW WITHIN ‖ 115

proves my point. You saw the look on his face when I confronted him. Did you ever think a man could turn that pale and still be alive? Abramm is as afraid of me as he ever was. I doubt it will be long before he abdicates of his own choice."

Simon was not at all sure he agreed with Gillard's assessment. Yes, Abramm had gone rigidly pale for a few moments, but nothing in his manner or voice had suggested fear. If Simon had to put a name on it, he'd say it was closer to fury. And something almost dangerous. That Gillard hadn't seen it was disturbing. As for Abramm's abdicating freely, Simon thought there was very little chance of that.

"So how was *your* meeting with him, Uncle? The private one after the Table. I understand you and Hamilton have been asked to report on the state of our defense."

"So you know about that already, do you?"

"I know about everything that goes on in my kingdom. For example, I know that you're frowning at me right now because you don't think I should call it *my* kingdom, even though it is. I know that for some reason you agreed to do his report instead of resigning. And I know that he actually questioned those Terstan rioters personally, which I find quite intriguing." Water trickled as he scratched his nose. "I also know he's riding in my preserve right now, with only six men and astride that young stallion Brentworth has been training."

"Warbanner? The one you've had your eye on?"

Gillard huffed. "The fool will set us back months with his feeble hands and weak will. That colt is headstrong enough as it is. He's probably already flung him into a ditch somewhere and run back to the barn." He snorted. "Maybe we'll get lucky and the fall will break his neck."

Abramm's neck, of course, not Warbanner's. Simon regarded his nephew with another twinge of uneasiness, though if he'd been pressed, he could not have said precisely what troubled him. Something in the young man's tone, perhaps. Or even the hope itself, which yesterday Simon would've shared with far less ambivalence than he did today. Things were growing more complicated by the moment, and not least his own feelings and convictions.

Gillard's voice interrupted his contemplation. "Is that all you wanted to talk to me about, Uncle? To be wary of insulting my pigeon of a brother?"

"You *will* be at the reception tonight, won't you?"

"You think I'd miss the biggest carnival to come to court in the last year?

Prittleman will be pontificating, Darnley will be in high form, lamenting the loss of his parties, and I hear our resident Chesedhan, that tiresome busybody Lady Madeleine, has composed a special song for the occasion. Which admittedly might not be as hilarious as it will be maudlin, but I hope for the best. And, of course, our new king will have to tell us *all* about his adventures in nauseating and intricate detail. I hope I can keep a straight face. Do you suppose he'll actually claim that business with the spear to be true?"

"I don't know, Highness," said Simon. So far as he knew Abramm was saying nothing about any of it, letting others spread the tale. Even when asked point-blank, folk said, he dodged the question and changed the subject.

One of Gillard's men hurried into the bathroom, sketching an apologetic bow to Simon before bending to whisper into Gillard's ear. Without opening his eyes, Gillard nodded, and Simon heard him whisper, "Keep me informed."

The man left, and a few moments later a smug smile bloomed across Gillard's clean-shaven face. Simon was on the verge of asking him what had caught his fancy when Gillard said, again without opening his eyes or moving his head, "I'd like a bit of time to myself before dinner, Uncle. You may go now. I'll see you over Harrady's roast boar."

———

Harrady's dinner party was held in the long dining room on the south side of his manor, one wall lined with windows overlooking the city and the twilight-purpled expanse of the bay beyond it. As the guests took their seats, the sky was turning to pale salmon streaked with clouds set afire by the golden orb now sinking beyond the western headland. To the south, far out in the harbor, the lights of Kildar Fortress on the eastern headland twinkled against the dark haze of the open sea, while the point of the western ridge remained dark, as always. Closer to hand, preparations were under way at the dock for the burning of the kraggin, the corpse being transferred from the crane of the harbor boat to that of an old whaler.

Harrady had invited the border lord Ethan Laramor and his wife, Lord Arik Foxton and his wife, Gillard, Ives, Moorcock (Matheson had had unexpected personal business to attend to), several young ladies to go with them, and Simon. As the city lights came up, the guests ate their way through a pastry-wrapped boar with its accompanying stuffed quail, boiled leeks and onions, a plum compote, fine white bread with butter and quince jelly, and a traditional apple pie. Afterward, the ladies retired to Harrady's drawing room, leaving the men to pursue more serious discussion.

Lord Foxton was nearly as enthusiastic about their new king as Admiral Hamilton and made the mistake of expressing it. For this lapse of judgment he earned a sarcastic putdown from Gillard and Harrady's disdainful disagreement.

"It's all an act," the old warrior declared, leaning back in his chair and drawing a pipe from a pouch at his belt. "No one can change that much."

"The very fact he's used an image opposite to what he was before makes it painfully obvious, in my mind," Ives agreed.

"You're just being played, Fox," Harrady added. "You and all the other gullible lords in the court."

From his place at the head of the table, Gillard fixed his gaze on Foxton. "You disagree, Arik?"

Foxton shrugged, trying not to let his discomfort show. "Well, we all have our opinions, Your Highness."

"Yes," Gillard said. "Some of which are more perceptive than others."

"Indeed," Foxton said quietly, fingering the brandy snifter before him.

Harrady busied himself with filling his pipe. "Mark me—we'll see the true man soon enough. Images have no substance, and one can only play a part so long before the strain begins to show."

"I think it's already showing," said Ives. "He's not been nearly so bold today as he was last night. Even you'd have to agree there, Fox."

Simon thought perhaps Foxton did not agree but was beyond making any further attempts at expressing himself.

"You thought him bold last night?" Gillard asked Ives incredulously.

Ives's head swiveled round. "Only until you arrived, Highness. Then, of course, it all went out of him. I thought he would faint when he saw you."

"But before that, you actually thought him bold? Abramm?"

"Only because his appearance was so different from what we'd expected, sir."

"Even then I can't imagine how you'd think that, Michael. As you said, it was just an act."

"Of course. But he always *was* good at acting."

"You mean singing," corrected Moorcock. "Remember the night of the red-tasseled hat?" He warbled a rendition of the song Abramm had sung for his mother's birthday celebration when he was twelve. Ives joined in with a falsetto harmony until they both dissolved into laughter.

Gillard scowled at them, even in this unable to find his good humor again. "I wonder where that hat is," said Moorcock.

"Do you suppose we could convince him to give us a reprise?" Ives asked.

The conversation wandered through various absurd suggestions before growing serious again, Ethan Laramor bursting out with the unshakable conviction that Abramm *was* the Mataio's man, that he wouldn't be surprised to learn that the Mataian leadership had not only hidden him away these last six years but had also orchestrated the entire affair with the kraggin to give him the credibility he needed. When pressed to explain how they could have known six years before the fact that there'd be a monster for Abramm to fight, Laramor maintained it was because the Mataio itself had made the thing.

Which triggered a sudden, awkward silence as everyone became very interested in their snifters. Simon cringed with embarrassment for his friend, despite knowing Laramor wouldn't care. Only a Borderer could make such a claim and be completely earnest. Springing from a culture where many still believed in ells and warlocks—and that the Mataio's primary objective was their own destruction—Borderers did not think like other men. Simon had no doubt Ethan thought his theories completely rational. But that only made them more discomfiting.

Harrady finally broke the silence with a harrumph. "Simon, didn't you tell us Shale Channon himself confirmed that Abramm wears the brand of an Esurhite slave?"

"Channon's just been promoted to Captain of the King's Guard," Laramor pointed out.

"But it's a claim easily confirmed by the physical evidence," Harrady countered, "so why would he lie?"

"He's right," Simon agreed, speaking for the first time in a while. "Besides that, Kinlock said Abramm showed up at the dock in Bre'el wearing Esurhite robes, that he paid with Esurhite gold and speaks the Tahg like a native. Facts confirmed by some of the others who came in with him on *Wanderer*. And we've *all* heard the accent in his voice." His gaze flicked over the faces surrounding him. "I think he's telling the truth."

Silence followed his words. The fire hissed and cracked, the clock on the mantel ticked, and outside a light breeze gusted against the windows.

Then Gillard burst out, "By the Flames, Uncle! Has he won you, too, then?"

Simon turned to him in surprise. "Won me? What are you talking about?"

"Just that I'd never thought to hear you defending Abramm."

"I'm not defending *him*," Simon retorted, "merely his claim that he was in Esurh these last six years as opposed to Laramor's that he was hiding out in some Mataian watchtower."

"Well, it sounded like a defense to me!"

Simon assured him again that he was simply being objective about the facts as he knew them, and could not see how insisting Abramm had indeed been a slave constituted a defense of him.

Gillard slouched back in his chair, still scowling. "Why didn't you resign when he called you in today? You don't mean to work for him, do you?"

Simon gaped at him. "He's the king, Gillard. I can't very well ignore his direct order."

"You could've stalled. All that business about improving our defenses is just talk. Rebuilding Graymeer's? That'll never happen. And this grand vision of an improved military? The lords will never fund something like that. Once they start missing their parties and plays and afternoon walks, you can be sure they will not be pleased." He picked up his brandy snifter, swirled the amber liquid, and sipped. "He's just trying to pull you away from me, Uncle. Win you to his side. You should have resigned the moment you entered that chamber."

"Gillard, I've known him all his life. He's not likely to win me away from you."

"Well, you'll not be doing any reports for him. In fact, tomorrow you'll go in and tell him you're resigning. That will take care of it." He set the snifter down. "I'll not have you helping him, Uncle."

Simon knew it must be hard for the boy, having lived as king for four years and accustomed to ordering folks about as he wished. He would count it force of habit that had produced those inappropriate commands and not fight it for now. But this denial needed to be addressed. In truth, he'd never seen Gillard this bad before. It worried him.

Before he could think what to say, though, Harrady's majordomo hurried in to whisper into his master's ear. The old warrior's eyes widened, and at his nod the servant rushed out again, leaving the host to turn to his curious guests. "It seems the king has been attacked."

The men at the table went rigid, their faces blank, their eyes, one after another, flicking to Gillard and away.

"When?" asked Simon.

"Was he harmed?" Laramor demanded simultaneously.

"Apparently not. Ah, here's the man to answer our questions," he said as the majordomo returned with the messenger from the palace.

According to him, assassins had followed the king when he left for his ride, hiding themselves along the road and striking when he returned. Fortunately his horse had spooked at the very moment the arrows released, saving him. One of his men took a shaft in the shoulder, but the only injury the king received was a gash to the cheekbone when his frightened horse had carried him into the woods and dumped him there.

"Was he hurt?" Gillard demanded.

The messenger looked at him in confusion. "Highness?"

"The horse. Was he hurt?"

"Oh. No, sir. He turned up at the barn without a scratch on him."

"Do they know who did it?" asked Simon.

"Only that the arrows used were royal issue, sir."

"What about the reception?" Ives inquired. "I assume it's been canceled?"

"No, sir. The king was not hurt and is determined to see the kraggin burned."

When there were no more questions, the messenger left, and as soon as the door closed upon him, the men at the table burst into excited commentary. A commentary, Simon noted, from which Gillard refrained. Instead he watched the golden brandy swirling in its snifter as he tilted it this way and that, a secret smile on his face. A smile, Simon thought sourly, that looked very much like the expression he'd worn earlier in the bath. One by one, the others fell silent, eyeing the prince uneasily until Simon spoke the question on everyone's mind: "Gillard, I hope you weren't involved in this."

Gillard looked up in surprise. "Involved in what?" His gaze roved up and down the table and understanding dawned. His brow furrowed. "Why in Torments would I take such a risk when all I need do is wait for him to self-destruct? Although I admit, I wouldn't have been disappointed if he'd been hit."

"This is the king we're talking about, Your Highness," Simon said quietly.

"He is a *pretender*, Uncle!"

"Nevertheless," said Simon, "he has the law on his side, and attempted assassination is treason. If you were found guilty—"

"Oh, please." Rolling his eyes, Gillard snatched up his snifter. "You really think *Abramm* has the courage to execute *me*?"

"Don't underestimate him, Gillard. He is a Kalladorne, after all. And he is not unsupported."

Gillard froze mid-sip, staring at him over the snifter's rim. Very deliberately he set the vessel down. "You *are* defending him."

"This has nothing to do with him."

"It has *everything* to do with him! You've done nothing but sing his praises all evening. Because *he* killed the kraggin and I did not. Isn't that right?" He didn't wait for Simon to answer, even had Simon chosen to. "Little Abramm comes back, allegedly slays the monster, and now you think he's worthy of the throne. Well, fine. At least I know where *your* loyalties lie." Throwing his lap cloth onto the table, he stood and, to the astonishment of all, took his leave.

12

If Abramm's first evening back in Kiriathan society had been a resounding success, his second fell just short of disaster, beginning with the unfortunate presence of Master Belmir and a coterie of Guardians at the reception and ending with the offering of insults to the daughter of the Chesedhan king, whom Kiriath desperately needed as an ally.

Coming on the heels of the affair with the Terstan rioters, Abramm was not at all pleased to find Master Belmir first in line to offer greetings and congratulations. Nor did he welcome the Mataian's enthusiastic commendations for Abramm's stand against the "evil, Shadow-serving Esurhites." Though Belmir didn't come right out and say so, it was clear he believed what Abramm had really said today was that he would soon see the realm cleansed of the corruption and heresies that had so long weakened the Flames that would protect it. He was especially excited by the prospect of purifying Graymeer's Fortress, something the Mataio had begged permission to do for years. Abramm's polite assertion that all fortress renovations would be accomplished by military hands, and not Mataian, seemed to pass unheeded.

At least when Abramm's newly installed staff had invited the Mataians, they had also invited a few prominent Terstans, though Everitt Kesrin, the Terstan merchant he'd met yesterday, was the only one of them to attend. And Kesrin was far less friendly tonight than he'd been on the docks, his cool and distant manner suggesting he had joined the ranks of those who believed Abramm to be under rhu'ema control. It didn't help that Prittleman made veiled references to the need for a Terstan purge within both Kesrin's and Abramm's hearing, nor that Abramm, distracted by Temas Darnley's mind-numbing prattle about dance steps and doublets, had failed to call him on it.

Finally it was time for the ceremony to begin, the song to be performed, and the kraggin to be burned. Listening to the song counted among the most embarrassing moments of Abramm's life, his discomfort made worse by the fact he had to endure it under the mocking regard of his dead ancestors, whose portraits surrounded him there in the South Gallery where the reception was held. Leaders of armies, founders of dynasties, winners of battles—*they* were the real heroes, while Abramm knew himself to be merely the befuddled recipient of Eidon's mercy and protection.

Things went from bad to worse when the kraggin's pyre was ignited in the harbor below them, for despite his orders that the platform be towed well out into the bay, it had, in fact, been moved even closer to the shore and the busy docks. Within moments after it was ignited, the prevailing winds had shrouded Springerlan's low-lying river district in foul-smelling smoke. Infuriated by the breakdown in communication, suspecting it had been some enemy's deliberate attempt to make him look stupid and incompetent, and disgusted with himself for not making absolutely sure his initial orders had been carried out, Abramm remembered little of the obligatory meeting and greeting he'd endured afterward. Only that it felt rather like being nibbled to death by ducks and that whenever he turned around he found Darnley and his idiot chatter, or Prittleman and his fanaticism, or Belmir and his pious smile—or his own armsmen, ever close at hand to prevent another assassination attempt.

Gillard surprised him by making an appearance, as did Simon, both managing to present themselves to Abramm with their congratulations and good wishes. Simon came early and was brief, brusque, and generally disapproving; Gillard arrived some time later, his cloak of smooth and courtly courtesy not quite concealing the hatred beneath it. He bowed his head the barest minimum protocol required, then asked baiting questions disguised as respectful interest. Was the king wearing that sword because he had finally learned to use it while scribing in Esurh? Where had he learned the kill point for a kraggin? Had he truly ridden the beast to the bottom of the bay?

Abramm kept his own responses to a polite minimum, neither admitting nor denying much. He was considering how he might end the conversation when his brother moved on to more recent events.

"I understand you took our young prize Warbanner out for a turn this afternoon. What did you think of him?"

No mention of the ambush, though by now Gillard certainly knew he was one of the prime suspects as its originator. That he would bring it up at all, even obliquely, could only be meant as a challenge. *Yes, brother, I was behind it. So what are you going to do about it?*

It was a well-used ploy, the old sword of intimidation that had never let him down where Abramm was concerned. Except now Abramm held that ice-blue gaze unflinchingly and found, as he had found at the Table last night, not fear in his heart, but a deep and fierce desire to challenge Gillard openly, sword to sword, in the ways of their ancestors. For a moment he almost did it. Then sanity reclaimed his thinking, and he recognized his arrogance for what it was. Unless it ended with one of them dead, such a contest would resolve nothing, and Abramm would just as soon leave Gillard in ignorance of his true skills with a blade as long as possible. Besides, Eidon had charged him with offering his brother the hand of peace, not the end of his sword.

Still he had to force himself to smile and play along. "He's a fine and willing animal."

Amusement glinted in Gillard's eyes. "They say he took you on quite a ride, from which it appears you did not escape unscathed." With cocked brow, he touched his own cheekbone on the same spot where a branch had cut into Abramm's.

There were times Abramm was convinced his brother could read his mind, so effortlessly did he hone in on the sore spots. That story—started by his own men, which made it even worse—still made him want to howl in frustration. Despite Channon's praise for how well Abramm sat a horse, the man clearly still believed him inept, still saw him as a scribe and a former Mataian scholastic, not a true horseman, and certainly not a warrior. It would never occur to him Abramm might have run Warbanner at his attackers on purpose. And he probably thought Blackwell had killed all those feyna.

The grooms had indeed smirked upon Abramm's return, though only when they thought he wasn't looking, and Blackwell could hardly come to his defense, since any elaboration on what had happened would do far worse than bruise his ego. Thus, he'd had to grit his teeth and bear it. As he did now, glancing as if unconcerned across the gallery. "He runs like the wind, and his gait is smooth as butter." *And his mouth is more responsive than that of any horse I've ever ridden.*

"He's fast, all right." Gillard glanced across the gallery, as well. "A bit too mellow for me, though."

"You won't mind, then, that I've taken him for my own."

Of course Gillard minded very much, which became obvious the moment Abramm's words registered. His nostrils flared, his brows drew down, and immediately he changed the subject. "That was quite a surprise last night, old Rhiad accusing you before us all of wearing a shield. Why do you suppose he did such a thing?" The pale eyes fixed on Abramm closely.

"From what I've been told," said Abramm, "he felt *he* should have been the one to deliver us from the kraggin and so seeks to discredit me. I also understand he is insane."

"He said you used Terstan power to kill the thing."

"Well, he was nowhere near us at the time, so I can't imagine how he'd know, one way or the other."

"Perhaps he sensed it."

Abramm cocked a brow. "Because of his deep awareness of things spiritual? Doubtless that was it. That would also explain why none of the other Mataians noticed anything." He knew Gillard did not believe any such thing and was only trying to rattle him.

His brother shrugged. "I am intrigued that, save for one man now on your payroll, all the others who were on the water with you—the only eye-witnesses—have disappeared."

Abramm smiled at him and decided he'd had enough. "I'm flattered you find the minutia of my affairs worthy of contemplation. However, I must warn you—" He leaned close and lowered his voice. "If you keep talking to me so pleasantly, everyone will think you've become a supporter."

A slight recoil, a blink of surprise, and the white-blond brows drew down in a frown. But just as Gillard opened his mouth to speak, Abramm said mildly, "Watch your tongue, brother. You must know that I would like nothing better than to lock you in the Chancellor's Tower for the rest of your life."

And again Gillard was brought up short, jaw clenched, eyes blazing. He glared at Abramm a moment, then leaned in himself and said in a low voice, "Fortunately Kiriathan law requires *two* witnesses to reach a conviction. Even for the king."

"And you were ever good at concealing your misdeeds, weren't you?" Feeling his anger rising, Abramm deliberately caught the eye of Blackwell, who had been watching for just such a sign. As the count started toward them, Gillard scowled, but he managed to restrain himself from making a comeback, and Abramm stepped away, dismissing him. His brother had no choice but to sketch a stiff bow, again no lower than he could get away with, and depart. He stayed half an hour longer, mingling with the guests to prove he was completely at ease, then left for good around ten o'clock, early as these things went, but not early enough for Abramm's taste.

He was given little time to dwell on the interchange, however, for Blackwell, despite knowing Abramm's willingness to marry for the sake of the foreign allies he was pursuing, had set himself the mission of introducing the king to every unmarried woman of standing in the court, including the count's own sister, Leona. All of whom smiled and simpered and batted their eyes in unpleasant reminder that, if not for the treaty considerations, Abramm would be the most sought-after bachelor in the kingdom.

Ironically, the only woman who didn't make eyes at him turned out to be the Second Daughter of the very king Abramm most wished to ally with. Lady Madeleine, noting his surprise and even alarm when she introduced herself, quickly assured him that as *Second* Daughter she was dedicated to Eidon and would never have to marry for politics. "Or at all, if I choose not to," she announced prissily. "Certainly I'd not choose a Kiriathan and *never* a king."

Which was welcome news, indeed, seeing as she was not only the plainest woman in court, but also the most outspoken. She'd proceeded to grill him on his reaction to the song, which by then had become a source of great irritation to him. Irritation he'd expressed freely, unfortunately, right before discovering she was, in addition to being Second Daughter, the official balladeer of her father's court and the one who'd penned the thing. Worse, she was in Kiriath not as part of the Chesedhan negotiating party but to research and write a ballad of the White Pretender. Seeing as Abramm had recently returned from Esurh and had admitted just today he'd seen the Games, she was certain he would be an excellent source of information. Her eyes were sharp upon him as she said this, and he could only pray Eidon had somehow blinded her to the shock her words produced in him.

Thankfully, Blackwell intervened then, ushering in another young lady for him to meet. Not long after that, when it finally dawned on him that, as king, he could leave whenever he wished, Abramm decided he had had enough.

Somehow Blackwell contrived to be among his escort back to the royal apartments—as he had contrived all night to be the man most often at hand to answer Abramm's questions or direct him in the next move of his social debut. Now as Captain Channon led them through the palace's blessedly deserted back corridors, Abramm asked why he'd brought all those ladies by.

"You know, I'll probably marry the Chesedhan princess."

Blackwell gave him a glance and a slight smile as they turned into a long, darkened corridor. "Don't worry about that, my lord. The Chesedhans are no more likely to approve your taking their First Daughter to wife than your court would approve her. Treaty or not, that is one thing that *won't* happen."

"Then why did they propose it at all?"

"Actually, I believe we did. As a sign of goodwill. You have to be amenable, after all. Offer the right things. No one expects you to go through with them, though." He flashed Abramm another smile. "Besides, I thought you'd enjoy their company. And there's no harm in playing the field before the vows are taken." He snorted softly. "Nor afterward for that matter."

"The Words forbid such things, Blackwell."

"Aye. The Words forbid a lot of things that people do all the time. And what would the court be without its romantic liaisons and passionate affairs?"

Abramm frowned at the gleaming marble floor stretched out before him, feeling put off. What he had known with Shettai was something precious and private, even sacred. He couldn't imagine flinging himself around like a dog with anyone who caught his fancy.

"In any case," Blackwell went on, "I did have a legitimate reason for my actions. The Harvest Ball is coming up in only three weeks. You'll need to choose one of those young ladies to escort."

"But I said just today that I was canceling all that nonsense."

"No, you said such affairs would be reduced in frequency and lavishness. And, sir, I strongly advise against moving too swiftly on that. You'll need the peers' goodwill if you hope to fund the military improvements you envision. The lesser amusements can go for a time, but we've been looking forward to the Harvest Ball all year. After what we've suffered this summer, taking it away will only make people angry and bitter." He paused, a sly smile spreading across his sallow features. "And think of all those young ladies who worked so hard to catch your eye tonight. Each hoping desperately to be the one who'll be dancing the Autumn Suite."

The Autumn Suite? As king he'd be the one dancing that, wouldn't he? Right out there in the middle of the ballroom floor, alone with his partner, and all the court watching. *Fire and Torment!* He'd never given thought to this aspect of wearing the crown of Kiriath, and the prospect made him quail. Worse, he'd have to choose among all those desperately hopeful young ladies.

He grimaced again. "And my choice, of course, will furnish an abundance of grist for the gossip mill."

"Unavoidable, I fear. But you *are* expected to go a-courting, sir. Chesedhan or not, you must take a bride soon, for the Crown needs an heir. Unless you want Gillard nipping at your heels for the rest of your life."

Was *that* why Eidon had told him to work with his brother?

But courting? Siring an heir? Khrell's Fire! The thought made his stomach sour. He still wasn't over Shettai, and not one of these women could even come close to replacing her. "Perhaps I'll choose Lady Madeleine and shock everyone."

"Lady Madeleine?" Blackwell's head swiveled sharply, his expression one of incipient alarm. "The Chesedhan Second Daughter? That wouldn't shock, sir; it would give the whole court apoplexy."

"Precisely why the notion appeals."

Blackwell fell silent, clearly trying to discern if Abramm was jesting. After a few steps, Abramm took pity on him. "I meant for the Autumn Suite, Blackwell."

"Ah." The count flashed a wan smile, and Abramm recalled that the man's sister had been among the contenders for his notice this evening.

They had reached the corridor's end and turned into a new one, shorter and brighter and hung with dark tapestries depicting the conquest of Kiriath. As their footsteps echoed around them, Blackwell said, "Be careful about the Second Daughter, sir. She is . . . quite the busybody and utterly without respect for propriety."

"I noticed."

"Or privacy for that matter. More than that . . . she's frighteningly quick-witted. They say her sister got the beauty and she got the brains. From what I can tell, it's no understatement. And you know Chesedhans cannot be trusted. She'll promise you discretion one day and the very next be trumpeting the matter to the world. If you have a secret you want to keep, best stay as far from her as you can."

"I assure you, Blackwell, it will be my pleasure to do so."

Blackwell studied him a moment more, then, apparently satisfied of his sincerity, launched into a new subject. "I don't know if you've noticed, but it seems a rift has developed between your uncle and your brother."

A rift? Between Gillard and Uncle Simon? "I did see that they came separately tonight."

"And strictly avoided one another for the duration. Your uncle's been at Gillard for months to go after the kraggin, but Gillard put him off, saying he'd only get men killed and ships sunk." Blackwell eyed him thoughtfully. "Perhaps he was right, if you killed that thing the way I suspect you did."

Abramm frowned at him and he went on. "In any case, your uncle spent the day checking out your story. And everyone agrees your speech to the Table today echoed things he's said for years. Many think he favors you now."

Abramm thought back to his earlier meetings with the man. "He sure didn't seem disposed toward me that *I* could tell."

"He's a Kalladorne. You're all notoriously hard to read. But he definitely had his eye on you tonight. Of course he's paranoid about the Mataio taking control of the realm and still isn't convinced you're not one of them. If you could persuade him beyond all doubt that you're not . . . I believe he might be won."

Uncle Simon? Won this soon? "But I've already done everything I can think of to show people the truth. What else is there?"

Blackwell glanced over his shoulder at the men trailing them, close enough to protect, far enough they couldn't hear if the words were spoken softly. "There is one other thing."

At first Abramm could not imagine what he meant. Then it hit him—as obvious as it was unthinkable—and he shook his head. "He'd find *that* truth even more repellent than his Mataian suspicions."

"There is that risk, of course, though the political advantages, should you succeed, would be profound." They reached the back stair to the royal apartments then, and Abramm paused as Channon started up. Blackwell glanced again at the trailing armsmen—who'd stopped when the king had—then shrugged. "I simply offer it as something to consider."

He sketched a quick bow and said his good-byes, leaving Abramm to climb the stair in thoughtful silence.

13

Had Abramm and Blackwell left the Gallery by the main entrance, they would have passed the gaming rooms and salons in which the diehard pleasure-seekers had congregated. Harrady had talked Simon into a game of dice soon after they had left the reception hours earlier. Predictably, Simon had lost money, and finally, despite Harrady's assurances that patience would win it back, he retired to one of the quieter salons and fell to playing uurka with Ethan Laramor. They were on their third game now, which Laramor was winning—again, to Simon's annoyance. He knew himself to be too tired, too brandy headed, and too preoccupied with the day's events to give his whole mind to the game, but it irritated him to lose all the same.

Gillard's too loud laughter rang through the doorway behind and to his right, the young man dealing with his troubles in typical fashion. No matter how drunk he became, he never slurred his words, which deceived those who did not know him into thinking the alcohol had not affected him. But Simon heard the bitterness in his tone and, as had happened last night, the blustering, unguarded tongue whining about Abramm's failure to have bared his chest and lamenting that the bowmen who'd staged the ambush had not been more accurate.

His companions took the words in jest, or so it seemed. Simon wondered how many actually shared Gillard's sentiments. Did they suspect him of orchestrating the ambush, too? Were the fires of rebellion being kindled even now in the king's own palace? Not that Simon could do anything to shut him up. His nephew was hurt and upset, and if Simon tried to speak to him now, he would only play more to the crowd. He had to get the boy alone. And since Simon would be leaving for the Briarcreek Garrison at dawn tomorrow to begin collecting information for his report to the king, it was now or never.

Thus he sat trying to concentrate on the game, one ear cocked on the door, while his mind roved back through the past six hours of the reception. Seeing Master Belmir, with his gaggle of Mataian attendants hovering in Abramm's vicinity all night, had filled him with great unease. As did the man's incessant talk of the prophesied Age of Light—one requiring the purification and dedication of all men—which he believed to be dawning on Kiriath's horizon. Meanwhile Prittleman bragged he would soon lead his Gadrielites in a purging of old Graymeer's, a claim Abramm had not denied. Though, with Byron Blackwell bringing by that steady stream of young ladies for the king's inspection, it was possible Abramm hadn't noticed.

"Well, that does it," Laramor said, breaking into his thoughts and finally moving his archer. "I believe you are besieged, sir. Would you care to surrender? Again?"

"Yes, yes. You win." Simon glanced over his shoulder at the door to the dicing room, from whence rang another burst of laughter.

"I'll not ask you for a fourth," Laramor said. "I think your chair could have played as well as you have."

Simon frowned at him. "You needn't rub it in."

"I don't know why you bothered to put on the pretense. You'd have done as well to doze on a sidebench until the boy's done with his playing. At least you'd have gotten some sleep."

"Aye, and missed my chance of speaking to him at all."

"Which might be for the best."

Simon began returning his game pieces to their starting positions. "He took what I said all out of context."

"But he'll be drunk now and even more sensitive. You'll only make things worse."

"If he was behind those attacks, he has to be stopped."

"Does he?"

Simon's hand froze on the figure of the archer he'd just set down. He looked up. Ethan was concentrating on carefully replacing his own pieces to their original positions, the light of the pedestal lamp beside him gleaming off the pewter-colored ring coiling around his index finger. Only when he had all the pieces put back did Laramor look up.

"It *would* be the easiest way to put things to right."

"Put things to right?" Simon went back to repositioning his own game pieces. "You could get yourself hanged for talk like that, man. And anyway, things have not turned out at all the way we thought they would."

"They've turned out almost exactly as I thought they would."

"Oh come, Ethan. You don't *really* believe the Mataio's held him in hiding all these years, do you?"

Laramor shrugged. "I'll admit, your evidence does refute that theory. But it's possible they sent one of their people to Esurh to find him and bring him home, one of those men on the water with him that no one can find." He rubbed the coil ring with his thumb. "Abramm's the Mataio's man, Simon. Didn't you hear Pritt going on about his plans for Graymeer's tonight? And the need for a purge? And Abramm standing right there, saying nothing?"

"I heard."

"It's only the start, you see."

"Maybe." Simon lined his footmen in their ranks. "And maybe not. Abramm's barely arrived. And what he said to the Table today . . . well, it was *good*, Ethan. You can't deny it."

Ethan's thumb stilled on the ring, his brow furrowing. "I thought you were with us on this. I thought you agreed he must not be allowed to rule." He leaned back in his chair. "Or is Gillard right and he has won you?"

"Don't be absurd. It's just . . . what you're talking about is not only dangerous, it could backfire terribly. It's a last resort, and I don't think we're there yet."

"So when will we be? When the purges begin? When we're forced to wear gray doublets with little red flames and commanded to surrender our wealth and our sons to the Holy Flames to keep the realm free of evil?" He tapped his ring on the tall brass form of his game king, gray eyes hard beneath shaggy brows. "It will be far too late by then, my friend."

Simon shifted uneasily. "All I'm saying is, give it a little more time. See how things settle out. You of all men know I've given my life for the good of this land, and I'm not about to let the Mataians have it. But neither will I run off willy-nilly. I want to get the lay of the land, if you take my meaning."

Laramor had no response to that, and Simon's glance dropped again to his friend's hands, where he was back at that habit of twisting the coil ring. *That really is an ugly piece of jewelry.*

"Where did you get that thing, anyway?"

Laramor followed the direction of Simon's gaze. "The ring? It's a family heirloom. Why?"

"I've never seen you wear it before. And it's—unusual."

"Aye."

Gillard's game broke up then, accompanied by much laughing and jesting as the players said their good-byes. Finally the prince appeared in the doorway.

Besides not slurring when drunk, Gillard rarely swayed or stumbled, either. But it did take him a moment to focus on Simon, another to recognize him, and a third to realize why he was there. A hard, desperate light flashed in his eyes. His lips tightened and he moved on without greeting or comment.

With a sigh, the older man followed him, feeling the twinge in his hip again and fearing Ethan was right—that this would do no good. He followed him all the way back to the Gallery's main rotunda before Gillard finally stopped and said without turning around, "I have nothing to say to you, Uncle, and wish less to hear what you have to say to me, so please stop following me."

His voice echoed across the hardwood floor and plastered walls, their ornately framed paintings hooded now in shadow. Lantern light shone dimly through the windows that lined the rotunda's outside wall, where the trees tossed in the breeze and scraped against the roof. Somewhere back along the corridors a door closed and voices echoed in indiscernible conversation.

Simon sighed wearily. "You're making this too personal, Gillard. And tormenting yourself over nothing."

Now, finally, the young man wheeled and stepped toward him. "Nothing? You said I was the son you never had. That I was more important to you than anything in life. That you would always stand by me no matter what. And there you were tonight, in front of Harrady and Foxton and all the rest of them, supporting him over me! Do you now intend to deny what I heard with my own ears?"

"You seem to have heard things that were not said. As for supporting him, I've done no such thing. All I sought to do was bring you to your senses." He glanced about reflexively, assuring himself they were alone, then closed the distance between them. "What you suggested this afternoon is a dire thing," he murmured. "A dangerous thing."

"It's not dangerous at all. Believe me, Uncle, if I wanted him dead, he'd be dead."

"As I said before, don't underestimate him. Even talking like this could get you arrested. Especially you. And with Shale Channon at the helm, it's not just Abramm you'd be facing. You know Channon will bring good men into the guard."

He could not see how his nephew was taking this, for Gillard's face, like the paintings, lay hidden in shadow beneath the gilding of his pale hair.

"And there's more to it than that—suppose you do succeed? The Mataio would surely censure you and, with grounds to stir up the populace against you, could force you to grant them concessions. . . . And it would start. Everything we're trying to avoid with Abramm would happen anyway."

His words died into a silence filled with the rushing of the trees, the faint scritching of the branches against the glass, the thumps and creaks of the palace at night.

"You're still committed to getting him off the throne, then?" Gillard asked finally, his voice hardly more than a whisper.

"I'm committed to the survival of this realm. That above all else." Whether or not that required Abramm's removal remained to be seen, but he wasn't about to say that now.

"Which means me on the throne and him gone."

"But not by means of assassination." It was unnerving not to see Gillard's face, especially when he did not immediately reply. "You know I'll always stand by you, son," Simon added quietly. He meant that sincerely, no matter what came of Abramm.

Yet still Gillard stood there as the branches squeaked and the wind blew against the windowpanes.

"I never meant them to hurt him," he blurted sulkily. "Only to scare him. I'd thought you'd realize that."

Simon blew out a long breath of relief, staring at the floor now. "But the men who did it know you hired them—"

"No. It sprang from another, one in the ranks who will quickly emerge as the source and be dealt with. He's accused me before, wrongly, so he won't be believed. Especially since I've recently called in a debt he owes me."

"Nevertheless, the gossips will blame you. And Abramm will suspect."

Gillard shrugged. "So what if he does? There *are* other suspects. The Ter-stans want him dead as much as anyone. And I wouldn't put it past some of the border lords, either, much as they hate Mataians. *They* certainly have experience—" He broke off, glancing toward the shadow-swathed doorway to the Gallery's rectangular west wing. A moment he stood listening, though Simon discerned nothing more than the sounds of wind and branches. At length, Gillard returned his attention to Simon. "I thought if I put enough pressure on him, he'd go back to Esurh. Or renounce everything, like he did before, and return to his Mataian devotions."

"Bonafil would never—"

Gillard whirled toward the shadowed doorway, his blade flashing from its scabbard. "Who's there?"

Silence and the wind answered him. And maybe the faintest whisper of someone breathing. Simon's hackles rippled.

"I know you're there," Gillard said. "Show yourself now."

Again, his words were swallowed by the quiet. Then the shadows moved, and a hooded figure glided out of the darkness of the doorway. It stopped before them, and a gnarled hand threw back the voluminous cowl to reveal a ruined face beneath a half-barren scalp. As Simon recoiled, Gillard voiced the recognition for both: "Rhiad!"

The holy man bowed his head. At his throat, the amulet of the Flames gleamed like an evil red eye.

"You're too late," Gillard said, almost flippantly. "The king has retired for the night."

"It is not the king I seek, my lord, but you."

"Me?"

"I sense we share a common interest, Highness."

"I can hardly imagine what, sir, since I am not Mataian, and do not wish to become one."

"I speak of our common enemy."

Gillard stared at him. "Go on."

"I know how it feels, Highness." Rhiad stepped closer. "Seeing him standing there before them all, applauded and admired, so straight and strong and handsome. He took it all from me, too, just as he is taking it from you. And it galls, doesn't it? Oh yes, it galls."

"*Abramm* did this to you?"

"*Yes!*" Rhiad bared his teeth in an expression more grimace than smile. "And I will see him pay!"

"But . . ." Gillard's eyes roved over the ruined face and barren scalp. "How could he do such a thing?"

The Mataian ignored him. "I know what he is. I know it as surely as I know your hatred. He is one of them."

Gillard went rigid again, his attention redirected to this new consideration. "Terstan, you mean? You've seen his shieldmark?"

"I was in the cistern, and it's the only way he could've gotten out. And that cow of a sister. They did it together. Her hands, his power. I'll get her, too."

The man was raving nonsense now, and Simon saw skepticism replace the hope on Gillard's face. "So you didn't see the mark."

Rhiad rushed on heedlessly. "It was *my* monster. *I* was supposed to kill it. And he stole it, just as he stole everything else. Just as he's stealing your crown from you." His head jerked up, eyes ablaze with their own fire as they fixed on Gillard. "Oh yes. I feel your hatred, my prince. Your jealousy. Your outrage."

Simon laid a hand on Gillard's arm. "Lad—"

The mad, fiery gaze switched to Simon. "And you—you only pretend he disgusts you. In your heart you admire him."

"*Admire* him?!"

But Rhiad had already dismissed him, returning his attention to Gillard. "Don't worry, my prince. I will take care of him for you."

Gillard was transfixed. "What do you mean, 'take care of him'?"

Rhiad smiled. "I know of your secret plans, the men you have hired, the orders you've given them. But their attempts will fail, just as the first attempt has failed. No mere man will get past *his* guard. Besides, assassination is too good for him."

"Gillard, this is treason," Simon said, tugging at Gillard's arm. "You cannot talk to this man."

"A moment, Uncle."

Rhiad paid Simon no mind. "I need only a few small things," he hissed, his face drawing near to Gillard's. "A lock of hair, a drop of blood . . . a few sovereigns."

The words whispered into silence. Rhiad smiled.

Gillard blinked, shook his head slightly, then frowned. "You're mad."

Simon stepped between them. "Away with you, sir," he said to the Mataian. "We want no part of this treasonous talk."

"*BE SILENT!*" Rhiad snarled, the amulet blazing at his throat. "*AND MOVE ASIDE.*" His voice was still hushed, but it carried the power of a battle cry, and Simon felt his mouth close. In the same moment, he stepped back to Gillard's side without any conscious intent to do so, and though alarm spun ever more wildly through him, he could not make himself move nor speak to act on it.

Rhiad's voice reverted to its insinuating croon. "What I have planned for your brother, my prince, is much more fitting than simple assassination. We will ruin him—crush that fine young body, strip the flesh from that handsome face, cripple that famous sword arm. And should he survive, so much the better, for life will only be a torment to him. People will shrink away from him, women will shudder at his touch. He will lose everything, my prince! His beauty, his strength, his position. Everything!"

It was a living nightmare. Simon could hardly breathe, but he could watch and listen and feel in a way he had never felt before. Horrified and furious at what this madman threatened to do against one of the royal family on the one hand, cringing inwardly at what he'd already done to Gillard on the other. The boy's pale eyes had glazed and his mouth hung open, breathless, the tip of his tongue just touching his upper lip.

"I'll even let you watch," Rhiad said, stepping closer than ever. Something metallic gleamed in his hand, down in the shadow between them. "I'll even let you participate. . . . All I need is a lock of hair. . . ." In slow deliberate movements, his eyes never leaving Gillard's, he lifted the knife he had produced and cut a pale blond curl from alongside Gillard's face, eliciting not the slightest response from his victim. He stuffed the curl into his robe and went on.

"And a bit of blood . . ." Now he lifted Gillard's left hand in his own, palm up. The knife flashed up, pulling Simon's eyes to it like filings to a lodestone. Then it froze as the Mataian's head jerked up and he peered intently over Gillard's shoulder.

Simon heard steps approaching in the corridor behind them.

Rhiad dropped the prince's hand. "You will remember nothing!" he hissed, pulling the cowl back over his head. "*Nothing!*" His amulet flared, and he whirled away as Laramor's rough voice intruded into the tableau. "Here! What's going on? Who are you?"

But the madman had already vanished into the shadows. Laramor stopped beside the two Kalladornes, looking at them in concern. "That sounded like Master Rhiad."

Gillard did not answer him, looking dazed and lost. And Simon could not help him much, struggling to understand how he knew that Ethan was right—it had been Master Rhiad—when he hadn't even seen the man's face.

"Simon?"

"He just approached us out of the shadows," Simon said. "Waiting for us, I guess. Whatever he wanted, he never got that far."

Laramor frowned at him, then glanced again at Gillard. "What happened to your hair, my lord?" He gestured at the short lock dangling on the young man's brow.

Gillard fingered it with an expression of bewilderment. "I guess it must've been cut in my contest with Tedron this afternoon."

"Really? I don't recall seeing it at dinner." Ethan's eyes darted once more to the shadows where Rhiad had disappeared.

"Well," said Simon, "he's gone now. And I'm off to Briarcreek at dawn. If I don't get at least a little sleep before then, I'll be falling off my horse all day. If you'll excuse me, gentlemen?"

————

Across the palace, in the semi-darkened bedchamber of the royal apartments, Abramm's stomach growled and he rolled onto his back, opening his eyes in frustration. He could not sleep. It seemed as if everything he had learned and seen and experienced today had been dumped into the pot that was his mind, where it boiled around in an endless, random tumble of images and feelings and fears. Already he'd lain here over an hour, and now he was hungry, as well. *Perhaps you should give up and try to go through those Table Records you asked for.*

He groaned. The last thing he wanted was more information! *Well, then read the Words or review your notes. It's better than lying here thrashing.*

He closed his eyes again, hoping maybe *now* the drowsiness would come. Only to reopen them a few moments later in the acknowledgment it was a lost cause. Sighing, he sat up, tossed back the covers, and swung out of the bed. As he pulled on the breeches left draped on the bedside chair, movement across the room drew his eye to the full-length mirror beside his wardrobe. As he straightened so did the man in the mirror, staring back at him with a stern, suspicious glare.

With his hair so short and that trim, old-style beard edging his mouth and jaw, his own reflection still gave him a jolt of surprise every time he saw it. At least now his clothes were merely commonplace, not the tailored silks and brocades a king must wear. But even in the linen undershirt, his shieldmark glinting between the untied open neck slit, he looked like a stranger.

He had changed in Esurh, and he thought he understood that. It was one of the reasons he'd come back. Now he was changing again, no longer the White Pretender, no longer the mysterious monster-hunter promising adventure and riches, nor even the lost prince returning to claim his birthright. Now he was king.

King of Kiriath.

For a moment he could hardly breathe. Awe. Wonder. Disbelief. And sheer, unadulterated terror. They clamped around his chest and held him motionless. He was riding those winds of destiny again, carried even now to the place Eidon had prepared for him, yet it still felt wrong. As if it were something someone else should be doing and he but an imposter soon to be found out and exposed.

But you are not an imposter, he thought at the reflection. *You are king, and this is your destiny. The Pretender was only a preparation.*

Then why does it feel so uncomfortable?

He turned from the mirror, padding barefoot to one of several tall windows, drapes open to the night.

And why do I feel so inadequate?

A blanket of yellow lights spangled the valley below him, cut through by the great dark swath of the River Kalladorne. Nine bridges arched over its width, their night lanterns casting evenly spaced circles of warm illumination along their lengths, a few night-lit barges drifting beneath them.

Terstans, Chesedhans, Gadrielites, courtier politics, grand balls, flirty young ladies, trustworthy councilors, war, rebellion, border raids, a crippled economy . . . So many problems to solve, so many options, so many people . . . and so many, many places to fail. His choices could bring success or disaster—and for all the glut of information he'd received, he still did not have enough to guide him.

Dare he trust Blackwell? Should he cancel the parties and symphonies and plays? Arrest Gillard on suspicion of assassination? Risk telling Simon his most precious and dangerous secret?

That, above all, haunted him. He remembered too well the look of horror on Carissa's face when she'd first seen his shieldmark, and he lived even now with the knowledge that it had driven her from his life. And *she* had started out loving him—sacrificing two years of her life to rescue him from slavery—

whereas Simon had never loved him at all.

The perpetual hint of revulsion had been missing from his expression tonight, though, a realization Abramm made only now as he sorted through the memory. A realization that filled him with almost as warm a glow as Blackwell's incredible assertion: *"I think he favors you."* Was it possible? And if it was, did he wish to jeopardize it by unveiling truths he knew the man could not appreciate? Wouldn't it be better to prove himself first, as Trap had done with Abramm himself? That would take time, though. Time he might not have, with Rhiad shrilling accusations and Gillard already prying at the edges of his secret. Was this pressure actually Eidon's hand, pushing him in a direction in which he was reluctant to move? Or was it merely another worldly distraction that appealed to his own desire to have it over with?

He sighed his frustration, fogging the window in front of him. *My Lord Eidon, it's obvious you've put me here. But now what? For all I know you may not even want Simon to be my ally.*

But once more all he received was an inner silence that was growing increasingly familiar. *I need to get to a Terstmeet*, he thought. By now he'd read his notes a hundred times, and they'd become so familiar he could quote them all verbatim. Reading them again would generate no answers, not like hearing the words straight from the mouth of the kohal as he spoke to the gathered Terst. When those words spoke precisely to whatever private dilemma Abramm wrestled with, or when they came shaped as a conversational answer to a question he'd asked earlier in prayer, that was when Eidon's voice was most clear to him. When the answers just drifted up in his own mind, he was never sure they weren't the result of some part of himself providing what he wanted to hear—or at least thought he *should* hear.

His stomach growled again, the hunger pangs increasingly insistent. After the ambush, and the fuss surrounding it, he'd been late getting back, then too nervous about the reception to eat a proper dinner. The decision was catching up with him now.

Opening the bedchamber door, he nearly tripped over young Jared, sprawled asleep in a chair against the study's wall, legs outstretched, an open red-bound book facedown in his lap. He looked up groggily.

"Jared!" Abramm exclaimed, embarrassed not only for nearly having fallen on the boy, but for the wild aggression that had surged through him in his surprise. "What the plague are you doing here? Have you no bed?"

The boy scrambled to his feet, white-faced, fumbling to keep hold of the book while bowing at the same time. "Y-yes, sir. But I thought you might have need of me." His gaze darted to Abramm's chest and away again, a reminder that the neck slit of Abramm's blouse remained untied, the shield-mark fully visible between its open edges.

A wave of horror doused the fire of Abramm's irritation, followed by cha-grined relief. Had he not stumbled over the boy, he'd have walked straight into the sitting chamber and one more person would suddenly have become privy to his secret. And surely adding Blackwell to the list was enough for one day.

Regaining his poise, he addressed the boy more civilly. "As it happens, I do have need of you. Fetch me some bread and cheese from the kitchen. And a pot of cider, too."

The boy bowed again, stammering his acquiescence, his gaze darting to Abramm's shieldmark and away again, as if he could not keep from looking and at the same time couldn't stand to look. Abramm wondered if he might not be the first Terstan Jared had ever known. At least openly. So far he had only given thought to the dangers of the boy revealing the secret, not what he might think of it all himself.

But already Jared was rushing off to do as he'd been bidden. When he returned, Abramm had retired to the desk in his study, reading through the scroll of Amicus in the copy of the First Word he'd found in his personal library. Jared set the tray of food on the desk, then asked if there would be anything else, his gaze darting skittishly to the shieldmark still visible behind the untied neck slit. Abramm said there was not, but as the boy turned away he reached to snatch the book now tucked into the back of his breeches. "You were reading this earlier, weren't you? Ah, *Alain's Aerie*. A good tale."

Surprise superseded the boy's wariness. "You've read this, sir?"

Abramm grinned. "About five times, I believe." He handed the book back.

"*Five* times?" Jared's standoffishness dissolved in the excitement of finding a shared passion. "I've only read it twice, but surely it is the greatest book ever written."

Abramm's smile broadened. "You've not read *Aerie*'s sequel, then."

Jared's eyes widened. "Sequel?"

"It must still be in the royal library. I'll find it for you tomorrow."

"Oh. Thank you, Sire!" His face glowed with excitement. Then his eyes dropped back to the mark, and uncertainty washed it away.

This time Abramm did not let it go. "Have you never seen one before?"

"Sir?"

Abramm gestured at his own chest. "A Terstan's shieldmark."

All the blood drained from Jared's face. "No, sir. Only heard about them."

"And what did you hear?"

The boy's eyes flicked up to his, to the shieldmark, to the chamber at Abramm's back, and finally to the floor. "That you serve the Dark One and drink the blood of goats and work evil spells to snare the unwary. . . . Wild tales, sir. Probably not true."

"Mmm." Abramm studied him, remembering himself at this age. *I would have been aghast. Horrified. In fear for my life. He doesn't seem so bad as that.* "Do you serve the Flames, then?"

"Yes, sir." Jared continued to stare at the floor, standing rigidly, book clutched one-handed to the side of his chest. "Sort of, sir. My aunt and uncle make me."

"Ah." Abramm leaned forward, folding his hands atop the open First Word. "You have many questions, I think," he ventured. "Perhaps you would like to ask some of them."

"No, sir. I . . ." Jared's voice died. He swallowed, his grip tightening on the book. Suddenly his head came up. "Did you really look into the Flames and fail, sir?"

"No. I never got that far."

The boy nodded, eyes dropping to the shieldmark, and staying there this time. "Did it hurt when they put it on you?"

"They?"

"The other Terstans."

"Terstans did not put this mark upon me, Jared. Eidon himself did. And no." He smiled at the memory. "It didn't hurt."

"Are you"—the eyes lifted to meet his own—"are you going to put one on me now?"

Abramm felt his brows fly up. "Of course not! I couldn't do that even if I wanted to. A man must come to Eidon from his own desire and will."

"That is not what the Mataian brothers say."

"I know."

Jared chewed his lip, hugging the book tighter, and Abramm sensed the window for this conversation had closed. Well did he know the horror stories children heard about Terstans. To press Jared too hard would hurt more than help.

"It's late," Abramm said. "We'll speak of this later."

"Yes, sir."

"Now get yourself to bed. And don't stay up reading all night, else you won't be fit for your duties tomorrow."

"Yes, sir! I mean, no. I mean—"

"Good night, Jared."

"Good night, sir." The boy's gaze caught on the mark one last time, then dropped away as he sketched a bow and hurried off.

Well, it was a better reaction than I got from Carissa. Maybe there's hope for Uncle Simon after all. . . .

14

The Terstan refugees were hidden away at Highmount Holding in a secret room beneath the unrestored garrison stables in the outer yard. The room's walls and floor finished with rough stone, it boasted a hearth whose chimney was shared by the still-working forge set up outside the stable above. Thus a fire could be kindled and vented without giving their presence away.

When Carissa joined them, a pot of stew was bubbling over the flames, a meal they later enjoyed with fresh bread brought down from the kitchen and a basket of new apples, crisp and tart from the holding's small orchard. A young couple with a baby, a single woman with a bruised and swollen face, and an elderly man—a university professor of some repute—with a bandaged right hand comprised the group who waited there at present. As soon as the storm abated they planned to thread the pass and make their way through the forests north of the Aranaaks to the next way station, a small trading post deep in barbarian country. Even to Carissa, who had lived her share of difficult journeys, it seemed a daunting prospect for such a group, especially this late in the season. She mentioned this to her new companions, impulsively offering a place for them here at the holding until spring came. But like scores of their fellows before them, they were determined to go on, confident Eidon would make them a way.

The two women, it turned out, were sisters, Grace and Clarity. The older one, Grace, had recently lost her husband to the Gadrielites, Mataian laymen sworn to the Order of Gadriel. The Gadrielites, they explained, took it upon themselves to find and reform heretics, Terstans being their primary targets. Anyone found on the streets was fair game for questioning, but more often the heretic hunters sought out the forbidden, clandestine worship services of their enemies, bursting in without warning and dragging off as many as they could manage. Lately they'd even been breaking into people's homes. Grace's husband, Brenlan, had been taken at a meeting in Southdock, then tortured to death in the effort to persuade him to renounce his shield and embrace the Flames. The elderly professor accompanying them had also been the recipient of torture, his hand crushed for writing "too many truths the Gadrielites did not like."

"'Tis not safe to be a Terstan in Springerlan anymore, my lady," said Clarity.

Certainly not for those as stubborn as Brenlan Throckmorton, Carissa reflected grimly. *Nor this Professor Laud.*

"Master Cooper told us Prince Abramm has returned to take up the throne," Clarity went on gravely. "When we heard that, we gave thanks we left when we did, for things will surely grow worse if he succeeds. Gillard, at least, only looked the other way. Abramm would surely make it a matter of royal command."

Carissa said nothing to this, her thoughts set hopelessly aroil by the mention of her brother, particularly in this context. Back in Jarnek he'd refused to come home in part because of the persecution toward Terstans that had existed in Kiriath when he'd left. If anything, things sounded worse now, and she doubted he would look the other way. Certainly he would be no less stubborn than Throckmorton or Laud should anyone demand he renounce that shield.

As the others continued to speculate about what would happen next in Kiriath, she busied herself washing their bowls and kettle. When she had finished, the professor, who had been watching her with such keenness of eye she suspected he had recognized her, led the others in prayer and a song of worship. From which, of course, she was excluded, unable even to pretend to praise a god who would allow such cruel injustices to befall his servants as had befallen these four. That night she dreamed of robed men—one of them, Rennalf—bursting into their hideaway to seize them all as heretics.

She awakened with a cry, staring around in the firelit dimness as the dream faded. The professor alone remained awake, puffing on the pipe she'd earlier watched Grace help him to fill and light. His eyes rested thoughtfully upon her. "Your dreams are troubled this night," he said presently.

Shivering, she sat up and crept with her blanket into the fire's warm radius.

"The men from whom you flee," he went on, "the men staying now in your own keep—they are evil."

She wasn't sure if he meant that as statement or question, but she took it as the latter and nodded. "Grace's husband may have died resisting evil men. Mine, I fear, has become one of them."

The old man formed a ring of smoke with his lips and sent it out into the air, watching it dissipate. Then he said to the fire, "I was given to understand it was Rennalf of Balmark who was guesting at your holding, my lady." Carissa glanced at him in chagrin, but he kept his gaze on the flames. "From what I sense up there tonight, you are wise to stay away from him. Although I fear that even down here his dark powers touch your dreams."

Her eyes flicked to him again. *Dark powers? So I was right about that amulet. The Lord of Balmark has changed for the worse.* With a shudder she trained her gaze back at the fire. "I don't believe he knows I'm here, sir."

"A man like that?" The professor snorted softly. "He knows, my lady. You are probably the reason he came here in the first place."

"If he knew I was here, Professor, he would be down here. Believe me." *Howling and spitting and promising me the beating of my life.*

"Oh, he can't find you just now. Eidon has woven a cloak of light over us to confound enemies like him."

She frowned. "Then how could he be touching my dreams?"

"He probably planted the seeds last night. That was when he arrived, was it not?"

Her frown deepened. He turned to meet her gaze soberly. "When he leaves," he said, "you should leave, too. Come with us if you like. Or head south to join your brothers. Only do not stay in Highmount."

She trained her gaze back on the fire. "I would be recognized in the south. And Rennalf would demand my return, which I could not abide."

"They say you were close to Abramm. With his Mataian ties, I can't imagine he would deliver you to a man said to deal in dark magicks."

"It is unlikely Abramm will succeed against Gillard." *The moment anyone finds out about that shield on his chest, it will all be over. They'll never accept another Terstan on the throne after Raynen.* "But if he does, Abramm would be more inclined to give me over than anyone. Gillard has only political reasons, whereas Abramm is constrained by the Words of Revelation—which forbid a woman to do what I have done." *He'd probably believe Eidon would make a way for me to survive it.*

They listened to the fire pop and hiss, to the wind rushing over the flue, then Professor Laud said casually, "According to the Words, there are times desertion is justified."

"In my case, there are other considerations." *Politics. Duty. The good of the realm.* All things her father had used to justify his decision to give her to Rennalf twelve years ago.

"Yes," Laud agreed quietly. "There are always other considerations." As he brought the pipe up to his mouth, firelight glinted off the marriage ring on his left hand, and she thought suddenly that his observation about desertion might be personal.

"You had to leave your wife behind," she guessed.

"And my children and grandchildren, too." He puffed a moment, then added, "They were happy to see me go."

Cloaked in the blanket, Carissa drew her knees to her chest and encircled them with her arms. "Why didn't you just tell the Gadrielites what they want to hear? At least, then, your family would have been safe."

"It was my wife who turned me in," he said without even a trace of bitterness.

She stared at him in astonishment. His hand crushed, his university position lost, his wealth taken, his children and his home and his friends left behind—and all of it thanks to the betrayal of the one person closest to him in all the world, all of it for the sake of a god who obviously didn't care? "And you still follow him?" she blurted, anger burning in her chest. "You still sing praises to him?"

Laud knew whom she meant and smiled gently. "I am alive, am I not? I am free. And I'm on my way to a new life in Chesedh."

"But—you've lost everything."

"Eidon gave me everything I had in the first place. He is free to take it all away if he wishes. I know it is not without purpose."

"Not without purpose? What sort of purpose is there in being betrayed by your wife? In losing your profession and your children and your hand?"

He puffed on his pipe a few times, the smoke's sweet aroma rising around her, then said, "I've been granted the opportunity to show I don't serve him because of what he gives me. To show I trust him even when it looks like I shouldn't." He smiled. "After fifty years in his service, I know this is not for nothing, my lady. In the end, all will be right and I will be blessed the more for having endured it. It is an honor to suffer for his name."

She frowned at him, tense and angry still, for he made no sense, and she could not imagine serving a god who deliberately hurt his people in order to bless them—and then had the gall to call it an honor. Even more upsetting was knowing Abramm served the same god and it was only a matter of time before he suffered a similar "honor." Even as she seethed, Professor Laud puffed at his pipe and stared into the fire with a small sad smile, and she knew he would never be swayed.

She awoke to find the storm over and Rennalf and his men already gone. According to Elayne, Ulgar's claim of seeing Carissa among the servants had been swiftly discounted when a blond maid wearing the clothing he'd described was presented for Rennalf's inspection and questioned closely. When she reluctantly admitted sneaking away to the barn for a lover's tryst, he'd seemed satisfied, had even teased Ulgar about it throughout that second evening. They'd left in the morning without further reference to the matter.

"We'll not see him again soon," Elayne declared firmly.

Cooper was not so certain. "Rennalf always was a sly devil, my lady. I remember more than once when he pretended indifference and was anything but. And I didn't like that amulet he wore, either. I think he'll be back."

Laud's warning not withstanding, Carissa sided with Elayne, convinced that if Rennalf truly suspected she was here, he'd have turned the fortress upside down looking for her. Neither woman, however, denied the man *was* up to something, and it irked Carissa that no one had an inkling what it was. He claimed to have strayed onto Laramor lands chasing barbarian raiders, though no news of such raiders had yet reached Highmount. Barbarians had figured heavily in the northmen's talk, however—one chieftain's name having come up several times—though whether they planned to defend against him or ally with him, no one was sure. But all agreed that it was unsettling to hear them laugh at the notion of Abramm challenging Gillard for the throne.

Of Abramm, naturally, there was a great deal of talk, though the servants closest to Carissa soon learned to avoid the subject in her presence. Those who believed she was Louisa and already regarded her as eccentric thought little of it. Those who knew the truth, like Cooper and Elayne and Hogart, stepped carefully and watched her with increasing consternation. Finally, three days after Rennalf left, four since they'd first received word about Abramm, Cooper broached the subject.

Carissa was in the solar, a small landinglike chamber whose inner half wall overlooked the Great Room below and whose outer held a thick-glassed window that let in a warm, bright light. She sat beside it, satin-stitching a ring of yellow daisies onto a pillow sham.

Cooper came and stood for a time before she finally looked up. "The pigeon loft is nearly full of our own birds again," he said. "It's time we took some back to Springerlan. I thought you might want to go along."

She focused again on her needlework. "Why would you think that? In fact, why would you think you should go at all? The weather will surely turn bad before you return, leaving your bride to pine for you all winter."

"I would bring her with us, of course."

"Well, I don't wish to go." She stuck the needle into the fabric directly alongside where the last stitch had entered. "Furthermore, with Rennalf out there scheming, I don't want to be here alone."

"My lady, Rennalf's scheming is a large part of why I'd like to get you out of here."

She tugged the last thread tight, then poked the needle tip through from the underside. It took her several tries to get it right and push it through. "If Rennalf suspected I was here, he'd have been back before now, Coop. And I'll not flee from the pot to the flames on nothing more than nerves and *what-ifs*. Send the pigeons down with Rolf and Jamison like you did last summer."

Silence stretched between them as she worked, gradually shortening her stitches to draw the petal to a point, then securing it with a couple of backstitches before starting on its neighbor.

"I want to see him, my lady," Cooper said finally.

Even the veiled reference pierced her like an arrow.

When she kept silent, he added, "I should think you would, too."

"Well, I don't!" She worked the needle rapidly in close, steadily lengthening stitches, then realized she had pulled them all too tight.

Cooper finally lost patience. "He's killed the kraggin, my lady! Challenged Gillard for the throne and won it! Do you realize what that means?"

"That Springerlan is free. That the people are pleased." She slid her needle under the last stitch she had taken and loosened it. "That Gillard is not."

Outside a gust of wind rushed against the glass. Voices drifted up from the kitchen as the front door opened and someone stumped across the Great Room. Moments later they dumped a load of wood into the hearth box, then stumped out.

As the front door closed again, Cooper sighed. "I thought this was what you wanted, lass," he murmured. "For him to come back and take up the royal scepter."

"I couldn't care less what he does."

"You hate him that much now? Him whom you went to the ends of the world to free?"

"I—" But her voice failed, and she had to pause in her needlework, blinking away the tears until she could see again. She resumed tight-lipped, her heart feeling like a knot of wood against her breastbone. "He made it plain back in Jarnek what was important to him," she whispered. "And it wasn't me."

Cooper's callused fingers tapped against the sides of his legs. Then, "You know that's not true, lass. Those last weeks he sought with all his might to reconcile. It was *you* who refused to talk."

The thread's tension finally to her liking, she started stitching again, the petal swelling outward from its origin. "I don't want to see him," she said finally. "Please don't ask again. I want you to stay here, as well. Send the pigeons down with someone else."

His reply was delayed, his tone carefully neutral. "As you wish, my lady." He started to go, then turned back at the door. "Would you send him a letter, at least? To let him know we are here?"

"No."

He stood in silence as she continued to ignore him. Finally, he sighed and departed. She was pulling the thread too tightly again and stopped once more to adjust it. But she'd barely begun anew when the thread snarled, and she tossed the hoop irritably into the basket at her side. She sagged back in the chair and stared at the window's clouded glass, blazing before her like a doorway of light. If only it really was a door and she could walk through it into another life, where threads didn't snarl and stitches didn't go all tight and tiny. Where people you loved didn't leave you for someone else.

Cooper was right. Abramm's return had been all that she had hoped for— the heroic slaying of the kraggin, the startling change in appearance and manner that had taken all the peers aback and set them wondering what would happen next. A post rider had reached Highmount Holding late last night with the full story—how Abramm had burst in on the Table looking like old Ravelin Kalladorne to face down Gillard himself and even the Mataian Master Rhiad—*Rhiad's still alive!*—who'd challenged him to bare his chest and prove himself not Terstan. And him fully willing to comply, halfway down the line of his doublet's buttons before someone finally stopped him!

It was a glorious tale, one that should have made her heart sing, yet she felt only cold indifference. And not even a reliable indifference, for she never knew when some random word or thought might churn up sudden tears or bitter, seething anger.

Down in the Great Room, she heard Cooper's low voice interspersed with his wife's higher tones. Discussing his conversation with Carissa no doubt, and lamenting her Kalladorne stubbornness. Well, he could just lament. She wasn't going south.

———

Abramm arose at dawn the morning after the reception and, still wrestling with the prospect of telling Simon about his shieldmark, went down to row around the lake, then take Warbanner for a ride. He returned an hour and a half later by way of the back corridors, avoiding the courtiers already gathered in the King's Court and Gallery in hopes of a glimpse of him. Or a word. Or a private meeting. As the Lord Pretender, he'd been something of a public figure back in Hur, but not even King Shemm had been the focus of as much attention as Abramm was now.

In the bedchamber he let Haldon and Jared dress him in silence, staring at his stranger's reflection as if it might provide him the answers he sought to all the questions that would face him this day. Afterward, he took a cup of heated cocoa and some cheese twistbreads into the study where he planned to eat while trying to go through those Table Records he'd eschewed last night. As he did, he spied a young woman perched on a white satin divan in the sitting chamber that opened off the study. Her skin touched with a swarthiness that said she saw more sun than was proper for a noble lady, she wore a scoop-necked gown of gray-blue silk and a strand of silver with a single Tortusan sapphire around her neck. No ribbons, no bows, no frills of lace, and her light brown hair was caught up in the distinctive braiding of the Chesedhan style.

He stopped at the sight of her, recognizing her at once and wondering if he might duck back into the bedchamber before she saw him. Too late. Even as he thought it she leaped up, her eyes widening like one who'd long sat on a riverbank and finally caught a fish.

"Lady Madeleine," he said as she swept into the study. "You certainly are up and about early this morning."

"But not so early as you, I see." She stopped about six feet away and dropped a belated curtsey, then stood with fingers interlaced before her waist. "Master Haldon let me in to wait for you. I hope you don't mind."

"It is a bit of a surprise," Abramm allowed. He set his cup on the nearest of the three desks and considered inviting her to join him for breakfast, then discarded the idea at the memory of Blackwell's warning.

He looked at her expectantly. She returned his gaze for a moment, then glanced about, her interlaced fingers working slowly back and forth. A flush crept into her freckled face. "I suppose I've broken protocol again, haven't I? It's just that I knew if I didn't see you now, there'd be no other time, and I wanted to apologize for my forwardness last night."

Abramm could not control the chuckle that escaped him. Her face flushed even more, and now she couldn't look at him at all. "And I suppose now I should apologize for my forwardness this morning. I fear I am not well suited to all this womanly reticence you Kiriathans find so attractive." She fell silent, her fingers working back and forth. Then she pulled them apart and let them drop to her sides.

"I wanted to apologize for my song, as well," she said firmly, lifting her gaze to his. "It was my intent to honor you, sir, not to offend you."

There was pain in her gray-blue eyes, and a vulnerability he would never have guessed to see. In that moment he knew, suddenly and sharply, just how she felt, for he had been there himself, far too many times. His annoyance and aversion turned to regret; sighing, he set down the pastry.

"No, it is I who should apologize, my lady. I had no call to be so harsh last night."

Her chin came up just a bit. "Actually, I prefer the honesty," she said. "As a king's daughter, I don't get it very often."

"I can understand that." He gestured at a nearby chair. "Please have a seat. Would you like some cocoa?"

"Oh no, Sire. I have said what I came to say and . . ." She trailed off, then drew a breath and blurted, "I was also hoping you might enlighten me as to how the song could be improved."

He blinked and almost chuckled again. She seemed heedless of the in-consistencies of her behavior. Or maybe she was just intent on getting what she wanted. He made a wry face. "I really don't think I'm the man to ask, my lady. In fact, I rather doubt there's any way you could rewrite it to suit me. Except perhaps to write it about someone else."

"Still . . . as you pointed out last night, I wasn't there. I had only what others told me."

"It wasn't an experience you'd want to write a song about, anyway."

"Why not? It's a wonderful story."

"It was a nightmare. Dark and wet and cold. The waves like mountains, the stench so bad you could hardly see for the tears in your eyes. The mast raining down, men screaming . . . and I assure you I had no such noble sentiments as duty and sacrifice. I was angry and more scared than I've ever been in my life. All I wanted was to see it dead."

She was staring at him wide-eyed. "You *did* hold on to that spear, didn't you?"

"It would definitely improve the song if you left that part out. It's just too . . ." He trailed off, searching for a word that would not offend.

"Heroic?" she supplied.

He felt his face go hot and she smiled. "Why, sir, now *you're* blushing!"

He scowled at her, and her smile vanished as she pressed her lips together and laced her fingers once more. "I'm sorry, sir. I didn't mean—"

"Never mind," Abramm said. "And yes, it is too heroic."

He would have elaborated but at that moment a quartet of servants arrived bearing a ladder and a rolled tapestry. The roll they laid on the floor while they set up the ladder and removed the existing tapestry hanging between the shelves of books that lined the walls of the high-ceilinged study. It was Gillard's coat of arms, which presumably would be delivered to his new quarters. That meant the roll they'd brought to replace it must be Abramm's. He stepped toward them, watching with interest as together they hung it from its hooks and carefully unrolled it down the wall.

Like all the Kalladorne arms, its overall shape was that of a shield, divided into quarters, white for the upper left and lower right, royal blue for the others. Against the white in the upper left flew the black hawk of the House of Kalladorne and in the lower right, the devices specific to the king in question. Abramm's consisted of a shield of gold bearing a red dragon rampant at its midst. Gold shield and red dragon. The sight of them drove the breath from his lungs, and for a moment he could only stare in astonishment.

Then he turned to the servant. "What is this?"

"Why it's your coat of arms, sir."

"*My* coat of arms." Abramm stared at the panel as anger chilled his belly. "Are you sure?"

"Yes, sir." He bowed and, when Abramm said no more, turned to helping his companions roll up the tapestry they'd removed, then fold up the ladder. In moments they were gone, and silence filled the chamber, Abramm, Madeleine, Haldon, and now Jared staring at the tapestry.

Then Jared burst out, "It's exactly like the brand on your arm, sir!"

Abramm turned to Haldon. "Is this some sort of jest? Because I'll tell you right now, I don't find it amusing."

But Haldon was staring at the device with as much apparent surprise as Abramm. "It's no jest, sir."

"You did not choose this design, then?"

"Of course not. It was created by Master Eckleston."

"Summon him at once."

Haldon's bushy brows flew up. "He's been dead ten years, sir."

"Well, then, how—?"

"This was designed when you were born. Held in reserve until you came to your majority."

The chill of anger became one of shock. Abramm stared at him open-mouthed, his flesh prickling.

Beside him, Lady Madeleine, whose presence he'd entirely forgotten, whispered, "Amazing."

Both men turned to her, for she had expressed the very sentiments they were feeling, though she'd been paying no attention to their conversation. Feeling their eyes upon her, she glanced at them, then pointed at the panel. "The dragon part of this device is very much like the brand of Katahn ul Manus."

Abramm went dead still, his heart thundering in his chest. *Khrell's Fire! If she guesses the truth, things will get very messy.*

"Who?" Haldon asked.

"Katahn ul Manus," she repeated. "A prominent Gamer in Esurh, until a few years ago." Her gray-blue eyes flicked to Abramm. "Surely you've heard of him, sir. You couldn't have lived down there any length of time and not. He was the one who owned the White Pretender."

"I've heard of him," Abramm said warily.

But already the wheels of that quick mind were turning. He could almost see it happen, see her backtracking, glancing at Jared, that little crease appearing between her slender brows. "Did I hear him say *you* wear this brand, sir?"

"It is not a thing I am proud of."

Understanding came to her in bursts. "Then you *must* have known—" She stopped, her glance flicking to his ear with its three tiny holes left over from the honor rings, to his arm where the brand hid beneath the silk and velvet sleeves, across his shoulders and chest—far too broad for a scribe's—and finally up to meet his gaze. Her mouth opened but nothing came out. Then her face paled beneath its scattering of freckles and she swayed so that Abramm leaped to catch her before her knees buckled.

He helped her into the nearest chair, and as the servants cried and chattered she looked into his eyes and whispered, "You're *him*!"

"Frighteningly quick," Byron had said.

"Katahn owned many slaves besides the White Pretender, my lady," he insisted.

"They said he really *was* a Kiriathan prince," she countered in kind.

"He was always seen painted and wigged. Rumor held it was because he *wasn't* Kiriathan and Katahn sought to cover the truth."

"But Beltha'adi offered him amnesty and a chance to wear the uniform of the Black Moon, the first among the northern peoples ever to be so honored."

"A political ploy. Nothing more. By then the Pretender was equated with Kiriath in everyone's mind."

The color had come back into her face, and her eyes blazed. "You're him," she said with quiet ferocity. "I see the truth in your eyes!"

"You have a very active imagination, my lady. And if you spread this theory of yours around, I guarantee you'll be laughed out of court."

"Are you threatening me?"

"Not at all." He straightened. "Tell the tale if you desire. But be prepared for the ridicule that will surely come your way."

He could not tell if she believed him, could not tell what she thought. Only that she was still far too excited for his comfort. But arguing with her would only make her more certain she was right. Better to let the disbelief of the court work on her for a while and distance himself as much as possible in the meantime.

He stepped back and gestured to the door. "Have a pleasant day, my lady. I'm sure we'll speak again." He turned to Haldon and asked when his first meeting of the day was scheduled.

If Madeleine was nonplussed, he didn't see it. He only caught her curtsey out of the corner of his eye and heard the rustle of her skirts as she was escorted back through the sitting room and out.

"Who's the White Pretender, Sire?" Jared asked as the door closed behind her.

"A Kiriathan slave who was unexpectedly successful in the Esurhite games, Jared."

"What happened to him?"

"He escaped from the great Val'Orda," Haldon said, his eyes fixed upon Abramm's face. "And later faced down Beltha'adi himself."

Abramm gestured irritably at the room. "Don't you people have something to do?"

Jared swallowed whatever he meant to say and hurried off. Haldon turned to plucking withered blooms from one of the flower arrangements on a table between bookshelves and Abramm returned to his uneaten twistbreads and now-cold cocoa. Annoyed, he called Jared back to bring him a fresh cup, but the boy had barely left before Abramm was again looking at the coat of arms and thinking that, while Madeleine had honed right in on the fact he had once been the Pretender, she had missed the greater significance. That the coat of arms had been waiting for him, with that device, long before he was ever born. And it was not just the dragon that astonished him but the golden shield, as well.

"How could this be, Haldon?" he whispered.

The old chamberlain was staring at it again, also. "I don't know, sir. It certainly does lift the hairs on the back of one's neck, though."

Destiny. The hand of Eidon had him, no questions now. No getting around it. At least he knew without a doubt that he *was* supposed to be here.

And it would only be a matter of time before Madeleine got around to figuring this part out, as well. Then there'd be another song. He groaned.

"Sir?"

"I was just thinking of Lady Madeleine."

"Ah." Haldon held silent for a moment. "Are you going to let her spread the tale, then?"

"Can you think of any way to stop her?"

"Actually it might not be such a bad thing."

Abramm turned sharply and saw his chamberlain struggling to suppress a smile. "You already knew about this, didn't you?"

"You mean the White Pretender?" Haldon let a bit of the smile escape. "You didn't get all those scars from your ink pens and books, my lord." He paused. "How long exactly *were* you a scribe?"

"Four days."

"Ah."

Jared returned then with the cocoa; Abramm accepted it wordlessly and waited while the boy went back to the bedchamber to resume his chores before continuing the conversation. "But the tale is so fantastic, Hal—so completely implausible—I don't understand how you could . . ."

"Even the most fantastic of tales spring from a kernel of truth. I suspected the moment I saw you in the bathchamber, and time has only borne out my suspicion. To say nothing of this." He gestured at the tapestry, then turned his gaze to Abramm. "Why have you said nothing about it?"

Abramm went around the desk and settled into the chair, sipping his cocoa. "I don't know. It just seemed—there was never an appropriate time. It's not a tale you tell about yourself."

"Well, now *you* don't have to tell it, do you?"

Abramm's head jerked up. "Is *that* why you let her in here this morning?"

Haldon did his best to look put out. "Sire, she is Second Daughter of Chesedh. She practically demanded audience. What was I to do?"

"I can't imagine. I'm sure you were totally helpless."

Haldon picked up a stack of books from the desk and began to reshelve them. "I really didn't expect her to pick up on it so soon. In fact, she wouldn't have, had the coat of arms not arrived. Had Jared not opened his mouth. Although—" He paused in the midst of sliding a slender blue volume between two larger gray ones. "I don't think it was coincidence, my lord." He pushed the blue book all the way in, then glanced again at Abramm. "Your people need to hear your story. Need to know how you defended them. It will give them heart . . . and make them love you even more."

"Love me? They'll laugh me out of court. Everyone will think I put her up to it. And may I remind you, Hal, I have no proof except my word."

"The proof, sir, is all over your body."

"Every slave has scars. And like mine, most are from the whip. Besides, if I show them the scars, I have to show them something else. Something that's far too mixed up in this tale of the White Pretender to separate. For apart from it, I never would've escaped the Val'Orda, and certainly wouldn't have defeated Beltha'adi." He paused. "Do you think it is time my people learned of that, as well?"

Haldon concentrated on his books. "That is a decision only you can make, sir."

And yet how could he make it? How was he to know the proper time?

His eyes went back to the coat of arms, the dragon and the shield there in scarlet and gold for all the world to see. How soon before people started to put the pieces together? Not long, with Madeleine out there leading the way.

Why have you done this, my Lord? Are you trying to tell me I can't really be king until I've acknowledged both? That I should come clean of all my secrets now and let you handle the explosion that's sure to follow?

But as with the matter of telling Simon, he got no clear answers.

15

On the eighth day of Abramm's reign, at ten minutes to two in the afternoon, Simon Kalladorne clattered up to the palace's main entrance on his big bay stallion and dismounted. Flinging the reins at the first lieutenant of his escort, he pulled his document pouch from its saddlebag and jogged awkwardly up the stairway to the carved and gilded front doors, pulling off his gloves as he went. He stank of horse and sweat and road dust, but he was scheduled to see the king in ten minutes, hardly time to get there, much less wash and change. He'd spent all day yesterday at the Briarcreek Garrison, finishing up the details of his report for the king on the status of the army and had intended to leave for Springerlan early this morning. But all sorts of things had come up at the last minute, delaying his departure.

He was in a foul mood and he knew it. Seeing the new conscripts always did it to him. Conscription regulations had been filled with so many exemptions of late that the only men they could actually draft were peasants or outright criminals. With military service having fallen out of favor among the peers years ago, fewer and fewer of Kiriath's aristocracy entered voluntarily. Not that the upper classes would be any better than the lower. Take that young fool he had encountered on the way here. The wheel had come off his buggy, stranding him, and the young dandy was in a dither, wringing his hands and screaming at his servants to fix it. When Simon and his escort had arrived on the scene, the peacock had all but fainted for fear they were bandits. A fine soldier that one would make.

Simon stopped at the entry to hand over cloak and gloves, brushing at himself in a futile attempt to remove some of the dust. As he straightened,

Temas Darnley and a coterie of adoring young nobles crossed the domed atrium on their way to the east wing. Darnley nodded a greeting, not even noticing that Simon only scowled back. They were all the same, a flock of pigeons decked in ribbons and lace with their ridiculous wigs and scented gloves and silly canes. They made him sick and angry, and sometimes he wanted to grab them by those lace cravats and—

He cut off the mental tirade. Raging did no good, and they were not all like that. There were still real men within the peerage—in military service, too. And Abramm's plans, if they were legitimate, would go far toward improving things. Even his person, if he continued to manifest the appearance and manner he'd adopted, would do that. Indeed, a number of the new men Simon had seen yesterday were there precisely because of Abramm, inspired by the way he'd dealt with both the kraggin and the court—to say nothing of his near miraculous escape from slavery. That they were also unemployed and suffering economic hardship likely had something to do with it, too, but at least they were claiming loyalty and admiration for their king. Simon just hoped Abramm would turn out to be worthy of it. Then frowned at himself for the thought.

He drew a breath and headed right, crossing the atrium to enter the spacious Hall of Mirrors leading to the west wing. Gold laced the marble floor and the mirroring of the inner wall, gleaming in the warm light of the row of windows opposite. He was halfway to the Fountain Court at its end when Leona Blackwell and her ladies-in-waiting emerged from one of the salons beyond the mirrored wall. A gown of magenta silk set off her ivory skin and flaxen hair to startling advantage and deepened the blue of her eyes, which today sparkled with an unusual animation. "Lady Leona," said Simon, bowing. "How lovely you look."

Her blush deepened as she curtsied and thanked him for the compliment, while he marveled anew at how much she favored her mother. He glanced around. "I thought the king had canceled the morning concerts and brunches."

She sighed mournfully. "He has. And everything else, too, I'm afraid. Well, except for his picnic to the western headland day after tomorrow, but that hardly counts. I've tried to persuade him otherwise, but he is set on conserving funds for his military projects." She affected an endearing pout. "The winter will be so very dull. . . . I don't suppose *you* could speak to him, my lord duke. . . ?"

The pout had evolved into a coquettish plea. But Simon shook his head sadly. "I fear, my lady, that Abramm is right." He was momentarily startled, hearing his own words, then went on. "It's a sacrifice we all must make."

"You really think those southlanders could be that much of a threat?"

Simon smiled at her. "Not so much now, my lady."

Leona sniffed and tilted her head. "Lord Temas says they're not. That Abramm's unnecessarily paranoid. That it's his Mataian background that's driving him—all those years of denying himself and seeing pleasure as something evil." She sighed again. "At least he has not canceled the Harvest Ball as he threatened to do."

Simon frowned as something she'd said earlier struck him. "Did I hear you say you sought to convince him of these things, my lady? Have you met with him, then?"

"Oh." A hint of pink touched her cheeks as she smiled. "I'm assisting him with the dances for the ball. We had our first practice this morning."

"Ah. And how did he do? I expect your toes must be rather bruised."

"It's just the patterns he's rusty on, sir. He's actually quite"—her blush deepened and she averted her gaze—"athletic. He's very athletic, sir."

And only now did Simon recall how Leona had all but swallowed Abramm with her eyes at his reception the night the kraggin was burned. The court gossips must already be chattering of a budding royal romance. "I assume your brother approves of this developing relationship?" *Since as Royal Secretary now, he's no doubt set it in motion.*

She blushed furiously, and her small hands fiddled with the ribbons at her waist. "I would hardly call it a *relationship*, my lord. I am only here to help with the dancing. As to my brother's approval"—her hands fell motionless at her sides and pique crept into her voice—"I should imagine he would be pleased if such a thing as you are suggesting developed. He was the one to arrange my tutoring sessions, after all."

"Ah." Simon suppressed a smile. The younger Blackwell had much of his father in him—particularly the ability to manipulate people into believing his plans for them were actually their own.

Now Leona blushed again, and her hands plucked up her skirt. "Well, it's been a pleasure speaking to you, my lord."

"All mine, I assure you," Simon said.

She swept away with her ladies, their skirts hissing, and Simon watched them go with a thoughtful smile.

"They're already taking wagers she'll be the next queen," Ethan Laramor said from just behind him, "Chesedhan negotiations notwithstanding."

Simon turned with an oath. "Plagues, man! You move like a spirit. Can't you give me a little warning?"

Laramor grinned and shrugged. "I thought I had. Maybe the problem lies with your ears, eh?" He wore the standard Borderer jerkin and britches today, his clanlord earring glinting alongside his jaw.

"My ears are fine," Simon growled. "And what the plague are you doing here, anyway? I thought you were avoiding the palace now that the Guardian-King has come to power."

"I was waiting for you, actually. And you, my friend, are going to be late for your meeting."

Simon scowled. "Is that a problem?"

"Unlike Gillard, Abramm is a stickler for punctuality," Laramor said. "He's already refused audience to several of the peers when they failed to arrive on time." He gestured along the gleaming corridor. "Come, I'll walk with you."

As they fell into step Laramor came quickly to his point. "What are you planning to say about the border situation?"

Simon glanced at him sidelong. "Is there something specific you want me to mention?"

"I'd rather you go easy on the subject. Don't give him reason to send his Mataian brothers up there to set things right."

"It sounds to me like Balmark is treating with the barbarians, Ethan. I can't very well not tell him."

"We don't know what Balmark's doing," Laramor said, hands clasped at his back. "And Abramm's got enough to deal with. He probably won't pick up on it if you don't do it for him."

They fell silent as a group of courtiers passed them, then resumed their discussion as they turned into the King's Court and started toward the broad convex staircase leading up to the Royal Apartments. "I have to at least mention it," Simon said, frowning at his friend.

"Just don't give him any more than he asks for," Laramor said quietly. "And try to keep him from asking for more than you give him."

"You know that sort of thing is not my style."

"Precisely why I'm bringing it up," Laramor said with a wry smile. They stopped at the base of the stairs, and the border lord's expression went from amusement to concern. "Be careful in there, Simon. Gillard's right, you know. Abramm *will* try to win you. He has to."

Simon scowled at him. "Do you really believe I'm so addlebrained I won't recognize flattery, manipulation, and double-talk when I hear it? And from Abramm, of all people, whom I've known since he was a babe?"

"Just see that you don't forget what you know of him," Ethan said grimly. "That his mentor was Saeral—as charming a snake as ever there was."

He left Simon to climb the stair alone, and five minutes later the old duke was ushered into the royal sitting room where, as Ethan had predicted, Abramm already awaited him. The new king sat upon the blue-and-white-striped divan near the fire, lost in thought, a glass of orange juice in one long-fingered hand. As happened every time since Abramm had come before the Table that first night to claim his birthright, Simon found himself startled anew by the change in his nephew's appearance. How much bigger he was than expected. How much more solid than he'd ever been as a boy. How confident and assured.

Clad in brown fine-wale corduroy breeches and vest over a full-sleeved ivory-colored blouse, Abramm's dress was austere, a decided relief compared to the excesses of his courtiers. As usual he wore no jewelry save his signet ring. Even the hilt and scabbard of the rapier he still wore—an odd concession to fashion when he so disregarded it in other respects—lacked all ornamentation, looking more like a service piece than the decorated broomsticks that were the norm.

As Simon stopped between divan and chair, Abramm took notice of him and indicated he should sit. "You look travel worn, Uncle," he said, leaning forward. "Would you like a drink? Something to eat?"

Simon allowed that he would, and both were swiftly provided. Once his guest's comfort had been seen to, Abramm nodded to one of the servants, who led the others out without a word.

Simon could not complain about his listener's attentiveness. The report was specific and comprehensive, yet Abramm never lost interest, never seemed lost, and did not hesitate to ask questions both intelligent and surprisingly relevant—not at all the sort that would be asked by a man who cared nothing for the military. Or who knew little about it. Nor did he allow any slighting of the border situation, questioning Simon closely when he tried to pass over it and ultimately extracting all the information Simon had to give before allowing him to move on. Which, despite Ethan's warning, made Simon warm to him all the more.

Until he brought up Graymeer's. Or, more specifically, the fact that Simon *hadn't* brought it up. "When I would expect it to be at the top of the list of deficiencies that need addressing."

It was like opening one's wardrobe and finding a nest of staffid inside. Simon frowned, all his goodwill smothered by rising suspicion. "Sire, you grew up in Springerlan. You know what Graymeer's is."

Cloaked in mists and infested with shadowspawn, the old fortress sat atop a honeycomb of dark passages so convoluted they'd never been thoroughly investigated, much less mapped and secured. For almost a century now, that lacking had doomed to disaster every attempt to reclaim the site, the lives lost to it grown too great to count.

"I know what it is today," Abramm said, picking up the glass of orange juice he'd set aside earlier and draining it. "But I also know it wasn't always like this. And I know that as long as it stands in ruin, the bay's west channel is an open lane for invaders to take the city. And yes, perhaps our navy can handle it, but why anchor a ship there defending the channel when a battery of cannon on the headland can do the job as well or better?"

His blue eyes met Simon's boldly, as if he expected to be challenged. But Simon smiled, feeling the irony of the moment. "Surely you know by now I would be the last to argue with you on that, sir. I just don't think spending more lives on Graymeer's is the way to go. Better to build elsewhere. I've already researched an excellent site at the mouth of the river."

"Which would let them get far too close to the city," Abramm pointed out, fingering the now empty glass in his hands. "Besides, we don't have time or funds to build anew. And it would be a foolish waste of both when all Graymeer's really needs, I suspect, is a good cleaning."

"A cleaning." The words sent a chill up Simon's back. "What do you mean to do, then? Set Brother Belmir and a pack of his Mataians to the problem? Or worse, Lord Prittleman?"

Abramm's head jerked up, his expression startled and indignant. "No! Why would I?"

"Because the Mataio has been screaming about cleansing that place for years. Now here you are, determined to do the same. It doesn't take much to add the figures. A worthy goal, I would say, for one who would be their Guardian-King."

"I am *not* their Guardian-King!" Abramm said sharply. "When I renounced my vows, I renounced it all. I thought I had made that clear." He was plainly irritated. But was it because of frustration at not being believed or because he feared his façade was being uncovered?

"Belmir claims your disbelief is temporary," said Simon. "That soon you will be back in the fold. Father Bonafil speaks of a coronation in the Keep."

"I'll be dead before I'm crowned in the Keep!" Abramm said fiercely. "And I've told them the truth to their faces. If they refuse to believe me, it's hardly my fault."

His passion seemed genuine. But Ethan's words would not go away. *"Remember his mentor was Saeral, as charming a snake as ever there was."* "So you're saying to me," said Simon, "clearly and plainly, that you are not a Mataian and never will be again."

"That is exactly what I am saying, Uncle."

"Why?" Simon burst out. "After all these years of stubborn allegiance, why do you reject it now? And how can you expect me to believe it is permanent? It's not like you hold another faith in its stead!"

He met Abramm's glance defiantly, expecting the boy to shrink back and avert his eyes. Instead, he found himself caught in a gaze suddenly piercing and intent, as if his nephew sought to see his motives or was perhaps gauging some other aspect of his character. Simon had no idea what he might have seen, but finally Abramm did look away, apprehension flashing inexplicably across the hawkish features as he set the glass down on the table beside him. For a long time he sat in silence, one finger circling the glass's rim, until finally he released a long breath and looked up. "Why, you ask?" His voice was grim. "Because I've seen it for the lie that it is. Since the day I discovered Saeral's true plans for me and fled, nothing that happened to me should have happened. By Mataian reckoning, I should have been blessed for my service—not chained to a galley and forced to break my vows or die."

"Chained to a galley?" Simon exclaimed, startled. "I thought you were a scribe."

"I was both. Scribe first, galley slave second." His lips twisted ironically as his hand left the juice glass and went to the opposite cuff. "Do you want to see the brand?"

No! Simon thought. *I don't!* And yet he said nothing as Abramm pushed the billowing sleeve upward to reveal a muscular arm slashed with white scars. On the swell of his bicep stood a red dragon rampant, somewhat distorted by the way the scar tissue had formed, but very clearly a dragon. Simon had already heard the stories that it was just like the dragon in Abramm's coat of arms, but hearing stories was not the same as seeing the thing in the flesh. Not only was it close enough to the dragon on his coat of arms to raise the hairs on Simon's nape, but it *was* a brand. The mark of a slave on the son of Simon's brother, now king of Kiriath. It was such an affront, such a shock, he could hardly bear to look at it. And now other details pushed themselves forward—the white scars, the broadness of shoulders and chest, the heaviness of his hands, thickened from hard labor. Galley slave. *That's how he's come back so changed. That's how he backed old Haldon up against the bedpost. Branded, chained to an oar, forced to row or die. Plagues! The steel was there. How could we all have missed it?*

Abramm looked away, jaw clenched, face touched with a hint of flush as he let the fabric fall back down his arm, covering the brand again. As he refastened his cuff he said, "I am no Mataian, Uncle, and I swear to you they will never rule this realm so long as I live. If my solemn word is not enough, I will swear it before Eidon himself, or upon any binding relic you wish."

There was that intensity again, a passion of declaration that rang with undeniable conviction. Simon did not know what to say to it, so he said nothing. The silence stretched between them, filled with the thumps and voices of the servants in the adjoining chamber, muffled and indistinct behind closed doors.

"I still don't think Graymeer's is a good idea," Simon burst out.

"I'll know better in a couple of days."

"My lord, that is another thing . . . you're not really going up there with all your courtiers—"

"Of course not. They'll only be there for the picnic. We'll be setting up on the flat above Sander's Cove. I'll spend a bit of time with them while Captain Channon and his men secure the fortress—as much as they can— then I'll go have a look. It'll be midday, and we won't stay long."

"But to even order the men to go inside—"

"They're all volunteers, Uncle."

And that brought Simon to silence. *Volunteers? He's gotten men to volunteer to enter Graymeer's? Then, Well, why not? They're already signing up for the army, why not this?*

Abramm smiled a little. "I've been in places like Graymeer's before,

Uncle. They're not uncommon in Esurh, so I do have some idea what I'm getting into."

"And you encountered these places while you were rowing your galley ship?"

The smile widened. "I haven't rowed a galley ship in years."

That's right. He'd come to Kinlock in Bre'el wearing Esurhite robes and carrying enough Esurhite gold to hire a trademaster and all her crew for his monster-hunting foray. Obviously much had transpired between his time on the galley and then. Much that so far he'd said little about.

Abramm's voice intruded into his musing. "To get back to your report—I'd like an addendum detailing all that will be necessary for reopening Graymeer's. Beyond that . . ."

He went on to authorize most of Simon's recommendations, and then, just when Simon thought he was finished, Abramm shocked him again. "I have one more request of you, Uncle: a list of men you regard as trustworthy and level-headed. And any other advice you deem important."

Simon gaped at him. "You ask *me* for a list of men you can trust? Knowing my ties to Gillard?"

Abramm leaned back on the divan, one elbow braced on the armrest. "Those ties are precisely why I am asking you." He paused. "And speaking of Gillard, what do you know of the plots he is hatching against me?"

Simon flinched. "I know of no plots, sir." A flare of red, a flash of fiery eyes stabbing into his own, a gleam of steel, a low, croaking voice . . .

"No plots?"

Only a strange, recurring, senseless dream. He straightened his shoulders and looked the king in the eye. "No, sir. In fact, I counseled him against taking such action."

"Did you?" Abramm ran his fingers along the silk upholstery of the divan's arm. "And was he involved in the ambush against me the evening of the reception?"

"He claimed he was not."

Abramm studied him thoughtfully. "You believe otherwise?"

"By all the gods, Abramm! Must you be so direct?"

"I serve only one god. And yes, I must be direct if we are to understand each other."

Simon looked away, hands clenched in his lap. He had not expected this level of audacity. Had not expected Abramm to face him eye to eye and challenge him like this. "Your Majesty, please. You must know the position you put me in with such a question."

Abramm's blue eyes stayed cool and flat. "These are hard times, Uncle. Few of us occupy positions we desire. I least of all." He paused, then repeated, as if Simon were perfectly at ease before him. "So was he involved, then?"

"Sire . . . please!" Desperate to escape that piercing gaze, Simon leaped up and paced to the hearth.

"This is not some bizarre competition for your affections, Uncle. We are talking about the fate of our realm, the lives of our people, the duty that comes to us because of our heritage and our name. A duty that does not ask us what we like or prefer."

Simon stared blindly at the dying fire. Those were words he'd uttered repeatedly over the years, though Gillard never really embraced them. That Abramm would use them now—as reproof, no less!—shook Simon deeply. And made him feel as wretched as he'd ever felt in his life, teetering on the knife edge of a decision he never dreamed he'd have to make. *Let me look into it, Your Majesty*, he wanted to say. But other words presented themselves, words he was loath to voice, even as he did. "He claimed at first he was not. Later he admitted he was, but with no intent to harm, only to frighten. To get you to abdicate and return to your Mataian towers."

Behind him, Abramm snorted softly. "I hope you know now, Uncle, that I will not do that."

After a moment, Simon turned from the hearth. "Even if it means igniting a civil war?"

Abramm watched his own fingers caress the silken armrest. "I do not wish war, Uncle. It is the last thing Kiriath needs. But if he takes it that far"—his eyes came up to skewer Simon's—"I will not back down."

And looking into that gaze, Simon knew he would not.

"The question is," Abramm went on, "which side of this struggle will you be on?"

"I am on Kiriath's side."

"Then you had best decide which of us is the better man for Kiriath."

Simon had nothing to say to that, and after a pause, Abramm stood to dismiss him. "Will you be coming with us tomorrow, Uncle?"

It took a moment for Simon to gather his poise and redirect his thoughts, "On the picnic? Or up to Graymeer's?"

"Whichever one you wish. Though I *would* welcome your commentary on Graymeer's."

Simon scowled at him. "Then I will oblige you, foolish and vain as I believe your project to be." He hesitated. "And the advice you asked for? Make sure you get yourself a horse you can control. No one expects you to be an accomplished rider, but even so, the sight of one's king on a runaway does not inspire confidence."

He had expected—intended—his remarks to be nettlesome, but they seemed to have missed the target, for Abramm only smiled. "I shall do my best to comply, Uncle."

16

Though the morning of Abramm's picnic and inspection of Graymeer's Fortress dawned calm, clear, and beautiful, the king himself awoke to an overwhelming sense of dread. For the first time since arriving in Kiriath, he'd had a nightmare. In it, Lady Madeleine tricked him into claiming before all his courtiers that he was, indeed, the White Pretender. As the peers laughed hysterically, Gillard challenged him to prove the lady's contention, and before Abramm knew it, the two of them were trading thrusts and ripostes. For some reason Abramm had only his dagger—not nearly long enough to counter his brother's rapier—and so was forced to retreat up the hillside where they fought all the way to Graymeer's peak and from thence into the tunnels beneath the ruin. All the while Gillard laughed, telling him he never should have come home, that he was a scrawny little loser who would only bring death to a people who didn't even want him. Finally, frustrated and furious, Abramm found an opening and plunged his dagger—suddenly become a sword again—into his brother's heart. The pale blue eyes opened wide with surprise, then glazed over as the body fell back off Abramm's blade.

The shock of realizing what he'd done jerked him awake, emotions churning with satisfaction and horror . . . and a paralyzing dread of what this day would bring. Last night, Shale Channon had told him Gillard planned a fencing demonstration as part of today's activities. *"He thought it'd be appropriate, in light of you wantin' to get the peers int'rested in military matters,"* Channon had explained. *"He's takin' all comers, he himself subject to whatever reasonable handicap they demand. We're having quite a time coming up with 'reasonable handicaps.'"*

He'd hesitated then, adding that Gillard would probably challenge Abramm to join him—as a matter of "courtesy" to the king. Not that anyone, Gillard included, would expect Abramm to accept such a challenge—or care should he decline—but Abramm would do well to prepare himself for the moment, since it could be embarrassing otherwise. Abramm had fallen asleep reviewing all the reasons why he must decline his brother's challenge, ruminations which had undoubtedly triggered the nightmare. But understanding its origins did little to alleviate the dream's effects, and for a time he didn't even want to get out of bed.

He might be able to postpone his inspection of Graymeer's—enough people had complained and warned and sought to persuade him against it that he'd likely be viewed as sensible rather than cowardly—but that wouldn't give him reason to cancel the picnic. Perhaps he could plead the grippe—Blackwell had come down with it last night, so why not the king?

Because it's a cowardly maneuver, he told himself, *and will only put off the inevitable.* He needed to win the lords' respect, not only for his projects but for his leadership, and he couldn't do that hiding in bed. He'd just have to leave Gillard and Madeleine and all the rest of them to Eidon.

Thus at precisely nine o'clock in the morning, King Abramm the Second rode into the Grand Fountain Court to meet his courtiers and begin the procession to the headlands. About half of those who'd claimed they were coming hadn't arrived yet—including his brother—but given that nine was early for most, he assumed they would come later. As the university clock tolled the hour, he threaded the gauntlet they had formed for him, those at the fore falling into line behind him after he had passed. He rode slowly, exchanging morning greetings and noting sourly that most were dressed more in keeping with an afternoon tea than a ride across the headlands. Lord Darnley was a show all in himself, decked out in a red velvet riding habit and an extravagant broad-brimmed hat complete with black egret feather. His saddle sported silver tassels, and his horse's mane and tail had been plaited into hundreds of braids trimmed with tiny silver bells. Looking at him, Abramm wondered if the Esurhites might have been more right about his countrymen than he'd wanted to admit.

Warbanner pranced and sidled nervously, impatient with the slow pace, rattled by the other horses—and perhaps the nervousness of his rider, as well.

As the last of the clock's deep tolls faded into the morning, they trotted down the bricked drive and out the western gate, following the Avenue of the King as it switchbacked down the populous hillside. At the bottom, it straightened, cutting through the city in a broad, tree-lined thoroughfare to the King's Bridge, the third span from the bay, and grandest of the nine. Spectators lined the route, most of them cheering and waving white banners bearing the shield and dragon of Abramm's still-startling coat of arms. The few who didn't, he noted unhappily, congregated nearest the river, many of them with shieldmarks exposed, standing silent and sullen as he rode by.

On the west bank the Avenue diminished to a wide street, which gave way to the hard-packed road that climbed the headland and ran on to Longstrand on the distant western coast. As storefronts yielded to farms and grassland, he gave Warbanner his head, and the colt exploded into a full run, leaving the others in his dust, as usual. This time Channon had posted guards along the way, and had himself ridden out with a couple of men in advance of the king. Though they had a sizeable lead by the time Warbanner started, he caught them easily, even nosed his way ahead for a time, before he'd finally had enough and slowed. Abramm's guards came up around him again, Channon and a subordinate abreast of him, a third man behind. It was a beautiful day, all blue and gold and sparkling. The sun shone brightly on the rippling grass, the sea gulls soared freely overhead, and the air was crisp with the chill of autumn, all working to erase the last trace of his dream-inspired dread.

He glanced at Captain Channon, riding stiffly beside him. The man had strongly protested his sovereign's plans to inspect the dreaded Graymeer's this day, and with good reason, Abramm supposed. Channon's father had been part of Simon Kalladorne's expedition to restore it the last time, so his knowledge of its dangers was more intimate—and accurate—than most. Nor did it help that the volunteers escorting Abramm today were not the Terstan soldiers Channon had hoped to enlist but were a mixed bag of men who mostly wanted the extra pay. It wouldn't matter for what Abramm intended today—just a quick look to get a feel for the damage and show everyone he wasn't afraid of the place—but in the days to come it would.

"How did your attempts go at recruiting from that private source you were going to tap last night?" Abramm asked. He was pretty sure Channon's private source was one of the Tersts that reportedly met in Southdock. "Did you get any more of the sort of men you wished?"

Channon glanced aside at him. "I did, sir, though not nearly enough."

"Only one, in fact, as far as I know," said the armsman to Abramm's right.

Annoyed at the man's uninvited intrusion, Abramm turned to reprove him—and swallowed his words as the familiar voice registered. Along with the recollection of the man's solidly muscled form, seen but not truly noted earlier, and now the sight of his freckled, red-bearded face, shaded under the wide-brimmed hat that was part of the King's Guard uniform.

As Abramm gaped at him, the armsman grinned back. "I must say the rumors about the dramatic change you've made in your appearance are resoundingly true, sir. Most impressive. You've become every inch the king."

"What the plague are you doing here?" Abramm blurted.

Trap Meridon grinned wider and lifted a finger to his hat brim in salute. "Caden Merivale, at your service, sir. And after that little ride you took last week—not to mention your plans for today—I'd say you're in sore need of me."

Abramm glanced forward and back again, checking the distance of the men around them, all but Channon out of earshot. "Are you out of your mind? What if you're recognized?"

"Nearly all the men I knew were transferred when Gillard came to power. As for the nobles"—Trap looked over his shoulder at the ragged line of riders trotting up the long incline below them—"I'm rank and file now. They don't see me even when they look right at me—you didn't yourself just now. Besides, I've changed almost as much as you have."

That, Abramm allowed, was true. Hardship, trial, and time had stripped the boyish roundness from Trap's face and set a flinty light in his eye. And with the beard and the swarthiness gained from seven weeks at sea, the whole feel of his countenance had changed.

"To say nothing of the fact that I'm supposed to be dead." Trap's glance came back to Abramm. "Anyway, I'll be spending most of my time today up at your fortress."

Abramm glanced round at Channon. "You knew about this."

"I asked him to come, sir."

"But how did you know he was—"

"I recognized him right off. And we talked a bit the night we fixed *Wanderer*."

Abramm glanced from Channon back to Trap again, thinking he had a good idea what they'd talked about. Trap had been loath to let Abramm go to the palace without him and must've wrung a promise from Channon regarding Abramm's safety. Which accounted for the man's overprotective zeal.

"So did you get to Sterlen at all?" Abramm asked Trap.

"I thought it better not to. Didn't want to draw attention to myself. I've been staying in Southdock, listening to all the rumors about you." He grinned again. "You look remarkably fit for a man dragged half a league through the forest on a runaway."

Abramm scowled. "Half a league, was it?"

They were interrupted then by a thunder of rapidly approaching hoof-beats, and at Abramm's nod, his guards separated, Channon trotting forward as Trap dropped to the rear. Warbanner's pale, dark-tipped ears swiveled nervously, and Abramm was just glancing over his shoulder when a huge black horse skidded up beside them in a riot of flailing mane and forelock. Abramm glimpsed an eye rolling white in a black face as the head whipped round in a spray of spittle to snap at Warbanner's neck. The young stallion squealed and dodged, then lunged at the black with a nip of his own. Abramm checked him with the offside rein, pulling him toward the road's edge, out of the black's reach. As the horses settled, he turned his focus to the rider, not surprised to find his brother, arrayed in cloth of silver this morning, grinning back at him.

"Fire and Torment, Gillard!" he snarled. "If you can't control that foul-tempered beast, why don't you take him back to the stable? Better yet, let *him* take you!"

Gillard had obviously expected a different reaction. For a moment he sat there, smile fixed upon his face. Then it vanished, leaving a hard light in his eyes as he spoke with careful courtesy. "I beg your pardon, sir. He's been a handful this morning. I thought the run had cooled him off a bit."

No you didn't, Abramm thought. *You knew exactly what you were doing.* He recognized the horse now, a five-year-old stallion whose reputation for nastiness exceeded even Warbanner's. Nightsprol was his name, and no matter how long he was run, it wouldn't temper his evil nature—though it appeared from his sweat-lathered coat that Gillard *had* run him hard, likely all the way from the palace.

"He doesn't get ridden enough," Gillard said. "Too much spirit, not enough riders skilled enough to handle him."

Or stupid enough.

"From what I've heard of your own troubles this morning," Gillard went on, more loudly than was necessary, "I thought you'd understand."

"My own troubles?"

"They said Banner needed two grooms to hold him and three to help you mount."

"No one helped me mount," said Abramm testily. "And the grooms' troubles were their own." He faced forward again, wondering how he was supposed to work with a man whose only intent was apparently to annoy him.

"Great day for an outing," Gillard said after a few moments. "And it was certainly needed. The courtiers get restless with all this idle time." Nightsprol was edging back toward the middle of the road.

"Perhaps they'll be moved to find some profitable way of filling it," Abramm said. Warbanner's ears had gone back, and so had Nightsprol's, the two of them eyeing each other unpleasantly. Gillard appeared oblivious, but Abramm knew he was not.

Hold your temper, Abramm, he reminded himself. *You know how to deal with this sort of man, even if he is your brother.* He drew a deep breath, then said very calmly, "If you can't keep that horse on your side of the road, Gillard, I'll ask you not to ride with me any longer."

Gillard flashed him a startled glance. Then, "I beg your pardon, sir. I didn't realize it was a problem."

Abramm regarded him evenly, started to tell him exactly what he thought of the lie, then stopped himself. Gillard had moved Nightsprol over, so for now he'd let it go. They rode in silence for a time before he let out a weary breath and said, "I know you hate me, Gillard, and I know it can't be easy having me come in and take what you've held these last four years"—*and lusted after for twenty-three*—"but the fact is, I have. And for good reasons, though I don't expect you to understand. At the bottom of it all, though, is that I want what's best for Kiriath." He shot a sidelong glance at his companion. Gillard stared stonily at the road. "Because of that, I'm prepared—" But the words stuck in his throat. *Forgive him. Let Eidon handle him.* He cleared his throat and tried again. "I'm prepared to let the past stay in the past."

Gillard barked a laugh. "You expect me to believe that?"

"No. But the truth is, you did me a bigger favor than you know, even if you didn't intend it that way. And . . ." Abramm's eye fixed on the lone sea gull floating lazily above the hillcrest toward which they climbed. "And we need to work together."

There. He'd said it. And just as he expected, once the words finally registered, his brother's head whipped around. "Work *together*?"

Abramm met his gaze. "Why not?"

Gillard's nostrils flared, and his eyes said, *I'll be dead before I work with you!* But as before, he kept his comments to himself.

"Kiriath will need both of us in the trials that are to come," Abramm said mildly, facing forward again. *Or so Eidon thinks, apparently.*

"Aye," Gillard said. "With all those Esurhite galley ships preparing to invade, we'd best get started immediately." His attempts at sarcasm had never been subtle. "What post will you offer me? Grand Marshall of the Royal Army?" He lifted his chin, looking archly down his nose at Abramm. "I hope so. It's the only one I'll accept."

I told you this wouldn't work, Abramm thought at Eidon. *It'll take a miracle to change his heart.* And while Eidon was very good at miracles, Abramm knew he wasn't going to reach in and forcibly change Gillard's will. *But I did try.*

"If you reconsider, let me know," he said and nudged Banner into a canter, leaving his startled brother behind.

They reached the picnic site around ten o'clock. The servants, who had set out earlier with the provisions, had been working all morning to get things ready. They'd erected the grand blue-and-white-striped pavilion on the wide flat at the base of the massive upthrust which supported Graymeer's—close enough the courtiers would feel a spice of danger, yet far enough none need worry he might actually be harmed. Smoke arose from the barbecue pits where spitted beef and mutton had roasted since dawn, filling the air with their mouth-watering aroma. Already a raft of sea gulls soared in elaborate patterns overhead, waiting to snatch up the spoils.

As Abramm dismounted and handed Warbanner off to a pair of waiting grooms, he saw Trap join the group of mounted armsmen gathering at the base of the road that switchbacked up to the mist-shrouded fortress. While Abramm ate and entertained his courtiers, they would scout the place out, then return to escort him up. Even from a distance he sensed their unease and was glad Trap would be with them.

The pavilion had only one canvas wall in place, the others drawn back to take advantage of the spectacular view: the bay to the east, scattered with the white sails of the many ships plying its waves; Springerlan to the north, the river gleaming at its heart; and the wide swath of grasslands tumbling into the distance to the west.

Taking time to greet his courtiers individually, Abramm worked his way through yet another gauntlet toward the oversized chair at the pavilion's rear where he would be served his morning chocolate and twistbreads. Halfway there, Lady Madeleine waylaid him. Clad in a blue woolen riding skirt and leather boots, her honey-colored hair plaited into a single thick braid, she was one of the few who had dressed appropriately for the day. Now as she greeted him with a curtsey and a keen-eyed gaze, he couldn't help recalling his dream and eyed her uneasily. That she had not yet told anyone of her suspicions regarding his identity as the White Pretender gave him hope she'd taken his warning to heart, but it was a hope soon dashed. Leaping over the formal pleasantries, she got straight to the point. "Is it true what they're saying, sir? That you spent your time in Esurh as a galley slave?"

As if some unseen rhu'ema had suddenly invoked a Command of silence, all the courtiers in their immediate vicinity stopped talking and turned to catch his answer.

"Where did you hear that, my lady?" Apparently Uncle Simon had a bigger mouth than he'd imagined.

"It's been roaming through all the talk this morning. We're evenly split between believers and unbelievers."

"And which are you, my lady?" As if he didn't know.

She smiled, her eyes sparkling with that look that said she had him. "Oh, I'm a believer, sir. You didn't get those shoulders copying inventory lists."

He felt his face heat as beside him little Leona Blackwell asked, "It's true then, sir? You really *were* in one of those galleys?"

The wave of silence was still spreading, more and more faces turning toward them. Uncle Simon and Ethan Laramor stood with Gillard not far away, their conversation interrupted. Simon looked embarrassed, while Laramor affected his usual blankly hostile expression and Gillard scowled as if he couldn't believe people would be so foolish as to even consider such a thing.

Abramm kept his expression neutral and said, just loudly enough for his brother to hear him clearly, "I was, yes. That's why I know so well what they can do."

Gillard looked away as Madeleine spoke again. "It seems an odd transition," she mused. "Slaves with scribing skills can't be common. Why would your master waste your talents by chaining you to an oar? Was it a punishment?"

Oh, you are good, my lady, he thought, his eyes coming back to hers. Leading him skillfully along the path to disclosing with his own mouth the truth she hoped to capitalize upon. Already she'd gained quite a bit. He wasn't giving her any more. With a smile and a nod, he said, "I'd rather speak of other things, Lady Madeleine. That period of my life was not pleasant."

She blinked up at him, her smile turning brittle.

Then Lord Prittleman was intruding with his numerous suggestions of what should be done during Abramm's upcoming inspection of Graymeer's, foremost among them that Prittleman himself be allowed to lead the way. Abramm told him he would consider it and managed to extricate himself, wishing for Blackwell, who always seemed to know just when Abramm needed him to intervene.

At length he reached his chair and had his breakfast, attended by a circle of faces that were not only becoming familiar but increasingly friendly. Foxton, Whitethorne, Hamilton, Bucklen—they spoke enthusiastically of his plans for Kiriath and for Graymeer's, opining that, since he'd succeeded in killing the kraggin, he might well succeed with Graymeer's, too, despite its grim history. They spoke of Esurh and of the border situation, of the Chesedhan treaty negotiations and the Harvest Ball, and then, inevitably, wound round to Gillard's demonstration—who would face him, what handicaps would be imposed. Gillard himself, standing now among his merry men not far from Abramm, kept eyeing him with a sly, amused expression that said it wouldn't be long before the challenge came. And in fact, Abramm had just given command that the games and amusements should begin when it did.

Abramm had spotted Trap outside the pavilion, back from his trip to the fortress, and was on his way to join him when Gillard confronted him. With a bow and a courtly smile he asked if Abramm would do him the honor of partnering with him for a brief exchange of swordplay. Abramm had prepared a polite declination, as Channon had suggested, but now that it was here, found himself staring wordlessly at his brother, startled by how fiercely he wanted to accept. In fact he was a hair from drawing his rapier and starting it right now. But he didn't trust this dark, angry current running through his soul, which did not seem at all like forgiveness, and which suggested that even if Abramm accidentally killed his own brother, wouldn't that be a good thing? Hadn't Gillard tried to kill *him*? Twice now? And wasn't one man's life worth saving the realm from destruction?

"I know it's been a long time since you've had to use a blade," Gillard said blithely. "But surely you remember some of it. And"—here he smiled again—"I promise to go easy on you."

The current rose closer to the surface: anger, wounded pride, years of mistreatment demanding justice. A justice Abramm could finally achieve with his own hand. He had no doubt he could fight his brother and win. Possibly within a very short time, since Gillard had no idea who he was really challenging. And if he died . . .

You said you would work with him. Offer him the hand of peace. Forgive him.

He doesn't deserve to be forgiven.

Neither did you.

I don't care.

And the moment he thought that, he realized it was the Shadow within him—hatred, outrage, pride, jealousy, the lust for vengeance and for the approbation of all these people who would watch. It was roiling around in his soul now, demanding to be satisfied. But it was wrong. There was no Light in it. And he was supposed to be king. *"A man cannot rule others,"* the prophet Remmath had written in the First Word of Revelation, *"until he first rules himself."*

And I said I would forgive him. Leave the injustice for Eidon to avenge.

He drew a deep breath and said with a faint, ironic smile. "Not today, brother. But I'm honored you asked."

Gillard looked quite smug as he bowed and turned away, calling to his friends and to the others whom he had elected to face first. As the crowd started moving again, Abramm caught Trap watching him soberly, and when their eyes met, his liegeman gave him a nod. He'd made the right choice. Even if it did mean he'd lost face. Perhaps he could make some of that up with the coming inspection—which would also relieve him of the disagreeable prospect of having to watch his brother show off yet again.

Before he could reach his liegeman, however, here was Lady Madeleine again, a group of ladies in her wake. "Sir," she said brightly, "what *is* that hanging from your belt? We've been discussing it all morning, and no one can figure it out. I guessed a coin purse, though it looks more like it's holding stones."

Abramm glanced at the leather pouch he'd tied to his belt this morning, fingering the smooth hard forms within. "It *is* holding stones."

Once again Madeleine had succeeded in drawing all eyes and ears his way, specifically now to the oddity on his belt. She looked up at him with raised brows. "Stones, sir?"

"After what happened on my last ride, I resolved never to go without it again. At least on jaunts like these."

"You plan to throw stones at potential assassins?" This from Uncle Simon coming up on Abramm's left.

Abramm allowed himself a smile. "In a manner of speaking. Stones can be deadly, after all. King Joktar was killed with one in the Battle of the Hulluk's Plain."

"Joktar?" Simon's bushy brows flew up. "He was killed by the Ophiran, Xantes. And Xantes used a sling."

"As will I." Abramm lifted the folded lengths of his sling where he'd tucked it alongside the pouch. The pavilion was only about a third full now, the majority having gone off with Gillard or to pursue their own interests, but among those who remained, all conversation had ceased, those around him staring at the sling with puckered brows.

"You know how to use one of those?" Arik Foxton asked.

"More or less."

"Bah! A stone and piece of leather!" Simon burst out. "It's a peasant's weapon."

"But a very effective one," Abramm pointed out.

"Real soldiers use bow and arrow, if not blades."

"Yet arrows can bounce off armor almost harmlessly, where stones can inflict great damage regardless. Arrows are subject to wind and weather, can be more easily seen and evaded. And from the hand of a skilled slinger, stones can fly as sure and fast as an arrow and be every bit as deadly."

Simon drew himself up, frowning at Abramm with his best stern-uncle expression. "Well, sir, I cannot allow that statement to go unchallenged. I propose a demonstration."

Abramm shook his head. "I said from the hand of a skilled slinger. I am only a novice."

"Ah. When the challenge is made, you back down. So much for your contention."

"I'm not backing down, merely pointing out that I cannot offer a true demonstration of the weapon's efficacy."

"But since your Esurhite friends are not present, you are the only demonstrator we have."

Abramm frowned, trying to read his uncle's expression and failing, as usual. "Well, perhaps I will consider it for another day. Right now I am off to inspect my fortress, and the rest of you have some fencing matches to attend."

"The fortress isn't going anywhere," Simon pointed out, with extreme neutrality.

"And we've seen a hundred fencing matches!" said Foxton. "Which your brother always wins. Nothing new there. I want to see if this sling is what you say. We're here and you're here, so let's see it, sir." He grinned.

At that, Abramm relented. But when he glanced at Lady Madeleine, who gave him yet another of her smug smiles, he realized she'd known all along what was on his belt. Her questions had been only to force him to this very position, laying more groundwork to ensure that her tale of him would be believed when finally told. And perhaps that was worth the opportunity she'd given him to save face in front of his courtiers.

It was decided Abramm's demonstration would be conducted down on the western slope where the steep rise of the cliffs could serve as a backstop. Foxton and Whitethorne prevailed upon the cook to provide them with some cabbages, one of which they fixed to the end of a pole driven into the ground before the cliffs. They stuck two apricot pits into it for eyes, then topped it with a jaunty, feather-trimmed hat and stood back to admire their work amidst hoots of laughter. By then the main body of the courtiers had gotten wind of the demonstration and came down to watch.

Abramm slid his hand through the loop cut into the bottom of the sling's length, adjusted the leather so it lay flat around the back of his wrist and then up across his palm. He flipped up the sling's slender tail, caught it between thumb and forefinger, and gave it a few practice turns and releases.

"Assassins come upon a man quickly, giving him no time for practice shots," a gruff voice said from the crowd, and Abramm was surprised to see it was Ethan Laramor.

"True." Abramm pulled a red, lozenge-shaped stone from his pouch, one of ten presented to him by the Dorsaddi king, Shemm, upon Abramm's departure from his land.

Lady Madeleine watched more intently than ever, while Trap positively smirked. The other men didn't seem to know what to make of it, though all were highly amused. Channon, as ever, looked worried. Perhaps he feared

Abramm would hit himself in the head with his own stone. His first shot, released too soon, dove into the grass only ten yards in front of him, raising a puff of dust at the point of impact. His second took the cabbage's hat off. He loaded a third, swung the sling a few times over his head to get the feel of it again, aware now of the smirks and elbowings and good-natured muttering. He was making a fool of himself and should stop. Just a few more tries, then he'd give it up.

He let the sling drop back behind his shoulder in the ready position, drew a deep breath, and fired up a quick prayer for help. Then, aiming right between the apricot pits, he flexed back, drew himself together, and flung the sling overhand, releasing it just as the two thongs pulled hard in his grip. The stone flew forward, too small and fast to see. He heard a faint *thunk*, saw the cabbage quiver, and noted, with some satisfaction, no puff of dust from either ground or cliff. He was pretty sure he'd hit it.

Everyone waited while Foxton and Whitethorne went to examine the target. After a few moments of hunting around in the grass, Foxton called back, "I'm afraid you missed it entirely this time, sir."

"No, Fox, I think I hit it."

"He's right," Laramor said. "I saw it shiver."

"Must've hit the pole, then." Foxton went back to searching the ground.

"Bring the cabbage here," Abramm ordered.

The cabbage was brought, Whitethorne turning it in his hands. "Not a nick on it, sir," he said apologetically, handing it to Abramm.

Abramm turned the "face" up and felt a chill of wonder when he found the hole he sought, for he knew he was not this good. The stone had pierced dead center of the apricot pits, its entry hole hidden by the edges of overlapping leaves and the fact Whitethorne had been looking for a large chunk of missing cabbage, not a narrow hole. *Thank you, Eidon.* "A direct hit," he said to the men, who examined the hole he pointed out to them, then looked up at him in surprise.

"So it is, my lord," Foxton affirmed. "And right between the eyes at that. Too bad it bounced off."

"Oh, it didn't bounce," he said. "Cut it open."

Doubtfully, Whitethorne set the cabbage on the ground and sliced it in half. At the middle of the densely packed, pale green leaves lay the red stone, its narrow entry track clearly visible. Whitethorne loosed an oath of disbelief as Foxton took the halves from him, inspected them himself, then handed them to Laramor. As the slain cabbage made the rounds, Simon looked at Abramm with that exasperatingly blank expression he was so good at. "I thought you said you were a novice."

"It took me three tries, Uncle. And I wasn't even moving."

"Well, I'll grant your claim of deadliness," Simon said as he passed on the evidence to Bucklen. "I still say it's a peasant's weapon."

"No argument there. In Esurh the peasants are forbidden to own swords or bows, and would lack the resources to maintain them, anyway."

"So the peasants taught you, then?"

Abramm grinned at the memory of King Shemm's painstaking tutorials. "Not exactly, sir."

And there was Lady Madeleine again, looking like a cat who'd finally caught her mouse.

About that time Gillard and his merry men arrived—Matheson, Moorcock, and Michael Ives. They halted just uphill of Abramm, Gillard's eyes sweeping the crowd around him. He was smiling in that way Abramm had learned long ago meant he was angry.

"I understand you are giving a demonstration, sir," he said to Abramm with a nod that again just satisfied protocol. "I should very much enjoy seeing the lethal aspects of a"—he glanced around as if bemused—"stone?"

"I'm afraid you've missed it," Abramm said. "I've just finished." He started up the hill to punctuate his remark.

"And was it a compelling argument for the use of stones as defense?" Gillard asked as Abramm came abreast of him and paused.

"It was, sir," Foxton said, holding up the split cabbage, Abramm's red sling stone still in place.

Gillard glanced at it and away as if it were a sight he had seen hundreds of times. "Well, if an army of cabbages awaits us in Graymeer's, I suppose we can rest easy knowing our king will deal with them decisively."

His own companions laughed at that, but it comforted Abramm to see the rest of the men did not—and that Gillard noted the lapse. He himself honed in on Gillard's choice of pronoun: "Us, brother?" he asked. "You wish to go to Graymeer's with me?"

Gillard's white-blond brows flew up. "Well, of course, sir. Did you not say earlier we should work together? If you really do mean to go, I wouldn't dream of letting you enter that dangerous place without my sword at your side."

Or in my back? Abramm wondered, chilled by the sudden resurgence of dream memories. Maybe it had been prophetic, after all. Madeleine had already come itchingly close to revealing his secret. Now here was Gillard, insinuating himself into the procession to Graymeer's, hurling Abramm's own words back at him as justification.

A smirk played at Gillard's lips as it grew clear that he had won. Again Abramm felt that dark current of rage arise in him, urging him to accept his brother's challenge after all. To stop lying and hiding and pretending to a forgiveness he did not feel. To get it all out into the open, right here, right now, in front of everyone. That would wipe the smirk from that beardless, hawkish face, wouldn't it?

His right hand came up to his belt and hung there, a gesture Gillard didn't even notice, or if he did, discounted completely. Abramm, after all, was no threat to him. Abramm was nothing but a scrawny little loser who never should have come home in the first place.

17

A shadow dropped over them as if a cloud passed before the sun. Except . . . the sky was cloudless today, was it not? The question and the concern it aroused, faint though it was, checked the momentum of Abramm's dark intentions. At the same moment he felt someone standing close at his right elbow, and Trap's familiar voice murmured, "Shall I have your horse readied, sir?" The combination brought him to his senses, the bitter current receding even as the sunlight returned, and a quick glance upward revealed there *was* a cloud there, the first of the morning. But likely not the last.

When he refocused on Gillard, he found his brother frowning at Trap, and stepped immediately to the right to block his view. Of everyone here, Gillard was most likely to recognize Trap, knowing, alone among the rest, just how and why he had not been executed six years ago. "Aye, Lieutenant," Abramm said. "Ready him." And now, having recaptured his brother's attention, he added, "If you really mean to come with me, Gillard, you'd better hurry."

Gillard took his words to heart, he and his merry men mounting even before Abramm himself and heading immediately for the track that led up to the fortress, obviously intending on leading the procession. Abramm sent Captain Channon over to tell him he'd be traveling at the *back* of the column.

"I doubt he'll be much problem once we get up top," Trap said, moving into Channon's place at Abramm's side. "The griiswurm auras are pretty strong. And he'll be susceptible."

"Aye, but with him around, so am I," said Abramm.

"Then you've made him a weapon in the hands of your real enemies, sir."

Abramm glanced at him sharply.

As usual Trap had drawn his perspective back to the big picture, reminding him there was more at stake here than petty, personal conflicts. If he continued to allow Gillard to provoke him, he would put himself under the Shadow's mastery as surely as if he'd never known the Light. Which was the last thing he needed going into a place filled with spawn, traps, illusions, real physical dangers, and possibly even the threat of Command, should someone be hiding up there capable of invoking it. And while he doubted there was, he couldn't rule it out.

No sooner had he resolved not to let Gillard distract him, however, than he had to deal with Prittleman, the man and his four gray-cloaked subordinates riding up in full expectation of leading the procession themselves. Having put off answering the man earlier, Abramm now had to inform him bluntly that his services would not be needed. And when shock drove Prittleman to the audacity of arguing, Abramm was forced to point out that since he no longer held with Mataian teachings, he did not believe the Flames would protect them, anyway. As the Gadrielite struggled to comprehend the sundering of his assumptions, Abramm thanked him for his concerns, asked him very coolly to move aside—he did so as one dazed—then trotted Warbanner through the resultant gap and onward, at last, to Graymeer's.

No one knew for sure how the fortress had come to be in its present state, but the most pervasive legend said the bulk of the damage occurred in the second barbarian war, during which it was captured and held for six years. Kiriath won it back in the final battle of that war, only to discover that more than its walls and gates had been damaged. The bedrock on which it sat had been tunneled through—by obviously arcane means—and the dark, twisting passages infested with shadowspawn. Since that time, a mist had hung between its walls, mysteriously warding both wind and rain. Garrisons subsequently stationed there suffered frequent accidents and disappearances, and there were constant reports of mysterious floating lights, disembodied voices, and agonized screams rising from the new-carved warrens below. Gates would not stay closed, weapons would not stay shelved, and worst of all, cannon would not fire from the ramparts, though the weapons could be transported just down the road onto the flat and work perfectly. No one had any explanation save that the place was cursed.

King Eberline had used it briefly as a prison, abandoning it when all the inmates went mad and died at their own or their guards' hands—or no human hands at all. A few attempts to restore it had followed, the most recent being part of the Chesedhan wars before Abramm's birth, which Simon himself had organized. But that attempt, like all the others, had ended in failure and death.

Abramm expected it to be much like the Dorsaddi capital of Hur, which had been cursed in a similar way and cleaned without too much problem. Though the warrens full of spawn would unquestionably add a complicating element, that was offset by the fact that the fortress stood in Kiriath, a land as yet unclaimed by the Shadow. The ghost stories he attributed to the effects of griiswurm auras and other spawn that those without the Light had been unable to withstand. The so-called disappearances were likely men who'd fled in terror, then deliberately vanished to avoid the punishment desertion merited.

As he zigzagged up the face of the rise, however, his optimism waned, and soon he was entertaining every misgiving anyone had ever raised about this expedition, from the potential distraction Gillard posed, to his need for a squad of Terstans experienced in dealing with shadowspawn, to Abramm's own lack of skill in unleashing the Light. He couldn't even kill a staffid without touching it, and was probably now rustier than ever, what with his lack of having found a Terst to learn with. What if there were feyna up there? What if there were *rhu'ema* up there? What if . . .

Halfway up the face of the rise he sheepishly realized his fears were all griiswurm induced. Trap had said the shadowspawn not only abounded in the fortress's yard, but likely filled all the passages underneath. It made him wonder just what they might be guarding. Unfortunately, as always, knowing the cause didn't immediately remove its effects, and it wasn't until they reached the final switchback that he finally secured a stable focus on the fact that the Light within him was more than sufficient to handle whatever might await him in the fortress.

At that point, Channon, who rode beside him now, and who, like Abramm, had not been up here yet, gave vent to his own inner turmoil. "You do know, don't you, sir," he said, "that Rhiad has disappeared?"

Abramm glanced at his companion. "You think he's come up here, Captain?"

"He's been exiled from the Keep. Where else can he go?" He paused. "They say *he* made the kraggin, sir. Or at least had a hand in it. That'd mean he can Command the spawn. An' if that's so, well, then, he'd be at home here."

Abramm doubted none of Channon's words. "You think I should fear him?"

"He hates you powerful bad, sir. There's talk he's sworn to bring you down."

"He's already tried that several times."

"He'll try again, sir. And sure he'll know you're coming up here now. The day, the time, who'll be with you." Channon eyed the crumbling barbican guarding the entrance just ahead of them now, its opening flanked by a pair of white standards.

"He could ambush you himself, sir. Or send feyna. Or . . ." He shifted uncomfortably as the barbican drew nearer. "They say he has . . . powers, sir. Powers of Command. That's when a man who has—"

"I know what it is, Channon." He'd been the victim of Command more than once—twice at Rhiad's behest, in fact—and knew he could easily resist it. At least as long as he didn't let the Shadow have him.

"He might use it to lure you down into the warrens, sir. Take you by surprise."

"With you and Lieutenant Merivale glued to my side?" Abramm raised a skeptical brow. "I think you're letting the spawn auras get to you, Captain."

"Spawn auras, sir?"

"Aye." *Doesn't he know about this?* "Griiswurm emanate a warding that stirs up all a man's doubts and fears, particularly about proceeding into the place they're seeking to keep him out of." He glanced up at the walls towering above on the right, the mist shredding over and between the crenellations. "There's probably thousands of them up here. That's why you're concocting these disaster scenarios. And why they seem completely reasonable."

But why so many? he wondered again. *Is it only to keep us from guarding the entrance to the bay and the river, or is there more at stake here we don't know about?*

As they came even with the standards, Abramm was surprised to see that each bore the dragon and shield of his coat of arms, marking the place as his, in position, if not yet in actual function. Trap had probably done that, he thought as they turned into the remains of a formal gateway. The guardwall itself was of old-style sandwich construction, ten feet thick, the space between inner and outer walls filled with sand and rubble. As they rode through the gap into a world of stillness and mist, Abramm felt something stir awake inside him, a sense of something precious here, and personal.

At the same time his neck prickled with the awareness of a hundred eyes opening and fixing upon him. He thought at first it was just the result of being surrounded by a mist that blocked out sun and sky and the fortress walls he knew encircled them. But after a moment, as the sensation intensified, he knew otherwise. *Rhu'ema*, he thought as the prickle swept across his back and arms and scalp. *They know I have come. And they know what this place is to me, even if I do not.*

The men Trap had brought up earlier had kindled a bonfire beside the old weed-grown pavement leading up to the inner ward, its guardwall mostly obscured by the mist at this distance. The shoulder-high blaze leaped and crackled, casting its amber glow across the fifteen men who had turned out to flank the road in acknowledgment of Abramm's arrival. He pulled up to receive the squadron commander's report of the day's activities—happily routine—then instructed the man to continue with his work and dismounted, his companions doing likewise. Several of the armsmen took their horses as their fellows returned to their duties, two feeding the bonfire from piles of old lumber and dying griiswurm while the rest went in search of more spawn.

Abramm started off on a quick circuit of the eastern half of the yard, while Gillard, unwilling to follow in his wake, immediately climbed the ramp to the wallwalk, merry men in tow. Before long shouts rang out from above, as they hailed their friends down in the flat, making sure that everyone saw them standing up there on the wallwalk of the infamous Graymeer's.

Abramm continued without comment around the barren yard, clumps of yellow grass crackling beneath his boots. It irked him that he hadn't thought of going up there himself—especially since part of his intent was to show his lords he wasn't afraid of this place. But it was too late now, and he was happy to have Gillard occupied elsewhere.

The outer ward had apparently served as little more than a barrier of protective space, and possibly as a training or storage facility. There wasn't much here beyond griiswurm, staffid, and several large piles of stones resulting from Simon's abortive efforts at clearing the inner-ward rubble years ago. As Gillard continued to engage in shouted conversation with the courtiers on the flat, Abramm moved on to the inner ward.

A ridged stonework ramp led up through the crumbling remains of the second gateway into mist so thick it reduced the world to a gray pocket less than ten feet wide. At its fringes a steeper ramp ascended to the left along the inner face of the inner curtain, heading for the mist-obscured eastern ramparts. A rusty cannon lay at the ramp's foot, half buried in hard, dry ground.

"We lost control bringing it down the ramp," Simon explained, noting Abramm looking at it. "We'd just learned they wouldn't fire and were taking them down to the flat. This was the last. It crushed a man to death, right here."

"And my father gave the order to abandon the place the next day," Abramm said, recalling the accounts he had read.

"Yes, sir."

"How'd it get buried so deep?" Abramm gestured toward their feet. "This ground looks like solid rock."

"Probably dirt washed down from the terrace up above."

They stood a moment more, staring at the cannon and listening to the echo of the men's voices and the fire's crackle drifting up from the lower yard. Then Abramm looked up, sweeping his gaze over the ghostly structures looming in the mist ahead of them, and finally fastening it upon Simon. "We're going to take it back, Uncle."

"I hope you're right, sir."

"Let's see what we have to do, then."

Though they'd all memorized the inner ward's layout, Simon was the only one to have actually lived and worked up here. Thus, he was elected to lead them through the crumbling maze of former barracks, eating halls, storage chambers, and stables that had once made up the heart of the fortress. Outside the wind picked up, hissing and hooting against the uneven stone in a way that sounded so much like murmuring voices Abramm thought he understood exactly where *that* rumor had come from. Until the words got a little too clear and personal:

You should not have come, Abramm Kalladorne. . . . Men will die because of you . . . suffer and die. . . .

He stopped abruptly, heart slamming against his chest as he scanned the walls of mist. "Did you hear that?" he asked Trap, already close at his side.

"I hear only the wind, sir."

"It was *in* the wind." He had Channon's attention now, and that of Simon and Ethan Laramor right behind him. None appeared to have heard a voice.

Go back, Abramm Kalladorne. . . . You do not belong here.

Abramm held up a hand, stopping their talk. "There!"

Their blood will be on your hands. . . .

He looked around at the others. But Trap was shaking his head, Channon had heard nothing, either, and Simon watched his nephew with worried eyes. *It was only for me,* Abramm thought. *Rhu'ema . . . trying to scare me off.*

"Do you want to go back now, sir?" asked Simon.

Abramm glanced at him in surprise. "Go back? We've only just started."

His uncle's brows drew together, but he said no more and they continued on. The voices dogged Abramm off and on for the entire hour they walked the ruin, which wouldn't have been pleasant in any event. Staffid virtually carpeted the ground, unfolding before their booted feet and scurrying away in constant rolling waves, crawling around and over the numerous griiswurm that lay among them. More griiswurm clung to the inner surface of every structure that still had a roof, the combined pressure of their auras so thick it was hard to breathe. Though no one else heard voices, they were all plagued by something—a rustle of fabric here, the quick, gritty rasp of a footstep there, the sough of someone breathing just beyond a gaping doorway when there was no one there. At one time or another all of them felt the nape-crawling touch of unseen eyes. Weirdest of all, though, was the dog they found caged at the back of the old powder magazine. Small, gray, and shaggy, the creature made no sound until they approached it, and then it yowled and scratched frantically at the cage door, only to back away as they got close. It barked ferociously all the while Laramor worked the latch free and opened the door, then wouldn't move until they'd stepped well away. Finally it burst from its prison and fled like a streak. No one had any idea what it was doing there, but all agreed its presence gave new credibility to their feelings of having been stalked: likely by whoever had been filling the dog's water bowl.

By the time they returned to Simon's half-buried cannon, all were thoroughly spooked and lost no time ascending the ramp to the wallwalk above. Free of mist, the world returned in a breathtaking vista and the bizarre sensation of the air growing lighter. As Abramm walked south toward the main watchtower rising from the fortress's most seaward point, he affirmed his earlier supposition that Terstans would have to form the bulk of the crew who worked here—and that his own hand would have to be among them. What form that hand would take he had no idea—beyond the fact that he would have to learn how to throw the Light very soon. Impaling and burning were simply too inefficient. And too dangerous.

The watchtower would be his last stop on this tour. He'd wanted to enter it from below, but seeing it was part of the guardwall, and by that linked to the warrens underneath the fortress, both Channon and Trap had warned him off. Plus it was filled near bursting with griiswurm. Better, they said, to enter from the wallwalk, above the mist.

Simon had had enough climbing for one day and stayed on the guardwall with Laramor while Abramm ascended the crumbling spiral stairway with his two armsmen. At the top, a makeshift landing provided opportunity to take in the spectacular view of Kalladorne Bay stretching northward on the right and the headland paralleling it somewhat left of front. Most of the latter lay now beneath dark and shifting clouds, and he could see that, while the picnic pavilions had not yet been taken down, dark blots on the track leading north showed at least some of the courtiers heading for home.

Up here, beyond the range of the mist's wind-damping effects, a stiff breeze ruffled Abramm's hair and beard and lifted his cloak around him. Out on the bay, it had whipped up whitecaps, sending the ships scurrying for port. From this point he clearly saw the dark coloration of the deep western channel leading to the mouth of River Kalladorne. He'd known from the maps and simple logic that Graymeer's was crucial to guarding that channel, but seeing just how much territory the fortress guns could command hardened his resolve to gain it back, no matter how difficult the battle.

A shout below drew his eyes to the men cavorting on the wallwalk near the guard tower joining the inner curtain and the outer guardwall. Gillard and his merry men dodged and thrust playfully at one another, long-legged griiswurm impaled on the ends of their blades. One man darted into the wallwalk entrance of the guard tower, then leaped out to surprise his fellow, who chased him back inside. Moments later both emerged, cackling with laughter as they tossed the griiswurm off their blades into the mist beside them.

Abramm rested gloved hands on the crumbling parapet before him and frowned at them. Then irritation turned to understanding as for the first time it dawned on him that Gillard had never grown up. His negligence as a ruler hadn't arisen from malevolence as much as from immaturity. From not really understanding the situation, or even the way acts committed in the present— or not committed—could have profound effects on the future. He'd just gone along, day to day, reveling in his power without understanding the responsibility that went with it. Selling Abramm to the slavers had been one such act of power, and Abramm was sure his brother even now had not the least inkling of its ramifications. He wasn't sure he understood them all himself.

Now, as Gillard played, Abramm's gaze tracked again to the bay, to the city at its far end, shining in the sunlight, and finally to that deep channel running toward it. He glanced aside at Trap standing not far off his right hand. "I mean to take this place back, Trap," he said quietly.

Lieutenant "Merivale" eyed him soberly and spoke no word of argument.

"There's no way I'll do it without Terstans, though. The job's too big. Somehow I have to get them to volunteer without telling them openly I'm one of them."

"I know a few people down in Southdock," Trap said. He leaned against the parapet and glanced downward. "Maybe I can talk to them."

"They won't believe you. They hardly know you." Abramm glanced down, as well. Gillard and his friends were now engaged in a contest to determine who could fling their impaled griiswurm the farthest into the mist, unmindful of the men working out of sight below them. Worse, they appeared to be using the nearby guard tower as their source of griiswurm. Frowning, Abramm told Channon to go down and put a stop to it before someone got hurt or lost.

As the captain left, Abramm returned to his earlier subject. "I have to go to Southdock myself. Attend the Terstmeet. Get to know the leaders, at least."

Now it was Trap's turn to frown. "My lord—you can't."

"I don't have a choice. Besides, I need it for myself. Studying old notes and reading the Words again isn't enough. I'm stagnating when I should be growing. I still can't even kill a staffid without touching it, and . . . and I'm not getting the answers I need."

"The Gadrielites prowl Southdock at will, sir. Much as you may hate to admit it, they are the law there. If you were to run into them . . ."

"It's the only option I have right now." He watched absently as Channon engaged two of Gillard's men in conversation. "You said yourself I'd be opposed. I never took you to mean I should just back down."

Trap released a long, reluctant sigh. "I suppose I can see if there might be some way to work it out. But—"

A ruckus erupted from the wallwalk, voices rising on the wind, loud and sharp, their words unclear, their alarm not. Channon and the other two were heading for the guard tower as several soldiers appeared out of the mist at the head of the ramp near the front wall, running along the wallwalk toward them. Simon and Laramor converged from the opposite direction, and Gillard was nowhere to be seen.

Abramm spat an oath. "He's gone and done it, hasn't he? Got himself lost, or Eidon knows what, and now I'll have to risk the men to find him. I should have known better than to let him wander about on his own."

He was about to call down that no one else was to enter the tower under any circumstances when a grit of leather on stone brought him around. And there was Gillard, standing at the top of the stairwall, grinning at them. "I didn't know you cared, brother," he said.

"How long have you been there?" Abramm demanded.

"Long enough." His blue eyes drifted to the parapet now at Abramm's back and he strode forward. "They're such idiots," he said, stopping before the wall to whistle and wave at his friends. He had a cut on his palm, a clean slice, bleeding freely, though he seemed not to notice it. On the wallwalk below, his men looked up in obvious astonishment and Gillard dissolved into cackles of amusement. One of them—Ives?—called up, "How did you get up *there*, my lord?"

Which only made the cackling louder.

Abramm scowled, irritated all over again. "They're not the idiots, Gillard. You are. What in the world were you thinking to go down there like that?"

Gillard waved him off. "It's just a little harmless fun, brother. Don't work yourself into a lather." He turned back to the parapet to laugh some more, and Abramm thought that something seemed wrong with him. His eyes held an uncharacteristic dullness, and his words were almost slurred. Was he drunk? The notion shocked, but after a moment he realized it probably wasn't out of character for him, or any other lord, to have brought along a flask of special vintage for the occasion.

His irritation mounted. "People have disappeared by the hundreds up here! And died by the scores. Even if you care nothing for yourself, those men—your own friends—could have been next on the list."

"Well, they're not, so no harm done." Gillard stood there a moment, staring down, then his face hardened, his mood shifting instantly from amused indifference to belligerence. He pushed back from the parapet, leaving a bloody palm print, and turned toward Abramm, his eyes narrow. "You've always been a little good-pants, haven't you?" he sneered, and there was no smell of liquor on his breath. "Follow all the rules. Make sure everybody does everything right. When are you going to learn you aren't the only person who knows a thing or two?" He cocked his head and smirked. "For someone who's so worried about the dangers in these towers, I have to wonder what *you're* doing up *here* . . . Sire."

Still smirking, he gave Abramm a perfunctory bow and disappeared down the stairwell, chuckling as he went. Abramm stared in blank astonishment at the space he vacated.

Beside him Trap stirred and said, "That was blasted odd, sir. Even for Prince Gillard. I wonder—"

And then the rage hit, that black current surfacing yet again, but fully this time, carrying him down the stair in angry pursuit, his hand gripping the hilt of his rapier, his mind filled with black thoughts of finally putting things to right.

It was when he passed the opening to the wallwalk and kept descending that he had his first inkling things were not right. But it was just an inkling, too weak to stand against the storm now raging in him. After all he'd put up with today, all the taunting, all the subtle jabs and hints of incompetence, this was the spark that lit the growing pile of kindling. And it wasn't just himself he defended, it was the office that he held. No one had the right to treat their king that way. No one.

Down the stairs he flew, moving lightly, quickly, ignoring the cries of alarm that reverberated behind him and the griiswurm brushing his arms as he passed, focused only on the echo of footsteps descending ahead of him. The stairs emptied into a corridor whose slick obsidian-surfaced walls should have alerted him to danger, but, like everything else, was lost in the shadows around the bright blaze of his anger. An opening gaped in the wall to his right—a short, vaulted stairway that descended to a domed cavern, lit with emerald light. The stairway had echoed loudly with his brother's footfalls, but when Abramm reached the cavern, it was empty, and he himself stood in one of three openings in the curved, black-ice wall. Gillard could have taken either of the others, and there was now no sound to indicate which.

The indecision stopped him where other things had not, and now he stared around the strange chamber in confusion and growing alarm. The emerald glow arose from a central pit, ringed by a low wall and presided over by a stone platform, all carved out of the same black glass as the walls. He could not see the source of the light from where he stood, but a soft chittering filled the room, and the place reeked like a poorly tended barn. On the curving wall above the pit had been painted in glowing green lines a great hairy beast with massive chest, low-slung hindquarters, wickedly long claws, and a mouth full of pointed teeth. Tiny orbs had been fixed into the wall for its eyes, glinting almost lifelike in the green light. Just looking at it sent a shiver through Abramm's rapidly waning anger.

He was backing toward the opening he'd just come out of, when the awareness of someone behind him set him whirling about, sword point up and ready to strike. *When did I draw my blade?*

The question was lost in the shock of recognition: Rhiad stood before him, unnerving in the combination of his remarkable physical beauty married to the horror that had become the left side of his form. They stared at each other a moment, then the Mataian laughed. "Now what are you going to do, my prince? Run me through? Poor, crippled ruin that I am? What can *I* do to you—the great Pretender, the killer of kraggin, the hero of the people?"

"What do you want?" Abramm said, keeping the sword up.

"What do I want?" Rhiad's one eyebrow arched. "Vengeance, brother."

"I have renounced the Flames. I am not your brother."

"Not yet. But you will be. My brother in pain. My brother in sorrow. My brother in loss."

"Are you threatening me?" Abramm stepped toward him, the blade reflecting the green light of the pit.

The Haverallan backed away. "So straight and strong and confident." His voice rasped harshly in the dark chamber. "Just as I once was. Before you took it from me." He slashed the air with one hand. "Put down the sword. You won't be needing it."

To Abramm's horrified astonishment, his rapier fell from suddenly nerveless fingers, and he found himself unable to move, his heart about to explode from his chest with alarm. *Command?! How can this be?* And then he realized what had happened: Gillard had knocked on the door to his anger, and Abramm, in opening it, had let the Shadow have him.

"Ah, my Golden Prince," Rhiad croaked. "You've made it so easy for me. Coming right into my hand after all this time of fruitless seeking. A fitting repayment, after you let my dog out." He turned to look at the monster glowing on the wall above them. "Do you like him? You will meet him soon. And what you took from me, he will take from you." He stepped closer and drew a fingernail down the side of Abramm's face, hard enough to hurt, hard enough to make him want to lurch back out of reach, yet still he could not move. His mind skittered wildly, caroming from fear to fear, for as in the battle against the griiswurm aura, knowing the Shadow had him did not always mean deliverance from it. The fear that it generated prevented the Light from freeing him, and even when he acknowledged that fear held him, that it was against the Words and the One he served and put it away, an instant later he was back in it, terrified to find himself so helpless as the doubts began to gather.

What if the Light really wasn't strong enough to fight it? Moroq had conceived the Shadow from the very start as a shield against Eidon's Light, so his own power might grow in its stead. Couldn't that be happening now? He swallowed hard, his heart pounding against his ribs.

Rhiad's eyes filled his vision. "Your boy already gave me quite a sufficient amount of your hair." He held up a length of blond braid bound into a circle, and dimly Abramm comprehended that it must have been the queue he had cut off the first day he'd arrived in Springerlan. "I couldn't think how I was going to get the blood, though. And here you've delivered it to me yourself." He paused. "Take off your glove."

Now for the first time Abramm balked, fighting the compulsion not with the Light but with his own anger and strength of will. He had thrown off more obvious Commands before, when he'd been the White Pretender back in Esurh. Why not now?

Rhiad's eyes flashed up to his as the voices returned. *You cannot win, Abramm Kalladorne,* they whispered. *You do not have the skill to stand against us . . . and you never will.*

No wind now, only the voices and a cold, inhuman presence he recognized as rhu'ema. Anger once more transmuted to fear as Rhiad repeated, more emphatically this time, "Take off your glove."

Numbly, Abramm watched his hands obey, then closed his eyes, seeking the Light and the thoughts that would free him from this bondage. "Now give me your hand." But again Abramm did not obey, both his arms hanging immobile at his side. He glanced up at Rhiad. Light pulsed briefly in him as he saw the other man's good eye flick to something past Abramm's shoulder. Too late he realized someone stood behind him. As he started to turn, something crashed into his head, and the strange room spun up away from him.

He hit the ground on his right side, gasping for breath. Dimly he felt himself rolled over and his hand seized. His eyes fluttered open in sluggish alarm. His palm lay in Rhiad's grasp, limp as a rag. A knife flashed, and dark blood welled in a thin diagonal line across his skin as he recalled an identical cut on Gillard's palm. *What is he doing? It must have been Gillard who hit me, but why?*

As if in answer, Rhiad laid the plaited hair against Abramm's palm, soaking up the blood, first one side then the other, finally wrapping it in a cloth and tucking it inside his robe. "Thank you, my lord," he said, dropping Abramm's hand and standing upright. "You may go. Don't forget your sword."

He moved out of Abramm's field of vision and spoke softly to his accomplice. "Go back the way you came. When you step onto the wallwalk, you'll remember none of this. You cut your hand on a piece of metal and you do not know where your brother has gone."

There was a rustle of fabric, a jingle of sword harness, and the grit of boot soles on stone. Then all was silent. It took a few minutes for Abramm to regather his wits, but it was the increasing volume of the chittering from the pit that really motivated him to get up. Thankfully, Rhiad had cut his left hand, not his right, so he picked up his sword easily, then climbed back up the stair.

He was never really sure how he found his way out, but he did so without much trouble, winding his way up the watchtower stair, past the griiswurm to the wallwalk level above the mist, stepping out through the doorway this time. Channon was over by the other guard tower questioning Gillard and the men with him, Trap staying prudently in the background. Thus Trap was the first to see Abramm emerge, and the first at his side. Then the others were there, too, exclaiming about his bloodied hand—"*Just like Gillard's, my lord!*"—and asking him what had happened. Once Channon heard the tale, he was determined Abramm should leave at once, and Abramm was content to oblige him. He'd seen what he'd come to see and learned far more than he'd expected.

You will fail. You do not have the skill to stand against us . . . and you never will.

As they returned to the outer ward for their horses, Abramm drew Trap aside.

"You have to get me to that Terstmeet in Southdock," he said fiercely. "As soon as possible. No more arguments."

Trap regarded him evenly for a long moment, then dropped a nod. "I'll need some time to arrange it."

"I'm talking days, Lieutenant, not weeks."

A frown creased Trap's brow. "Very well, my lord."

THE

MORWHOL

PART THREE

18

I'm not ready to go south yet. Why can't he see that? Why does he have to keep at me all the time? Carissa stood on Highmount's south wallwalk, frowning at the featureless gray clouds that blanketed the sky. This high on the mountain, they hung low and close, but from the distant hills and valleys tumbling away below her, she knew they would look high and flat and unpromising. And even though they were spitting snow now, the small, hard flakes held precious little moisture, certainly not enough to heal the woes of the lowland crofters and herdsman so desperately in need of it. Not enough to block the high roads and passes southward, either. And all that had been laid down by the last storm two weeks ago had already melted off. Even the Kolki Pass was clear. It wasn't too late to change her mind, and though Cooper had already sent Rolf and Jamison south with the pigeons, he reminded her daily that she need only give the word and they'd follow in a heartbeat.

A gust of snow crystals ticked against the flat face of the stone beneath her hands and stung her cheeks. Her fingers were starting to ache with the cold despite her woolen gloves, but she didn't want to go back inside. She'd spent too much time inside these last weeks, what with the cold and the mysterious men lately lurking around the fortress. Her gaze dropped to the steep, grassy slope at the foot of the Holding's high walls, a hundred yards of cleared ground tumbling down to the front line of the spruce forest that extended south and west and north as far as she could see. Berry pickers, mushroom hunters, messengers up from New Holding, even the wall guards had spotted them during the last week—cloaked riders who'd vanished into the shadows the moment they were seen. Cooper liked it not a bit, certain the men were Rennalf's henchmen. This morning he'd pressed Carissa more strongly than ever to use some sense for once and go south. She'd refused. He'd lost his temper. She'd lost hers. They were no longer speaking.

So here she was, standing on the wallwalk between two guard stations whose men carefully avoided looking her way, alone, estranged from her friends and miserable, as always. More and more her gaze drifted northwest-ward to the distant shimmer of the Ruk Pul—the "River of Tears"—and the great northern plain beyond. Balmark lay just this side of that river. She could almost pick it out from here.

A hawk soared into her field of vision, swooping low over the line between forest and grassy slope, then flapping up to circle around, ranging wider with each pass. *I wish I could fly away*, she thought. Then realized she'd already spent six years trying to do that—and had come away more empty and frustrated than ever.

Cooper thought she just didn't want to see Abramm again, and he was right. She didn't. But at the same time she wanted to see him more than anything in the world. In the last weeks she'd at least come to admit that, even if she didn't understand how she could be so conflicted about it. But that wasn't why she refused to leave Highmount. Not anymore. With the passage of time and the strangers lurking in the forest, and the increasingly unnerving character of her dreams, her convictions had changed. Although she'd never admit it openly, she was now more convinced than Cooper him-self that her husband knew of her presence here.

The problem was, Cooper's solution to run south was exactly what Ren-nalf hoped they'd do. She was sure now that Professor Laud was right—Ren-nalf *had* known she was here before he came. She suspected he'd stopped by just to rattle her, hoping she'd leave her stronghold and bolt straight into his waiting arms. Her only salvation, she knew—*knew*—was to stay safe behind Highmount's walls. And yet, even as she acknowledged that, she also feared that each day spent here brought her increasingly under his sway. Which made no sense. Yet the fear remained, combining with the other to lead to the inescapable conclusion that it didn't matter what she did. Perhaps she should just get it over with. Go down to the stable, saddle up Heron, and head for that sparkle on the horizon to which she'd sworn never to return.

"Milady? Are you all right?" The guard had left his station to approach her and now stared down at her concernedly.

She must've been standing here a long time, for her teeth hurt from being clenched together, her back ached, and she was cold to the core. Philip's orb, resting against her skin beneath her undertunic, formed the single warm spot on all her body. And the hawk was nowhere to be seen.

"I'm fine," she told the man, trying to smile reassuringly and failing.

His blond brows drew down farther. "You were . . . moaning, my lady. And you're shivering awful bad."

"I'm fine," she said again, though her chattering teeth belied the claim. She glanced again at the forest's edge and sucked in her breath. "There's another one!" A rider, hidden in shadow at the forest's edge. She had only a glimpse before he vanished, but it was enough to scare her back inside.

The warm moist air of the Great Room hit her like a blow when she entered, stinging her cheeks and making her nose and ears ache along with her fingers. She went straight to the fire, not even removing her cloak as she held her hands before its roaring warmth.

Elayne—Mistress Cooper now—sat in one of the tree-limb chairs before the hearth, knitting the front of a sweater out of delicate gray wool. "How is the weather?" she asked in her soft, alto voice.

"As you predicted," Carissa said, keeping her eyes on the flame. "Spitting snow with no sign of doing more." She paused. "I saw another rider."

The rhythmic click of Elayne's needles stopped. "Just now?"

"Yes. The guard didn't see him, though."

"In broad daylight. They're getting bolder."

"Yes." Carissa heard the needles start up again as she unfastened the ties of her cloak and let it fall into Peri's hands, the girl having followed her from the door. She stood for a time in silence, listening to the fire snap and the needles click.

Then Elayne said quietly, "We don't have to go to Springerlan, my lady. We can go to Sterlen. Rent a place on the outskirts. No one has to know who you are, and you needn't see your brother at all."

Suppressing a shudder, Carissa stripped off her gloves and gave them to Peri. "I can't afford to leave now," she said, holding her bare hands to the fire. "Not with all the repairs this place still needs." It was a lame excuse, and she knew it, for there'd be precious little repairing done once the snows started. Elayne knew it, too.

"My lady, you're not safe here. Besides, with everything else that's going on—the raids, the rumors of that army Rennalf's gathering—Felmen feels that Abramm needs to know."

Felmen. Carissa was still getting used to hearing Cooper addressed by his first name, still found it odd sounding and wrong. She grimaced. "I'm sure that, as king, Abramm has his own ways of gathering information." He'd made it clear enough back in Jarnek what he'd thought of Carissa's attempts to help him, hadn't he? *"You should never have come. Everything you've done only makes things worse. . . ."*

"Not if there's a secret border-lord rebellion being hatched against him," Elayne pointed out.

"I doubt Coop can tell him any more than his own spies have already seen for themselves."

Her front almost too hot for comfort, Carissa turned to warm her back, glad Elayne was concentrating on her knitting. A few moments later, though, the woman admitted her husband had more reason than to report on border matters. "He wants to see his king, my lady. It's been four years."

"Coop swore an oath to Raynen, not Abramm," said Carissa. "With Raynen dead, he *has* no king. If he owes fealty to anyone, it's to me."

The needles continued to click for a time. Then Elayne said softly, "My lady, Felmen was liege-sworn to Abramm before you even left Jarnek."

And now, finally, Carissa looked at her, a sinking feeling in her middle. *Liege-sworn?*

Elayne put down her handwork to meet Carissa's gaze. "When you originally left Springerlan, Raynen had charged Fel with killing Abramm should you find him. That's why he worked so hard to prevent you from succeeding. He failed, and so, after Abramm defeated Beltha'adi, he tried to make good on his oath. And a poor job he did of it, too, hoping Abramm would kill him in the process, I think, or if not that, then afterward." She glanced down at her knitting, adjusting the needles a bit. "When your brother offered forgiveness instead, Felmen gave him his oath." Mistress Cooper paused. "And took the Star, as well."

So that's when it happened.

"He never told you," Elayne went on, "because you were so against anything Terstan. He was afraid you'd cut yourself off from him, too, and have no one."

It was a lot to digest, a lot Carissa did not want to think about, so she turned away and collapsed into the other tree-limb chair, saying nothing.

She'd known for some time that Cooper wore a shield, but she'd had no idea he was liege-sworn to Abramm—and she felt somehow betrayed.

"Even if you do not wish to see Abramm for yourself, my lady," Elayne murmured after a moment, "or care about the good of his reign, could you not at least go down for Felmen? He is in agony over this, for he understands how few real supporters your brother must have. And the things going on up here have made him very uneasy."

"If he's sworn to Abramm, why doesn't he just go to him?" Carissa asked bitterly. "Why concern himself with me at all?" *He's already deserted me. Might as well make it official.*

"He won't leave you here alone, my lady. And even if he would, Abramm has charged him with staying by you."

And that brought her up short. "*Abramm* charged him? You mean he's only stayed with me because he was ordered to?"

Mistress Cooper looked pained. "My lady, Felmen loves you like his own daughter. He would have asked for the assignment even if it hadn't been given. And it breaks his heart to see this rift between you and Abramm. He longs to see you reconciled, and knows that won't happen with you hiding up here."

"That won't happen regardless of where I am," Carissa snapped. She stood and went back to the hearth, standing in a silence filled with the fire's crackle and the bump and thud of the butter churn being worked in the kitchen.

They said nothing for a time. Then Elayne released a long low breath behind her and murmured, "Why do you hate him so, my lady? Surely not just because he chose to wear a Terstan shield?"

Carissa felt herself growing tight and tense again. "That shield ruined everything," she said bitterly. "He was supposed to come back to Kiriath a hero and take up the crown. He would've been a great king."

"But he has come back and he is king."

"Only until that shield on his chest is discovered. Or, more likely, is revealed by Abramm himself." Carissa's voice shook with emotion. "Then he'll be forced out in disgrace. It may already have happened."

"And it may not have. It may be they'll find out and not depose him." Elayne paused, then added, "Eidon is with him, my lady."

"Aye!" Carissa cried, her tone more biting than ever. "The same way Eidon was with the Throckmortons and Professor Laud. The same way he was with Raynen." She turned from the fire to face the woman behind her. "I *saw* the curd in Ray's eyes, heard the madness in his voice, and I will *not* watch that happen to Abramm!" Even now the memory of that awful moment when Raynen had broken down completely, raving about spies and birds, twisted knifelike in her heart.

"What happened to Raynen was a tragedy," Elayne said gently. "But one of his own making. Neither the curd nor the madness is inevitable, my lady. They are the result of many, many decisions made over a long period of time."

"And what about the Throckmortons and Laud? I suppose you'll say their sufferings were their fault, as well. Or that they should be grateful to be alive and free and honored to have been smitten. Never mind they lost everything. Never mind they probably won't survive the Kolki Pass." She scowled and shook her head. "If that is how Eidon stands by his servants, all the more reason to believe Abramm has already been cast down! And if he can't save himself, how can he possibly save me?"

Mistress Cooper held her gaze evenly, but after a moment a look of dawning comprehension came into her face. "It's not Abramm you hate, is it?" she said finally. "It's Eidon himself."

Carissa's laugh was tight and brittle as she turned back to the flames. "It's difficult to hate someone when you don't believe he exists. As for Abramm— I gave up everything for him, and he turned me away. That's not something easily forgiven."

Elayne had no answer for that. After a moment her knitting needles began to click again. Carissa held her hands out to the fire, staring at the rings glittering on her fingers. Rings she had acquired on her travels—the starfire from Andol, the little ruby from Thilos, the other three from the great bazaar in Draesia. Trinkets meant to bring her pleasure and, as with all else, failing to do so. Behind her Mistress Cooper spoke again, very softly. "Will you tell me about your dreams, my lady?"

"My dreams?" Carissa turned from the hearth.

"Peri says she's found you three nights now, standing before the open window, shutters thrown wide to the night, staring and moaning, and she could not wake you up."

A chill washed up Carissa's back. "Perhaps it is Peri who's having the dreams."

"She says other times you toss and moan in the bed, and even with the shutters closed the room is like ice." *Click, click, click.* "That it all started after Rennalf was here."

Another chill. *"I fear his dark powers touch your dreams,"* Laud had said. Carissa wrapped her arms about her chest. "I know my sleep has been unsettled, but I'm sure it's just the uncertainty of everything. I would have remembered getting up and opening the shutters."

"What about Rennalf? Do you dream of him?"

"I told you, Elayne, I haven't had any dreams." But suddenly she wasn't so sure, as recognition seemed to stir in her soul.

"They say he's a powerful warlock," Elayne remarked. "That he summons the ells to do his bidding. The ells can speak to people in their dreams."

The barbarians and many of the border folk believed the ells to be servants of the dark gods that lived in hill and sky, spirit folk possessed of mystical powers that could be harnessed and used by men who learned the secrets of commanding them.

"I'm sure I would remember if ells had spoken to me," Carissa said. "And if he *is* a warlock"—just saying the words sent another shiver through her— "well, then all the more reason to stay where we're safe. If he sees our every move, what good is fleeing?"

"He cannot see our every move. Nor are we helpless to conceal ourselves from him." Elayne's needles stilled again, and she stared at them for a long time before looking up. "I fear he seeks to draw you to him, and that eventually you'll go to Balmark all on your own."

Carissa smiled. "It's a long way to Balmark, Elayne."

"Not by the Dark Ways of the Warlocks, ma'am. And Felmen suspects there's a gateway up the pass. Perhaps in the old watchtower." She paused. "You *are* still wearing that staffid warder Philip gave you?"

Carissa scowled at her, annoyed again. "Has Cooper told you *everything*?"

Elayne ignored the question. "It will provide you some protection. But really, it would be better for us to leave."

Carissa said nothing to this, and presently Elayne returned to her knitting. They spoke no more of it, but Elayne evidently relayed the conversation to her husband, for Cooper did not join them for dinner as he usually did, claiming a need on the northern wall required his attention. He ate quickly in the kitchen and disappeared, leaving the women to dine alone in silence, Carissa alternating between guilt over depriving her beloved guardian of his opportunity to see Abramm and indignation that he'd given her brother his fealty four long years ago and never told her. It felt as if everyone were conspiring against her, talking about her behind her back—even her sleeping habits were subject to discussion and evaluation!

She went to bed early, as always, hoping she would feel better in the morning. As always. Sometime in the night she was jerked awake, gasping for breath. The air was thick and chill, and the fire must have gone out, for heavy darkness filled the room, pressing down upon her as if an ox had settled onto her chest. She lay rigid beneath her elk-hide cover, pulse pounding as she listened to a silence so complete not even Peri's breathing broke it. Had the girl gone down to the main hearth to get warm?

Wait. She sat up, almost surprised that she could, trying to hear past the blood rushing in her ears and the rasp of her own breathing. *There.* A faint, high wail, like the wind keening through the towers up the pass. Except there was no wind tonight. Shoving the elk skin aside, she stood and strode to the window, where she unbarred the shutters and pushed them outward with a creak, a brief, alarming sense of déjà vu stirring within her. Beyond the wall-walk outside, the steep, barren slope descended like a swell of ice to the forest's dark edge. Snow-covered peaks ran northwestward to her right, gleaming feebly beneath a sky as black as a hole to the underworld.

It was singing. Long high notes in a minor key, following a patternless melody. And this, too, felt familiar. It grated across her senses like steel across slate, raising the hairs on the back of her neck. From the wallwalk came the scritch of footsteps as the guard patrolled his circuit. He met his fellow halfway to the corner tower and they halted briefly in quiet conversation.

The song grew louder, promising comfort, relief, and a sense of belonging, even as it filled her with aversion. A tingling started over her heart, spread across chest and shoulders, and ran down her spine and the backs of her arms. Perhaps she should close the shutters and go back to bed.

She stayed, caught by the tantalizing hope that somehow all her sad, lonely days would soon end, and her life would be changed forever. The music grew louder, but the guards paid no heed. Out over endless forest, something flickered, vanished, then flickered again, and a skein of crimson light undulated across the horizon, pale at first, but growing steadily brighter. Another joined it, then another. Crimson, violet, azure, each wove among the others with serpentine grace. Her breath caught. The eerie music played over her like icy wings, and the tingling at her breast became a tiny fire.

Below her, one of the men said, "There's those lights again. Remember I was tellin' you?"

"Aye. They're winter lights, like I said."

"Never seen winter lights like that before. And not this early in the season, either."

The mystical serpents drew nearer, vast veils of color billowing overhead.

She stared enrapt, floating on tone and light, on long plaintive purples, discordant trills of scarlet, and low vibrating blues. They filled her mind, her heart, her vision, drawing away the weight and wetness of her flesh, until she became as dry and light as a puffball, ascending into the empty hole of sky to dance among them—

And still that fire burned upon her breast, illumining scenes from the lower, harder reality through which she now seemed to be walking, even as she floated among the colors in the sky. The door of her chamber swung open before her, revealing the shadow-swathed corridor beyond. Narrow stairs gave way to the dimly lit interior of the Great Room, scattered with the humps of sleeping servants, which gave way in turn to the cold silent space of the inner yard, and then the outer, with its pale clumps of weed and dead bramble. And finally, here was the old north gate looming before her, closed and recently fitted with brackets and a heavy bar, now in place.

She reached for that bar and suddenly a man blocked her way, his scarred face and tender eyes as inexplicably familiar as the rest of this. For a moment he looked like Cooper, though Coop's face was not scarred. Then, as in the way of dreams, he shifted into Abramm, whose face was not scarred, either. The man was neither of them, and yet, in some strange way, as close to her as both. Reality shifted—

And she floated in the sky again, the veils of color swirling about her, welcoming her into their embrace as she watched a young woman robed in white far below, standing in the Holding's dark and lonely outer yard before the north gate and a man whose body blazed with a hideous white light. Pale curls tumbled to the woman's hips, and phosphorescent mist enfolded her. Why did she just stand there? Why didn't she push around the blazing figure to lift the bar and open the gate? And—no! Now a second man with short gray hair and a salt-and-pepper goatee burst from the keep, clad only in jerkin and britches, his chest afire with the same ugly white light that shone on the figure blocking her way.

"Hurry!" she yelled at the woman. "If you don't get through that gate, they'll catch you and take it all away!"

Again she stood on the ground, facing the gate and the scar-faced man who'd stopped her. From this vantage, only his eyes flashed with the hideous light—a light she hated. And loved. He'd stopped her when she had sought to flee this prison before, she recalled—an evil being who would deny her all the warmth and comfort and companionship the Others wished to give her.

Anger flared through her detachment. "Why do you hold me here!? Why do you hate me? Why won't you leave me alone and let me pass!"

"I do not hold you here, Carissa, daughter of Lissandra. Nor do I hate you. But I will let you go, if that is truly your wish."

"Yes! Get out of her life," the voices whispered around the part of Carissa that drifted in the sky. "Let her pass! Free her to have what she has longed for all these years." While to the woman at the gate, they said, "You must tell him these things yourself. Say the words, and you'll never see him again."

Yet no sound came from the tiny woman far below. She simply stood there, facing the bright figure, its hideous light reflecting off the tear tracks on her face. Behind her, the tall man with the goatee finally reached the outer yard and started toward her, a small, dark-haired woman now hurrying in his wake.

"Go!" the voices shrieked. "Do you want to belong to something? Do you want to be loved by someone? Then tell him to get out of your way and go through the gate! NOW!"

But still Carissa stood, staring at the scar-faced man and weeping at her inability to speak the words that would grant her the freedom she craved.

And suddenly here was Cooper pulling her into his warm, strong arms and hugging her to his chest like a rag doll, though she could hardly feel him at all . . . *as she floated high above and watched the lights withdraw into the distance from which they'd come. Their weird song faded until all that remained was silence and a shifting mist suspended between the forest and the eternal darkness overhead.*

Abruptly she was back, returned to all the weight and wet of flesh chilled by a coldness such as she had never known, even though Cooper was holding her tightly, praying for Eidon to bring her back to them.

The scar-faced man's voice whispered in her heart, *"Go to your brother, Carissa. He has what you desire, and he will need what you can give. I will make a way for you."*

"Fire and Torment, lass!" Cooper muttered over her head. "You're like ice!"

"We've got to get her inside to the fire." That was Elayne.

Cooper was picking her up now, carrying her in his strong arms back up the yard toward the inner gate. Halfway to the keep, she found her voice. "Coop?"

"What is it, lass?"

"I'm ready to go south now."

19

Five nights after the episode at Graymeer's, Trap pressed a spot on the paneling in the back of the royal bedchamber and a portion of wall swung silently inward. A musty stairway descended from there, so narrow its cold brick walls brushed Abramm's shoulders as he followed his liegeman downward. Behind him, he left the partially sewn suit that was still not correctly fitted, the ever-changing guest list, the endless and picayune protocols, the dance steps, the unending meetings with peers, advisors, supplicants, hopeful young ladies, and his own servants. He could not believe all the fuss—and all the time consumed—for something that was little more than entertainment. One would think he was in the midst of planning some massive campaign on which the fate of the realm depended, and he'd been hard pressed not to express his irritation with it all.

Now as they descended, with the light from Trap's kelistar casting weird, jerking shadows around them, he felt like a boy again, hiding from his tutor. Trap led him to a locked room furnished with chest, cot, and chair beside a full-length mirror. They left it twenty minutes later, transformed from Kiriathan nobles to Southdock ruffians of Esurhite extraction. Stained and worn woolens hid beneath heavy full-length cloaks. His skin already deeply tanned from his weeks at sea, Abramm had only to blacken his beard with charcoal and pull a black curly wig over head. The wig, tied into the standard knot of an Esurhite warrior, was further secured by a floppy, wide-brimmed hat.

"Just don't let anyone get a good look at your eyes," Trap had warned. Though he'd appended the disclaimer that even then it was unlikely they'd guess the truth. *"No one will be looking for the king of Kiriath under all that!"*

"And certainly not in the company of one as rascally looking as you," Abramm had retorted, for Trap's disguise included a bushy black beard that Abramm thought looked obviously fake. Trap maintained it wouldn't matter where they were going.

If he was no more at ease with this endeavor than he'd been when Abramm first suggested it, at least he was resigned. And confident that he'd prepared, as much as it was possible to prepare, for the dangers that might meet them in the lawless warrens into which they ventured.

A second long stairway dead-ended in a small stone chamber where Trap extinguished the orblight and they stood in silence, listening for any sounds that might betray a furtive follower. After a few moments, Abramm heard the rustle of his companion's clothing, then a faint clank and muffled rattle. Moments later a breath of air washed across his face and stirred the edges of his robe as the heavy stone door swung outward. In utter darkness they stepped through the opening, waiting again to be sure they were alone before closing the door.

The ground sloped steeply away from them now, and they descended through the barely visible support stilts of the building overhead, emerging onto a muddy track on the fringes of Portside. Moments later they strode among the bustle of men unloading one of the many newly arrived vessels lined up along the waterfront and from there made their way to the Avenue of the Keep and beyond into the maze of twisting stairways, narrow dog-legged passages, and dank, muck-bottomed drainage tunnels that was South-dock. The air grew chill and so strong with the kraggin's stench it was hard to breathe. Shreds of mist floated eerily around them, reflecting the feeble illumination of the occasional lantern or lighted second-story window. Com-munal fires started up in squares and alley ends by the homeless only added to its netherworld feel. The place literally crawled with staffid, scuttling into the street litter alongside the rats and slinking cats, while feyna rustled in the eaves overhead, peering down with tiny, coal-like eyes.

It seemed to Abramm that they walked forever—Trap was likely taking a circuitous route to lose any followers—but finally they reached a square on the riverbank, tucked at the foot of the dark, looming bulk of Bunman Bridge, first of the nine spanning the river. Lights winked along its top edge, curving in a line across the starlit sky, while beneath it, the first of its three supporting arches swept up in dark silhouette against the river's gray gleam. A group of raggedy men and women congregated about a central fire pit, talking quietly, but Trap ignored them, skirting the gathering to head for a ramshackle three-story boardinghouse on the far side, and then around back to its rundown stable. Two men armed with rapiers stood guard, one of them nodding a greeting to Trap as he and Abramm entered.

Inside, a narrow aisle led past the loft ladder and several stalls into a high-ceilinged room smelling of straw and grain and horse. Orblights clustered near the ceiling, illumining a clutter of crates and barrels and about ten roughly dressed attendees, most of them men. Others were coming in behind them as Abramm and his liegeman found seats on bales of straw stacked at the back.

Trap leaned close and spoke quietly in the Tahg, "The nobles usually gather up in the loft, where it's darker and folk leave them alone. I thought it best not to draw undue attention, but if you'd be more comfortable—"

"This is fine," Abramm said, studying their surroundings with interest. Trap kept his expression neutral and said no more. Not long after they had settled, a black-haired, thick-bodied man in a green woolen jerkin and dark trousers approached and introduced himself. "Seth Tarker. I don't believe I've seen you here before." His beard, Abramm noted, was nearly as bushy and wild as Trap's fake one.

"I'm called Anahdi," Trap said, his Kiriathan suddenly heavier with the Tahg lilt than Abramm had ever heard it. "I've been coming for about a week."

"Anahdi, huh? What kind of name is that?"

"Esurhite."

The man's brows drew slightly downward. "We don't get many Esurhites here."

"The name is Esurhite, but I'm actually Kiriathan. I was night-shipped as a boy."

"Ahh." Tarker's gaze drifted to Abramm, and Trap took his cue.

"This is my friend Alaric, and no, that is *not* an Esurhite name. His mother was Kiriathan."

"And her night-shipped, too, then?" Tarker guessed.

"Aye."

He nodded. "So you've just come in then, on one of the new ships."

"We did," Abramm said, increasing the Tahg lilt in his own speech. Trap glanced at him blandly, but Abramm read the warning in his eyes.

Too late. Tarker was already on the trail. "Wouldn't have been *Wanderer*, would it?"

"Aye. It was," Abramm admitted. Trap was now focused on the folk surrounding them, clearly displeased. In their turn, the other attendees had broken off their own conversations to listen with sudden interest.

"You were there?" Tarker said. "You saw what happened?"

"We were there," Abramm allowed. And it seemed now that every eye in the room was upon him.

"So"—Tarker squinted at him—"did he do it? Did he really kill that monster?"

"It wasn't exactly a sporting event with everyone standing alongside the gunwale watching."

"So you didn't actually see him do it."

"No." Was it lying to speak the literal truth and still give a false impression?

The answer served him well, though, for immediately the others went back to their own conversations and the energy drained from Tarker like water from a broken jug. He asked where they were staying, more for something to say than for interest, and then one of his fellows approached to mutter something about Gadrielites and both went off to confer with their confederates at the back of the stable. After that the newcomers were left alone, save for occasional furtive looks darted their way. New arrivals continued to pour in, among whom the topics of conversation centered still on the unjust imprisonment of the rioters last week and the fiasco of the king's project up at Graymeer's.

"The mist's gotten thicker up there since his visit, have ye noticed?" a woman sitting in front of them remarked. "Spilling out the gate and down the walls. Those as live closest say they've got more spawn than ever before."

"Aye," said her companion. "Vermin'll be all over the headland afore long cause o' him. Mark me on it."

It went without saying that Abramm was evil. Just as with Belmir, it didn't matter that he'd renounced his vows, refused to attend Mataian services, and been about as cool toward Mataian leaders as protocol allowed. The Terstans considered it all an act, and had the stories to prove it, all passed on from "a friend" or "my brother," who had gotten the tale from someone else, who'd heard the tale from someone else. And none of the reports were even questioned, no matter how absurd, preposterous, or downright impossible the stories were.

He'd known he wasn't popular with these people, but seeing the antagonism, hearing it on every side, so dogmatic, so imbued with the passion born of wrongs suffered over years, brought it home in a profoundly discouraging way. *Trap's right*, he thought. *Even if I stood up right now and told them everything, they would think it a trick.*

At length the rumble of conversation quieted as a grizzled older man in a leather jerkin and dark woolen breeches stepped out of the shadows into the center of the gathering. His steel gray hair was cropped close around craggy, coarse features, pale and age-wrinkled, though his brown eyes snapped with life, piercing as crossbolts. Abramm recognized him with a jolt: Everitt Kesrin, the Terstan he had met when he'd first arrived in Springerlan. The man who owned the Westland Shipping Company and strode about with his mark bared and had a penchant for baiting high-ranking Mataians.

Kesrin welcomed them all, made some announcements regarding the apparently safe escape of some of their number to Chesedh, then paused, sweeping the audience with his gaze. "Many of you have been asking me a question over the last few days that I have been reluctant to answer. A question I remain reluctant to answer, not only because I do not have all the facts, but because I feel it borders on slander and violates the admonition that we respect those whom Eidon has put into authority over us."

With that sentence he had Abramm's full attention.

"Yes. King Abramm rules at *Eidon's* behest and we must not forget that. But if it is for the cursing or blessing of our people, I cannot say. Abramm may well be what we all suspect—a spineless puppet of the Mataio, possessed by a servant of Moroq. Then again, he may not. After all, when Master Rhiad accused him of wearing a shield, he could have bared his chest as demanded and proven the charge false then and there. But he did not."

His audience erupted into a paroxysm of muttering as Abramm kept his face expressionless and flicked a glance at Trap. When the outburst died away, Kesrin continued. "I know half of you are ready to lynch him. Yet for every alleged grievance he's committed, I could offer a reasonable explanation in support of his innocence." He held out his hands to stay another outburst. "I'm not saying he *is* innocent, only that we don't know for sure. Since we have no real information, we have no business making any judgments about the matter. And to take action based on mere speculation is completely out of line.

"Worse, in all this worry about where this man's loyalties lie, we've forgotten he *is* the man Eidon has given to rule over us and that through him we've been delivered from the kraggin. We should be grateful for that above all else." He paused, raking them with a gaze that snagged briefly on the two Esurhites at the back before going on. "That is all I have to say on the matter for now, so please don't ask me any more."

With that, he changed the subject, pointing out the various exits to the newcomers and assuring them that should the meeting be interrupted, the Terst had men assigned to stand in the gap while the others slipped away. Then he surveyed them all in silence, and when they had settled, said, "Let us seek the Light."

It took Abramm but a moment's reflection to realize Kesrin's recent speech had provoked the Shadow within him to project a fog of fear, worry, and discouragement into his soul, none of them compatible with the fact that he bore the very Light of Eidon in his flesh. But it was hard to let them go all the same. Still, even if he couldn't quite dismiss them as irrelevant falsehoods, he could refuse to consider them further, especially when he had something else to concentrate on. And thankfully, Kesrin was soon speaking again, asking the One who'd given them the Light for guidance and understanding and protection during their meeting.

"Now, to return to where we left off last night." He pointed casually at the empty air to his left and a crystal tablet formed out of nothing, floating shoulder height above the straw. Trap, who'd been the Dorsaddi's primary teacher, and thus Abramm's, as well, had told him of kohali who possessed this skill but that he had never seen one. Now he was surprised and fascinated by the tablet, which seemed to project the kohal's thoughts as either images or words as he progressed through his lesson.

The lesson itself was on a passage he had apparently been teaching for some days, which told the story of Shadiel and the Black Heron. Abramm had memorized it as an acolyte of the Mataio, though he had never heard it taught in the context Kesrin was now teaching it—that is, that Shadiel was a Light bearer and the heron a feyna. It made a good deal more sense than it ever had when Brother Belmir had taught it. Even so, Abramm found his mind straying back to his troubles.

He had hoped to find a way to connect with someone here, preferably the kohal of the Terst. That was before he learned it was Everitt Kesrin, however, who he recalled all too vividly from the night of the reception when Prittle-man pronounced the need for a Terstan purge, and Abramm had been too wool-witted to call him on it. Thus giving Kesrin more reason than most to be suspicious, no matter how convincingly Abramm might plead the case of his break with the Mataio. Even the sight of the shield on his chest might not do it, and Abramm had heard some rhu'ema would even counterfeit kelistars, which was at this point about the only Lightskill he possessed.

The whole thing looked hopeless. Unless he meant to announce the truth to the entire realm and stand by it, he didn't see how he could convince any of these people he was actually on their side.

Kesrin had been teaching for about half an hour, when Abramm finally put aside his fears and frustrations and forced himself to attend to the man's words, surprised to find he had gone from the subject of the feyna, to the system that produced them. And the enemy that had devised that system: Moroq and his rhu'ema minions.

"They will hide in the shadows and the darkness, hoping you will forget they exist. Hoping you will focus on the pawns they send against you, instead. They will seek to wear you down, to fill you with fear, to get you to doubt your ability, your destiny, your very place in the Light."

Abramm sat rigidly, his eyes locked upon the kohal. Chills crawled over his flesh as memories of his struggle over the last few days paraded through his mind. It was as if the man were speaking directly to him. No. Not the man. Eidon himself.

"They will seek to keep you from using the power that is your heritage and rely instead upon human power. And they have myriad ways of doing that, starting with their inside ally—the Shadow that dwells within us. Never think you have conquered it, for you won't. Never think you will escape it, for you will fight it until the day that you die. Constantly it will project its selfish and arrogant desires into your soul, seeking to turn you back to the self-dependence you lived in before you took the Star. And living in the Shadow's power always brings one back to fear.

"You have a destiny. Do you know what it is? Are you willing to embrace it? Lay down your very life in its service? Or will you let your enemy hold you back with fears and illusions, keep you from trusting him whom you should trust above all others? He knows exactly what he is doing in your life, and he has everything under control. You know that, but do you *believe* it?

Will you go forward in the direction he has led you and rest in the knowledge that he'll see you through it? Or will you back away?"

He fell silent, leaving the words to echo in Abramm's hearing, igniting a fire of wonder in his soul. For it was as if Eidon himself had stood before him, and he knew without doubt that he was being told in no uncertain terms what to do. *Trust me, Abramm. Carry on with the plan. Let me take care of the details.*

Abramm frowned at the gray-haired man standing at the head of the group beside the glowing tablet. Nothing about him looked any softer, any more inviting than before. He could not imagine how he could be persuaded.

Leave that to me.

Very well, my Lord Eidon. I will speak to him and see how you do it.

"Know that the Light within you is greater than anything the enemy possesses," Kesrin said. "And that *they* are afraid of *you* going forward in it. Know that. Believe that and you will be—"

There was a bang, a rapid thumping of footfalls, and one of the men who had stood guard at the door burst into the main room. "Gadrielites!" he cried in a low voice.

The kohal flicked his crystal tablet into oblivion as the gathering arose en masse, hastening to their chosen exits with well-practiced silence. A whip skirled to the ceiling and with a single crack extinguished all the orblights, shrouding the stable in darkness. Someone grabbed Abramm's arm and pulled him to the side of the room opposite the entrance. He heard the soft hiss of others' breathing, the shuffle of feet, the jingle and rustle of clothing, and his main reaction was not fear, but intense irritation. Why did they have to be raided *now*, just when he'd decided to release his secret? Now he'd surely have to wait, and who knew what might happen in the interim?

Before he had reached the safety of the exit, he heard a faint, brief staccato of clinking that was the strangely benign sound of clashing rapiers. More bangs and thumps preceded the invasion of new light, murky and flickering, as four gray-cloaked figures burst into the main room, armed with chains and sandclubs. One of them carried a lantern, which he hung immediately on a wall peg as the others fanned out.

At that moment all thought of fleeing passed from Abramm's mind, and he turned, his rapier leaping from its sheath. It was not anything consciously thought out, indeed was in violation of all the plans he had agreed to, all the warnings he had heard. But these were his people, and just like with the kraggin, he would not stand by and allow them to be violated.

He flicked a score of kelistars into the air for light, wrapped the cloak around his left arm, and stepped forward, the long blade of his sword advancing before him. Beside him, Trap had done the same, but their adversaries seemed not to have divined their danger. Within their cowls they only chuckled and kept coming.

The leader, a stocky, muscular man, swung his heavy chain once over his head, then let the end fly. Abramm blocked it with his padded left arm, twisted his wrist to grab the heavy links, and drove his rapier into the man's shoulder, piercing muscle, bone, and ligament. As the man staggered back howling, Abramm jerked the chain free of his assailant's grip, then snapped it back against the side of his opposite, uninjured shoulder. He staggered away and Abramm switched focus, slashing at the sandclub that was tumbling toward his head and dissolving it in a spray of sand and an empty fabric tube, fluttering downward. Snapping the chain again, he caught the sandclub wielder at the hip, knocking him to the ground.

Trap was meanwhile disarming his opponents with equal ease, and soon all six were scrambling for the door. Abramm dashed after them, taking the original man down with his chain and leaping upon him, knee driving into the broad back. The ruffian had come prepared with binding cords, which he'd looped around his waistbelt under his cloak, and now Abramm plucked them free and used them on their bearer. Then he rolled the man over and pulled back his cowl.

The face beneath was broad, bearded, and pocked beneath a receding hairline of curly brown hair. It looked vaguely familiar. The black eyes slitted with fury. "You'll pay for this, filthy Shadow lover!" the graycloak hissed. "No one touches Eidon's chosen and gets away with it."

"A warning you'd do well to heed, friend," Abramm retorted mildly, standing upright. By then, Trap had secured another of them, but the other four were gone.

As they pulled both men to their feet, Abramm grew aware of the audience that had gathered in the shadows beneath the rear loft: Seth Tarker and four of his fellows stood frozen, watching the proceedings in horror.

Now Abramm addressed him, remembering his Tahg lilt only at the last minute. "Ah, Mr. Tarker. Sorry we didn't get all of 'em. Maybe next time we'll do better."

Tarker stepped out of the shadow, his face twisting with some intense emotion. "Are you *insane*, man? Do you have any idea what you've done?" He stepped forward and pulled the Gadrielite from Abramm's grasp. "What did you think to do with them? Take them to the borough magistrate? They'll be let go before you can leave the jail. And then they'll be back, angrier than ever."

"Perhaps if you stood up to them more," Abramm said sharply, "they'd be afraid to come back."

"We'll never be afraid of the likes of *you*," the graycloak muttered, glaring at him.

"That's because you don't know me very well," Abramm said with a wicked grin.

"Stop it!" Tarker snapped. "You have no idea what's going on here, *Alaric*." He turned to the stocky captive. "These men are strangers to us, Mr. Skurlek. We've never seen them before tonight, and we certainly didn't ask for their help."

Abramm stared in astonishment as Tarker passed Skurlek off to one of his associates and another took possession of Trap's man. Then the two were escorted—still bound, at least—out the door under the rear loft. Tarker lingered, his dark-eyed gaze flicking between his two befuddled listeners.

"One thing taught among us is the importance of not meddling in affairs you know nothing about. Thanks to you, it'll be days before we can gather again. Maybe weeks. And now we'll have to find another place to meet, too."

"And another after that if you keep caving before them," Abramm said, gripped by a rising anger of his own. "They're nothing but bullies and lawbreakers, and they'll never stop taking from you if you don't stand up to them."

Tarker's frown deepened into a scowl. He started to speak, but apparently thought better of it and closed his mouth again. Finally he shook his head and stepped back from them. "Please do not try to find us again. You will not be welcome if you do."

And with that he took his leave.

20

"Well," Abramm said some moments after the sounds of Tarker's passage had faded. "That certainly did not go as I had hoped."

He was still in shock. To find himself deprived of his opportunity to speak to Kesrin and forbidden even to try again was bad enough, but to have it come as punishment for just action against the unlawful persecutions of the self-righteous Gadrielites was infuriating. It also showed him how much he had settled into the role of king, for he was having a very hard time accepting the fact that he'd just been ordered not to do something by a commoner.

"So what do we do now?" Trap asked, breaking into his mental tirade. His liegeman was looking around the small yard with obvious unease, and the recollection that both their lives and reputations remained in peril jolted Abramm back to the present.

"Go back, I guess." He shook his head. "They had blades themselves and were using them! So it's all right to fight, just not to win? What kind of sense does that make?"

"None. Which only underscores the truth of Tarker's words. We really don't know what's going on down here." He paused. "As I understand it, the last time some of them stood against their enemies, a good number ended up in the royal dungeons for their trouble."

"There was nothing that could be done about that," Abramm protested quietly. "None of them would testify."

"I know, sir. I'm not casting blame, merely pointing out the complexity of it all."

They reentered the square where the fire had been, finding it silent and deserted now. Even the boardinghouse stood dark and still.

Abramm sighed. "This is a fine fix I've gotten us into. One I have no idea how to get out of."

"Eidon will make us a way."

"I thought he already had." Abramm grimaced at the boardinghouse and the Bunman Bridge looming behind it, tendrils of fog drifting in front of its dark bulk. When no brilliant solutions presented themselves, they headed back down the alley through which they'd originally come. Halfway along the narrow passage, Abramm laid a hand on his liegeman's shoulder. "You don't happen to know where the Westland Shipping Company is, do you?"

Meridon's face was hidden in the shadows beneath his hat and he was a moment replying. "The office or the warehouse?"

"Both, I guess."

The warehouse stood along Springerlan's waterfront and at this hour was, not surprisingly, locked up for the night. An overseer supervising the unloading of a nearby merchantman gave them directions to the company offices, of which there were two—one along prestigious Banker's Row, way up in the hills off the Avenue of the Keep, the other on Hyde Street, only three streets up from the waterfront. They had to follow it some ways around, though, and back into the outskirts of Southdock.

By then the fog was thickening rapidly, curling around the tops of buildings and piercing their cloaks with its damp chill. An increasing number of taverns made for more activity, the narrow streets alive with revelers recently come ashore. The smell of liquor mingled with that of vomit, garbage, and tobacco smoke. They walked into two private duels and had to detour around a square of brawling sailors before they reached the company office, only to find it also closed for the night.

Abramm stood in front of it scowling, even as he berated himself for his disappointment. *What did you expect?* he asked himself. *It's nearly midnight. Of course there'd be no one here.*

Beside him Trap muttered, "They're still after us, sir."

"I know," Abramm said irritably. They'd been shadowed by graycloaks since leaving the stable, and he did not doubt Skurlek was among them, eager to avenge his wounded pride. Right now he almost wished the man would attack him again, just so he could release some of this frustration.

"I've seen six of them now."

And they'd have to lose all six before they dared to return to the palace.

Finally conceding defeat, Abramm glanced down the street to his left where store and office fronts lined the narrow way, their darkness highlighting the activity swarming around the inn they'd passed coming up. Ruddy light spilled from its open door and windows across the damp cobbled street and illumined a weathered sign whose peeling paint proclaimed it the *Golden Loaf.* Laughter, loud singing, and the wheedling of a reed pipe echoed faintly up the street.

Not the most reputable establishment perhaps, but it looked crowded and chaotic enough to serve their purpose. He pressed through the crowd outside the door and into the smoky stone-floored room beyond, Trap on his heels.

Oil lanterns hung on chains from the rafters, adding their smoke to that of tobacco and the great crackling hearth fire on the left, a haunch of mutton spitted over its flames. Wooden tables packed with patrons filled the floor space, a fact Abramm noted peripherally as his eye went first to the only two exits besides the door they'd just come in—the mouth of a hallway at the top of a short bank of steps leading leftward beyond the hearth, and a swinging door just beyond the long bar to the right. No guarantees on the hall, but the swinging door clearly led to the kitchen.

They found a space at the bar's far end, hidden from the entrance by the other patrons. The innkeeper attended them swiftly, and they arranged to rent his last room for the night, then ordered themselves each a slice of the mutton with cups of mulled cider. As the man went off to get them, Abramm glanced over his shoulder at the crowd. Though no one was looking at him, he knew every person in the room was focused on him and his companion, being strangers *and* Esurhites. Anyone coming in to ask about them later would certainly be rewarded, although hopefully it wouldn't matter.

He did not expect the Gadrielites to follow them in here. Despite Tarker's claims to the contrary, invasion, kidnapping, and assault were still illegal, and Abramm doubted they'd be so bold as to act with this many non-Terstan witnesses. More than that, he did not believe the others would stand by and do nothing should they try. Most of these people, while common and rough, looked like decent folk. Anyway, they wouldn't be here that long. They'd eat, go up to their room, and in a little bit, slip away out the back door. Or the window, if need be.

The barkeep returned with two mugs of steaming cider, and shortly thereafter a girl brought their mutton, pink and hot in its own juices with a thick slab of dark bread beside it. She looked vaguely familiar, but as she was already regarding Abramm with far too much interest for his comfort, he didn't feel free to return her stares. Trap paid her with a half crown and she went away.

They had barely started to eat, however, when the crowd at the door stirred and muttered, finally parting to admit four men in Gadrielite gray. Their cowls were pushed back, their faces boldly revealed—it *was* Skurlek and his cronies—and with their arrival every head swiveled toward them and silence gripped the room. As they scanned the crowd with narrowed eyes, Abramm saw the others flinch, avert their gazes, and almost sink into their own tunics. So much for his prediction of Gadrielite timidity and civilian boldness.

Still mostly hidden from view, Trap leaned close against his side and said, "Might be time to leave, sir."

To reach the hallway where the stairs led up to their room, they'd be spotted for sure, and considering the way the Gadrielites had barged in here, and the way they had the others cowed, he wasn't sure going to the room would solve anything anyway. There were four of them in here now, which left only two to guard the back door. He and Trap could easily handle two.

The Gadrielites fanned out, peering at individual patrons as conversation started up again. Abramm and his liegeman could stand and fight, of course, but recalling Tarker's fear of retribution, Abramm was reluctant to bring trouble on the innocent innkeeper.

As the serving girl passed by again, carrying a stack of dirty plates, Abramm stopped her and asked if there was a back door through the kitchen. Her gray-blue eyes flicked up to his, then darted toward the Gadrielites in immediate comprehension. Her mouth tightened, but she gave a quick nod, then hurried on her way.

Abramm glanced at Trap, and together they pushed casually away from the bar and slid around it. They were noticed immediately, Skurlek's rough voice barking a command to halt. Which Abramm would have ignored had not the other two graycloaks pressed through the swinging kitchen doorway at the same moment to block their exit. They stopped together as the room quieted again, the silence broken only by the crackle of the hearth fire and the hissing sizzle of the meat juices dripping into it. All along the wall between them and the hallway, men had gone stiff and alert, eyes flicking from quarry to pursuers and back again.

"These men are Terstans!" Skurlek declared, his booted feet loud on the

stone floor as he approached. "They have profaned the Flames and Hands of
Eidon, and will be held accountable—as will any who dare to aid them."

With a sigh, Abramm turned back to face his accuser, partly regretful and
partly rather pleased. Flicking his cloak over his right shoulder, he checked
his immediate periphery to be sure nothing would hinder the draw of his
sword as Skurlek now drew up before him, his breath sour with rotten teeth.

"Mr. Skurlek," Abramm said. "We meet again."

Skurlek puffed out his chest, drawing Abramm's eyes to the little tongue
of flame stitched to the breast of his cloak. His hand patted the leather-
wrapped hilt of sword he now wore belted to his hip. "Except this time we're
evenly matched."

Abramm looked the man up and down. Skurlek was stout with muscle
but carried more fat on him than Abramm did. He showed no sign of the
injury he'd received earlier, though Abramm had stabbed his left shoulder,
and it appeared Skurlek was right-handed. No matter. The greater injury by
far was his wounded pride, for the man was clearly consumed by his need to
avenge it. And convinced of his ability to do so. It was a combination that
could be easily goaded into the mindless fury that bred mistakes.

Abramm smiled. "I'm afraid it will take a good deal more than that pig-
sticker at your side to make us evenly matched, sir."

He watched the pocked face redden as the other patrons, divining what
was to happen, scrambled up and out of range, tables and chairs screeching
and chattering as they were shoved aside and a ring cleared for the combatants. As the sound of murmured wagers hissed around him, Abramm felt the
mood of the place shift from fear to flickering hope.

"We'll see what Eidon has to say about that, Shadow lover," Skurlek
grated, yanking his sword from its scabbard and lunging for Abramm's heart.
Abramm's own blade sprang to hand in the same moment, sweeping the
other's blade aside in a looping stroke that let him come in left-handed with
the dagger. Skurlek barely dodged it, the short blade slicing his leather tunic
and grating along his ribs.

A susurration of surprised approval arose from the onlookers, and the
combatants began to circle one another. Then Skurlek flung the end of his
cloak at him, the heavy folds entangling Abramm's rapier as the fabric
flapped up into his face. He dodged to the left, out of the line of attack, let
the cloak fall as he blocked another strike with the dagger, then lunged with
the rapier before his opponent could recover, slicing the tendon at the base

of the man's thumb and loosing his grip on the blade. Skurlek watched it clatter to the floor in disbelief, his hand bleeding freely, dangling at his side, thumb no longer useful for holding anything.

There were times Abramm felt regret at dealing an opponent a blow that could cripple him for life. This wasn't one of them. He was starting to relax and straighten from his crouch when the Gadrielite sprang at him, a hidden blade flashing in his hand. Abramm's sword flicked back, driving through his assailant's throat and into his brain almost before he realized what had happened. Skurlek stiffened and stepped back, his face slack with disbelief. Then he crumpled lifeless to the floor.

The inn was so quiet Abramm could hear the hiss of the oil lamps and the jingle of his harness as he wiped his sword clean on his cloak and sheathed it. The gazes of the others were like a burning on his skin. He felt cold now, and mildly nauseated, for though he hadn't hesitated to cripple, he also hadn't intended to kill. Which surprised him, considering how many times he had killed in Esurhite arenas. But this was one of his own subjects.

Skurlek's companions stood over the body, staring down at it. It had been at the back of Abramm's mind that cutting off the head might paralyze the body, and that seemed to be what had happened. With Skurlek dead, his followers seemed lost.

"I guess Eidon has spoken," Abramm said as drew even with them.

Only two of them even looked up at him. "Keep following us," Abramm continued, "and you may end up following him." He gestured at Skurlek's body. "Harm this place or anyone here out of retribution and I'll seek retribution of my own."

He looked each man square in the face and marked the others, as well, seeing in them the first flickerings of fear, confusion, and outrage. He pressed by them, and they stepped back as if wary of touching him. Whispers of conversation started as the crowd opened before him. From this he surmised that Skurlek had been regarded as a man of some skill with the blade.

The innkeeper met him at the door, sober faced and grateful. "The man needed killing, sir. More than you know. He's caused a world of hurt around here. But being a favorite of Lord Prittleman himself, there was nothing anyone could do."

"They could take their grievances to the king," Abramm said quietly, at the same time thinking, *Prittleman! That's where I've seen Shurlek before. He was at the picnic!*

"The king would do nothing," said the innkeeper.

"Certainly that will be the case if he doesn't know about them." Abramm paused. "I regret to say we'll not be needing your room tonight after all."

"Sir, it would be an honor to put you up. At no charge."

"We have other arrangements. But you may keep the sovereign for your trouble."

As they left the crowd outside the Golden Loaf's door and continued down the street toward the river, Abramm gave thought for the first time to the bigger picture. The whole room had been watching. "What in Hur's Hollows was I thinking?" he muttered. "I should have at least drawn them outside into the night. What if someone recognized me?"

"I wouldn't worry about that," Trap said wryly. "Our king, after all, is not yet known for his skill with a blade. And *no* one would expect to find him in Southdock, rubbing elbows with the rabble."

That was true, but it only reminded him of the reason he was down here—and how this most recent incident would only widen the gulf between him and the skittish Terstans he sought. He had no illusions that his warning to Skurlek's Gadrielite friends would restrain them longer than an hour or two, after which "Alaric" would be a marked man. He'd have to figure out another way to meet with Kesrin. And summoning him to private audience was not an option.

As they reached the inn's far end, a figure emerged from a narrow passage and stepped into their paths, receiving for his audacity a sudden and very close look at the business ends of their rapiers. But the stranger, who stood as tall as Abramm, was already holding out both hands, palms up. "Peace, gentlemen. I wish merely to talk." He had an odd accent. Thilosian, maybe?

"Who are you?" Abramm demanded, his sword still unsheathed.

"I am Yacopan. I understand you have an interest in the Westland Shipping Company."

"How would you know that?"

"I watched you stand before the office door some time earlier. My employer—owner of that company—wishes to speak with you. If you have the time."

A thousand thoughts flew through Abramm's brain. Was this a trap? Some clever dissembling on the part of the bereaved Gadrielites? But no, those men had been genuinely cowed—and far too shocked to put together something this quickly. In light of Abramm's desire—his need—to speak with

Everitt Kesrin, this seemed like an opportunity made by Eidon himself. He could not let it pass.

"I would like that," Abramm said.

The man led them back into the passage from which he had emerged and into a side door of the Golden Loaf. They walked past a stairwell and down a narrow corridor, sounds of the Great Room at its far end echoing around them. Yacopan stopped three rooms down, knocked, and the door swung open.

They entered a rectangular room with a stone fireplace and overstuffed chairs at one end, a good-sized table at the other. Plain woolen rugs covered the floor, and dark drapes hid windows along the wall opposite the door. The only light came from the fire on the hearth, but Abramm recognized Everitt Kesrin at once. He sat at the table alone, finishing up a meal that looked like it came from the roast out on the main hearth, with a crust of white bread and boiled greens. He had not started his meal alone—four mostly empty plates scattered the table around him. Whoever his guests had been, they were here no longer, only Yacopan and one other man, who was smaller and fairer in coloring but no less intimidating.

Now Yacopan conjured a kelistar and held it near the newcomers so Kesrin could study his guests as they entered, his hands resting against the table edge, knife in one, fork in the other. For a few moments after the door closed he regarded them, his eyes traveling up and down their forms. Then finally he snorted and went back to his mutton. "Alaric, is it?" he said, content to let them stand as he sliced off another bite.

"Yes, sir," said Abramm as Yacopan extinguished the orblight.

"And I hear your mother was Kiriathan."

"Yes."

"That accounts for the blue eyes, I guess." Kesrin poked the meat into his mouth, chewed, swallowed, then took several more bites before he finally leaned back in the chair to look up at him. "You seem determined to draw down the fires of torments upon me, Alaric. I'm curious as to why."

"What do you mean?"

"It will hardly escape the Gadrielites' notice that one of their own was first humiliated by an attendee of the Terstmeet I was conducting, then killed by him the very same night in the Great Room of the Golden Loaf, an establishment I am well known to frequent."

"*He* came looking for *me*!"

"And you didn't know he was following you?" Kesrin demanded. "Didn't know what he intended?"

"I knew what he intended," Abramm admitted. "But everyone present saw how it came about."

"Yet the story will not be told that way. The Gadrielites will connect you with us, regardless of whether you are one of us or not. Then we, I fear, will pay the price."

"Only because you keep backing down from them."

Kesrin frowned and went back to his meal. For a time the only sounds were the clink of his utensils on the pewter plate, the hiss and crackle of the fire, and muffled laughter from the crowd in the Great Room down the hall.

The meat and greens were gone by the time he spoke again. "Seth told you to leave us alone. That you were no longer welcome among us. Why did you not heed him?"

"Because I need to talk to you."

"And here I thought this conversation was *my* idea." He picked up the last of the bread and broke it in two.

"In truth, I believe it was Eidon's," Abramm said.

Kesrin looked up at him sharply, brows drawn together. "You are an odd man, Alaric." He ate one of the pieces of bread, then said, "What is it you need to talk to me about?"

This, too, was not going as Abramm had intended. For now that the question was before him, he found himself blank headed and wordless, terrified to blurt out the barren truth, yet seeing no other way before him. He was more certain than ever that Kesrin would not believe him. Memories of Carissa's rejection plagued him. As did the endless arguments that burst out among the Dorsaddi, first over the need to take the Star at all, and then, among those who did, about everything else imaginable.

One thing he had learned in all of it was how very difficult it was for men—or women!—to admit they were wrong. Once an opinion was formed, it was as easily turned as the current in a flooded wadi. Especially if the opinion had been made public, and even more especially if it had been lauded and embraced.

But perhaps this was just the Shadow again, blinding him to the possibilities and power of the Light, seeing only the negative, the obstacles, the potential for disaster. At the moment that seemed all he could see.

He glanced at Yacopan, standing by the door, then at the other man, a silent sentinel near the hearth, and finally at Trap, who clearly understood his dilemma and just as clearly had no solutions.

"Whatever you have to say to me," Kesrin prodded, "can be said in front of Yacopan and Parsival."

"It is my secret to share, sir, not yours."

Kesrin laughed outright. "You've already aligned yourself with Terstan heretics, man. What other secret could you possibly need to guard after that one?"

When Abramm had no answer for him but still refused to relent, the man sighed again and shook his head, finishing off his meal and pushing the plate away.

Before he could speak, though, the door opened and a serving girl slipped in—the same girl who had served them back in the Great Room. Now, seeing her with Kesrin, Abramm realized she'd been with the merchant on the dock the day he'd arrived, the fawn-haired girl who'd stared at him as if he were some kind of god. Now as then, her gaze kept coming back to him, making him glad for the poor lighting. As she gathered up the plates she asked Kesrin if she should bring his tea, and he said that she should.

"The wellberry blend tonight, I think, if you please."

"Yes, sir." She paused, balancing the plates, and leaned closer to him. "Are they *really* from Esurh?"

"You are here to serve tables, lass," he told her firmly. "And table servers don't ask inn patrons personal questions about their guests."

Her disappointment was palpable. Half pouting, she flicked another glance at Abramm and hurried out.

As the door snicked shut, Kesrin returned to their conversation, letting Abramm off the hook for the moment as he pursued another line of inquiry. "Your victim this night wore a shield, as well. Did you know that?"

"No," Abramm said, surprised. "Was he one of yours?"

"Years ago."

"I'm sorry, then."

"So am I, though in truth he brought it on himself."

Abramm allowed himself a small smile. "I expect his gray-cloaked friends will have a bit of a shock when they find that."

"Oh, he covered it up years ago. I doubt he even remembers that he wears it."

Abramm frowned at him. "If he wears the shield covered, where was the sarotis?"

Kesrin arched his brows. "The sarotis is not always manifested outwardly, son. It depends on the individual, and of course, the powers of the rhu'ema— or even certain spawn spore—can be used to mask it." He smiled wryly. "Terstans are not the only ones who get it, merely the ones who have been chosen to bear its stigma."

"Covered shields, false ones, hidden sarotis—how can you ever tell who's genuine?"

"You can't always. It takes wisdom. Sometimes a good deal of it." A staffid folded itself over the edge of the table and skittered toward Kesrin. "That's why we're told to be careful who we choose to walk with," he said as if it weren't there. "And why we aren't to judge by appearance. Although I think there wasn't much question as to where Skurlek's loyalties lay." The spawn was only inches from his hand when the Light flickered out of it, impaling the creature and frying it on the spot. "And do not think," he went on as if nothing had happened, "that you are free of his friends simply because you have bested him with such finality—or even because you have threatened them. They *will* come after you. Seth's advice was as much for your good as ours."

As Yacopan picked up the dead spawn and carried it to the fire, the serving girl returned with a tray bearing cup, water pot, and infuser filled with tea, going around to the left side of the table this time, passing by Abramm close enough for her skirt to brush his cloak. She set the tray on the table and unloaded it, then placed the infuser into the cup and poured the steaming water over it. When that was done she took the tray and stepped back, standing just behind the kohal's elbow, her eyes flicking from Abramm to Trap and back again, so piercing Abramm felt as if she had somehow stripped away all his disguise and now knew exactly who he was.

"You may leave us now, lass," Kesrin said.

"But—"

"Now."

She argued no further, but took her opportunity to peer even more intently into Abramm's face as she passed him, though he deliberately kept his gaze on Kesrin and hoped the room's dim light hid the flush that had crept into his face.

As the door shut, Kesrin swirled the infuser around in his cup and said, as if there had been no interruption, "I don't think you understand the situation here, Alaric."

"I understand that evil has power only because the righteous fail to stand up to it."

"Or are too few in number to do so. Especially when the law of the land is not on their side."

Abramm felt his own brows rise. "It is against the law in Kiriath to protect oneself and one's property from criminals?"

"Technically no, but when the magistrates look the other way, and the testimony of a Terstan no longer holds equal weight with that of other men, and those others are either too afraid to come to our defense or else agree with the Gadrielites, well, it may as well be."

"And what about your new king?" Abramm asked, his heart suddenly pounding. Kesrin had already noticed his eyes. If Abramm mentioned the king, it was possible the kohal might make the connection, though he still wasn't sure that would be a good thing. Nevertheless he plunged on. "You're all so sure he won't support you—why don't you go to him and find out for sure?"

"How do you know we haven't?"

"Have you?"

"I doubt he'd see me."

"Surely with your social position, you'd have no problem gaining an audience. You attended the palace celebration of the kraggin's death, after all."

"Yes," Kesrin retorted sourly. "And was there to see Abramm agree with Lord Prittleman, who is leader of the Gadrielites, that a purge of Terstans is needed."

Abramm grimaced. "You *heard* him say that?"

"He didn't *say* anything. But he was standing right there when Prittleman said it, heard him clearly and offered not one word of reproof."

"Maybe he was distracted," Abramm suggested.

Kesrin shook his head, setting the tea infuser aside and lifting the cup to blow on the hot liquid. "No, I fear he is possessed, quite frankly, and that if I went to him he would merely use the situation as an excuse to station more men down there, in order to decrease our freedoms further." He leaned forward to gingerly sip his tea.

Abramm frowned at him. "Yet you said in your message tonight that Abramm is the one Eidon has placed over you as ruler. Are you not charged, then, with the duty of taking your grievances to him if the lower authorities will not give you justice? You urged us to trust Eidon in this, yet it seems to me you have need of listening to your own advice."

Kesrin continued to fuss with his tea, blowing and sipping and keeping his eyes off Abramm. "Your suggestions are very bold, Alaric," he said presently. "But I can't help noting *you* would not be the one to pay the price should the king find such boldness offensive."

"From all that I have heard, sir, boldness is hardly an approach you are unfamiliar with." He paused, aware of his heart pounding wildly again. "In fact, you were quite bold with the king himself that day you met him on the dock, bandying words with him and Master Belmir about the authority of Kiriathan law."

"That was different. That was—" Kesrin's voice choked off. His head came up sharply, brows drawn together, his gaze as intent on Abramm now as the serving girl's had been earlier. Abramm matched him stare for stare, watching as his face went blank. The moments stretched out in a silence broken only by the creak of the old building and the muffled wheedle of a reed pipe from the Great Room. A sap pocket burst in the fireplace, pluming sparks onto the stone hearth.

Finally Kesrin spoke, his voice quiet and strained. "Yacopan. Parcival. You may leave us now."

Yacopan's mouth fell open. "Sir?"

"Take up your posts outside the door. I'll call you when I need you. For now I will speak to Alaric alone."

The servants looked at one another in befuddlement but did as they were bid. As the door closed, Kesrin turned his gaze back to Abramm. After a moment he stood and came around the table to face him, a kelistar blazing to life between them. It floated in front of Abramm's chest, casting its illumination across his face. Kesrin's gaze passed slowly over that face and then he stepped back.

"May I . . . may I see your mark, sir?"

"Certainly." Abramm flicked back his cloak and loosened the ties on his jerkin to reveal the shield on his chest, glittering like newly minted gold in the kelistar's clear light.

Kesrin peered at it, picked gently at its edges to see if it would peel off, then touched it with a flicker of Light that elicited an answering flicker from the Light that lived in Abramm's own flesh. He drew back with a muttered

"Light's grace!" and whirled to pace to the table's end where he stood with his back to them. After a few moments he expelled a burst of air and turned again to face them. "Your pardon, Sire, but I haven't been this surprised in a long, long time."

"You're sure I'm not deceiving you? That my mark is real and not some sort of trick? That the Light in me is genuine?"

Kesrin smiled slightly. "I can feel it now from here, sir. In fact, I remember thinking there might have been something that first time we met—there on the dock. The way you looked at me, the way you took my hand. I almost believed I felt a spark of the Light there."

"Actually I was thinking of conjuring a kelistar," Abramm said with a smile, "but it seemed inappropriate."

"But then the night of the reception—" Suddenly Kesrin's expression changed again, this time to a flustered dismay that seemed completely out of character. Memory of the reception had apparently caused another realization to click in his mind, and now he jumped to the table and pulled back one of the chairs. "Here, sit down, sir. I don't know what I was thinking, making you stand all this time. Would you like some tea? I pray you'll forgive my incivility—"

"I can hardly hold you accountable for believing a deception *I* initiated," Abramm said with a laugh. He sat and, seeing his host hesitate beside his own chair, motioned for him to sit, as well. "Please, kohal, let us forgo the social formalities of my station and speak with each other as men."

Kesrin nodded and sat, but it was plain this was a situation outside his ken.

"You did not know my brother Raynen, did you?"

"No, sir. Not personally." Kesrin picked up his mug, stopped, then put it down and asked again if Abramm wanted tea.

"No thank you." A few more moments under that nosy serving girl's gaze and she'd be recognizing him, too. Then all the world *would* know. "Please, kohal, be at your ease. I am little more accustomed to being a king than you are to entertaining one. Whatever protocols you might break, it's unlikely I would notice."

"Of course, sir."

"Now, you were saying something about the reception?"

"The reception. Yes." Kesrin picked up his mug again. "I was saying that it wasn't just the Prittleman thing that put my hackles up. I also felt a strong sense of evil associated with you. I see now it must have been coming from someone else." He sipped thoughtfully at his tea. "Undoubtedly he was trying to put me off of you."

He fell into a contemplative silence, his eyes fixed on the pewter candlestick—minus its candle—sitting on the table in front of Abramm. After a time, he said, "There are others among the peerage whom I'm sure our enemies have manipulated as they have me."

"That is part of why I came to you, sir, hoping you might do something about this rumor that I am the Mataio's puppet."

Kesrin looked up at him gravely. "Unless you're prepared to have me state openly that you wear a shield, I can do little more than discourage it. And even then I doubt the majority would believe me."

Abramm frowned. "If I state it openly now, I'll lose the Crown for sure. Unless . . ." His frown deepened as he fingered the base of the candlestick. "Unless I've misread things and Eidon doesn't intend that I be king so much as simply stir things up." He looked up into Kesrin's dark eyes. "Am I *wrong* to hide it?"

"That is between you and Eidon." Kesrin contemplated his tea, swirling it gently in the cup. "We are to be purveyors of the Light, it's true. But there are many ways to do that, and I've long said that timing is everything." He swirled the tea some more, then sipped. "There *are* some who need to know the whole truth now, though. One man in particular. One who would be a valuable and loyal ally, and who, at the moment, is anything but."

"Who is he?" Abramm could think of far too many possibilities.

"I'd rather not say just yet. For your own sake as well as his. And I'm a little worried about him for other reasons, too. But I'd like your permission to tell him the truth, if you'll trust me to determine whether that would be best or not."

Abramm didn't hesitate. "I'll trust you. Go ahead and tell whomever you think should know."

Kesrin nodded, then took his thoughts further than he cared to share for a few moments before rousing himself. "Is that all you needed to speak to me about?"

And now Abramm smiled sheepishly. "Actually, no. What I wanted most was to beg *your* permission to return to your Terstmeets. I have much to learn, and many questions, and I feel as if I am starving."

Kesrin looked surprised, then somewhat pleased. "It was Alaric who was banned, I believe, not Abramm. But I'm afraid it will be days before—" He broke off, apparently seeing on Abramm's face the chagrin—maybe even the desperation—that his words caused. He tapped his forefinger against the cup for a moment, then relented. "There will be smaller meetings throughout the sector until we can regather the whole group. Perhaps we can work out a way for you to join us."

"Thank you, sir."

They went on to speak of other things and it was not until the wee hours of the morning that Abramm and Trap finally took their leave. "Send word to the king of your troubles," he told Kesrin as they left. "Give him a chance to prove he will help you."

"He could get into very big trouble helping us."

"We have as a people long held that all should be free to worship as they wish. Why should Terstans be an exception?"

"I'm sure Lord Prittleman would be happy to explain that," Kesrin replied with a grin. Then he sobered. "Be careful of him, sir. He's a ruthless fanatic. And rest assured news of Skurlek's death will get back to him. Alaric is a marked man already. He'd do well to leave the city altogether."

"Well, seeing as he's outlived his usefulness, I rather suspect he will."

21

Late the next morning, as Simon was leaving the Royal Fencing Hall on the far eastern side of the palace grounds, he was waylaid by Ethan Laramor. After several hours spent at hard weapons practice, followed by a leisurely dip in the hall's outdoor baths, Simon was feeling more relaxed and content than he had in some time. And after all the trouble he'd taken to avoid meeting with his Borderer friend over the last few days, finding him waiting in the hall's main yard was as dismaying as it was surprising.

Laramor, though he did make use of the archery range, rarely came to the fencing hall itself. In fact, few did, and the great high-ceilinged room where scores of young men once gathered to practice now echoed with the sounds of but a few. The stars of the sport, and those who would become stars, practiced there, but few of those were noblemen anymore. The decline had begun in Simon's youth and was now in full swing, the art that had once been the full measure of a nobleman reduced to sport. Nowadays, while the courtiers were happy to spend an evening watching—and wagering on—various matches, to actually pick up anything more than a decorative sword themselves was increasingly unthinkable. Gillard's skill and interest were tolerated as an amusing eccentricity, neither emulated nor aspired to by most of his peers. Thus the hall often stood empty, its lofty spaces mocking the few who dared intrude.

Abramm had come down to watch some of the practice matches yesterday, and everyone was still buzzing about it this morning. Why had he come? Would he be back today? Was he thinking of taking lessons? No one knew, but the visit had elicited more excitement than Simon had seen in some time, and everyone from Headmaster Tedron to the lowliest towel boy had only good things to say about their new king. They were especially enamored with that sling of his, which he had been persuaded to demonstrate again. Another cabbage had died—though he'd needed five attempts—and today the young boys, some of them noblemen's sons, were out in the sparring yards practicing with makeshift slings of their own.

Only boys, perhaps, but it marked a watershed: Yesterday, if they'd been practicing with any weapons at all it had been swords. Today it was slings.

A large part of the fascination undoubtedly sprang from the thing's novelty, though Simon had to admit the weapon had its good points: simple and cheap to make, easy to carry, and you never ran out of ammunition. And seeing the ease and accuracy with which Abramm used it the day of the picnic had done much to revise his view that it was a crude weapon used only by the unskilled and uncouth.

Nor was that the only thing about which his views had been revised that day. His opinion of Abramm himself, already on the rise, had taken a major jog upward, thanks not so much to the business with the sling or even the courage he'd shown in Graymeer's, but to the way he'd handled his horse. With a light, sure hand and a well-balanced seat, he reminded Simon poignantly of his own brother Meren, Abramm's father. Despite Simon's fears, the animal's antics hadn't fazed him, though in truth, Banner had indulged in far less of that than was his wont. Instead of making Abramm look foolish and inept, the fiery young horse had actually enhanced his regal bearing.

Simon believed one could tell a lot about a man by the way he worked his horse, particularly a horse like Warbanner. The best riders were not oppressive or overbearing, yet somehow you knew they were unquestionably in control. Clarity of purpose, strength of will, unshakable self-confidence, an instinctive underlying respect for others—Simon wasn't sure exactly what it was, but Abramm had that indefinable quality that made some men natural leaders. His courtiers had responded in the same way as Banner had, and even Simon had felt the pull of it.

Which only intensified the ambivalence that had raged within him since that afternoon in the royal audience chamber when Abramm forced him to reveal the truth of Gillard's plottings. At first he'd told himself it was only politics, that there was nothing else he could have done. Abramm had asked, and Simon had to comply or ignite disaster, personal or otherwise. But when he ran into Laramor shortly thereafter, he'd felt suddenly and intensely ashamed, as if he had so despoiled his honor it would never recover, even while he told himself he had done no such thing, that Abramm was the rightful king. And the king had asked for his advice in implementing the very plan Simon himself had been begging Gillard to start for four years now. Even now Gillard seemed more concerned with his own position of power than with what was right or good for Kiriath.

But all those observations could not assuage the sharp pang of guilt he felt, and so he'd spoken to none of his oldest and closest friends—nor to Gillard, either—since the picnic, burying himself in his work and telling himself he lacked the time. That he'd talk with them if they ran into each other, or after he'd gotten this expansion project under way. And then he didn't think about it anymore.

Just as he hadn't thought about the rumor sparked by Abramm's visit to the fencing hall, which said he'd asked Master Tedron to prepare him to face Gillard in a challenge for the Crown. It was a speculation as ridiculous as it was ominous. Ridiculous, because a few fencing lessons would never make up for the disparity in their skills. Ominous in that people were sure Gillard *would* challenge him, one way or another.

But this morning Simon had put all that out of his mind, losing himself in the complex dance of feint and parry and lunge, in the requisite boasting and inevitable demands for proof, and all the technical talk of who did what that came afterward. For a few hours he was young again, with no more concerns than what happened at the end of his blade. But the moment he exited the hall and saw Ethan Laramor sitting on that bench in the shade of the old oak, it all came rushing back.

"Ethan," he said warily as Laramor fell in beside him. "I didn't expect to see you here this morning. They said you'd gone down to the city."

"I did." Laramor's dress confirmed it: black, broad-brimmed hat, suede leather doublet, white cravat, and brown leather riding gloves, which he was in the process of stripping off. His riding cloak he had already removed and folded over one arm. He looked pale and hollow-eyed, as if he'd been up all night.

"You heard about the killing?" he asked, tucking the gloves into his belt and shifting his cloak to his hand.

"Prittleman's man, Skurlek?" Simon made a face. "How could I not? Father Bonafil's already issued a statement demanding Abramm apprehend the murderer at once, and Abramm, to his credit, is dragging his feet."

"Only because he hasn't gotten out of bed yet," Laramor said.

Simon looked at his friend in surprise. "The master of the dawn? Still not up at this hour? Are you sure?" Since the day he'd arrived Abramm had consistently risen at first light to spend an hour exercising Warbanner or rowing circuits of the Lake of the Moon.

"I guess he had a late night," said Laramor.

"I heard he turned in early. Closed his doors around seven, in fact."

They entered the forested ravine adjacent the hall, a path of finely crushed gravel winding ahead of them through stately elms and oaks just starting to turn color. Ferns, already brown and curled from the first frost, bordered the path, while birds chirped overhead, their songs underlaid by the constant chuckle of the stream at the vale's midst.

"All I know," said Laramor, "is that he still wasn't receiving visitors when I went through on my way here. And it's already after eleven. Maybe he was attacked by an assassin sneaking into his bedroom again," he added dryly, "and is making up for his lost sleep."

Simon snorted a laugh. "I'm sure we'd have heard by now if that were so. More likely he's just sick. Quite a few have been down with the grippe lately."

"True," Ethan allowed. He ran a finger under the edge of his cravat, as if it were too tight. "I've been feeling poorly myself of late."

As they started over the first of two stone bridges spanning the stream he half laughed, half snorted. "Wouldn't that be something if Abramm contracted lung fever and died? Eidon just takes him out and all our problems are solved."

Or multiplied, Simon thought sourly, and this time he did not chuckle along. Instead he returned to their earlier subject. "So what did you learn about this murderer? They're saying he was some half-Esurhite Terstan just off one of the boats."

"Aye. And quite a hand with the blade, I guess." Laramor paused. "But it wasn't murder, Simon. Skurlek attacked *him*. In front of at least thirty witnesses. Though, of course, his being Terstan and Skurlek being one of Prittleman's, there won't be many willing to testify."

"He's probably long out of the city by now."

"I *hope* he's heading back to Esurh. He's done us a service, and I'd hate to see him have to pay for it."

Simon knew Skurlek more by reputation than personal encounter. In addition to linking him heavily to the officially illegal Gadrielite persecutions, rumor attached other crimes to his name—extortion, rape, even murder.

"He was a hooligan in fancy pants," Laramor declared with some degree of heat, "just looking for an excuse to bully people. He probably wasn't even Mataian, though you'll never get Pritt to admit it. He's like to blow a lung with the fit he was throwing outside the king's chambers just now."

"He was doing that three hours ago when I left to come here!"

"Well, now he has a score of other petitioners to watch his antics. Haldon just kept repeating, oh so patiently, that the king was not yet receiving visitors. I wanted to laugh, but the crow scowled at me so evilly, I couldn't."

They left the shaded hollow for the bright expanse of the East Terrace, a long, almost barren formal garden separating the forested glen and the palace itself. The lay of the land was such that the wide Keharnen Plateau took a sudden rise just before sheering off in the steep escarpment that formed the eastern boundary of the Kalladorne river valley. Built along the edge of that escarpment, the palace stair-stepped down from that higher point toward this more level prospect, where Queen Katerin had built her East Terrace seventy-five years ago.

Bounded on the south by a stone balustrade lining seaside cliffs and on the north by a stand of mature oaks and elms blazing gold against the hot blue sky, the terrace was a long, graded rectangle, marked out in a network of graveled promenades interspersed with well-groomed plantings. Ribbons of purple flowers swirled with low hedges and close-clipped lawns in embroidery-inspired motifs, and a grand walkway accented by three round, placid pools bisected the terrace's length.

At this hour the midday sun glared off the gravel with hot, eye-searing intensity and the terrace lay nearly deserted. The two men strode along the sea-cliff balustrade in silence, each engrossed in his own thoughts. Having avoided Laramor all this time with the assurance he would talk to the man when opportunity arose, Simon now faced the reality that he'd said nothing because he feared to widen the gulf that had already opened between them. Ethan had declared himself firmly in Gillard's camp. He had already warned Simon that Abramm would seek to win him, almost as if he believed it would be accomplished by supernatural means. With his Borderer upbringing and beliefs, that was entirely possible. Which meant anything Simon said by way of defense on Abramm's behalf would probably be discounted.

The Borderers were a proud and stubborn lot, fiercely loyal to their chosen causes and intolerant of those who chose differently. In matters of religion and politics; schisms, rivalries, and feuds abounded, and though to an outsider their differences might seem so slight as to be irrelevant, Borderers took them very seriously. A large minority of them were Terstan, whole clans in fact, descended in a long unbroken heritage from the days of Avramm the First. The majority worshipped the gods of hill and field and wood, an even older tradition in the mountains along the Ruk Pul. Superstition and black magic were pervasive, and a clan chief might as likely be a powerful warlock—able to summon the dark spirits they called ells—as the leader of a local assembly of Terstans. Since many believed both sprang from the same source, it was hard to understand why they fought. But easy to understand why they all hated the Mataio.

The Holy Brethren had repeatedly sought to "convert" the border clans, then castigated them for refusing. Never having had a Mataian king, however, the Brethren lacked real power to do more than castigate. Lay believers had occasionally marshaled armed groups like Prittleman's Gadrielites to try to cleanse the borderlands, but it never worked. That didn't mean they had given up, though. In fact, with the kraggin and the recent influx of spawn, more and more calls had sounded for physical action to be taken against those the Mataio deemed impure.

So Simon could understand the threat Ethan saw in Abramm. He just didn't think the threat was being realized.

As they reached the terrace's midpoint, Laramor slowed to a stop, turning toward the balustrade to stare over the bay, now deep blue in the midday light. Vessels of every shape and size cluttered its surface, though most of the bigger ships had already sailed out with the brisk land breeze of the morning, a breeze that had by now died away to the stifling stillness of midday.

Simon stopped at Laramor's side, leaning his bottom against the sunbaked balustrade—his hip was already starting to ache from the morning's exertions—and turning his gaze across the terrace. Sweat trickled down his sides beneath his underblouse, and all at once his doublet became so constricting he could not bear it another moment. Yes, it was improper to go about in one's underclothes, even scandalous out here on the terrace, but he was too old to care about such things anymore, and there was no one to see him anyway. Only those tiny figures on the farthest walkway heading for the stair up to the palace. He began to undo the row of front buttons.

Beside him, Ethan finally spoke. "He's won you, hasn't he?" he asked quietly.

Simon's stomach clenched with nausea and irrational shame. "It isn't what you think, Ethan."

"Isn't it? You've been avoiding us ever since the day you had your meeting. Me, Harrady, Gillard—all of us. Almost as if you can't bear to look us in the eye."

That wasn't far from the truth.

"Word is you've agreed to become his advisor."

That took Simon aback. "Who told you that?"

"Does it matter?"

Simon continued with his buttons. "I'm Grand Marshall of the Royal Army. Of course I'm going to advise him in some capacity." *You're sounding defensive, old man. You did what you had to do. And now, somehow you have to convince him to do it, too.*

"You were supposed to resign," Ethan said. "And I've heard something about a list of reliable men you're compiling."

Simon unfastened the last button and shrugged out of his doublet.

Beside him Ethan stood stiffly. "Gillard is hurt that you are not with him on this, you know."

Just exposing his sweat-soaked undergarment to the open air brought instant relief and for a moment Simon reveled in that. Then Ethan's words registered and he looked sharply at his friend. "Is that a *threat?*"

"A reality." Laramor had propped both elbows on the balustrade and stared out to sea as he absently twisted the coil ring on his forefinger. "He feels like you've betrayed him, and . . . I feel like that myself."

"And I think the true betrayal lies in encouraging him to oppose the rightful king." *Might as well just lay it out there.* "He's risking his life, his reputation, and the peace and freedom of this land for little gain. Perhaps no gain at all."

Ethan rounded on him angrily. "How can you say that, Simon! Knowing what Abramm is."

"What I know of Abramm," Simon said with deliberate calm, "is that the crown is his by right, and he appears well suited to wear it. Far more so than I ever would have guessed or even hoped."

Ethan gaped at him. "Gillard's right. You *do* admire him!"

The words sparked a strange burst of memory—fiery eyes in a ruined face, a flashing knife, a white-blond curl, and those same condemning words hurled at him. *"And you! You admire him!"*

Then it was gone, like a dream image popping into the mind and popping out again the moment one tried to seize it.

But although those words had elicited shocked denial from him the first time—*How do I know that? How do I know it was even real?*—now he acknowledged their truth. He draped his doublet over the balustrade beside him and said, "Why shouldn't I? He's turned all of us on our ears, out-performing by a hundredfold every expectation we had."

"It's only been two weeks, Simon. Anyone can perform well for two weeks."

"I don't believe it's a façade. The boy's survived slavery among the Esurhites! Light and Fire, Ethan! Shouldn't we *expect* him to have been changed by that?"

"He certainly *has* been changed. I just don't think it was slavery that did it."

And with that Simon's patience gave out. "Why are you so insistent he's involved in some mysterious Mataian conspiracy? It's like you made up your mind beforehand and won't even consider the facts."

"Facts are subject to interpretation."

Simon sputtered an oath. "He's done nothing but stall them, deny them, and reject them. He's declared freely and frequently that he's not only renounced his vows but his beliefs in the Flames altogether."

"I do not trust a man who gives up one set of beliefs and has nothing with which to replace them."

"So what are you saying? He has to be *Terstan* before you would support him?"

An odd startled expression passed across Ethan's weathered features. Then he frowned. "Not at all. In fact, if he made such a claim I would be more suspicious than ever. Just because a man wears a shield doesn't mean he serves the power behind it. And there are paper shields, pigskin shields, some even made out of gold foil."

"Why would anyone *pretend* to be Terstan?"

"The Gadrielites do it all the time in order to penetrate Tersts and betray their members." Ethan pulled off his hat and fanned his face. Sweat trickled down the side of his check, turning his strawy hair dark along temple and neck, and staining the upper edge of his cravat. "In Abramm's case, it would be the perfect way to convince people he really wasn't in league with Bonafil and powers of the Flames."

"So the boy has no chance with you at all," said Simon. "No matter what he says or does, in your eyes he's guilty and there's no amending it. And all this without you ever having spoken to him directly."

"I already know what he is, and if I spoke with him, he would only deceive me—as he has apparently deceived you." He glanced at Simon, then replaced his hat. "There is much here you do not understand."

"So enlighten me!"

"You wouldn't believe me."

Simon rolled his eyes. "Plagues, Ethan! I've never seen you so pigheaded before!"

Ethan stared grimly across the bay and said nothing.

Simon felt at his wit's end. It was as if his old friend had turned into someone else. "What if you're wrong?" he asked finally. "What if Abramm has come in good faith and is *not* in league with the Mataio at all? Do you truly believe there's no possibility *you* could've been deceived? Or merely have misperceived events as they unfolded? Are you that infallible in your judgments?"

Laramor kept his gaze fixed stubbornly upon the bay, his jaw set, his fingers once more twisting the coiled ring on his left hand.

"Light and Fire, man!" Simon exploded, goaded past all thoughts of diplomacy. "You're engaging in treason! That's an execution-worthy crime. At least talk to him face-to-face, one on one if you can. At least give him a chance to prove himself to you."

Finally his friend moved, scowling fiercely down at his hands, the silver ring gleaming in the sunlight as it twisted round and round beneath his fingers. "I've tried," he said finally. "He refuses to see me."

"I don't believe that."

Ethan looked at him askance. "You think I'm lying?"

"I think you may have been told that. I don't believe he refused."

The other man turned with a sigh to face the terrace, squinting out over its brightness, then shutting his eyes and massaging his temples as if his head hurt. It was some time before he spoke. "I was told he was angry with me because of Carissa."

"*Carissa*? You had nothing to do with that mess! Besides, everyone *knows* you and Rennalf are practically in a blood feud." Sudden suspicion hummed like a hive of stirred bees. Could someone in the palace be deliberately driving a wedge between Laramor and the new king? Gillard, perhaps? It seemed a bit subtle for him, but he surely stood to gain the most.

"Talk to him, Ethan. If they refuse to admit you, *demand* to see him. Prittleman does it all the time. Go and see him *today*. Before you go too far to back out."

Laramor had gone back to his ring, not twisting it now, just rubbing his fingers along its coils while the sea gulls wheeled overhead, their raucous cries sharp in the still, hot silence. Finally he looked up. "No, Simon. It's you who's wrong. In the end, perhaps you'll see that. I just hope it comes before you lose everything you really care about."

He pushed off the balustrade and strode away. Simon followed slowly after him, frustration bitter on his tongue.

22

As Simon was leaving the Hall of Fence, Abramm stood at the largest of the three desks in the royal study and let a gray-green bracelet slide off the tip of his dagger into a narrow-necked flower bowl. The flowers it had recently held lay piled in disarray upon the desk, their wet stems spreading a wrinkled stain of moisture across the papers scattered beneath them. The water he had dumped into the mostly empty ash pail and sent off with Jared to be disposed of.

The bracelet hit the bottom of the bowl with more of a click than the clank it should have made, were it really metal. But it lay there all the same, unchanged and benign, trapped without knowing it. Or at least Abramm hoped it was, counting on those still-wet glass walls to prove too steep and slippery to climb. He set aside the dagger and glanced up. After sending Jared away, he'd dismissed the other servants and told them to close the doors behind them, that he did not wish to be disturbed for a time. He was alone.

Returning to the palace from his meeting with Everitt Kesrin shortly before dawn, he'd skipped his usual morning routine for the sake of a few hours' sleep. The fact that he was keeping his courtiers waiting, that a nearly hysterical Darak Prittleman was terrorizing everyone out in the ante-chamber, had disturbed him—until he remembered he was king and could elect to see supplicants or not, as he chose, regardless of the fits they threw. And at the moment, he had no desire to face Prittleman and his demands. After last night, he was more inclined to throw the man into the royal dungeons and lose the key. Nor was that his only reason for delay. Kesrin had provided him a portfolio of notes, which he had started reading as soon as he had awakened. In them was a brief discussion of the technique for striking shadowspawn with the Light from a distance.

Now he eyed the creature in the bowl, still looking like a harmless heavy bracelet rimmed with gold scallops, a piece more suited for a man than a woman. Which made sense seeing as it had taken on the guise in a man's quarters. To see it in its true form, he had to see it through the Light, a concept he still didn't entirely understand. Trying to apply it, though, even if he failed, would surely teach him something.

He drew a deep breath and laid his hands flat around the belly of the bowl, cradling it between them, the nearly healed cut on his left palm still tender at the contact. Kesrin's notes said it was a matter of perception. A matter of recognizing the fabric of deceit, for it was the same pattern with all things born of Shadow. Recognizing it with hand and eye and soul and spirit, all of them. There should be a slight pressure, a sense of vibration—yes! He did feel that, though so faint it might be only imagination. Except now, knowing how to look, he also saw the shivers of the illusive cloak the staffid had wrapped around itself, the sickly throbbing luminescence of the green. He felt a strong wave of revulsion, and suddenly the lines and shadows came together in a new way—like the old vase/face puzzle—and he *saw* the staffid in the bracelet. At the same moment a thread of light shot from the index finger of his right hand, penetrated the glass, and struck the creature in the center of its back.

Immediately it whipped out of its curl, arching back as if in pain, its many legs wriggling into view. He zapped it again without even thinking to do it, and the thing flashed up the side of the bowl, undulating like something that should be under water. But the slick glass sides defeated it, and it fell back, rolling and arching and writhing about the bottom.

"Your pardon, sir," came a familiar feminine voice from the doorway behind from him. "I hope I'm not interrupting."

He jerked around in horror. "Lady Madeleine! What are you doing here?"

"Oh, Jared let me in the back way." She swept toward him, as if completely unaware both of his horror and the fact she should not be here. "Lord Prittleman is making such a scene in the antechamber, I knew if I wanted to see you before tomorrow, I'd better go around."

"And did it happen to occur to you that the reason for Prittleman's distress was that I am not receiving visitors?"

"Jared said you'd been up for a while. I only wanted to make a quick check of your titles here." She gestured at the book-lined shelves around them. "And Master Getty sent me with a message. I promise not to bother you. How is your hand, by the way?"

"My hand? It's fine. Why would it not be?"

"I was afraid you might have reopened that cut on it," she said, looking around. "It's awfully dark in here. You'll ruin your eyes trying to read like this, you know." Her own eyes fell upon the staffid, quivering now on its back in the glass bowl. "What happened to that?"

"It, uh . . . seems to be injured."

Her gaze climbed to meet his, one brow lifted. "Injured?"

"I think someone might have stepped on it."

"So you scooped it up in a vase and set it here? For what purpose? A desk ornament? I think the flowers were more attractive."

He frowned, giving up the contest in a wash of annoyance. "I don't see that it concerns you, my lady. You said you have a message from Master Getty?"

She shook her head, half smiling. "You are a terrible liar, my lord."

"I beg your pardon?!"

"Never mind. Yes, Master Getty sent me to tell you he doesn't have the book you asked for."

He frowned at her, suspecting a deeper story here. She was not, after all, the lackey of the royal library. "The university said he does."

"And he says the university has it." She paused. "It is not the first book to go missing in this way. And I've been through both libraries, top to bottom. *The Histories of the Hollyhock, The Journals of Ravelin, The Records and Forth-tellings of the Kings of Light—*"

"Kings of Light?" Abramm asked, startled out of his annoyance.

"That's what they called your ancestors in the early days of your family's reign. You didn't know that?"

"No."

"I think it's because they were Terstan, though that's not widely known anymore, either. Back then it was the *Terstans* who were called Guardians. And Guardian-Kings, if you can believe that. Unfortunately, all records that would confirm that have gone missing in this ridiculous back and forth between Masters Getty and Dewes. They have no love for one another, you know. Each believes *he* should be the sole custodian of historical texts." She paused, her gaze shifting around the room again. "So I thought I'd have a look at your personal library and see if the books got moved here."

He recoiled, taken aback once more by her forwardness. "I think I can look through my personal library myself, Lady Madeleine."

"Yes, but you are so busy, sir. And there appear to be a number of fascinating volumes here." She was already moving toward the nearest wall of books.

He stepped to cut her off. "Undoubtedly there are. If you give me a list of the titles you require I'll let you know if they're here."

"I'm sure I could see it for myself if there was more light in here—"

And suddenly, right in front of his face hovered a grapefruit-sized orb, fragile as a soap bubble, filled with glowing threads of gold that swirled around coruscations of white. Its soft illumination spilled out across the darkened room, over the paper-littered desk, the tumbled flowers, the book-lined shelves, and the amused and freckle-spattered face of Lady Madeleine, whose gray-blue eyes were sharp upon his own.

He stared back at her, shocked beyond hope of concealing it, and it seemed as if his heart had jumped into his throat where it was all but choking him. It wasn't just that she wore a shield herself, but that she had revealed it to him, and so casually. Before he could follow the implications of it all, however, her eyes flicked to the side of his face, and the dove-wing brow lifted. "You have three holes in your ear, Sire."

He just concealed his start of surprise, put off balance yet again. Was the woman unable ever to follow a single train of thought to its end? "Yes. I am aware of that."

"The Pretender wore three rings in his left ear. Esurhite honor rings, the third gained within his second year of combat, though a third ring isn't usually given until at least the fifth year."

"It was no doubt done for the notoriety," he said, feigning unconcern, wondering—hoping—she had not guessed as much as he had feared, her orb-making but a ploy to win more information on the Pretender. "His master would make more money that way."

"Mmm. They say it so enraged his master's son, Regar, who had only two rings, that it drove him into the priesthood. They say it's the reason for his all-consuming hatred for the Pretender."

"Your knowledge is considerable, my lady. So great it makes me wonder why you even asked to interview me on the subject."

"There is still much I do not know. And as I told you—I always go to original sources, if possible."

Original sources. Back on that, are we? Abramm grimaced. "Well, if you know anything, you must know my reputation here. And surely it is obvious from that that I cannot be your White Pretender."

She smiled. "Your reputation is six years old, sir. And sadly out of date, I fear. Katahn ul Manus was famous for his ability to develop his fighters. From the way you ride, you obviously carry the Kalladorne athletic skills as much as their looks. Besides, I saw how you conducted yourself last night after Terstmeet . . . *Alaric*."

He gaped at her, and she grinned back, an expression that might have been endearing in its impishness had he not been so aghast. "I don't know who you thought to fool with that ridiculous disguise," she went on. "Your eyes are a dead giveaway to anyone who's seen you as Abramm."

It came to him in a stunning rush: *She* was the serving maid for Kesrin! The girl who'd brought the tea and couldn't keep her eyes off Abramm. No wonder she'd seemed so familiar. Nor was it surprising he hadn't recognized her—what was the Second Daughter of the Chesedhan king doing in South-dock waiting tables? The answer came immediately: looking for original sources.

"Fire and Torment, woman!" he burst out. "Are no secrets safe from you?" His mind tumbled with revelation upon revelation of what this would mean and what he must do.

"None that I want as badly as I've wanted yours," she said, picking up one of the roses and sniffing it. "Don't worry, though. Your secret is safe with me."

He snorted. "Whyever should I believe that, Lady Madeleine?"

"I suppose you shouldn't." She returned the rose to the pile and looked up at him. "Shall I pack my bags and return to Chesedh, then? Or perhaps you mean to throw me in the Chancellor's Tower."

"I doubt you'd stay there long if I did. And it would ruin all chance of an alliance with our countries, as I'm sure you're aware."

"So you admit it—I have you."

"I admit I don't know what to do about you."

"Tell me your story and you shall have no fear."

"On the contrary, my fears would only grow worse."

He turned away from her, ready to pace, and stopped himself, lest he look more agitated than he already looked. He had no idea what to do, and all he kept hearing was Byron Blackwell's warning. *"She'll promise you discretion one day and the very next be trumpeting the matter to the world."* Maybe Blackwell would know what to do.

"Oh look," she said from behind him. "It's died at last. Now you can put the flowers back."

He came over and peered into the bowl where the staffid lay stretched out, motionless, its colors drained to lifeless gray. He poked it with the dagger, eliciting no response.

She was looking at him again with that keen expression he'd come to dread. "You struck it with the Light, didn't you?"

He sighed and surrendered. "Tried."

"Succeeded I should say."

"It took an awful long time for it to die." He frowned. "Are you trying to distract me, my lady?"

"Believe me, sir, I have no intention of it." She picked up the bowl and gestured at the fireplace. "Do you mind if I get rid of the evidence, though? I've never been able to abide these things."

At his acquiescence, she carried the vessel to the fire and dumped the dead staffid into the flames.

"How long have you been marked?" she asked, setting the bowl back on the desk and beginning to replace the flowers, one by one.

"Four years," he said testily, annoyed anew at the way she had taken command of the conversation.

But now she looked up at him in surprise. "Four years?! I'd have thought surely it had been longer. After all, you slew Beltha'adi—"

"That was Eidon's doing. And not at issue here—"

"So you *do* admit it. You *were* the White Pretender!"

Abramm held on to his temper. "If I may drag your skittish mind back to the subject of concern—you really don't seem to understand the jeopardy in which you have placed yourself."

She concentrated on the flower arrangement taking shape beneath her hands. "If you were Gillard, I would be afraid. But you are not."

He watched her for a moment, then said quietly, "I have killed more men than Gillard ever has, my lady."

And that stopped her. She stared at her hands, now motionless, her face gone pale, bringing the freckles spattering her nose into sharp relief. Finally she started to life again, carefully placing the last three stems of foliage before she looked up, and he saw that all the sparkling banter had left her.

"But you would not kill anyone for this, sir. Nor even, I think, throw them into a tower to shut them up. At least, not those who wish to be your friends."

"And do you wish to be my friend?"

"I already am, whether you know it or not." She smiled thinly. "I had hoped you'd credit me with more intelligence, though. Do you think I don't realize the price that would be paid should word of your shieldmark get out prematurely?"

"It is hard to tell what you realize, my lady. Harder still to tell what you might say."

She gave a small *harrumph* and continued to push and pull at the flowers. "I can keep secrets every bit as well as I can find them, sir."

"Perhaps, but did you give any thought to the fact that unfriendly ears might be listening to this very conversation?"

"Of course. Why do you think we're cloaked?" She glanced over at Jared, who had returned from emptying the water-filled ash bucket, and sat on the chair by the door, his nose, as always, in a book. She grinned at Abramm's startlement. "You didn't even notice!"

He hadn't, and it irked him. It irked him further that he had not thought to cloak them himself, though of course he'd had no inkling of what she meant to discuss until they were in the midst of it. "Very well, I'll concede you showed foresight, but my secrets are such that I can't help asking why you should even want to keep them when you would gain such notoriety spreading them about."

Her hands pressed flat onto the table as she leaned toward him. "Because I serve Eidon, too," she said with quiet intensity. "Because you'll probably marry my sister. And because my people *need* Kiriath's help—as you'll need ours—if we're to survive against the Armies of the Black Moon and the evil that's driving them northward. A threat I believe *you* understand far better than your brother ever will."

He stared at her in astonishment, realizing she grasped what more than half his nobles did not.

She straightened. "Let me tell the story of the White Pretender publicly."

"Haven't you already begun that?" he asked, scowling.

"I mean the way it really happened. Something people will believe."

He turned away from her, struggling with that squirming uneasiness in his belly. "You didn't come here because of Master Getty, did you?"

She was a few moments answering him. "He did send me about the book."

"But you used it an excuse, came right in, even knowing I wasn't receiving visitors, hoping to get me alone for your interview." He turned back to face her, anger rising in him again.

She had interlaced her fingers before her waist once more and was working them back and forth. "I'm sorry if I've overstepped, sir. I figured if I asked openly, you'd turn me down again." She looked up at him, sober faced. "I have nothing but the greatest respect for you, and I believe with all my heart that this story should be told. Your people *need* to hear it."

Just what Haldon had said. Perhaps what Eidon had said to him last night, as well. *"You have a destiny. Are you willing to embrace it?"* Kesrin had asked. *"Will you go forward in the direction he has led you and rest in the knowledge that he'll see you through it?"* And anyway, hadn't Abramm already decided to let her tell this tale when she'd first gotten wind of it? No, he'd decided to let her tell *a* tale, and that by default, since he didn't see any way to stop her. Now she was pressing him for the real story, one that would only be told if he chose to have it so.

He glanced at the tapestry of his coat of arms, the golden shield with its red dragon device gleaming in the lower right quadrant. He'd thought the Pretender was only a brief passing, a part of his larger experience in Esurh, but what if he was more? As the Pretender had been used to rally the Dorsaddi, might he not be used to rally Kiriathans? Maybe he represented something Abramm had not yet discovered, a greater part of his destiny than he could imagine.

Across from him, Madeleine had turned her gaze to the tapestry, as well, and took up his thought as if it were her own. "Your arms bear the truth of who you are, sir," she said. "Designed for you before you were even born— who can deny Eidon's hand in that?" Her eyes came back to his. "They go together, the dragon and the shield. And I think in revealing one, you will smooth the way for revealing the other."

Let me tell it, her expression pleaded. Why was it so difficult for him to yield? Because he truly did fear to embrace it? Because he feared what that would require of him? The sacrifice? The pain and loss? Or was it because he feared he would be unworthy, unable to meet the challenge?

Out in the sitting room, a door banged loudly, breaking into his thoughts.

Angry voices echoed, growing rapidly louder until, to Abramm's astonishment, the study door wrenched open and Lord Prittleman burst into the room, trailed by three of his cronies and a grim-faced Haldon.

"Sir, I apologize for intruding," Prittleman said, "but time is crucial. The longer we wait—" His eyes fell upon Madeleine and narrowed suspiciously. "What is *she* doing here?"

Abramm felt his face flame as the implications of Prittleman's question battered him like debris in a gale: king sleeps late, refuses to rouse even in the face of a murder investigation, only to be surprised in his privy chamber with a young lady of dubious reputation who had sneaked into the royal apartments at an hour far too early to be respectable. Across from him, Madeleine was blushing, as well, clearly having reached the same conclusion. Seeing her discomfort, Abramm's own erupted into fury.

"That is *my* question to ask of you, sir," he replied, his voice rough with the effort of keeping it level. "Barging into my privy chamber uninvited to accuse me to my face of being both inept and immoral? Are you insane, or are you simply so swollen with your own pride you can no longer see your place? I am tempted to throw you into my dungeons to remind you where you stand, and if you dare to speak another word or fail to leave my presence at once—indeed, these entire premises—I swear before Eidon himself that I will do it."

Prittleman's face turned bright red except for his lips, which were white and pressed tightly together. Somehow he managed to keep them that way as he folded himself forward in a quick bow and left.

"Make it known he is unwelcome until further notice," Abramm said to Haldon.

"Yes, sir."

Haldon left them standing there, the king and Lady Madeleine, neither of them able to find their tongue for a few moments. Madeleine, of course, recovered first—she did not likely have this hot rage to wrestle down—but when she spoke, her voice was lower and almost chastened. "My, but you can be downright ferocious when you wish it, sir."

"I cannot abide that man. He sets me off almost worse than my brother does. Especially the way he assumes we are so like-minded. I cannot wait for the day I tell him what I really am." He glanced again at the tapestry of his coat of arms, and suddenly the decision he'd refused to make was made. "You are right, my lady. It is time I told them the story of the White Pretender. At the very least it should keep idiots like Prittleman from barging in on me unannounced. Did you bring something to write on?"

She stared at him wide-eyed and pale-faced. "You wish to do the interview right now, sir?"

"Unless you have some other engagement that requires your attention."

"No, sir. Right now is fine."

23

Four days down from Highmount Holding it was colder than ever, and still nary a flake of snow nor drop of rain to be seen. Carissa's chestnut mare swayed sharply and stepped down hard on the steeply canted trail, bumping into Elayne's mount beside them and banging Carissa's right leg against Elayne's left for perhaps the hundredth time today. The kindling-dry forest loomed close around them, veils of mist shifting between dark pines and pale aspen trunks, the silence echoing with the cracks and thumps and jingles of their passage. Only three men rode ahead of Carissa and Elayne—Cooper on point and two of the five armsmen he'd drafted from New Holding—but even that was too many for comfort. Each planted hoof exploded little puff-balls of powdery silt from the drought-parched ground, raising a cloud of gray dust around them. It coated everything—horses, tack, riders—and even Carissa's hands felt gritty beneath her leather gloves. Worse, she didn't think she would ever get this musty, metallic taste out of her mouth.

Peri, Hogart, and the three additional New Holding men who brought up the rear had it even worse, so she restrained her inclination to complain. The snow would be here soon enough—she hadn't expected to get this far without it—so she might as well cherish the luck while she had it.

No snow, and no Rennalf, either. It had been too much to hope for. Or perhaps, just affirmed Cooper's contention that her former husband had sent the ells for her at Highmount because he was busy elsewhere, hoping to draw her not to a trap in the forest but to the watchtower up the Kolki Pass, with its possible entrance to the Dark Ways. They'd found her stopped at the north gate, after all, not the south. Cooper suspected her nocturnal visitors had planted that fear of a trap in the forest to keep her from doing just what she was doing now. Rennalf, he said, was no doubt scrambling to dispatch agents to intercept her—which was why Coop had pushed them so hard these last four days.

Carissa had doubted him only in his assessment that Rennalf was not actually waiting for her out in the forest, a fear she'd been unable to banish despite knowing the ells had probably implanted it. And while the words of promise spoken by the man in her vision had carried great power at the time, that all seemed like a vague dream now, with no more authority than her own yearnings. For days she'd ridden in abject terror, certain at any moment they would round a bend and find Rennalf's men awaiting them.

But they had not, and once she reached the inn at Raven Rock tonight, she thought perhaps she might finally relax. Rennalf could not stage a kidnapping this deep into Laramor lands without igniting a blood feud, and not even Carissa believed he was that arrogant and foolish. Besides, just having four stout walls around her would do much to ease her anxiety. And with the majority of folk at Raven Rock being Terstan, the combined influence of their Light would protect her from the seductive songs of his ells—at least, that's what Elayne claimed.

They reached the Owl Creek fording around midafternoon, shocked to find yet another sobering evidence of the drought that gripped the land. The mist-hung creek had sunk far down in its banks, exposing boulders and rocks not normally seen. Cooper called a halt so they could drink and wash and refill their water bags and casks. But as the men dismounted, Carissa's neck suddenly crept with the sense of unseen eyes. Uneasily, she scanned the opposite bank, evergreens and aspens looming ghostly in the mist. Except for the noises of her own party, the world lay silent around them, no bird calls, no chattering squirrels, not even the sough of the wind in the trees.

Hogart took her mare, and she swung out of the saddle, joining Peri and Elayne upstream from where the men were watering the horses.

"It's going to snow soon," Elayne announced, gazing at the misty sky as Carissa walked up. "I can smell it."

Carissa glanced at the sky, as well, gave the far wood another uneasy sweep, then set to shaking the dust from her clothing and washing her hands and face. Already crystalline shards of ice congealed along the stream's edge and by the time she finished, her fingers were red and aching with the cold. Swirling her cloak back over her shoulders, she walked over to where Cooper and Hogart were inspecting the road where it entered the water. "Ten or fifteen at most," she heard Hogart say as she joined them.

Cooper grimaced and squinted back up the track.

"Ten or fifteen what?" Carissa asked and saw at once that something was wrong.

Cooper's grimace deepened. "Riders," he said finally, gesturing at the ground. "A sizable troop crossed recently."

Fear dropped upon her like a net. "Heading for Raven Rock?"

"Heading away. And several days ago, from the look of it."

She drew a deep breath. "We're too far south for it to be Rennalf, though, right?"

"Unless he's lost his mind, yes." He kept his voice carefully neutral and now stepped back and around to tell the men accompanying them it was time to go. "Snow'll be on us soon," he said. "I can smell it."

Elayne drew up at Carissa's side, smiling fondly at him, though he didn't notice, occupied now with his preparations. "It'll be all right, my lady," she said quietly, pulling on her gloves. "Eidon will make us a way. You'll see." At that, a puff of wind coursed down the rocky streambed, rustling the evergreens and showering them in fluttering gold leaves shaken loose from the aspen on the riverbank behind them. The world turned briefly golden, and for the first time in days Carissa felt that sense of promise she'd known so briefly back in Highmount, as sure and compelling as it had been that night. *Go to your brother,* a familiar voice breathed in her ear. *He will protect you. . . .* The voice died with the breeze as stillness returned.

She was just about to mount her horse again when she saw the owl, perched on the dead limb of an evergreen. It was one of the great gray ones, earless, round-faced, with large yellow, probing eyes. The moment she looked at it, a vision flashed in her head, something horrific and bloody, but then Elayne stepped between them, even as the orb on her breast grew hot, and the images vanished before she grasped them.

The bird blinked, its head swiveling away, gaze moving over the rest of the company, none of whom had yet seen it. Then it unfolded its great wings and launched into the air, bringing them all around to watch it flap soundlessly up the creek bed into the mist. Silence followed. Then one of the horses snorted and Cooper growled, "We'd better hurry. Weather'll be turning anytime now, and the sooner we reach Raven Rock the better. Make sure you all have your slickers to hand."

He was right about the weather. Barely had they crossed the creek when the wind stirred, and shortly after that, the first flakes fluttered to earth. By late afternoon they were falling steadily, frosting the road and the trees and the crests of the horse's manes. In other circumstances Carissa would have been enchanted, for she had always enjoyed riding in softly falling snow. But now she was cold and wet and feeling grimier than ever, her discomfort bearable only in the knowledge that the inn awaited, with its bath and roast boar and hearth fire. She held those images in her mind, drawing from them not only strength but also the power to ignore the worry at the back of her mind.

Thus when they came around the bend and into the flat beneath the granite formation from which Raven Rock drew its name, she couldn't at first make sense of what she saw. When she did, she wanted to cry.

The village of Raven Rock was no more. In its place stood a lumpy, snow-dusted field from which protruded a few blackened timbers, the charred and tottering remains of one wattle-and-daub wall, and a huge soot-stained stone hearth and chimney—all that remained of the inn itself. There was no one here. No cheery hearth fire, no smiling faces, no warm food, no stout walls to stand against the darkness. Not even a place to take shelter from the storm.

Cooper and Hogart rode a quick circuit of the meadow and the village as the snow continued to fall. Carissa sat her mare and watched them, trying to accept a reality that seemed more like a nightmare, while Peri shivered and made little breathy cries of dismay at her side. The two men returned to confer with Elayne; then Cooper came to Carissa. "We have to move on, my lady. Get as many hours away from here as we can."

His words hardly registered. "How could they have destroyed a whole village this deep into Kiriathan territory?"

"I don't know, lass. But we've no time to speculate. The faster we get you south, the better."

"You think Rennalf had something to do with this?"

"I don't know. I am only sure that he is after us, and I like nothing that has happened this afternoon. That owl . . ." He shook his head. "We've got a few hours of light left and must make the most of them. The snow's not falling hard enough it'll hinder us yet. And the farther down we go, the less of it there'll be. More important, it's chased the birds to roost and the ells to their hollows. And it'll cover our tracks."

His meaning finally penetrated. She stared at him. "You're talking about riding on *now*? Right-this-minute now?"

"Yes."

"But we've been traveling all day—"

"I know." He scanned the lumpy field again, his jaw tightening. He'd lost friends here. His wife had lost family members. "There's a pack trail off this road before too much farther," he went on. "We can take it down to Kerrey and on to Springerlan from there."

"Springerlan!?" Alarm fired through her. "I thought the turnoff to Springerlan wasn't until after we'd gotten out of the Highlands—past Breeton and Aely and Old Woman's Well."

"That's the coach road. This is a pack trail. Traders and trappers use it." He paused to let her absorb that. "Once past Kerrey we'll be in lowlands—free of the snow, away from any of those cursed Dark Ways and out of Balmark's reach."

His reasoning was sound, but her heart constricted all the same. *Springerlan!* She had not expected to have to make this decision so soon. Choosing to flee south, *away* from Rennalf, was not at all the same as choosing to go *to* Abramm in Springerlan, despite the advice of the man in her vision—and the more recent voice at Owl Creek. If anything she'd been leaning toward Elayne's suggestion of wintering in Sterlen. Now she frowned. "Riding down a pack trail in a snowstorm in the middle of the night does not sound like the best idea in the world, Coop. Not as tired as we are. And if the trail loses elevation as rapidly as you say, I can only imagine it's precarious."

Cooper's face revealed that it was. "We wouldn't go down it tonight."

"Tomorrow when it's covered with snow and ice hardly seems better."

He shrugged unhappily. "If you'd rather take the long way through Breeton and down the Goodsprings Valley, fine. But I fear that's the route Rennalf will expect us to take."

"Or he might think I'd fly to Abramm as fast as I can," Carissa countered.

"I'm sure he's aware of how you feel about Abramm, my lady."

The implication of his words jolted her. *Did* he know? If so, he must know her indecision, and thus couldn't be sure what she'd decide at this point. And there was that treacherous trail down to Kerrey to consider, as well. What good would it do to go that way only to fall off the precipitous path to their deaths? And what if the path turned out to be impassable after the storm cleared? They'd have to come back or be stuck there in the middle of nowhere. On the Breeton road there'd be farmhouses to provide food and shelter. Maybe even help if they needed it. They wouldn't have to worry about falling off a cliff, or getting lost . . . clearly it was the only rational choice. Clearly.

She looked up at him and exhaled as decision crystallized. "We'll head for Breeton," she said firmly. After that, well, she'd decide when she had to.

24

"No, no, no!" Dance Master Aubury burst out yet again. "To the left, sir. To the *left*! The first turn's to the right, the second's to the *left*. Let's try it again from the beginning." He glanced over his shoulder at his trio of musicians as Abramm and Leona resumed their starting positions.

"He's enjoying this," Abramm muttered dryly.

"Yes," Leona agreed with a small smile. "I believe he is."

"And make sure you keep your shoulders squared, sir," Aubury added as Abramm held out his right hand for Leona to place hers in. "And your back straight."

They were in the Queen's Ballroom, and it was early on the morning of the Grand Ball of the Harvest, early enough, in fact, to make spectators unlikely, even if all the ballroom doors hadn't been closed and locked. Abramm did not doubt there were those who would count it worth the effort to rise at this outrageous hour to watch him blunder his way through this final practice. And he *was* blundering, no question of that.

Already he'd stepped on the toes of all three ladies who'd turned out this morning to help him, had blanked so badly during the chingipan he'd actually had to follow Leona's lead at one point, and now could not for the life of him remember that it was *Left, you fool! Left!* Not that Aubury would ever call him a fool to his face, or even with his tone. But he knew the man must want to pull his own hair in frustration.

He had three waltzes, a chingipan, and two circle dances—the paquay and the rondella—to know for tonight. The paquay he recalled from childhood, but it was this rondella that was driving them all mad. He wanted to go to the right because all the flow and momentum of the movement carried to the right. But it was part of the dance's eccentricities that demanded he stop that flow at the precise moment when all looked completed and turn to the left, the movement echoed by every other dancer in what would tonight be a large circle of ever-changing partners. "A charming reversal," Master Aubury assured him.

They tried it again, and this time he managed to check himself in time, though while he didn't actually commit left, he still made an awkward bobble. And there must be no awkward bobbles tonight. Especially from the king.

So they did it again. And again.

The horns, loud and brassy in the wood-floored room, were giving him a headache. And the pastry he'd eaten this morning wasn't sitting well, either. He would have been better off eating nothing today, knowing how nervous he would be until this ball was concluded. Ironically, it was not the potential for assassination that distressed him as much as that for social humiliation. He would be watched tonight as he had never been watched before—even as the White Pretender—scrutinized by hundreds of courtiers who'd made it their major tasks in life to observe, catalogue, and evaluate the clothing, manners, mien, and conversation of their peers, especially those peers who outranked them. Their new king, who had come in so brashly and canceled all their parties and games and dances for the last three weeks, would be under especially stringent observation.

It was commonly held that he'd canceled them because he feared to look the fool trying to compete with a court far more sophisticated and erudite than he could ever be. That facing down the Table of Lords and riding into Graymeer's was one thing, but mastering the graces of culture and high society was quite another. He would be judged tonight as harshly as he'd ever been judged.

And all this bungling of the dance merely brought into crystal clarity the fact that of all the things he'd done, he had least confidence in his ability to handle not only chingipan and rondella but all the small talk and double-talk and endless suggestive flirting that awaited him this night. Then there were the rules of etiquette and proper address—so many, so convoluted, they made the rules of the Vaissana's household in Qarkeshan seem simplistic. Fortunately, he had Blackwell to assist him; otherwise he would certainly be lost.

"To the left, sir!"

He switched midstep, *again*, and grimaced apology to Leona.

He never did get it perfect, and finally decreed they had practiced enough and would just have to hope for the best. A bobble in the rondella would not bring down the kingdom, after all. At least he hoped not.

He was surprised to see Lady Madeleine waiting alongside the wall by the door where Jared and Abramm's guards, Will Ames and Philip Meridon, were stationed. She wore a gown of muted burgundy this morning, accented with silver stitching, and clutched a large hide-bound book to her breast, one finger stuck among the pages—a position that made her curtsey somewhat awkward.

"Lady Madeleine," he said, joining her. "I thought we were done with the Suite."

"Oh, we are, Sire. I'm not here about that." She nodded to Leona, still at Abramm's side. He now turned to the young woman himself and, removing her hand from his arm, thanked her for her assistance and bid her good day. She took her leave unwillingly, flashing Madeleine a tight-lipped glare, and he thought it a good thing this was the last practice session. Having a full schedule before him, and already behind on it, he suggested Madeleine walk with him back to his apartments. As they left the ballroom, Jared just a footstep behind him on the left and Will and Philip trailing farther, he sighed with heartfelt relief.

Beside him, she observed wryly, "Rough morning, huh?"

"I'd rather fight with Warbanner. And I don't even want to *think* about tonight."

"You'll do splendidly, sir. It's not as if you are unaccustomed to performing." She glanced aside at him, one slender brow arched. "Or was that back *there* a performance?"

"Believe me," he said grimly, "that was no performance. Maybe I'll just plead the grippe and skip it all."

"You know you can't do that."

"No. It would hardly be fair to Master Aubury or Lady Leona, after all the effort they've put in."

"I'm sure neither of them regrets a moment of it. Aubury gets the pleasure of being able to order his king around, and Leona . . ." She paused. "She certainly does have her eye on you, sir."

"Indeed." He clasped his hands at his back as they started up the corridor, gray morning light flooding through the line of double doors running along its left side.

"And yet she seems unaware that her interest is not returned."

He looked sideways at her, amused. "And you are not unaware?"

"*Is* her interest returned?"

"No. Though I'm sure she has set herself to change that."

"With little hope of succeeding, I trust."

Again he fixed her with his gaze, partly annoyed, partly amused. "And how is that any of *your* affair, my lady?"

She lifted her chin and said primly, "I am only looking out for Chesedh's interests, sir." An errant tendril of fawn-colored hair dangled against her cheek.

"I thought that was the ambassador's job."

"Cheede? He can barely manage to sugar his tea!"

He burst out laughing. "My lady!"

"Well, you've met him. Muttering and peering at the furniture. He reminds me of a mole." She tucked the errant tendril behind her ear with her free hand, still clutching the big book with the other. "He hasn't a clue what's going on, and certainly has no intent of working anything to advantage. The only reason he was sent—oh, never mind." She paused, cocking a brow at Abramm's laughter. "I have amused you, sir?"

"Your pardon, my lady." He restrained himself and indicated she should continue.

"In any case," she said, "I stand ready to do my best to discourage any lady who happens to spark your interest."

"I hate to think what that would entail." As they reached the end of the corridor and turned left, he added, "Thankfully none of them have sparked my interest yet."

"And you wanted them all to know it, so you chose me to be your partner for the Suite tonight. Don't think I haven't figured that out."

"I had every confidence you would." He glanced down at her sidelong, his bantering mood turned abruptly serious. "I did want to speak to you about that, though. . . . I had no idea the gossip would be as vile as it's been."

"For which we can thank Lord Prittleman, I believe."

"And the debut of your new song the other night. It will only worsen from here. If you'd rather I find another partner, I'm happy to oblige you."

She lifted her chin again, and the tendril of hair dropped against her cheek. "I will only withdraw at your direct command, sir. As for the gossips, I would never give them the pleasure of believing they had chased me off."

"You don't care at all what they think, do you?"

She tucked back the tendril. "I learned long ago that caring only makes you miserable. People don't like it when you're different. You can change to be like them, or fret about their criticism—or accept who you are and go your way." She glanced up at him. "It seems to me you've done your share of that yourself."

"Never so consciously. And *I* can't leave them and go my way."

"Which is why I am grateful I will never be a king." She lifted her chin in that prim way of hers and faced forward again. "Or a queen, for that matter. It's Eidon alone I serve, not people."

"And yet often it is in serving people that we serve him."

She frowned slightly, keeping her gaze fixed on the vast, gleaming hall before them. "Well, thankfully he's already shown me how he wants me to serve him."

"Ah yes." Abramm returned to the bantering tone. "Running about sticking your nose into other people's business."

The frown returned more deeply now.

"Only a jest, my lady," he said, grinning. "You can't deny it—so, please, do not take offense." He waved a hand at her. "Why are you holding your finger in that book?"

She looked down at it. "Oh. I wanted to show you this picture I found. It seems like it might be a match for that monster you found painted on the wall down in Graymeer's."

She laid the open volume in his hands. The bottom half of the left page displayed an engraving of a huge beast with powerful shoulders and tapering hindquarters. A spiky bristle of hair sprouted from head and shoulders, framing the doglike snout and wicked teeth. Its one visible eye had been starred with white lines as if to make it glow. Just looking at it raised the hackles on the back of Abramm's neck.

"This is it," he said, turning his attention to the text above and beside it. "What is it?"

"A morwhol. A few pages earlier there's a story about some border lord who made it to slay a rival. After ravaging a good number of the rival's kinfolk, the beast killed the rival himself, then was recaptured by its maker and caged. For years afterward he used the threat of its release to ensure his people's obedience."

"A man made it, you say?"

"Yes, sir. In the end, the thing escaped and turned on him—killed him and all his kin—then lived on in the area for some time after, a danger to all who strayed too near."

"And I suppose it's still up there to this day," Abramm suggested wryly.

"No. It finally died, though the narrative doesn't say how. In fact, the implication is it can't be killed. At least not by natural means."

He frowned at her, then flipped to the title page: *Tales of the Highland Lords*.

"I haven't read the whole book," she said, "so there may be something more. And I don't know how much of what's in it to believe. Some of it's pretty wild."

He went back to the picture. Made to slay the rival in a blood feud, she'd said. Rhiad's accusations of heresy had apparently failed, so if he was as committed to revenge as he claimed, why wouldn't he try something else? And if the rumors were true about him having made the kraggin, why not one of these morwhols? The mad Mataian's words still haunted him. *"Do you like him? You will meet him soon. And what you took from me, he will take from you."* Abramm shuddered, realizing for the first time that Rhiad might be more dangerous than he'd thought; more dangerous even than Gillard.

Lady Madeleine was staring up at him with a bemused look, and he realized she had asked him something. "I beg your pardon, my lady?"

"I was just wondering where you got that ring?"

"This?" He lifted his right hand from the book. "It's my signet."

"No, the one on your left hand. Coiled around your index finger."

He looked at it, puzzled, for he didn't recall even seeing it before, much less putting it on. "I guess Haldon brought it out with the other clothes."

"You guess? Do you have nothing to say about it, then? You just let them dress you like a doll?"

"Well, hardly like a doll."

"I've never seen you wear it before."

"Are you keeping catalog of my apparel now, too, Lady Madeleine?"

"No, but this is . . . your pardon, my lord, but it is singularly ugly."

"It's a family heirloom."

She frowned up at him. "A moment ago you didn't seem to know *what* it was."

"Is this all you came about?" He closed the book and handed it over. "If so, you'd best get back to your business. Let me know if you learn any more about this morwhol creature."

To her credit, Madeleine knew a dismissal when she heard one. "Yes, sir. Of course, sir." She dropped a curtsey and he continued on alone.

But once she was gone, he looked at the ring again and admitted she was right: it *was* ugly. And how *did* he know it was a family heirloom when he could recall no family member ever having worn it? He felt he should probably examine that question but found he had no interest, and a moment later his thoughts ran off to other more compelling subjects.

Trap Meridon was waiting in the sitting room when he arrived, returned from what Haldon had said was an "urgent mission." Now the first thing he did as they came together was to flick a hand, producing a drift of music and a tingle of Light as the cloak that would protect them from unfriendly ears settled around them. Abramm noted it and cocked an expectant brow. "What's this about?"

"Remember how Kesrin told you the night you revealed yourself to him that one of the peers needed to know your secret? One who was probably being put off from you by the rhu'ema just as Kesrin was?"

"I've been wondering what came of that."

"Kesrin only made contact with the man a couple of days ago. I guess they'd had a falling out. For the same reason, it turns out, that the man's been so hostile toward you—someone put a ring staffid on him the very day you arrived. If that tells you anything about his importance in all of this."

Abramm leaned his backside against the nearest divan and folded his arms. "So did Kesrin tell you this man's name?"

"Yes, sir. In fact, I've just come from the man's flat. He's been sporesick for days, telling everyone it's the grippe." Half the court had fallen victim to the ailment in the last two weeks, and all blamed Abramm's picnic—not because they'd been drenched on their way home, but because they believed it was part of the curse that had been loosed by his ill-advised intrusion into Graymeer's. The epidemic seemed largely over now, though a few still—

"Khrell's Fire!" Abramm cried, coming forward onto both feet as all the pieces fell together. "It's Ethan Laramor, isn't it?" The man was a border lord, sprung from a culture in which everyone hated Mataians and a large minority were Terstan; whose own lands were crossed by the Terstan underground on its way to the Kolki Pass in the Aranaak; who'd been irreconcilably hostile toward Abramm from the start and was said to be actively supporting Gillard; and who had been very sick now for almost a week.

Trap smiled grimly. "Very good, sir. He is absolutely flailing himself for his error—would've renounced his clan lordship and sent himself into exile had Kesrin and I not dissuaded him." He paused, his eye catching on Abramm's hands, the right slowly twisting the ring on his left.

Noting the direction of his gaze, Abramm stopped the movement and lowered his hands, feeling a mild irritation. He half expected his friend to comment, but Trap went on with his tale, relating how, in the attempt to make amends, Laramor had confirmed their own predictions of what Gillard had planned for tonight. The attack would come during the Autumn Suite, with two knife-throwers, only one of whom knew about the other. They'd be striking in close succession from different positions, since the chaos that would arise after even one attack would preclude any further attempts.

"Unless they want to get in close," Abramm pointed out.

"Laramor said no. One of them has refused to go anywhere near you. Apparently he heard about the man who tried to kill you in your bedchamber last week and does not hold with Gillard's contention that he failed because he was inept."

Stunned by Abramm's unexpected skill with a blade, the bedchamber assailant had been easily disarmed. Stunned in his turn by the golden shield glittering between the edges of his attacker's leather jerkin, Abramm had let the man escape.

"The problem is," Trap went on, "Laramor's been out of touch with the plotters for days now. The plans could well have changed, especially with all this talk of Lady Madeleine's new song—about you being the White Pretender and all." He was frowning again, for he'd not been pleased with the timing of the song's debut. Better, he said, to have waited until after the ball. "If the men Gillard's got lined up were already uneasy because of the tales your bedchamber assailant told, they might quit altogether if faced with the prospect of going after the Pretender."

Abramm rolled his eyes and went back to lean against the divan. "Nobody really believes I'm him, though, and you know it. They all think I paid her to write the thing, and I can't imagine Gillard's thugs turning down the kind of money he must be offering because of some crazy rumor."

"Well," Trap said, "it will certainly make our lives easier if you're right." His gaze caught again on Abramm's ring, which Abramm was again stroking, and this time he stepped closer to get a better look at it.

Abramm dropped his hands and stepped back from him. "Yes, Madeleine has already informed me of how ugly it is."

Meridon looked up at him, puzzlement moving toward suspicion. "Where did you get it, sir? I don't think I've ever seen it before."

"It's a family heirloom."

"An heirloom." Trap glanced up at him. "Are you sure?"

"Of course I'm sure!" Abramm snapped. "And why are you even asking me about it? My selection of accessories is hardly your concern."

Meridon regarded him uneasily. "My lord, according to his description, Ethan Laramor wore an ugly ring very much like that one. He wore it for almost three weeks, in fact, without realizing what it was."

A squall of horror blew through Abramm, quickly squelched by incredulity. "You think this is a *ring staffid*?" He held up his hand.

"Take it off and we'll see."

But Abramm was already turning away from him. "Ridiculous! I know a staffid when I see one. And I'm certainly not going to pick one up and put it on."

"You might if it was delivered to you personally."

"So now you're saying I'm not only stupid and blind, I'm also a witless fool?"

"I said no such thing, my lord! Why are you taking such offense?"

"I'm not taking offense. Fire and Torment, man! It's just an ugly heirloom."

Trap met his ire stolidly, his face blank, his voice quietly calm. "If so, sir, then you should have no trouble taking it off."

"My wrist always starts tingling whenever I'm near them, and it's doing nothing of the kind. Besides, you of all people know how sick spore makes me."

"Some spore is subtle, and some types of staffid have auras that are almost undetectable, especially to those not well skilled in the Light."

"Now you're saying I'm not well skilled in the Light?"

"Oh, for crying out loud, Abramm!" Trap exclaimed, patience finally worn through. "Just show me you can take the blasted thing off and we'll be done with it."

"How dare you speak to me like that!"

"I dare because I am responsible for your safety!" Trap wrestled his temper back under control, his voice softening. "I am your liegeman sworn, sir, and your friend. And this uncharacteristic temper of yours is only confirming my fears. All I'm asking you to do is take it off for a moment. After that, I'll bear whatever punishment you deem just."

Abramm glared at him, mollified but still feeling obstinate and violated. Yet he could not deny the reasonableness of Meridon's request. Nor the peculiarity of his own fit of pique over it. "Oh, very well." He yanked the ring off, slid it back on again, and then looked up defiantly. "Now can we go on?"

Trap's gaze bored into his own. "You didn't take it off, my lord. You didn't even touch it."

Abramm's protest died in his throat as he realized Trap was right. So he tried again, forcing himself to take hold of it, and, very deliberately, pull it off his finger. Illusion told him he had. Feel told him it was still on his hand. And the moment he realized his eyes were deceiving him, the illusion vanished, and there was the ring—an opalescent gray-green spiral, coiled around the entire first joint of his left index finger.

He began to tug in desperation, panic arising in tandem with the compulsion to give up—and even now to hope it wasn't what he feared.

"Let him do the work," Trap murmured.

The admonition brought him up short. *Yes, you are trying to do it yourself. . . .*

Deliberately, Abramm drew a deep breath, confronting the panic and rejecting it as he turned his thoughts toward the One behind the Light. Immediately a sharp pain shot up his arm and he felt the prickle of hard insect legs against the soft skin on the sides of his finger. Then the thing gave way. Revolted, he tossed it onto the end table. As it landed, the Light tingled through him, leaping unbidden from his finger to strike the spawn in a tiny bolt of white. Struggling to right itself, the creature arched back at the blow, writhed in one last corkscrewing convulsion, and stilled.

Rubbing his now-tingling finger, Abramm stared at it, the chagrin of being wrong offset by the surprise of having struck the thing with Light—when he hadn't even thought to do so. It seemed his practice had paid off, though he had no idea if he could guarantee the same results next time. And now the chagrin was renewed as he recalled his protest that he was not unskilled in the Light—a blatant self-delusion if ever there was one.

"How long do you think you were wearing it?" Trap asked quietly.

With a sigh Abramm dropped into the chair beside the table. "I don't know. Since this morning, maybe."

"Do you remember how you got it?"

"Someone did give it to me—I remember that. But not who and not when." He looked up. "So it *was* deliberate."

"You've known from the beginning they would be close to you, seeking to hinder or control you."

Yes. He knew it. It was just too easy to forget it when he couldn't see them or feel them, and he had all these human enemies to contend with. Human enemies who were, in the end, merely pawns of his real antagonists.

"Did you give Jared the orb yet?" asked Trap.

"Jared!" Abramm's head came up in surprise. "You think it's *him*?"

"I don't think he's possessed. But he's already been used once. You haven't given it to him, have you?"

"Not yet. I've been distracted. And . . . frankly I'm not sure he'll accept it." *And if he doesn't, I'll have to send him away.* He poked at the dead staffid on the table, pushing it around on the waxed surface, then sighed. "I'll give it to him this afternoon."

Meridon nodded, then went on to ask him what he wanted to do about the ball, seeing as it couldn't be an accident this thing had come to him today. "Whoever did this probably knows of your sensitivity and hopes to incapacitate you enough you won't be able to defend against Gillard's attackers tonight."

"Or else scare me into backing out altogether."

Trap's glance flicked up to his, discerning Abramm's unspoken intention at once.

"I feel fine," Abramm told him. "And you said it took Laramor three weeks to get sick. I've only been exposed a few hours and can't have picked up more than a trace."

"Even a trace can waken the rest."

"But it's not wakened, that's the point. If it does, we'll reconsider. But for now—plagues, Trap! Gillard's practically delivered himself into my hands. And anyway, if I don't attend, think what that'll do to me politically. The peers are irked enough that I've canceled all their other parties. And pleading illness?" He shook his head. "It won't do. Even if I really did feel bad, I'd have to go."

Trap did not give up easily, either, but in the end Abramm prevailed. The ball would go on as planned, and they would trust Eidon to see them through it.

———

Later that day, Abramm found a moment to speak to Jared alone. Having sent the other servants away, he called the boy to his desk, where, riffling through the various parchments and papers, he retrieved a gray-bound book which he offered to the boy. "Since you enjoyed the *Aerie* books so well, I thought you might like this."

"*Blue Mountain!*" Jared's eyes went wide and he took the volume reverently. "This is the one you told me about, isn't it? Thank you, Your Majesty!"

As he had promised that first night, Abramm had found the sequel to *Alain's Aerie* and presented it to the boy. Jared had taken it wide eyed and pale faced, struggling to get out a thank-you. But the next day he had appeared at his duty post with his brown locks cropped close in obvious imitation of Abramm's own, and from then on Abramm had become increasingly aware of how the boy hung upon his words and hovered about him in hopes of performing some service, his admiration and deference bordering on worship. He was counting on the depth of that regard to serve them both now.

Already starting to open the book, the boy remembered himself and dropped it to his side. "Will that be all, sir?"

"No. I have something else, as well. Something a little more important." Fighting a twinge of guilt at having so shamelessly maneuvered the boy into a position of gratitude, he extracted a small leather pouch from his pocket and gave it over.

Inside was the Star of Life Abramm had instructed Trap to have set into a chain, its light blazing brightly across the boy's palm.

Jared looked up at him. "What is this, sir?"

"What does it look like?"

"A white pebble on a chain."

A white pebble? Well, that's encouraging.

The boy's brows were drawn together in obvious perplexity as he dangled the orb before him. "Is it a gift for my mum?" His tone said he would find an affirmative to be completely incomprehensible.

"No, Jared. It is for you, if you agree to take it. It will protect you from the staffid. And other things. You should wear it under your tunic, and never take it off."

Jared lifted the orb with his free hand to examine it more closely. "What sort of other things, sir? Feyna?"

"Those. And lost old men who bid you do things you don't remember doing."

Jared's face fell, and he looked at the floor, so intensely and immediately shamed by the memory, Abramm regretted having to bring it up again.

The evening of his return from Graymeer's, Abramm had asked the boy about the queue of hair he'd been sent to burn with Abramm's reeking Dorsaddi robes. Jared swore he had burned both and that, even though he'd had to go all the way to the kitchen to find a fire on that warm afternoon, no one had delayed him nor questioned him on his way. Indeed the only person who even spoke to him was an old underservant who'd strayed above his station and gotten lost.

Quietly indignant at the very idea he might have given such a creature the queue of royal hair, Jared had also admitted to having no clear recollection of casting it into the fire, either. When Abramm had gently explained that he believed the boy had been put under Command, Jared was horrified.

"I told you that wasn't your fault," Abramm said now. "So don't you go studying your feet again."

Slowly the brown head came up.

Abramm gestured toward the orb on its chain. "This will help protect you from him and others of his kind."

Jared's eyes darted toward it. But still he did not put it on and, after a long moment, asked quietly, "Is it a Terstan thing, sir?"

"It is."

"And will it put a shield on me?"

"I told you, Jared, the shield only comes to those who desire it and freely choose to accept it."

"Do I have to wear it?"

"No." He hesitated to say this next, but knew that he must. "However, if you would rather not, I must find you another assignment. I cannot afford to have one so close to me who is not protected."

"Yes, sir. I understand, sir." He squared his jaw and drew a deep breath, then shook open the chain and dropped it over his head, threading the orb underneath his white shirt.

His eyes came up to meet those of his king, his look one of a proud determination to serve no matter the cost, a look that sent a chill racing up Abramm's back and put a lump in his throat. *Oh, my Lord Eidon, if only I can be worthy of his regard.*

"Thank you," he said to the boy. "That will be all."

25

"Oh, come, Gwynne," said Lady Jenevieve Harrady. "The king only chose Lady Madeleine to keep the field open. You can't imagine he'd really be interested in *her*."

Lady Gwynne Worslen, whom Simon had escorted to the ball this night, sniffed and waved her lace hankie. "I'm not saying *that*, only that he could've picked a Kiriathan lass by lot if he doesn't want to choose a favorite yet. It *is* the Autumn Suite after all. The honor should go to Kiriath not Chesedh." Gwynne, thick-waisted, white-wigged, and wrinkled with age, was ten years a widow, and old school, like Simon. She had never trusted the Chesedhans and never would.

They stood near their assigned places at the head of the wide King's Court stairway, surrounded by the highest lords and ladies of the land. A gauntlet roped off in red velvet led to the king's apartments, from which Abramm would shortly emerge to start the procession for this year's Grand Ball of the Harvest. In the court below, a chamber orchestra provided music composed by Roemert, the strains of his Seventh Concerto underlying the rumble of conversation while servants mingled amidst the nobles, bearing trays of appetizers and glasses of watered white wine.

"Ladies, ladies," said Harrady, standing to Gwynne's left. "You're forgetting how handsomely the Second Daughter has paid him for this privilege."

"Aye," Gillard agreed, resplendent in a doublet of cloth of gold. He glanced down at the buxom Lady Amelia, hanging on his arm. "What's it been now, four times in the last week already?" He grinned salaciously at the others. "If our formerly celibate king is not careful, we'll end up with a Chesedhan bastard on our hands. Which will be a lot worse than a few turns about the dance floor."

Gwynne sniffed again. "I cannot believe he could be enamored of her. She is so plain and so . . . forward. As well as being Chesedhan."

"He's been a slave so long," said Gillard, "he probably needs a forward woman."

As the others laughed at his joke, Simon managed to keep the scowl off his face and plucked a bite-sized rusk mounded with scarlet roe from a silver tray as a servant bore it past. Popping the morsel into his mouth, he turned his attention to the vast court at the bottom of the stair where the lesser nobility and wealthy freemen had gathered in a sea of silk and feathers and sparkling jewels. There were wigs galore, and walking sticks, and the hideous and silly-looking pear-bottomed breeches—but among them were sprinkled an increasing number who had taken their cue from the new king and dispensed with the frippery to echo his more conservative tastes.

Simon detested gossip in all its forms but especially that which he knew to be untrue. Since the day that stick Prittleman had burst uninvited into the king's private chambers and had been banned from the palace indefinitely, he had enthusiastically revenged himself by spinning out ugly accusations, one of which was that he'd surprised the king in bed with Lady Madeleine that morning. Gossipmongers had seized upon the tale and run with it. It had not helped matters that Abramm had taken to retiring at seven-thirty most evenings, refusing to receive visitors for any reason. Simon had asked him bluntly yesterday morning whether they need worry about any half-Chesedhan offspring, and Abramm had heatedly denied having any such relationship with Lady Madeleine, declaring that she would never consent to such a thing, and nor would he, that Prittleman was a pox-mouthed liar, and that he would thank Simon not to contribute further to that vicious rumor. It had taken him a while to regain his composure, after which he apologized for his harsh words and his own unfair accusation.

Now, listening to Gillard and the others joke about it, Simon wanted to walk away, or at least offer a word in Abramm's defense. But his relationship with Gillard was strained enough these days, and he wouldn't make it worse over something so petty as the vulgar gossip of the court. Especially since more than half the nobles on this balcony were saying the same things.

Realizing after his conversation with Laramor that Gillard needed to hear other opinions besides those of a fanatical border lord, and that Simon was doing the boy no favors by shutting him out, he had forced himself to pay a visit to the crown prince three days ago. It had been a prickly encounter, very similar to the one he'd had with Laramor. Hurt and bitter, Gillard had accused Simon of having been bought off and refused to believe that Abramm was committed to the plan he'd proposed—that he was even capable of being so, in fact. The king's sole purpose in all this, he'd claimed, was to ruin and humiliate Gillard himself. Simon had bitten his tongue before the conversation had gotten out of hand, striving to convince Gillard as gently as he could that Simon had not abandoned him, that he did *not* care more about Abramm than he did Gillard, and that his sole consideration was the good of Kiriath. He wasn't sure how much of it got through, but at least by the end Gillard had stopped arguing and begun to listen sulkily. And had invited Simon to attend the pre-ball party he had hosted at Harrady's estate the other night, an affair Simon had attended primarily to prove he was neither ignoring nor avoiding Gillard, nor had he "gone over" to Abramm. When he left, he thought he'd been moderately successful.

Tonight he was no longer sure. Gillard had been tense and cool toward him from the moment he'd arrived, unable to speak without mocking or criticizing his brother. Just now he and his companions had launched yet another round of ridicule for Lady Madeleine's preposterous song about the Esurhite slave-turned-gladiator/hero, the one so obviously modeled upon Abramm. Mawkishly fawning, disgustingly overdone, and a sheer flight of fantasy they'd dubbed it. If the kraggin tale had strained credibility, this one burst all bounds of reason, so outrageous it was laughable. And while Lady Amelia contended that writing it had been part of Lady Madeleine's payment for the privilege of dancing in the Autumn Suite, Gillard argued that the *king* had paid *her* to create it. "He needs to capitalize on the kraggin thing, after all. Keep his hero status going."

"Especially after that fiasco at Graymeer's," added Harrady. "Though I can't imagine who he thought would believe it."

"Frankly he would have done better with Graymeer's," Gillard said, "although I have to say that the Pretender title's certainly appropriate."

A commotion at the far end of the gallery cut into their laughter, and conversation echoed into silence as Blackwell emerged from the royal apartments, list in hand. Simon grabbed another roe-piled rusk and ate it as the ordering of the procession began. By the time the King's Court clock had finished striking eight, the nobles were all in their spots and a herald exited the King's Suite to proclaim Abramm's advent. The orchestra burst into fanfare as first came the royal attendants, then Abramm himself, clad in a clean-lined, close-fitting doublet of deep blue brocade, stitched with thin, vertical lines of gold. As usual, his only concessions to the glory of his position were the golden circlet on his brow, the five gold chains of his kingly rank looped across his chest, and a trimming of diamonds on his deep-blue satin cloak. He'd also consented to replace his worn rapier scabbard with a finely tooled, gold-chased sheath more in keeping with his status. And he'd clearly won the rumored tussle over the long cloak with train that Raynen had instigated as part of royal formal wear—Abramm's dark cloak fell no farther than his hips.

He advanced slowly, mindful of the dignity of his position, greeting first Gillard, then Simon, then the high lords after them. He had been well coached, though Simon sensed he was nervous for perhaps the first time since his return. Even so he conducted this initial portion of the procession flawlessly, and they started off, down the stair, across the King's Court, and along the Hall of Mirrors to the Grand Ballroom, Simon following on his right, Gillard on his left.

The ballroom's four crystal chandeliers filled the vast chamber with light. Oak-leaf garlands draped the walls, entwined with masses of red, gold, and russet autumn flowers. More flowers decked the tens of buffet tables lining the perimeter of the vast marble floor, accented by the traditional wheat sprays, crimson-spiked fire gourds, and brown shepherd's bowl. Among these sat countless platters of meat cakes, sandwiches, pasties, plum coudles, grapes, fruits cut into all manner of shapes, and crimped and curled candies and chocolates.

They were met at the edge of the dance floor by the ladies chosen to dance the various waltzes with the king, Lady Madeleine among them, looking her plain and pained self—these affairs were not to her liking—a sad contrast to Lady Leona, who, having drawn the honor of being Abramm's first partner, stepped forward into a graceful curtsey. As always the sight of her caught at Simon's heart for the way she resembled her mother, especially in that russet gown, its décolletage filled with a necklet of diamonds and sapphires, her flaxen curls piled elegantly atop her head. She looked up at Abramm with open adoration as he took her hand and complimented her beauty, while those in their periphery smiled and traded speculative glances. The couple started toward the dance floor, and from the far corner, the orchestra burst into an introductory fanfare. Traditionally the king and queen—or king and his lady—danced the first round of this opening piece, to be joined by the other attendees on the second. The guests hurried to find their places around the silver-and-white marble floor.

Anticipation intensified. At Simon's side, Lady Gwynne caught her breath. Her old friend Lady Jenevieve rested a hand on her arm and watched with keen attention. Even Simon felt a fascination for what would happen next, interest piqued by the rampant rumors of Abramm's bungling efforts at practice this morning. But those who expected the former Guardian-slave to be tentative and uncertain were disappointed. Abramm led Leona to the center of the marble ring with a confidence that belied his religious past, and at precisely the right moment he moved into action, sweeping her dramatically around the floor, as graceful and sure of himself as if he had had years of practice.

At Simon's side, Lady Gwynne sighed. "Goodness. He's exquisite. Who would have believed it?"

"He ought to be," Gillard said acidly. "He spent weeks practicing."

Abramm and Leona completed their portion of the dance and returned to floor center, finishing with a flourish perfectly timed to the music's end. The chamber filled with the rising sound of the onlookers' murmurs of approval, then the rustle of hundreds of satin skirts and trousers as the other dancers joined the king to complete the second half of the dance. After that, judging his obligations to Gwynne fulfilled, Simon left her and Jenevieve deep in their analysis of the king's performance, his dress, his manner, the way he had received Leona—"*I don't believe she has a chance of winning his heart, Jen!*"—and a host of other minutia Simon could not imagine even thinking about, much less dissecting and debating in endless conversation. Nor was Gwynne's and Jenevieve's the only such conversation here tonight. All around him the ladies eyed their new king and compared notes on their observations. It was times like these Simon was truly thankful he'd never been in line for the crown, for he knew he would never be able to bear such scrutiny.

He wandered around for a while, visited with a few friends, and finally found himself on the mezzanine overlooking the dance floor. The two side loges had been closed and darkened, leaving only the front balcony open. For not the first time he thought there were too few royal guard in attendance tonight—although Abramm had already gained a reputation for being difficult when it came to matters of his safety. Not only did he tend to take blatant risks—the trip to Graymeer's, for example—but he was also given to riding alone and rowing alone, and he absolutely refused to go about surrounded by a cadre of guards.

But he always wore that sword. And the dagger, too, Simon had noted the other day. Sheathed on the right where his left hand could draw it, instead of at his back, where most right-handers kept theirs. If they kept one at all. For where the sword was yet a piece of fashion, the dagger was not.

He found himself thinking of that song of Lady Madeleine's again, toying with the possibilities, recalling her question the day of the picnic as to why Abramm had gone from scribe to galley slave. She was right: it was an unlikely transition. Unless the man who owned him had suddenly become aware that he had in his possession no mere scribe but the crown prince of Kiriath. A slave who, even if he died in his first game, would still bring in much money, and who, if he didn't, would be very profitable indeed. There was the matter of the red dragon that had been burned into Abramm's arm, as well, a device Madeleine claimed was the brand of the same prominent gamer as owned the White Pretender of her song. . . .

Reason overtook him then, and laughing at himself for entertaining such ridiculous thoughts, he put them aside, aware once again of the anxiety that weighed increasingly on his spirit. It was as if something terrible was going to happen tonight, though what it might be, he did not know.

Below, the dancers swirled in intricate, ever-changing patterns, Gillard shining among them in his golden doublet. Tall and regal, he glittered in and out of the line of ladies that passed through his arms and into those of the next man in line. On the surface he seemed relaxed, smiling, sometimes even laughing as he moved through the repeating cycles of the dance. But Simon perceived the tension in him; he looked like a man about to do battle, and his gaze strayed repeatedly across the circle to the dancers moving opposite him, where Abramm, no less striking, also met, danced with, and passed on the cycling progression of ladies.

Well, of course it must be hard for Gillard to be here, to go through the motions as if nothing were amiss, when the bitterness of being cast out of the starring role for this evening was surely eating at him. Especially so since Abramm had not been the bungling fool his detractors had hoped, but was, in fact, carrying it all off quite well. Too well, perhaps. For in one way, Gillard was right: all the admiration and acclaim that had but a month ago gone to him was now being directed toward Abramm. Not because Abramm was taking it; because he was *earning* it. That was what Gillard didn't see. Maybe couldn't see.

And maybe that was what was making Simon so uneasy. In their talk last week, he had not brought up the question of Gillard's involvement in the continued attempts on Abramm's life. Perhaps because he'd wanted to believe Gillard had kept true to his promise to desist. Now, as with every other conclusion he'd come to that day, he wasn't sure, and wondered if he really knew his nephew anymore. *But surely he wouldn't try to kill his own brother.*

Simon blinked and gripped the balustrade before him, startled by his own thought, and then revolted by it. *No, he wouldn't do that. Much as he hates Abramm, much as he hates being supplanted, he wouldn't do that.*

But what if he does? Then what will you do?

A thump and a muffled clatter drew his eye to the loge on his left where the guard so recently standing at the rail had momentarily left his post. Given the nature of Simon's thoughts, it was not surprising he would see the absence as ominous, but then the curtain at the back swayed and here was the man back again, straightening his uniform jacket and taking up his post, his gaze trained alertly at the dancers below. Or, more precisely, on the king he was sworn to guard, who'd just settled on his throne at the far side of the dance floor to receive the respects of his courtiers, the line of them snaking around the side of the dance floor. Probably just a simple shift change.

Then again, it would be easy to steal a uniform and come up here, kill the real guard and take his place. Or even buy off one of the men already so employed. With loyalties as confused as they were these days, it might not take much to persuade a man he was serving the true king and not the pretender.

Below, Abramm continued to chat with his nobles, Captain Channon standing guard to his right, Will Ames to his left. Across the floor from him,

Gillard stood with Lady Amelia on his arm again, laughing with Matheson and Moorcock. Ives, it seemed, was not in attendance tonight, though perhaps Simon simply hadn't spotted him yet. As Gillard's biggest supporter, it would be unlike him to miss the biggest social event of the year. Unless, of course, he was sick.

Simon looked at the guard again and a chill of foreboding swept over him. For a moment he stood there, thinking he really needed to do something. Then, realizing he was being paranoid, he laughed it off and went to find the food.

26

As the smiling, smarmy Lord Denniston bowed his exit from Abramm's presence and the next peer approached to take his place, the king glanced up at the darkened loge again. The missing guard had returned to his station seemingly without incident. Abramm ran his eye across the balcony to the opposite loge and the other guard, noting the straight-backed, gray-haired figure leaning against the balustrade between the two loges. Simon was looking toward the wandering guard himself, and Abramm wondered again if he knew about the plot. Laramor said not, but Simon had recently mended the breach in his relationship with Gillard. Was it coincidence that it had happened shortly before this attack of Gillard's was to take place?

It didn't help that Abramm himself still didn't know where he stood with his uncle. While Simon had done everything Abramm asked with full effort and efficiency and perfect decorum, he had maintained his cool professionalism. Possibly Abramm's own directness regarding the man's loyalties had something to do with that. He knew he'd not improved relations between them when he'd forced his uncle to betray Gillard's involvment in the assassination attempt in the royal preserve. Nor did he doubt that part of the reason Simon had avoided Gillard these last two weeks was so he wouldn't have anything to report should Abramm ask him for such information again.

Then again, most likely the guard really was just a guard, not the assassin in disguise Abramm's jumpiness was making him. Channon had kept the possibility of an attack close to his chest, and by Abramm's order had assigned only a minimum of obvious guards for the affair—although many of the usual servants were enjoying some unexpected time off this night, replaced by men whose swords were concealed in back-mounted scabbards under their tabards.

Abramm received a few more of the peers, including several young ladies put forth by their fathers and brothers for his consideration, and when he looked up again, Simon was gone. Then the orchestra signaled it was time for the paquay, and couples formed up, all of them selected by rank or lot for this honor. This was a dance Abramm had learned before he'd taken his First Vows in the Mataio, and after a year of almost daily practice, it was one he felt completely confident with. Instead of maneuvering around each other with a complicated series of steps and passes, this one had only a small number of steps, turning each couple in unison as they all revolved around the floor in a great circuit. Once they had completed two circuits, the couples split, each finding a new partner as in the rondella and dayard.

Abramm's first partner was the shy young daughter of the Count of Runningvale. Probably not more than fourteen, she was overwhelmed at finding herself in the arms of her king and could hardly speak, even when asked a direct question. After the first few turns, he gave up and they completed the round in silence.

And then, here came his next partner, twirled off the hands of the first man into his own. He recognized her with a mixture of surprise, relief, and trepidation, for it was Lady Madeleine.

They had barely come together, however, when he realized something was wrong. She was cool, clipped, and kept her gaze fixed over his shoulder. Surely she wasn't still miffed at the way he had dismissed her this morning.

As they finished their first turn he said, "Something has disturbed you."

Her lips tightened a bit; then she tilted her chin up and finally looked him in the eye. "I understand you expect there to be an attack upon you tonight."

He just kept himself from gaping at her, briefly considered denying the charge before realizing denial would be useless. Then he chuckled, shaking his head ruefully. "Your reputation as a busybody is very well deserved, my lady."

"I won't be put off by insults, sir." Her chin came up even higher.

"It wasn't meant as an insult. I begin to think I should enlist you as part of my intelligence network."

"Compliments will serve you no better." She was openly frowning now. "You are mad to be out here tonight if you are truly in such danger."

"I have taken precautions."

"Yes, I thought you looked a bit thicker about the waist than normal. But I was referring to the spore you must be carrying. I know very well you've not had time to do a decent purge."

Again she derailed his train of thought. "Spore?" And then the connections came. "You knew what that ring was and you didn't tell me?"

"You hardly gave me a chance. Even had I said anything, I doubt you would have believed me." When he said nothing, she continued. "How long were you wearing it?"

"Only a few hours. In any case, the attack will not come from that direction."

"You don't know when that spore will start making you sick."

"There can't have been that much."

"Unless you put the thing on last night."

"I feel perfectly fine."

"You *look* a bit flushed. And you're obviously sweating."

"Well, I *am* wearing a lot of clothing."

For a moment their eyes met, as if both shared the same startling solution to the problem of too much clothing—a solution that jacked up his internal heat even more and turned Madeleine's face bright red. For the first time in his memory she looked flustered and shifted her gaze past his shoulder.

They said no more, for already the cycle was coming to a close, and they soon moved on to new partners. When the paquay ended some ten or twelve ladies later—he'd lost count—it was Leona Blackwell who'd found her way into his arms again. She beamed up at him as the orchestra played the dance's closing measures, then dropped into the deep finishing curtsey. Immediately the orchestra started into its next selection, a filler piece that signaled an intermission.

"There, you see?" Leona said as she accompanied Abramm toward his chair on the dais. "You haven't missed a step. I knew you would do it perfectly."

Abramm smiled down at her. "I couldn't have done it without your help."

As they approached the dais where Ames and Channon waited, he became acutely aware of the heat. A rivulet of sweat trickled along the edge of his temple and down his chest under the leather-covered metal of his hidden breastplate. It had seemed a heavy encumbrance when he'd first donned it before the ball, but he thought he'd gotten used to it. Now it weighed upon him like a millstone. And his heart pounded a rhythm that echoed in his head as if a kettle drum marked time somewhere off in the palace, barely audible. Alarm flared in him as he wondered if Madeleine was right—if he was finally reacting to the staffid spore.

Suddenly Leona fanned herself and cried, "It is beastly hot in here, don't you think?"

The pounding faded into the rumble of conversation and seeing the sweat that glistened on Leona's own brow, Abramm assured himself his own discomfort was only the result of his exertions combined with the heat of the chandeliers and all the guests themselves.

"I believe I'd like to step outside for some air," Leona said, glancing suggestively up at him.

He hesitated, balancing the prospect of temporary relief against the likelihood that such an act would set the gossip mill racing. And would also tell him if his feeling of being overheated really was just the result of exertion and too many clothes.

"That would feel good right now," he said finally. "I think I will join you." She looked so unabashedly triumphant, he felt immediately guilty.

Abramm could tell that Captain Channon was displeased with the plan—in the dark solitude of the terrace gardens, Abramm would be more vulnerable, his assailant more able to escape—but he said nothing, merely following along as he should. Abramm was convinced Gillard wanted drama and an obvious alibi, however, things a secret attack would not provide.

As they strolled toward the doorway, Leona's hand on his arm, he caught Madeleine watching them with that sharp look of hers and almost smiled. For the second time this night, he had put uncertainty and even alarm on her face, and he found that it felt good. Nor was she the only one to notice and that was good, too. If the gossips thought him interested in Leona, it would divert the court's attention from Madeleine. As much as her own actions would allow it.

The chill evening air hit his face like a splash of cold water, washing away the last traces of his disorientation. Believing that it had, indeed, arisen from nothing more than being overdressed, he began to relax. It helped, as well, to be out of the public eye. The scrutiny tonight had been every bit as intense as Byron Blackwell had warned, and Abramm was feeling it.

He led Leona down the wide terrace stairway, and they walked side by side along a pebbled pathway lined with sculpted animal topiaries—ghostly shapes in the shadows limned with the soft light from the terrace behind and the lamps that dotted the path. They spoke of the dances, the food, the music and then, in a way Abramm didn't quite follow, Leona wound the conversation around to Lady Madeleine and the rumors that had come out of Prittleman's ugly accusation.

"Which I don't believe for a moment, sir," she assured him hastily. "I know Lord Prittleman, after all, and I'm sure whatever reason you had for entertaining Lady Madeleine at that early hour, it was perfectly proper. However, there are those who believe she's seeking leverage with you in order to persuade you to accept the Chesedhan alliance offer."

"But, my lady, I've already stated publicly that I *want* an alliance with the Chesedhans."

She blinked. "Oh. Well, what they're *saying* is that by choosing Madeleine you're sending a clear signal to her father, the king, that marriage to her sister is a possibility."

"It *is* a possibility. Which I've also stated publicly. Though how it could be a clear signal to her father, I can't imagine. Who would be the channel for it? Ambassador Cheede? I don't believe he'd perceive a signal if it bit him. He has a hard enough time with outright declarations."

She giggled. "He *is* somewhat obtuse."

They came to a walled terrace perched on the hillside, affording a south-facing view of the sparkling city and the broad gleaming river running through it. Its bridges twinkled with lights, and overhead a blanket of cloud had obliterated the stars, reflecting the city lights in a dull orange glow. Across the river, the scatter of lights decreased as they mounted the western headland, finally giving way to darkness. Somewhere in that expanse lay Graymeer's Fortress, where, according to Kesrin, something evil was brewing. The mists that had been spilling out of it lately and the sharp increase in the number of spawn that had plagued the people who lived nearest the place supported his contention, and more and more lately Abramm found himself thinking about Rhiad and the monster painted on the wall. *"You will meet him soon."*

Leona went on talking about the alliance and how concerned everyone was because "really, no one will accept a Chesedhan queen," while Abramm sighted off the end of the eastern headland, sliding his gaze due west to where Graymeer's lay hidden behind velvet curtains of night and distance. At first he saw only the darkness, imagining the chamber walled in black ice that lay out there somewhere. Glowing green lines shaped the beast Madeleine had called *morwhol*, floating above a pit of spidery things crawling in the luminescent soup of their own secretions, and all around them a chittering in the darkness and a deep, distant throbbing—

He broke free with a start, the throbbing that of his own heart slamming against his breastbone, the imagined scene echoing in his mind with unnerving realism. He had almost smelled the must-cloaked astringency, felt the eerie warmth of that pit on his face.

Before he could analyze it further, Leona jarred him from his thoughts by taking both his hands in hers and pulling him round to face her. She was looking up at him with an odd mixture of shyness and aggression, the network of jewels that filled her décolletage gleaming in the light of the garden lantern.

"You must know how handsome you are," she said quietly. "How all the ladies in court are completely smitten with you. Even the married ones." She paused, and her eyes fell away from his as she added, "Even me."

Abramm stared down at her, feeling as if he had suddenly come awake in some horseless cart, bereft of rein or brakes and careening down a mountainside. Something clamored at him to respond, but his tongue lay still, his mind blank. What did one say to such a declaration? *Thank you very much, my lady? Now shall we go back inside?*

She glanced up again and stepped closer to him, returning his stare with an earnestness that only added to his discomfort. "I know this must all be new and a little bewildering for you—given your background. But you needn't fear your attentions would be rebuffed. . . ." Letting go of one hand, she watched her fingers walk up his arm and leaned closer. "I assure you, sir, they would be most welcome." Her eyes flicked up at him beneath lowered lashes as her hand came to rest on his upper arm.

He did not move. Did not speak. Her advance had taken him completely by surprise, and now as he finally comprehended what she was about, a vision of Shettai flooded his soul, with her dark eyes and glorious hair, her regal cheekbones, and that slightly mocking smile. In an instant all the wonder of her soft curves and exotic scent welled out of his memory as if he had only discovered it yesterday. After four years he still hadn't gotten over her. He doubted he ever would. Which just now made the thought of romancing another in her place—any other—completely abhorrent. Even in his distress, though, he recognized that to express that abhorrence would be needlessly cruel and supremely stupid. Leona was the sister of one of his top advisors, a lady of the highest rank and well liked in court. To offend her as harshly as that would not only humiliate her, it would make of her a bitter enemy. And he had more than enough enemies already.

But if he knew enough not to fling her away, he did not know what to do instead, and finally settled for easing back out of her embrace. He caught her falling hand in his and forced a smile as he forced out a breath. "You're right, my lady. I am not accustomed to this, and you've taken me quite by surprise. I hardly know what to say."

She smiled, apparently undeterred, for at once she closed the small distance he'd opened between them. "You needn't *say* anything, Sire." And again her hand was on his arm, sliding up to his shoulder, to the back of his neck, the diamonds and great amber stone glittering ferociously beneath her uplifted chin.

Again he stepped back, feeling flustered and helpless. "My lady, I'm . . . I'm . . ." He shook his head, risked a small, apologetic smile. "I'm afraid you're moving too fast for me."

At last she understood. But if she looked disappointed, she was by no means devastated. Her hand came down from his neck, sliding across his chest and stopping as a crease formed between her slender brows. Her glance dropped to her fingers now pressing against the breastplate under his doublet.

The crease became a frown. "Why, sir . . ." Her eyes came up to his. "Are you wearing . . . *armor* under this?"

He stepped back yet again, enough that her hand had to fall completely away from him. He caught it and smiled. "I *told* Lord Haldon there was far too much stiffener in the backing on this thing." He gestured at his doublet. "I suppose I should take comfort from knowing that tonight at least I shall not have to worry about my safety should I be attacked."

She thought it the joke he meant it to be and laughed with him. Then he lifted his head, listening. "Is that the orchestra tuning up? I believe so." He grimaced. "Which means it's time for the rondella."

"We could always stay out here," Leona suggested.

He smiled at her. "And give the gossips even more to play with? No, they'd accuse me of cowardice—which is what it would be. Might as well go in and get it over with."

She squeezed his hand. "You'll do fine, sir."

He got through the rondella, though not without the bobble—and the kingdom did not come down because of it. After that he received more of the peers, including Everitt Kesrin, Brother Belmir—who requested an audience with him at a later time—and finally, his brother Gillard, who was uncharacteristically pleasant. Which in itself was a threat worse than his usual baiting and left Abramm confident things were going as he had hoped. He continued to be plagued by the headache and the heat, but since in the case of the latter everyone else was plagued by it, too, he didn't let it concern him. Eventually they opened all the line of doors along the outer wall to let in some cooler air. The evening crept by, his impatience mounting, until at last it was time for the Autumn Suite.

Madeleine joined him on the dais as the courtiers hurried to take their places, forming an aisle for them and encircling a considerably smaller portion of the floor than had been used so far. She had that tight-lipped look again, prompting him to note it aloud. Most women would have demurred, denying anything was wrong. Not Madeleine. Here came that lift of the chin, that direct look of the eye.

"If you must choose to go through with this madness, I would have liked warning to have taken precautions similar to your own." She tapped his metal breastplate.

"Why? You are not the target."

"No, but I am dancing with it. I could well come directly into the line of fire. I'm sure he'd be pleased to get me as well as you."

"I assure you, my lady, you need have no concerns." He lifted his bent arm for her to take as the music began, and cocked a brow at her.

She took it grudgingly. "What then? You expect me to rest in the knowledge that the White Pretender will protect me?"

"Or if he is not up to the task, perhaps Eidon will do."

She tossed her head and turned her gaze forward. "Eidon will not suffer himself to be tempted by fools, sir."

And suddenly it dawned on him that it wasn't anger making her so tight and tense, it was fear. Which surprised him, for she seemed in so many ways fearless.

"My earlier offer stands, my lady. If you would rather not do this—"

"It's a bit late for that, sir." She glanced up at him. "You aren't feeling ill yet?"

"I'm fine."

And then they were being announced, the herald's clear voice ringing through the crowded ballroom as, in accordance with tradition, they walked along the gauntlet formed by the peers chosen as Suite attendants and out onto the cleared floor. As they moved to the center of what seemed to Abramm to be a great well of space, his gaze flicked over the onlookers who stood foremost, shoulder to shoulder as they ringed the dance floor, here and there a steward or a guardsman—Ames, Channon, Blackwell, Simon . . . Gillard. His brother stood with his arms crossed, his expression benign.

Reaching floor center, Abramm stopped, Madeleine beside him. He held his breath as all the subtle rustlings stilled to silence in the ballroom. A moment they stood thus. Then the horns blared, the strings pulled out a swelling melody, and he swept her into his arms and started around the floor. She looked up into his eyes as dance protocol demanded, her face now perfectly calm. He returned her gaze with only half his mind, concentrating on peripheral vision, as they turned and turned in the course of the dance. Faces and eyes and hands, all the things that might give away a person's intent to someone sharp eyed enough to see it.

His awareness caught on one of the servants standing in the inner circle, just in front of the first set of outer doors, now open to the terrace. He recognized the man as one who had earlier tried to serve him canapés he did not want, who had let his gaze flick up to meet Abramm's in a startling display of audacity. Abramm had figured him for one of Channon's armsmen in disguise. Suddenly he was not so sure. Holding no tray now, the servant's gloved hands hung at his sides, half obscured by the sides of his tabard. Dark eyes watched Abramm a little too sharply. Another turn and another as round the floor they went, their days of practice paying off handsomely.

They were on the inner side of the circle when the music suddenly grated on his ears, and someone started playing a deep drum wretchedly off rhythm. His middle twinged and so, finally, did his wrist. He nearly panicked. *No! Not now!*

Protest did no good. The tingle became a rush of fire.

. . . and suddenly he was in the chamber again, the morwhol's outline pulsing over a pit alive with green tongues of fire. Before it stood a wild-haired giant of a man robed in darkness, arms flung wide. A woman clad in translucent veils stood on the level below him, teetering at the pit's edge, her body silhouetted against the green light. A mellow chanting accompanied the drumbeats, hypnotic and disturbing.

Then it all vanished, and he was back in the ballroom, missing a step in the sudden disorientation of the shift, but quickly regaining his rhythm.

Madeleine stared up at him, white-faced, looking as disoriented as he felt, as if she had seen it, too. Her warning echoed through his mind. *"Eidon will not suffer himself to be tempted by fools."*

I do not wish to be a fool, my Lord, he thought. *My life is in your hands, and I know that well. If I have overstepped, I pray you will be merciful. . . .*

They turned again, past Gillard, the guards up in the loges—both standing by the railing now—and then the servant by the terrance door. Abramm caught only a quick, moving glimpse of the latter, a flash of white skin, dark eyes, and the turn of the dance put his back to the man. It was enough. Something piercingly familiar registered in Abramm's brain, the set of the shoulders, the tension in the stance, the cock of the arm, some indefinable expression on the face—he never knew exactly how it worked, but suddenly the world slowed around him, and he felt the decision to attack.

He had only an instant to make his own decision, and then he was shoving Madeleine away as he wrapped his left arm in the cloak and flipped it up, continuing his turn to meet the coming blade with perfect timing, deflecting the pinwheeling sliver of steel moments before it would have buried itself in the side of his neck. At the same time his right hand closed on his sword hilt and the long blade sang through the air, parrying away the second dagger that had come spinning down from the balcony a heartbeat after the first attack was launched.

He continued the turn, aware of blank faces and wide eyes, most of the onlookers still not having registered what had happened, even as the second dagger now clanged to the floor. Madeleine stood off from him, fiercely scanning the crowd—

Then chaos broke loose, everyone crying out at once. He heard Channon bellowing orders, saw Simon throw himself forward out of the circle of onlookers, saw the servant-assailant already running through the open door he'd positioned at his back, a step ahead of the royal guards now leaping to stop him. A great thundering erupted from somewhere on the balcony and suddenly here was the drum again, loud and heart-shaking, pounding in his head as if it sought to part the bones of his skull. Simultaneously the spore in his wrist sent hot pain stabbing up his forearm. His middle cramped so violently he barely kept himself from doubling over. The tumult around him continued, vague and indifferent behind the darkness and the green fire and the pain.

But here was Madeleine, her face a tiny flower at the end of a long dark tube. She slid under his right arm, his fist still gripping the sword, her shoulder propping him up just as he was about to collapse. For a moment she stiffened, clinging to him as fiercely as he to her, and Light flowed into him, steadying him, pulling him out of the miasma of darkness and searing yellow-green, easing the pain in his head, quieting the nausea. The vision passed. He drew a deep shuddering breath.

"What is that place?" she murmured. "Your chamber in Graymeer's?"

He nodded.

It's the spore, he thought. *I didn't expect it to hit this hard and fast. I've got to do a purge now. . . .*

Channon had come to stand beside him and was speaking to Lady Madeleine, though Abramm could not make out what they were saying.

He swayed, light-headed, clinging to consciousness as again the spore rippled through him and the green-lit chamber overlaid the ballroom. Again the warning to purge now came.

Just a little longer . . .

A pair of soldiers pressed through the crowd, gripping a man between them. Two more soldiers followed with another man.

"The one who struck from the loge is dead, my lord," Ames reported. "His throat was cut by this one." He prodded one of the two men with the tip of his sword.

Abramm drew a long, unsteady breath, blinking at the man Ames had indicated as he tried to regather his thoughts. Then—*that's Michael Ives!* His gaze shifted to Gillard, full awareness returning in a flood. His brother smirked openly, believing they had nothing to tie him to this crime.

Steadier now, Abramm stepped free of Madeleine and sheathed his sword, then turned to Ives. "I hope you were not expecting to be delivered by your sponsor, Ives. He'll watch your head roll and count it good riddance."

Ives held his regard defiantly at first, then faltered. He had not expected to find himself in this position at all, Abramm realized. Caught and accused, perhaps, but with Abramm dead and Gillard on the throne again, he would have been pardoned. The fact that that wasn't going to happen was just dawning on him. His dark eyes flicked to Gillard.

"We already have Ethan Laramor's testimony regarding this plot on record," Abramm said. "You would be the second witness of the truth." He let that information sink in a moment, then murmured, "Is your loyalty so great that you are willing to take the blame for tonight's actions yourself and let the true culprit go free? Because you must know that is what you are about to do."

Ives traded gazes with Gillard for a long moment, then wilted, his face turning slack and gray as he took a small step back. Gillard's smirk faded.

Ives turned to Abramm, opened his mouth to speak—

"The plague with that!" Gillard snarled. And he flung himself at the king, steel rasping in the silence. Only it was not one, but two blades that suddenly saw light as Abramm's, redrawn, came up to meet his brother's. Abramm turned Gillard's thrust aside with hardly a thought, then flicked the point back and, as with his bedchamber assailant, capitalized on the total shock he'd produced in his opponent to disarm him. Gillard's blade flew from a suddenly bleeding hand, clattered to the floor and slid into the feet of the onlookers as he staggered forward off balance. He stopped at the point of Abramm's own blade, pressed against the base of his jaw. Profound silence dropped over the room. Even the assassination attempt had not provoked so great a shock as this layered concoction of unexpected events.

Slowly Gillard drew back, his eyes fixed blankly upon Abramm as he plainly struggled to understand—to accept—what had just happened. At his side, Channon stared, wide-eyed and slack jawed. A little farther down the line of onlookers, Uncle Simon looked as if he'd been struck a blow to the head.

And seeing them all, Abramm had a moment of supreme satisfaction, a sense of vindication unlike any he'd ever known. It was a moment he would savor for the rest of his life. But only a moment, swiftly lost.

A sudden ear-piercing howl ripped through the room, a monstrous gale blasting through the ballroom's open doors, banging them violently against the wall, tearing free the curtains, knocking over arrangements and candlesticks and chairs, even entire tables. Wigs were torn loose, skirts hurled every which way, lamps extinguished.

As darkness descended, Abramm saw Gillard bolt past him for the open doorway, but before he could move to stop him, reality shifted back to the man in black, the girl, the flames—

And now another man. One with only half a face, whose long gray hair covered only half his head. The chanting filled Abramm's ears, harsh and savage, pouring fury into his blood, turning his vision to scarlet around a tall blond man with heart-stoppingly familiar features: his own. He saw himself standing at the center of the crimson whirlwind, the force shrieking around him, tearing at hair and beard, ripping them from his face, battering his body, until it lay broken and crushed. The world spun away. His blood burned. His chest heaved. His own voice sounded deep and feral in his ears. The girl screamed, not of fear but of shared rage. Steel flashed in the darkness and she fell backward into the fires.

Abramm wrenched himself free, gasping, trembling, on the verge of vomiting. His head felt as if it were about to split. The pain in his arm exploded, and he felt, far out on that distant headland, the arrival of a new creation. A creation of blood and shadow and hatred. A creation made for him.

Now! said a voice behind the Light. *You must do it now!*

Yes, my Lord. And, as his legs buckled beneath him, he dove inward, riding the Light into a surging blue sea of spore.

27

Simon was still reeling from the shock of seeing Abramm effortlessly disarm his brother when the wind blasted into the ballroom and chaos erupted for a second time that night. He saw Abramm stagger and double over, as if something in the wind itself had felled him, saw him drop to his knees as Gillard bolted around him. Fighting the gale, the younger Kalladorne dashed for the nearest open doorway and disappeared into the night as Abramm collapsed upon the marble floor among his guards. At that point, Captain Channon broke free of his own paralysis, his barked orders sending armsmen racing off in pursuit of the crown prince, while he himself turned to the king. He had just reached Abramm's side when the wind died.

A moment of relative silence ensued, broken only by the residual thunk, rattle, and clack of things still falling and coming to rest. Then the servants bustled into action, righting tables, relighting lamps and candles, picking up plates and flowers and various articles of clothing. The guests drew a deep collective breath and vainly attempted to regather their shattered poise and grooming. More royal guards raced out the doors, but Simon was already pressing his way through the crowd toward Abramm, who so far as he could tell had not yet risen. Concern twisted at his heart. He'd thought the boy had withstood the attacks upon him virtually unscathed. Apparently he was mistaken.

He found Captain Channon and Lady Madeleine kneeling beside the king's unconscious form, blood spattering the pale marble at his side. As Simon squatted with the others, his eyes swept Abramm's torso, searching for sign of the injury that had felled him. But the only wound he found was on the king's left arm, likely the result of blocking that first dagger—

Memory flashed, of the dancing couple moving gracefully into the turn and coming suddenly apart, Lady Madeleine flying backward as Abramm whirled in a swirl of cloak to block the first blade and then that sudden as-if-by-magic appearance of his long sword sweeping through the air to block the second. Just recalling it raised anew in Simon the sense of having seen the miraculous.

But certainly there was nothing in it that should have left the boy unconscious.

"What's happened?" he asked quietly.

Channon jerked around. His eyes widened and he seemed uncharacteristically flustered. "Uh . . . I'm, uh . . . not sure." He stood and waved back the gathered onlookers. "Please, my lords, ladies . . . give him some room. And you two"—he motioned to the pair of guards nearest—"bring me some mantles for a stretcher."

As the armsmen rushed to do his bidding, Simon arose also, his concern escalating. He could only think of one thing that could have laid the king out cold from what appeared to be a minor nick. "Has he been poisoned?"

Channon's eyes widened even more. "Oh no, sir. Uh . . ."

"I think he's simply fainted," Madeleine offered, still kneeling at the king's side. "He was feeling poorly earlier. Thought he might be coming down with the grippe."

"Aye," Channon agreed hastily. "That's likely it." He looked over the crowd. "Hurry with those mantles, gentlemen."

Simon seized his arm, drawing him back. "Are you *sure* those blades weren't poisoned?"

Channon looked wildly uncomfortable. "Not sure, my lord, but—"

"There are very few poisons," said Lady Madeleine, close beside them now and speaking quietly, "that would have such an immediate effect."

Simon frowned down at her, annoyed at her intrusion.

"As I said," she went on, "he was feeling poorly anyway. I don't think he's eaten much today, and between that and this heat and all the clothing he's wearing, well . . . I expect he'll be all right shortly."

"Yes, my lord. I'm sure he will be," Channon said, shaking free of Simon's grasp as the men arrived with the mantles. Simon watched them lift the unconscious king to the makeshift stretcher, not remotely reassured.

Channon sent a man for the royal physician, instructing him to meet them in the king's apartments. Then he nodded to the guard at the other end of the cloak and together they lifted the king and started for the side door. The crowd swallowed them up. As they reached the door, a collective gasp arose from those nearest. Simon glimpsed Channon's head as he moved through the doorway. The gathering erupted in chattering wonder, and rumors fled by him, tales of a halo of light enfolding the king as he was carried out.

"I know I saw *something*," someone up ahead of Simon murmured.

"I didn't. But Lewis did. He was closer."

"Lord Faxton touched it and was not burned," someone else said.

"It is a sign from above."

"He is the King of Light! The Guardian-King!"

People swirled around him, their excitement growing as the story swelled and took on ever wilder forms. Simon stood where he was, bumped occasionally by those moving past him, yet hardly aware of them. A cold sick feeling congealed in his middle. *A halo of light enfolding him? Oh, please, no. Not that!*

And yet he vividly recalled the day he had challenged Abramm about his claim of having renounced the Mataio. *"How can you expect me to believe it is permanent? It's not like you hold another faith in its stead!"* And Abramm had looked at him long and piercingly before turning away to contemplate the glass beneath his hand. In the long silence of his consideration that followed, was he wondering how much to tell?

Rhiad's accusations. Gillard's hoping. Abramm's unwavering refusal to even humor Mataian requests . . . his open antagonism toward Prittleman. And all the other things that had happened: the voices he'd heard at Graymeer's, the imagined assailant in his bedchamber, his shunning of all but a few personal servants.

The thoughts were piling up, making it hard to breathe. Simon had virtually turned his back on Gillard for this man, and now to find out he was nothing more than another Raynen?

Abruptly he came aware of someone speaking to him. It was Gwynne, asking if perhaps he might escort her back to her lodging. He very nearly swore at her, but captured his tongue and his frustration in time and assured her that he would, thinking perhaps a trip away from the palace would clear his head and make things seem less dire.

It did not. He returned as torn and distraught as he was when he had left, and after a period of time spent wandering halls now mostly deserted, found himself entering the anteroom of the king's apartments. The guards wouldn't let him go any farther, however, and were arguing about it when a disheveled Byron Blackwell emerged from the royal sitting chamber to assure him the king had not been poisoned, just overcome by the stresses of the day. "He's sleeping peacefully, sir. No need to worry."

"I should like to see that with my own eyes, if you please."

"I'm afraid that won't be possible, sir. The king is very jealous of his privacy, and we could not violate his direct orders—"

"I don't believe you, Blackwell," Simon said quietly. "I believe I know exactly what he is doing right now, and it's not sleeping. I demand to see him."

Blackwell frowned. His eyes shifted uneasily behind the distorting lenses of his spectacles. Then he drew a breath and turned toward the door. "I will announce your request."

"Which you and I both know will be a waste of time," Simon growled, "since at the moment I suspect he cannot speak to anyone."

Alarm crept into Blackwell's face.

Simon went on. "I have seen these halos before, sir. On my father and on my brother, who was Abramm's father. I know what they are."

"Halo?" Blackwell chuckled as if relieved. "Is that what this is about? Sir, I assure you that was nothing. A trick of the light mixed with the people's excitement. Nothing more."

Simon held his ground, staring at Blackwell relentlessly. "If you will not let me see him, I shall have to address my frustrations and suspicions to my friends. Is that what you want?"

Blackwell stared back at him, his glasses reflecting the light in twin discs. He seemed unable to find his tongue.

"Oh, come, Blackwell," Lady Madeleine said testily as she emerged from where she had been listening behind the half-open sitting room door. "At least fifty people saw it as we brought him here. And if the duke has already guessed, there is no point in putting him off."

"Guessing is not the same as knowing for sure."

"Well, with that remark, sir, you've just transformed the guess to a certainty anyway. Might as well go all the way." She pulled the door open farther and cocked her head at them.

Blackwell capitulated with a sigh, stepping aside as Madeleine gestured Simon toward the open door.

Abramm lay on his back on the canopied bed of the royal bedchamber, stripped down to britches and hose, his body enfolded in a corona of white light, so bright one could hardly see his face. Simon stood at the king's bedside, regarding him for a long time, shocked beyond words or feeling, despite the near certainty of his suspicions. After a while he sank into the chair Haldon brought for him and continued to stare. As if staring would somehow ease the awful pain in his breast. Or make the light go away. Or give him a clear vision of what he was supposed to do now.

Slowly his mind began to work again, throwing up vignettes of memory, one after the other in no particular order—Abramm and Gillard and Meren and Raynen. . . . In the end he found himself mostly reliving those last few moments of the ball, the way Abramm had handled himself in the attacks upon his life. The clock had just finished striking—he didn't know how many times—when he said to Haldon, "Do you think he really might have been this White Pretender Lady Madeleine made the song about?"

Haldon stood beside him, hands clasped at his back. "I know he was, sir."

And now, finally, Simon looked at him, surprised by the conviction in his voice. "How could you *know* that, Hal? Just because a man can throw you up against a wall—"

"I've seen the brand on his arm, sir." He paused, his eyes going back to the form on the bed. "And the scars on his body. The light is fading now. If you wait a bit, you'll see them, too."

And so he waited, and the light did fade, and the lines of Abramm's muscular torso emerged and on it, gleaming white around the golden shield, was a network of scars, both long and short, wide and narrow, clean-lined and ragged. More battle scars than Simon bore on his own body, and Abramm still a very young man.

The White Pretender.

Comprehension shook him to his core. *How much of Madeleine's song is true?* Had he really stood and fought the great Beltha'adi to the death? Little Abramm, the skinny-legged boy who'd been the only student ever to rank lower than twenty-five in the Qualifying Order of Fence, who'd excelled at song and scholarship and refused his princely warrior training to take up the vows of peace and contemplation? And then run even from them. To survive the nightmare of slavery in a galley ship and the even greater nightmare of whatever training he must have received to fight in the Games.

The steel was there. And the stubborn Kalladorne will. Simon wondered how he had not seen it. How he could have been so completely wrong about this boy. And about Gillard, as well. For if there might have been question as to who was behind the initial assassination attempt tonight, Gillard had removed all doubt by attacking the king in full view of everyone, no pretending, no façade of scare tactics. If Abramm had not deflected his brother's blade, he would be lying here dead, surrounded by mourners. It was a despicable thing Gillard had done. A crime worthy of death. A dishonoring to the family name far worse than anything Abramm had ever done.

Yet something in Simon would not let him give up on the boy. This was Gillard, whom he'd doted on since infancy, the six-year-old who'd told him he wanted to be the best swordsman in the land just to make Simon proud. Now he'd tried to kill his own brother in front of all the peerage, and Simon couldn't seem to get his mind to match the deed with the person. Confusion roiled in a bitter, murky froth—guilt and regret mixed with disbelief and the cold brutal truths of life. Was some of this his fault? If he had resigned his position as Grand Marshall and refused to work with Abramm, might he have been able to bring Gillard to his senses? To have stopped this before it started?

And now what was he to do? Go back to Gillard? Stay with Abramm? He didn't know. His loyalties had become more bitterly divided than ever, his sense of honor teetering on the verge of cracking apart. Even his confidence in his ability to rightly judge a man's character lay in ruin.

Only as the last of the light faded from around Abramm's body did Simon leave, and by then it was almost dawn. He trudged back to his quarters, feeling alternately miserable and completely empty, wanting only to fall asleep in his bed and awake to find it all a terrible dream. Instead, he found his servant Edwin awaiting him with a message that had come in hours earlier. Edwin didn't know who it was from, for its wax wafer was sealed with a generic mark. He knew only that the person who brought it had stressed that Simon must read it as soon as he returned.

"Why didn't you send someone out to find me?" Simon asked, turning the envelope over in his hands.

"He told me not to, sir. Though I did try. Discreetly, of course. No one seemed to know where you'd gone."

Stepping away from the servant, Simon opened the envelope. It was from Harrady, requesting his presence at the man's lodge at once, *regardless of when you read this. Make sure you are not seen.*

It didn't take much to deduce what this must concern. He tossed the letter into the fire, then stared at the flames, frozen with indecision. If he dallied, perhaps the choice would be made without him. . . . *Coward!* he thought with a grimace. Besides, was there really a choice to be made? As Simon had figured out the meaning of the corona of light on Abramm's body, so would the Mataio, and likely soon. They'd force him to reveal what he was and remove him from the throne. Gillard would be reinstated, and all Abramm had done and planned would dissolve like mist in the morning.

The only real winner would be the Mataio.

KIRIATHAN

AND

KING

PART FOUR

28

Carissa and her party approached the town of Breeton nine days after leaving Highmount Holding, five after bypassing the ruins of Raven Rock. Those last five had been especially miserable—plagued with snow, rain, mud, and dwindling supplies. They saw no sign of Rennalf nor his men. No ells, no birds, no animals, and few travelers, though given the weather that wasn't surprising. The farmsteads she'd hoped to shelter in had been intact, but deserted and emptied of foodstuffs. And as the snow turned to rain, dry wood became increasingly scarce, making their fires small at best. The last night they'd had no fire at all, sharing round their last portion of biscuit and washing it down with icy stream water which, even after most of the particulates had settled out, still tasted like dirt.

The ninth day had dawned like all the rest: cold, gray, and rainy, the clouds hanging low and thick above them, the trees dripping, the leaf-covered road puddled with water. In retrospect Carissa wished now she'd chosen the Kerrey route, especially in light of the probability Rennalf really could use the Dark Ways—which she suspected were similar to the ether-world corridors of Esurh. If so, Cooper was right to fear she wouldn't be safe from him until they reached the lowlands.

As for going to Springerlan, what was so awful about that, anyway? It was warm, civilized, populated, and as far from the Highlands as she could get and still be in Kiriath. Abramm was certain to be occupied with his kingly duties and unlikely to seek Carissa out, especially if he knew she didn't want to see him. They'd been able to avoid each other in the confined cave system at Jarnek, after all. Surely they could continue to do so in the sprawling environs of Springerlan. Though, truth be told, she wasn't sure she even wanted to avoid him anymore. For the part of her that longed to see him had been inexplicably gaining ascendance over the last few days. Perhaps it was escaping Highmount and the influence of the ells. Or spending nine days in the company of Elayne Cooper, who somehow always brought the conversation around to Eidon. Or perhaps it was Elayne's observation back in Highmount that it wasn't Abramm Carissa hated, but Eidon himself.

They had talked of that some on this journey, a word here, an exchange there. Never more than a few lines, but Elayne had made Carissa think. *Was it Eidon she hated?* She certainly had reason. He'd taken Abramm from her—twice—and also her mother and father and everyone else she'd ever cared about. He'd refused her a husband's love, refused her the child she'd yearned for, and by that condemned her to humiliation and unending misery in Balmark. Then he'd refused to let her save Abramm—from slavery or the Terstans—and had turned her own travels in search of fulfillment to an extended exercise in futility. Wherever she turned, it seemed, he was there to slam her down again. What else could she do but decide there was no just creator directing things? It had to be fate or evil, or maybe just people randomly running up against one another, making each other miserable. Whatever the answer, if Eidon did exist, it seemed he had no hand nor interest in any of it and must be occupied elsewhere.

"Or perhaps he is simply trying to get your attention," Elayne had suggested.

But if that were true, then why had Carissa not been marked with the shield when she'd tried to take the star back in Jarnek? She hadn't voiced that question to Elayne, for to ask meant admitting what she had done and what had come of it, and she wasn't ready to expose that humiliation yet. She'd abased herself before him and he'd rejected her. Made herself willing to take on the curse that was his shieldmark for the sake of her brother and been refused. Eidon had already gotten her attention, only to reject it outright. If she did hate him, it was only because he hated her first.

It was midafternoon when they reached Breeton, which, despite her fears, stood untouched. Unfortunately, it was so full of people and livestock it could hold no more. Its gate stood locked, though dusk was hours away, and the gateman would not open it. "We got refugees from Raven Rock," he told them through a small opening cut into the gate at eye level. "Ye know them barbarian demons leveled it, don't ye?"

"Aye," Cooper told him. "And we've been nine days on the road now because of it." He paused. "So it *was* barbarians, then?"

"That's what they say. And now we've got not only the Raven Rock folk, but those from the outlying crofts, too afraid to be out alone, plus all the travelers wanting to get out o' the rain or fearful o' going on. Even if we could squeeze ye in, there'd be no place for yer animals. There *is* a place south o' here, though—maybe a league and a half. Old fortress, used to house royal soldiers, 'til Gillard pulled 'em out a couple years ago. Been empty ever since. Roof's still decent, though, and the hearth works. I sent a couple groups there yesterday."

"For the hearth to work," Cooper argued, "we'd need dry wood. Supplies, too." The man grumbled that both wood and supplies were in need by all, but finally he went away, returning eventually with another man, who gave them a bag of biscuits and volunteered to bring down a load of wood on his own donkey. In fact, he'd even show them the way if they wanted to wait for him.

Elayne did not want to stay at the fort, and argued with Cooper about it for a bit, too quietly for Carissa to follow, but it seemed to hinge upon some old tale of magic and warlocks which might or might not be true. In the end, seeing as the place had once been manned by the king's soldiers, and the Breeton gateman had sent other folks to shelter there already, Cooper believed it would be safe. The Breeton people wouldn't be sending folks on to a place that sheltered an entrance to the Dark Ways. Besides, after nine days everything was wet and soggy, and they could all use some time out of the weather to dry out. It was at least four days more down to Aely.

From the outside, the fortress appeared deserted, its heavy front gate aslant and ajar, bottom edge so buried in a buildup of earth it could not be moved. The keep windows stood dark, but a wisp of smoke arose from the chimney, quickly swallowed by the lower edges of the clouds. Old outbuildings, a clump of bathweed interspersed with dried corn stalks, an old stock pen, a stone well and adjoining trough—they all stood glistening with moisture in a thick growth of grass marred by a single trail leading up to the keep itself.

The Breeton man led them to a musty stable, which they were surprised to find empty, if recently used. "Looks like the others must've gone on already," their guide said as they dismounted. "Guess you'll have the place to yourself." He grinned at them, but Carissa felt a twinge of uneasiness all the same. She'd been looking forward to enjoying the sense of safety to be found in the company of common folk.

Leaving two of their men to see to the horses, they trooped up to the box-shaped keep after the Breeton man and his wood-laden donkey. The front door suffered from the same ailment as the main gate, torn partly free of its hinges and scraping the floor. Cooper shoved it aside in a great echoing screech, and they stepped into warmth that was almost painful. That the inside of an abandoned, broken-down keep could feel this warm, Carissa thought, was a measure of just how cold she had become.

As the remainder of their hired guards unloaded the wood, their guide led them up a narrow corridor into a dark chamber whose size Carissa only sensed at first by the feeling of space and the way sound echoed around her. As her vision gradually adjusted, she picked out the stone stairway rising along the left wall, the dim shape of a long table at the room's end, and the glowing bed of coals on the hearth to the right.

The Breeton man surprised them by conjuring an orblight over by the hearth, directing the men to stack the wood beside it. Following his lead, Cooper and Elayne each conjured one, as well, though their combined light still barely reached the Great Room's surrounding walls. As the men started to lay the fire, Carissa and her companions continued across the chamber toward the long table, its surprisingly clean surface gleaming in the kelistars' pale light. Tall, wide-backed chairs presided at each end, the near one empty and the far one—

Light pierced the shadows of its embrace, glinting off the long, frizzy hair of the bearded man who sat there, elbows propped on the arm rests, fingers steepled before him, and they all stopped at once. Cooper's muttered oath drowned out the unladylike word that left Carissa's own lips. Simultaneously, a cadre of northmen burst from a doorway in the left wall with torches and drawn swords, while another group trooped through the front door, now at Carissa's back. In a heartbeat, they were caught, led by the Breeton man into the very trap Carissa had feared. She turned to look at him in question, and saw he had known all along.

"I'm sorry," he muttered miserably, staring at his feet. "They said they'd turn Breeton into another Raven Rock if we didn't deliver you over."

Cooper growled another epithet as Carissa forced her gaze back to Rennalf, who watched them with amusement. As the man Breeton from fled through the front door, Rennalf's underlings swiftly disarmed Cooper,

Hogart, and the others, then herded all out the side door save Carissa.

As the rest of Rennalf's men scurried about setting torches in wall brackets and stoking the newly kindled fire, she stood looking down the table's gleaming length at the man civil law designated her husband. He met and matched her gaze, his face hard between the side braids, his eyes reflecting the light of the candelabra that had been set upon the table between them. He still wore the green-stoned amulet on his throat, and now she clearly sensed his unsettling aura of dark power. Warlock. Master of the Ells. Walker of the Dark Ways and Servant of the Shadow. No wonder he'd reminded her of the priests and Broho of Esurh.

"Well," he said. "Ye've have decided t' return at last, my vinegary, headstrong little wife."

"What are you going to do to my friends?" she demanded.

"They'll be fine. I have what I came for."

She stared at him wordlessly.

"Ye heard my little Illik died?" he asked.

No answer. He grinned. "That means ye still have a chance t' produce an heir for me."

The words were not unexpected, but hearing them sent a shudder rippling through her, and for a moment she thought she couldn't stand here another moment. He saw her reaction, and snorted. "Ye should be grateful, woman. If I didna need ye, I'd kill ye. In fact I may yet, if ye're too displeasin'. Or truly barren." He waved a hand. "I'm preparin' t' eat. Join me. I'm sure ye're hungry after all yer travels."

Actually, her stomach was drawn up into a knot, her breath coming in shorter and shorter gasps as if all the air was somehow being used up and she couldn't get enough of it. A plate of mutton and rye bread was set before each of them along with a tankard of mead. She loathed mead and he knew it, though right now even water would have been hard to swallow. He pulled out his knife, using it with his fingers to cut and pull away pieces of the meat, then stuff them into his mouth in great, awkward gobs. Fatty juices gleamed off his beard, and he kept grinning at her every time he caught her looking at him, showing his teeth along with the food he was chewing. She soon learned not to look.

In the relative silence her thoughts finally came round to the acknowledgment of how he had gotten here. For there'd been no horses in the stable, and she doubted they'd been hidden in the woods. It was cold and wet, and Rennalf couldn't have known when she'd arrive. Besides, horses in the stable would have been no surprise. If they weren't there, it was because Rennalf hadn't used them.

He waved his knife at her plate. "Eat. Drink. We'll be leaving soon and I want ye mellow." He grinned at her as he chewed. "This very night ye'll be back in the big bed at Balmark."

She swallowed down rising terror and came suddenly aware of the Terstan orb, hanging from its chain around her neck, warm against her skin. Elayne said it would protect her against the ells. Maybe it would protect her from Rennalf, as well, though it hadn't done much of a job so far. *You said you would make me a way,* she thought reproachfully at Eidon. *But just like always, you only make things worse.*

Rennalf scowled at her. "Are ye deaf, woman? I said eat. The food'll help settle yer stomach."

She began to pick at the bread. After a while he said, "I want t' see ye drink, too."

In the past, it had been his custom to force her to choke down a tankard of mead to make her more "biddable." It had worked to a point—under its influence she could actually bear to have him touch her. But it never took away the tension, the revulsion, the utter contempt for him. Or for herself. She lifted the heavy tankard and sipped, controlling the gag reflex with all her will. It was even more bitter and rotten-smelling than she remembered.

"More," he ordered her. "A good hefty swallow."

As she struggled to obey, a red-haired man jogged down the stone stair from the second level and stopped at tableside. She recognized Ulgar at once. "Aistulf's demanding t' see ye now, sir, and gettin' flamed about it. Should I bring him through? I'm na sure he'd agree to it."

"Tell him I'll be there soon."

"Yes, sir. Will ye be wantin' the others here t' go through, too? Because Dorniuk'll need help if ye do. It's too many too soon, he says."

"Tell him t' get some help. But start them going through now. I'll need everyone in Balmark if things get touchy with Aistulf."

Ulgar left, and Rennalf continued to eat while Carissa toyed blank-minded with her food. Her hands were trembling so badly, she could hardly hold the dull-edged eating knife they'd given her, and the mead gurgled acidly in her stomach. Rhiad had needed to drug Abramm to bring him safely through the corridor, he'd said. Rennalf must be doing the same here. Not trying to mellow her to make an heir, but to bring her through the Dark Ways back to Balmark.

Panic roiled through her, and she must have made some sound or movement because suddenly the flickering eyes glared down the table at her. "By the Stone, wench, what're ye mewing about now? Drink another draught of that mead."

She was jittering, her whole body shivering with the terror and helplessness sweeping through her. At the sharp tone of his voice, she flung out a hand to obey, seized the tankard in weak, shivering fingers, and lost hold of it halfway to her lips. The vessel clanged onto the plate, its rank, golden contents splashing out across the table and into her lap. She was on her feet in reaction almost as it happened, but did not save herself from a dousing, even as Rennalf's profane exclamation rang off the stone walls.

As the sound faded, she looked up at him, new terror eclipsing the old. In time past, a beating would have followed such a performance. Indeed, from the look on his face, she was sure that was precisely what was to happen.

Then Ulgar was back again. He'd spoken to Dorniuk and sent several men through and thought Rennalf should go next. "Tis flickerin', m'lord. Likely only good fer one or two more 'fore it goes down. Could be an hour or more 'fore the other waymakers get there. An' I do na like the sense I'm gettin' from Aistulf, m'lord. I think there'll be trouble."

Rennalf blew out an angry breath and shoved his plate away, then stood, the chair scraping across the stone floor. "All right." He strode down the table's length and seized Carissa's arm. "Ye're comin', too. Sane or not, ye can still bear me a son."

He dragged her up the stone stairway to the second-level landing, then down a hallway to a windowless storage chamber in whose far corner a column of dancing green threads stretched from floor to ceiling. Like the etherworld corridor Rhiad had made in Esurh, this one's presence buzzed unpleasantly across her skin, even as it stirred the orb on her breast to fire.

Rennalf shoved her forward, but she veered away, aware of the fact that she was jibbering with fear and unable to stop. Terror gave her strength as she fought him in earnest, slipping free of his grasp, then running mindlessly into the wall. Cursing ferociously he seized her on the rebound and dragged her toward the column. They were still several strides away when a searing heat exploded on her chest and rushed down her arm, loosing his grip and flinging him back from her.

Regaining his balance, he stood holding his wrist as if it hurt and staring at her in confusion. Then the amulet flared. Understanding hardened his lips. "So—ye're one of *them*, are ye?"

Lurching toward her, he grasped the front of her tunic with his good hand and yanked downward, the sound of the ripping fabric loud against the buzzing. Cold air rushed over the suddenly exposed nakedness of her chest as she gaped at him, as taken aback by his action as she was by what he did next: nothing. He only stood there staring at her chest as if he had never seen it before.

Comprehension dawned. *He thought I was a Terstan! Expected to find a shieldmark and now that it isn't there, he doesn't know what to think. Unless— he's seen the orb!* But a quick look down showed the orb had vanished. Her gaze came up, scanned the room, and found it, slid up against the wall in a crumple of chain, glowing with white-hot fire. Any minute now he'd turn, see it—

Don't let him see it, Eidon! If you live, please! Don't let him take me!

Frowning, he looked down at his hand, then up at her chest again, and burst into a stream of muttered blasphemies. Then he turned to Ulgar, standing in the open doorway. "Post a guard in the hall, lock the door from the inside, then follow me through. We'll send someone for her later."

At Ulgar's nod, Rennalf wheeled and strode into the column, vanishing in a flicker of green and blue. A moment later, Ulgar pulled the door shut, his key grating as the lock tumblers turned and the tongue engaged. Then he followed his master into the green-and-blue oblivion of the doorway into the Dark Ways, and Carissa was alone.

29

Abramm awoke from his purge late in the morning after the ball. For a time he lay in his great canopied bed, staring at the folds of gold-threaded fabric overhead and groping mentally after fading dreams. Normally after a purge they were filled with light and wonder, but this time he recalled only disturbing snatches of scenes that made no sense. Huge dirty clouds had towered over him, menacing in their size and bellowing like angry bulls. But just as his terror swelled to the breaking point, they vanished in a puff of feathers floating in the darkness while a dog barked in the distance and a flock of chickens squawked in frantic agitation. Then a child's face loomed out of shadow before him, wide-eyed and openmouthed . . . and he awoke.

Why would he dream of such things at all, much less following a purge? And why did it all seem to carry such resonance for him, such a sense of reality and dire portent?

But chasing the memories brought no answers, and as he grew more awake, the threat in them dissipated, replaced by one far more immediate—and real. For the return to consciousness brought with it memories of the ball, and he realized he had fallen into his purge in front of everyone.

He sat up and Haldon was right there, dressing gown in hand. As he stood and let the chamberlain slide it onto his arms and up over his shoulders, he said, "So how bad was it last night?"

"They were carrying you out of the hall when the corona took form."

"It was seen, then."

"By a fair number, I'm afraid, though most didn't know what to make of it."

"That won't last long." *Not with Prittleman on the prowl. And now Gillard. He will know what it is for sure.*

"No, sir. And, uh . . . your uncle was here last night."

Abramm rounded on him. "What do you mean here?"

"Sat by your bedside for hours. He left a little before dawn."

"And went straight to Gillard," came Byron Blackwell's voice from near the door.

They turned as he stepped into the bedchamber, leaving the door ajar behind him. Behind his spectacles, brown eyes darted to Abramm's shield-mark, then up. "Captain Channon's looking for him now. Simon, I mean. Apparently he had a predawn meeting with your brother out in the Farthington sector, after which he disappeared."

"So they both know, then," said Abramm.

"It would seem so, sir."

I waited too long. . . . Abramm turned back to his reflection in the long mirror, the Terstan shield glittering between the embroidered edges of his dressing gown. "They'll force me to reveal it now," he murmured.

"Yes, sir," Byron agreed. "The Table is meeting as we speak."

Abramm muttered an oath and turned from the mirror, shedding the recently donned dressing gown. "This is *not* how I wanted to do it." He pressed the gown into Haldon's hands. "I'll wear the black again."

"Yes, sir. You're not going to eat first?"

"No."

And still Haldon hesitated. "Sir, your brother did commit an act of treason last night. Trying to kill you, in front of everyone—"

"The Mataio will surely absolve him of that," Abramm said. "They'll laud his courage and dedication to Kiriath's welfare, while they take over the Crown. . . ."

He wanted to let loose another oath but restrained himself.

"Perhaps you could use a patch," Haldon suggested, flicking a glance at Byron before moving to the wardrobe to hang up the dressing gown.

"Just wear it long enough to show them you have no shield," Blackwell said. "It would buy you some time."

Haldon began riffling through the other garments in the wardrobe.

"But it would be a lie," Abramm said. His eyes returned to the mirror, now across the chamber from him, the mark glittering prominently against his scarred torso. For a moment he considered the proposition, then ran a hand through his hair and grimaced. "And I'm not sure I even *want* to hide it any longer."

"If you don't," said Blackwell, "they'll destroy you."

Haldon pulled out an underblouse.

"I have the materials," Blackwell said, lifting a small black pouch. "We could do it now."

Abramm frowned at him.

"You know they'll ask you today, sir. Probably send a delegation straight to your chambers and demand you reveal yourself to them. It could come at any time. And . . ." He paused, exchanging another uneasy glance with Haldon. "You should know that most of your servants have fled. A sudden resurgence of the grippe." He paused. "A few remain loyal, but you must understand—if the Mataio brings you down, all who served you will go down, too, whether they knew your secret or not."

Abramm met his gaze soberly, sick at the realization that he was right, understanding now why he'd taken the initiative to bring those patch materials. And why he was pressing it so insistently. The patch made sense. And why fuss about its being a lie, when he'd been lying from the day he'd arrived? It was just that . . . he'd had enough of lying and hiding. He wanted to be known for who and what he was. It was there in his coat of arms. It should be in the people's minds and hearts, as well. And the idea of actually covering up his shieldmark with a piece of pigskin was revolting.

If only others didn't have to suffer the consequences of his decision.

I've made a real mess of things now, my Lord. What should I do? Is the time for discretion truly past?

Hurried footsteps heralded a new arrival moments before the door creaked farther open and Lady Madeleine burst over the threshold.

"Sire! Word has just come that—oh!" She broke off, her gaze roving across his bare chest, sticking on the shieldmark, then darting up to meet his eyes as a tide of red suffused her face. Immediately she turned away. "Your pardon, sir. The door was open and I thought you would be—I'm sorry, sir. I'll wait outside." And with that she fled back to the study.

"That woman has no sense of decency whatsoever," Blackwell muttered.

"Was she here last night, as well?" Abramm asked, glancing aside at Haldon who still stood at the wardrobe with the shirt, ready now for Abramm to don.

"I'm afraid so, sir," Haldon said.

"You should have had *her* banned from the palace, not Prittleman," added Blackwell.

"*Not* Prittleman?"

"Well, at least along with him." He held up the dark bag again. "Shall we get on with it, sir?"

"No," Abramm said. "I'll see what she wants first." He moved back toward Haldon and turned to let him slide the shirt up both arms.

"Sir, the patch will need to dry and cure enough so it looks real," said Blackwell. "We don't have a lot of time."

"I said I didn't want to do that yet, Blackwell."

"Yes, sir."

Madeleine waited by the pair of windowed doors leading out onto the balcony on the west wall. They were closed now, and she stared through the glass toward the western headland, her face pale beneath the freckles, her eyes cupped by deep shadow. She wore a simple high-necked gown of gray tapestry, and her fawn-colored hair was drawn into a single long braid down her back and secured with a slender golden circlet set upon her brow.

"So what is this news you have for me?" Abramm asked as he crossed the chamber to join her.

She turned with a start, blushing again at the sight of him, then dropping her gaze and finally glancing back toward the window. "Have you seen what's happened to the western headland?"

He came up beside her and saw it was completely blanketed in a low-lying mist, though the rest of the land was clear. She told him that witnesses claimed Graymeer's had exploded with green lightning last night, just before the wind that had disrupted the ball. Then the mist had boiled out of it, swallowing everything down to the river's edge and as far north as Tripletree. "People on the west side won't even open their doors," she said. "And now there are tales coming in of mauled sheep—tens of them, apparently—of flocks of chickens slain in their coops, and sightings of a strange beast with big shoulders and skinny little hindquarters."

"The morwhol," he breathed.

She nodded. "But they say it's only the size of a dog, which is not what I expected."

"Maybe it has to grow."

"And feed?" She gazed out the window. "Except it's eating very little of what it kills."

"Maybe it doesn't feed on flesh."

She glanced at him again, one slender brow cocked.

"The Esurhites believed power was gained in the taking of life. If this beast *is* what was made in that chamber last night, then it's Shadow-spawned. Maybe it feeds on life rather than flesh."

As she considered this, his own thoughts returned to what she'd said about the mauled sheep. Maybe those weren't clouds in his dream. Maybe they were sheep. Was it coincidence he had dreamed of them last night when the morwhol had been out slaying them? His visions at the ball last night he'd attributed to the influence of the ring-staffid spore, but what if they weren't? He fingered the thin scar running across his left palm, recalling that Rhiad had needed both hair and blood from him to make the beast. Had that created some sort of mystical bond between them?

Beside him, Madeleine roused herself. "There's more. It attacked a little girl—a crofter's daughter."

A little girl . . . the child's face! Nausea began to churn in his middle. "Please tell me she's alive."

"Barely. The crofter and his sons drove the beast off, but— Where are you going?"

"To talk to them myself," Abramm said over his shoulder as he headed back toward his bedchamber. "Where's Lieutenant Merivale?" he asked of the guard on duty.

"He left with Captain Channon, sir."

"Find them both. And see that Warbanner's saddled and brought round to the front." He stepped into the bedchamber as the man raced off. "I'm changing into my riding clothes, Hal."

Blackwell was not happy. He insisted that Abramm must deal with the controversy regarding his shieldmark before things got any worse. Surely others could investigate rumors of the beast. Abramm told him plainly that he was not interested in his opinion, adding that if he killed the thing, perhaps that would counterbalance everything else.

Half an hour later, Trap and Shale Channon met him at the front entrance anteroom, as full of objections as Blackwell had been, if for different reasons. Channon still had not found Simon and was clearly invested in the search. Yet he could not leave Abramm to traipse off into the mist-covered headland in search of a monster without his presence. Trap considered the excursion unnecessary and dangerous and pled for Abramm to send him instead. He refused. And no sooner had he settled things with them than here was Lady Madeleine, waiting outside with the horses, arrayed now in her riding woolens and already straddling her own mount.

"Oh no," he said before she could even open her mouth. "You're not going. And don't talk to me about researching any more songs. This is too dangerous."

"More so for you than I," she said, lifting her chin. "And I wasn't thinking about a song at all. The fact is, I know more about this beast than anyone here. I can help." Her fingers provided added persuasion as they fiddled uncharacteristically with the buttons on her blue jacket, all but pointing to the shield that lay beneath it.

She was right. Not only was she the local expert on the morwhol, but from all appearances she knew more about wielding the power of the Light than Abramm himself—and maybe even Trap. In the confrontation he was seeking, she could be as much of an asset as any of the men he was bringing. Besides, if he said no, she'd just follow anyway.

"Very well," he said, continuing down the stair to take up Warbanner's rein.

Today's ride was different from the one he'd taken last week for the picnic. The streets stood silent and deserted, even at midday. Furtive faces peered from the windows as he sped by, and though he rode cloaked and with plain gear, he knew that word would soon spread of what he was doing.

They crossed the King's Bridge and trotted into the woolly wall of mist looming at the river's edge. It closed about them swiftly, blotting out all sight of the city and river behind them. Unlike a normal fog, this mist carried no moisture, and by that Abramm knew it to be unnatural, a byproduct of whatever had happened at Graymeer's last night, perhaps to provide a covering environment in which the young morwhol could grow.

The crofter's holding nestled in a broad valley some distance off the Longstrand road, where the family lived in a sod-roofed hut built half into the side of a hill. A sheep cote and chicken house, also of stone and sod, huddled not far down the slope, and it was here the beast had ambushed the little girl. Two horses stood ground-tied in the yard, their riders—the men originally sent to investigate the attack—talking to the family clustered by the hut's open doorway. As Abramm and his party emerged from the mist, they were spotted immediately, the armsmen hurrying to attend them.

The little girl, they had learned, had gone out to collect the eggs, only to find the chickens slaughtered and the beast awaiting her. Her screams had brought the dog to her defense, which had held the creature off until the man and his sons arrived with ax and staves. But the beast was too small and quick for them, and perhaps too smart, as well, leaping to attack the father's face where his sons could not use their weapons. They had pulled it off him only to let it slip their grasp and flee into the mist. After that they'd been too frightened—and too preoccupied with the girl's injuries—to search further.

"We were just getting ready to start that, Sire," the investigating armsman said to Abramm. "I doubt it's still around, but there might be a track we could pick up."

Abramm nodded his approval, then gestured to the people huddled by the door—a tall, sun-weathered man in homespun clothing, his slender gray wife, and two boys, one nearly grown to manhood. "I think I'll talk to them myself now."

"I'm not sure they'll talk to you, sir. At least not . . . coherently."

Abramm eyed them again, noting how their gazes flinched away. "Why not?"

"They've been bad enough with us. They're sure to be . . . overwhelmed by your presence. On top of everything else. The girl was chewed up badly. They say she's got the wound fever."

"How could she have wound fever? She was attacked only a few hours ago."

"I know, sir, but the poor babe *is* burning up. Likely won't live the day."

"She may be spore-sensitive," Madeleine murmured at Abramm's side.

That *was* the most likely explanation. He felt a dull anger rise within him—that a little girl should suffer because of a madman's thirst for vengeance. . . .

"It's probably gone back to the fortress by now," Trap said from Abramm's other side.

"No doubt at first light," Abramm agreed. "Still, I want to see her."

The armsman was right that his presence had overwhelmed the crofters, but not, he thought, because they counted it an honor. They reminded him more of the poor folk of Esurh, afraid of authority, afraid that if the king so much as noticed them, they would lose their heads. Perhaps with good reason, for it wasn't just fear he saw in their faces. The woman, especially, bristled with a latent hostility that suggested she believed this was his fault. That *his* audacious invasion of Graymeer's had stirred this evil up, and now *she* was paying for it. The man would hardly look at him as he answered Abramm's questions, his fear and anger and grief making him all but inarticulate. At length Abramm gave up and asked to see the child herself.

"Talia? She is abed, sir. Sore sick. We dare not bring her out."

"I never thought you should. I will go in to her."

Wide-eyed expressions of alarm passed among them. "But . . . she cannot speak to you, Your Majesty. She is wild with fever."

"Nevertheless, I will see her."

They looked at one another again, then scrambled out of his way.

"Keep them out here," he said to Channon. Then with a glance at Trap and Madeleine to accompany him, he ducked beneath the weathered lintel and entered the house.

A small fireplace stood to the left of the single large room, pats of sheep's dung smoldering on a bed of ash. Across from it stood a roughhewn wooden table and several chairs, and beyond them, rolled sleeping pallets lay stacked in the corner. The air hung close and moist, sour with the stench of smoke, vomit, feces, and the irritating musk of spore. The girl lay near the fire, drenched in sweat, tossing restlessly on a straw-filled mat. Her blond hair lay in lank, wet strings, and her face was a network of already suppurating scratches and bite marks. Red blisters lined each cut and her little nose was swollen twice its size.

Abramm knelt beside her, the accusations he'd received at Graymeer's echoing through his head. *You should not have come, Abramm Kalladorne. . . . Their blood will be on your hands . . . your hands. . . .*

Before him lay the first casualty: young, innocent, completely undeserving. *It waited for her. Hid in the croft and waited for her!* Rage bubbled up through his guilt. *If it was for me, why didn't it come after me? Why this poor little child?*

"Talia?" he asked softly. "Can you hear me?"

She did not stir, though beneath closed lids her eyes moved back and forth.

"I fear you won't get much out of her until it's passed," Madeleine said, standing at his side. "If it does pass."

He shuddered at the thought of her death, and the same sense of personal responsibility that had claimed him when he'd gone after the kraggin claimed him now. "Maybe we could heal her," he said.

And even as he spoke the words, he knew that was what he had to do—

touch her with the Light and draw away the spore that was ravaging her tiny body. Whatever he couldn't remove would be residualized, placed into a dormant state her body could better tolerate. It was not a skill at which he was adept—he'd never even used it before—nor was it without risk. In drawing off the active spore, he could easily transfer it to himself.

"You know," Trap said. "She may not be spore-sensitive at all. This thing strikes me as being closer to veren than feyna. Its spore may just be more virulent. Perhaps you should let me do it."

"Or maybe all three of us," Madeleine suggested.

"No," Abramm said. "It was made for me. I'll do it. Although . . ." He glanced over his shoulder at the family standing outside, watching him through the doorway. As usual, Trap picked up his meaning without his having to speak and stepped into the opening, blotting out light and the family's line of sight at the same time.

Abramm drew a breath, reminding himself that Eidon's power could easily match anything lurking in this girl. Then he took her hand—it was limp and hot—and called her name. She did not move. He felt the spore in her as a faint buzzing irritant and reached cautiously toward it. At once she moaned and shivered, her eyes moving under the closed lids, her hand twitching against his palm.

"My lord," Meridon said from the doorway behind him, "stay alert. This may be a trap—"

The girl shuddered, the tiny hand twisting to wrap her fingers tightly about his thumb. Breathy little whimpers burst from her throat as her head began to toss and the shudders increased in magnitude. Then, before he could assimilate what was happening, she rose up on both elbows and opened her eyes. They blazed with a green malevolent fire, twin suns in a black sky that snared his own gaze and in a heartbeat carried him into her memories. He stood, small and frightened in pungent-smelling darkness from which emerged a vision of blood and feathers and torn flesh, of a small, dark, man-like face with a short snout and gleaming teeth beneath bright green hate-filled eyes. A torrent of fear flowed into his soul, spinning new visions out of old, visions of blood and death and screaming pain all centered about the same beast—no longer small, but huge and powerful, with massive head and shoulders, sloping hindquarters, whiplike tail, clawed feet. It roared and ripped and spat, slashed and clawed in a blood-spilling frenzy, leaving its victims—men, women, even children—to wheeze out their lives in field and yard and street, mauled and maimed, attacked for one reason alone—because they were Abramm's subjects, and thus were hated as much as he was hated. *Watch and remember, Golden Prince. For as I do to them, so will I do to you.*

Dimly he heard the girl screaming, felt her hand tugging hard at his. He knew he must focus the Light and burn off this poison rushing into him, but the thought was carried away by new visions of horror and death. *You cannot stop me. No one can stop me!*

He heard other voices, sharp with concern and warning, knew they were telling him something important. But they were so far away, and so faint . . . lost in the roaring of the beast and the screams of its victims.

The monster became his only reality, its green eyes boring into him, the rankness of its breath raising his gorge. Suddenly he lay pinned on his back as a dark shape, impossibly big, loomed close above him. Hot, stinking breath washed into his nostrils as a clawed hand hovered above his face, then slashed downward, tracking fire through brow and cheek. Blood trickled hotly down his temple and he gasped, as much in shock as in pain. The claw struck again. And again, slicing arm and chest and hip and leg, shredding skin and muscle into blood-soaked ribbons as his terror rose like a head of boiling foam. *You will lose it all, Abramm Kalladorne. Crown and people and station. Face and skill and body. I will take it all and no one can stop me!*

And it was truth. He knew it was truth. This was a vision of what awaited him and he could not elude or evade it. It *would* happen.

Then something closed upon his shoulder and white light burst through his darkness, swift and searing as a bolt of lightning in a howling storm. And no mere flash, either, but a current sustained and widening as it linked with the Light that lived in him. Night turned to day in an instant, the black torrent of fear boiling away like steam.

He was left panting and dazed at the girl's side, still on his knees, the scar on his wrist twitching and searing as if all the pain that had wracked his body had been drawn down into that one point. A twinge of headache, a ghost of the nausea brought on by recently active spore, and all was gone.

The girl lay quietly before him, sleeping now, the flush of fever gone, the wounds themselves mere slender scabs rapidly on the mend. The hand on his shoulder withdrew itself as he breathed deeply and rocked back, feeling weak and dizzy. Outside a woman was wailing. *Her mother,* he thought. *She must have heard the screams. Some of which were mine, I think.*

He wanted to go and reassure her, but the prospect of gaining his feet seemed a major enterprise. A moment later he tried anyway, and here were Trap and Madeleine to help him, their faces drawn and concerned, Madeleine's in particular. Indeed, she looked as ravaged as he felt, her skin pale and damp, her eyes sunk into hollows of deep fatigue, as if she had been sleepless for days. It was her hand that had laid on his shoulder, he realized with a start. Her sharing of the Light that had delivered him, not Trap's.

"Are you all right?" she asked.

"I'm not sure." He still felt weak. "You?"

"Tired. It was only after you." She regarded him with concern.

"What happened?" Trap demanded as outside more clamor erupted. Channon's voice, firm and commanding, quenched it.

Abramm frowned. "I think I saw what the girl saw when she was attacked. After that, the fear just took over and there were visions of—" He broke off, unable to speak as the memories came rushing back—the mist and the beast and the carnage. The green-flamed eyes with their vicious hatred. *You cannot stop me!*

Not me, perhaps, but the One who lives within me can! But he had no sooner affirmed this truth to himself than his breath caught and his heart raced anew with the certainty that the beast was still here, watching him from some hideaway, waiting for its chance. Because it wasn't just Abramm's people it wanted, it was Abramm himself. And not merely to kill him, but to ruin him, little by little. Nightmare images flashed through his mind, stoking the fear into a panicked, neck-prickling certainty that if he didn't get out of this hut *right now*, it would kill him.

Swallowing, he forced down the rising terror and reembraced the Light, wondering if he might have some odd form of sporesickness. He could sense no active spore in him, though, so he forced himself to go on. "Visions of what it *means* to do, I think," he said. "Not anything it's already done."

"When it's grown to full size maybe," said Madeleine.

"Which is why we must destroy it today," Abramm said firmly, leaning away from Trap and balancing on his own two feet.

"But it could be anywhere on this headland," Trap protested. "The chances of finding it—"

"It's gone back to Graymeer's."

Trap frowned at him, looking suspicious and half alarmed. "How do you know?"

Indeed, how did he? A moment ago he was certain the beast was in this hut with him, breathing down his neck. Now he was just as certain it was in Graymeer's. He looked from one to the other of them, helpless to explain and caught in a rising urgency to be off. "I know," he said. "And we have no time to lose."

The other two gaped at him as he lurched toward the doorway, staggering when the room spun yet again. Meridon caught him just before he fell, then suggested he sit down. He wouldn't. Shaking off the dizziness, he tried again, striding unsteadily through the doorway into gray daylight and the white-faced regard of the crofter family, standing in a semicircle before the hut.

Talia's mother clutched her husband's broad chest, her tearstained face turned toward Abramm. "She's gone, isn't she?" the woman cried, no longer attempting to hide her hostility. "You overstepped your place, and my little Talia has paid for it!"

He stared at her uncomprehending.

And here was Madeleine again, coming up close at his side to deliver him. "Actually, ma'am, the fever's burnt out. Your daughter's sleeping peacefully and should be up before long."

The woman's eyes narrowed, shifting from Madeleine to Abramm and back again.

"See for yourself," Abramm said, finally recovering his wits enough to speak.

The woman flashed a disbelieving look at her husband, then rushed past them into the hut. As soon as she was gone, Abramm dismissed her from his thoughts, striding on toward Warbanner, who was prancing and tossing his head as if he sensed the turmoil in his master.

"See that their chickens are replaced," Abramm said to Channon as he took Banner's reins and leaped to the saddle. "And bring them one of Hilda's pups."

As they rode out of the yard, heading back toward the Longstrand road, they heard the crofter woman's shriek of joy. Abramm took little pleasure in it, though, for in his mind's eye all he saw were the mutilated corpses that would soon litter lane and yard and field if he did not find this beast in time.

30

They were just turning onto the Longstrand road when Everitt Kesrin and Ethan Laramor came riding out of the mist from Springerlan, Kesrin's bodyguard Yacopan in their wake. They were bundled in leather and wool, and Laramor's craggy face was pale—almost gray—and sheened with a film of perspiration. He did not look well enough to be out of bed, much less on horseback halfway up the headland. He also had trouble meeting Abramm's gaze, his former hostility replaced by embarrassment and shame.

After the requisite greetings, Abramm directed his attention to Kesrin. "So what brings you gentlemen out here?"

"You, sir," Kesrin said. "Ethan thinks he knows something about this mysterious beast that's roaming the headland. And when we heard you'd ridden out to find it, well . . ."

He turned toward Laramor, who met Abramm's gaze stolidly and confessed he'd had an idea someone planned to create such a beast when they'd found the caged dog in Graymeer's that day. "It's called a morwhol, sir."

Abramm glanced at Lady Madeleine. "Yes, we found a reference to it in some old texts."

"I should have said something earlier, but . . . I was a suspicious fool, sir. Your uncle tried to warn me, but I wouldn't listen. Now the thing's loose."

Uncle Simon tried to warn you? Well, it's nice to know I made some headway with him, even if everything has gone over the walls by now. He turned his thoughts back to the man in front of him. "We all make mistakes, Laramor. Had I made it clear from the start what I was, perhaps things would be different. And I doubt we could've stopped Rhiad anyway. Now, what can you tell me about this morwhol?"

The border lord met Abramm's gaze for a long, hard minute, then gave a little nod and proceeded to tell them of the blood feud of Lords NakNaegl and Breen. "Breen was the Terstan," he said, "NakNaegl the powerful warlock who commanded the ells. He created the beast and set it loose. It killed most of Breen's family in its hunt, finally cornering Breen himself not far from where Breeton stands today, where it slowly tore him apart. Afterward, bound to him even in death, it stayed beside the remains, feeding on all who lived nearby or happened along. It took nearly fifty years to starve to death."

"According to the record I found," Madeleine interposed, "the beast was captured by its maker afterward and used to intimidate serfs until it turned on him and consumed him. That it was *his* remains it stayed with."

Laramor shook his head, his clanlord earring glittering. "The beast turned on NakNaegl before it slew Breen. And it was NakNaegl's son who claimed to have captured it, but it was really only a wolf in a cage." His gaze came back to Abramm. "The beast itself was made for Breen and stayed with him until the end."

"So if this one kills me here today," Abramm said, "you're saying it will stay and feed off people in Springerlan until everyone moves away. And Graymeer's will be twice cursed."

"I think it's too young to kill you today, sir." Laramor's gray eyes met his own grimly. "Which is why *you* must find it first." He proceeded to corroborate Abramm's earlier speculation that it fed on the life energy of its victims, and that the more it killed the larger and stronger it would become.

"Then we have no time to lose," Abramm announced when he had concluded, the old urgency rising up in him. "We ride to Graymeer's."

Laramor looked startled. "You know it's there?"

"I do." He told them what had transpired at the crofter's hut. "It seems I have some kind of link with it. At least I hope I do." It would be dreadful to waste the time riding all the way up there needlessly, but at the moment he had nothing else.

Laramor and Kesrin were exchanging frowning glances and then, as

Abramm was about to turn away, Kesrin said, "We would like to come along, sir. Perhaps we can be of assistance."

"I'd welcome it, sir." He glanced at the border lord. "But your friend here looks like he should be in bed."

"Your uncle would say I always look like that," Laramor retorted with a wry grin.

Abramm eyed them both, then gave his consent, wheeling Warbanner around to set him at a canter back up the Longstrand road and then south along the crest-line track to Graymeer's. And all the way, he was beset with the recurring sensation that the beast he sought was actually seeking him, that it was not in Graymeer's but following unseen somewhere in the surrounding mists, from which at any moment it might attack. That it had not, made him think the sensation was a ruse, designed to frighten him off, like the griiswurm auras. It also made him wonder if he'd guessed right after all, if perhaps the beast only wanted him to think it was at Graymeer's, when it was actually fleeing across the headland in the opposite direction.

The final upthrust appeared without warning out of the mist, the ground taking a steep upturn as the trail turned crosswise to the slope. As they ascended the switchbacks to the ruin itself, the sound of the surf crashing in their ears, Abramm's sense of imminent attack redoubled, his neck hairs rising again and again with the sense of something coming at him. Warbanner grew even more jumpy with his rider startling at every little clack and thump, and the desire to turn back became so intense it took all Abramm's will to keep his hands from pulling the reins around.

They reached the top without incident, however, passing through the barbican and crumbling gateway into the mistbound outer yard, where the internal pressure fell suddenly and completely away. Unnerved, Abramm reined in Warbanner by the ashes and scorched earth that remained where his men had burned the griiswurm on their first visit. The mist hung thicker now than before, boiling around them as if disturbed by their presence, visibility only a few feet, even in the outer yard. Already the spawn were making a comeback, a few dark, tentacled shapes crawling alongside the road, a sprinkling of staffid unrolling between them and skittering away.

Unable to sense the creature's eyes on him anymore, Abramm feared that he'd been right: the draw to Graymeer's *was* a ruse. But when at last he dared to seek it, it was still there, no longer a looming menace, but a tiny ratlike thing, scrambling to escape his notice somewhere in the inner ward. He rode forward without comment, aware of his companions' uneasy eyes upon him. Past the second gateway, he stopped beside the half-buried cannon at the foot of the ramp to the wallwalk. The mist was so close now, he wouldn't have recognized the few feet of ramp that he could see had he not known it was there. Most of his companions were obscured, only Trap and Channon clearly visible, with Ethan Laramor a vague shape beyond them, Madeleine and Kesrin vaguer still. The others he could not see at all. Nor could he see any of the broken walls of the inner ward's crumbling storage and living quarters, though he knew they lay before him.

He hesitated, seeking the way to go as he ignored the aversion that pulsed within him, the almost overwhelming compulsion to turn and leave.

And then the scene shifted.

He raced down a narrow corridor whose stuffy air was sharp with the tang of spawn. Staffid lay hard and quiescent under his paws and a faint green light glimmered ahead of him, gleaming off the irregular surface of the roughhewn, griiswurm-covered walls. His urgency to escape was mounting. The Other must not come near. Not yet. He needed the master. The master would know what to do.

The light grew closer, brighter, and at last he burst into a familiar place—the domed chamber with the pit full of spidery things swimming in their own secretions. The master lay sleeping on the wall bench, cloaked in dark wool, his half-barren head pale in the green light.

Abramm gasped and was back in the mistbound inner ward again, staring at the half-buried cannon. "They're here," he said, dismounting and striding into the mist. "The beast and Rhiad both. And the beast knows I'm after it."

There was a scramble of activity behind him as the others dismounted and some hurried to catch up, but he barely noticed, all his awareness fixed upon the mind-scent of the creature he sought. Afterward, he could never say how he found his way—nor retrace his steps—but somehow he did, almost as if he were being drawn, despite the beast's now-desperate attempts to ward him off. Again and again he was struck with the sense of imminent attack, wave after wave of neck-prickling alarm washing through him. Ironically, each incident, rather than increasing his fear, served only to strengthen his resolve, confirming his belief that none of them were real.

He was vaguely aware of men walking closely beside him, kelistars shining in their hands—

He nosed desperately at the sleeping man, whining. But the master would not wake up. He knew the man wasn't dead—the scent of life billowed out of him, and blood still wept from the cut across his palm. And the blood . . . he paused to sniff the wound, the aroma filling him with a golden rush of delight—then remembered his need. The Other was coming! The Master must save him! Another shove with his nose, another jostle with his paw. Wild with fear now, he nosed the limp hand again and sank his needlelike teeth into the gnarled thumb. The master leaped up, howling, and, seeing him, began to rage.

Abramm blinked and came back to himself, jogging now down a narrow stair, with staffid scrambling away before him and griiswurm brushing his shoulder. The stair emptied into a long passageway walled in obsidian, equally choked with spawn. It smelled familiar, as if he had only moments before known this acrid stuffiness. Down the passage he went to a second short stair, green light glowing at its end. His heart began to pound.

But the great domed room with its green-lit pit at the bottom stood empty. He paused only an instant, then dashed for the left opening. Passages led to stairs to more passageways to more stairs, and finally he emerged in a low vaulted chamber, supported by three pair of squat stone pillars. At the far end stood a dais from which sprang another pillar, this of one red light. And at the base of the dais, a half-bald man with a silver braid carrying a small, doglike thing with heavy, maned shoulders and slim, dangling hindquarters.

Abramm's eyes darted back to the pillar of red, and suddenly his breath left him. That was the opening of a corridor through the etherworld!

If they reached it—

He bolted across the chamber, rapidly closing the gap as shouts rang out behind him—but the malformed pair had too much of a lead, and even as he ran, Abramm watched them fly up the low stairs and fling themselves toward the scarlet column. There was only one possible way to stop them.

As he launched himself after them he heard a shout of warning, felt a hard jerk on his cloak just as he collided with the corridor itself. The world erupted in a firestorm of white and red and green as the Shadow lurched up in him and residualized spore burst alive. A horrible screeching tore at his ears as a million fire-footed ants raced across his skin. He glimpsed a passage of impenetrable darkness, felt for a moment as if he were being turned inside out. Then the Light poured out of him, a vast current of it, that blasted upward through rock and earth and cloud and sky. Spears of it penetrated every passage the main beam crossed, flashing through all the warren that honeycombed the great rock under Graymeer's.

Something slammed into him from behind, and suddenly he was lying on his back, gasping for breath in air turned biting and sulfurous. Shimmery violet afterimages danced before his eyes, and he wondered if he were even alive, though Tersius was not here to meet him and surely Eidon's Garden of Light wouldn't feel like this. . . .

When he could see again, he realized he lay on his back at the edge of the dais, still in the underground chamber. Someone lay beneath him, grunting and squirming in the effort to get free. Abramm rolled off him and sat up, not surprised to find it was Trap. "Are you all right?" he asked his liegeman.

Meridon sat up, as well, staring at Abramm oddly, then at something over his shoulder. "I think so," he said. "What did you just do?"

"I thought I could destroy the corridor before they got through it. That if I touched it with the Light, I could do what Carissa did to the one Rhiad made back in Esurh."

"You did more than that, though. You pulled the Light out of me."

"And me," Kesrin interjected, looking up at them from where he stood at the foot of the dais.

"And me." Laramor stood at his shoulder.

"Me too," added Madeleine, while Channon nodded agreement behind her.

Abramm stared at them in consternation. They were all looking at him quite oddly. "Well, not because I was trying," he said finally. "I can't even throw the Light reliably, let alone draw it out of someone else."

They began to frown, exchanging puzzled glances. Kesrin shifted and swept the chamber with his eyes. "Nevertheless, you did. Maybe it has something to do with Graymeer's itself. Something here that you tapped into."

"Something like . . . what?"

"I don't know." He turned to scan the back of the chamber. "There are stories of the old kings and their impenetrable fortresses. Their 'walls of fire' and 'hearts of flame.'"

"Yes!" Madeleine exclaimed, stepping up beside him. "During the age of the Kings of Light."

Abramm frowned. "Those are myths, my lady. Wild things."

"So say some of the story of the White Pretender, sir." She smiled impishly at him, and he felt his face flame.

"Well, it's not something we're going to figure out today," Trap said. "And we have more important concerns at the moment." He gestured across the dais toward the corridor. "At least we can rest knowing no one will be coming back through *that* anytime soon."

Abramm turned to look at the dark, smoking disk that was all that remained of the pillar of light. But instead of triumph, he felt only profound dismay. *I have no corpse to bring back to the lords. I may not have even killed the thing.*

Trap, as usual, was on the same thought track, putting the uncertainty into words and adding, "You were sensing it before. Can you still?"

Abramm flung his senses outward, seeking the beast's bitter mind-taste. A long moment he searched, then shook his head. "Nothing." Not even the small ratty thing.

"It must be dead," Madeleine concluded.

"They might just be out of range," Laramor argued. "Young as it is, it's not going to be that strong." He gestured at the smoking disk. "My guess is that thing was part of what we in the Highlands call the Dark Ways, Shadow paths conjured by powerful warlocks to take a man leagues across the land in a heartbeat. One of them probably used it last night to help Rhiad make the creature. If your beast is alive, it's likely up in the Highlands, and out of range."

"So we're back to not knowing," Abramm said.

"I'm sorry, sir," said Laramor. "Time will tell. If I'm right, it will be drawn back to you."

"Killing as it goes," said Abramm. "I've got to go after it, then."

"No." Kesrin's quiet voice stopped him short. The kohal's dark gaze flicked up to him. "You don't, sir. In fact, you shouldn't."

"If it's killing my people, kohal—"

"You don't know that. You don't even know it's alive. Don't you see?" He stepped up onto the bottom stair. "It's a distraction. As Lieutenant Merivale just said, you have more important concerns."

*Gillard. The Table of Lords. The Mataio and their accusation. My own reve-
lation of the truth.*

Abramm's stomach tied itself instantly into a knot. "If I go back without
the corpse no one will believe a word I say. Not about the morwhol nor the
corridor nor anything. And they already blame me for all of it."

"If you leave now, they'll say you've run away. And if I may say so, sir, I
have to wonder if they wouldn't be right."

Abramm stared at him, stricken.

"The Table won't wait. If you don't go back there now and face them,
your enemies will defeat you."

"But if that thing is killing my people—"

"Your concern is noble. But as I said, I believe it's a distraction."

"You think Rhiad used the beast to lure me up here just so I wouldn't
admit what I am? He's the one who accused me in the first place!"

"Not Rhiad—he's only wrapped up in his desire to ruin you. But the thing
that lives in that amulet on his throat? That one knows exactly what it's
doing."

"Rhu'ema, you mean. But they've been trying to expose my secret, too.
Now you're saying they want to hide it?"

"Abramm, you stand on the verge of publicly proclaiming the truth of
who you really are. A proclamation that will profoundly impact us all. The
rhu'ema know this." He paused. "You don't know if this beast is even alive,
or if it is, where it's gone. Eidon does. But he's chosen not to give you that
information, and without it there's little you can do. Which tells me you must
dismiss it for now and turn your mind to the more important task."

"Go back to Springerlan and tell the lords I wear a shield."

"Yes, sir."

As soon as Ulgar disappeared into the column of green light, Carissa
lunged for the orb, plucked it off the floor, then pressed herself back against
the wall, clutching the talisman and her torn tunic to her breast, fighting back
the desire to laugh hysterically.

She could hardly believe Rennalf had caught her, only to let her go . . .
until the emotion waned and she realized she'd only received a reprieve. With
the door locked and Rennalf's henchman outside, she wasn't going anywhere.

And the fact of his imminent return precluded the possibility of her inducing her guards to open the door.

Sagging against the wall, she contemplated the faint shaft of light across the room from her. Ulgar had said the waymaker was growing tired, that the corridor wasn't working as well as it might. But he'd also said reinforcements were coming, which meant she didn't have a lot of time. If only there was some way to turn it off—

She opened her hand around the orb she'd been clutching and looked down at it. Its white glare had dimmed considerably. In Jarnek, she'd over-heard talk that her possession of this very orb had been what enabled her to shove Rhiad into the corridor he had opened in that cistern, triggering its destruction. Perhaps it would do the same with this corridor. *Except I have no one to shove through this time. Only myself.* Which defeated the purpose. Throwing the orb into the column of light might do the job . . . but then again it might not, leaving her trapped here without even that protection. Still, the thing had flared strongly when Rennalf had tried to pull her through earlier, so maybe just bringing it near enough would trigger something. . . .

Interlacing the broken chain around and through her fingers, she stood and faced the column, aware again of its buzz grating against her skin and teeth and ears. New uncertainties gave her pause. What if she were pulled in and sent on to Balmark? Would she even go to Balmark? What if the whole thing just exploded as it had in Esurh?

She stood there chewing her lip and rolling the orb between thumb and forefinger. Whoever Rennalf sent back for her, he'd bring a soporific, some-thing that worked faster than mead. Then he'd take her through, and shortly Rennalf would apply himself to the matter of siring an heir. Swallowing hard, she decided the quick death of an explosion—even lifelong madness—would be better than that.

With another gulp she clenched her fists and approached the column. It was like forcing her way through a swarm of invisible bees. The buzzing beat against her skin and sucked the air from her lungs. The orb's heat flared against the backs of her clenched fingers, but she kept going, gratified to see the green column flicker—

Suddenly she found herself facing a crowd of people she did not know. People of exquisite beauty, with kind faces and intelligent eyes, people who offered by some wordless communication a haven of safety and belonging the likes of which she had yearned for all her life. But the moment she started forward again, the orb flared hotly. She'd have to drop it to go on. Uncertainty returned. Why did it seem the people had no faces? They were smiling. Their eyes were warm and kindly. How was it she could not tell one from another, could not tell if they were male or female? How was it they kept reminding her of thin ice on Balmark Pond?

She stood buffeted by the invisible bees, unable to hear the voices of those before her for their buzzing. Then orb's heat seared against her knuckles, the buzzing crescendoed, and as if it were only a painting on a wall, the crowd flattened and tore open before her, revealing an endless black hole and a distant pale figure flying toward her.

Horrified, she was already flinging herself back when he was upon her, looming over her as a white wind came up behind him, seeming to ignite the very air as it bowled her over, sweeping her along until she slammed into a wall, buffeted there for an instant by a terrible screaming gale—

Then it was gone. She lay in utter darkness on her side, pressed into the corner made by wall and floor, the broken chain of her necklet still laced through her fingers, the Terstan orb lying hard and warm beneath her palm. The etherworld corridor's annoying buzz was gone, along with its light. Outside the hall guards banged on the door. "My lord? Everythin' all right?"

The latch rattled.

Beside her something snuffled and whined. She heard a grunting rasp, a rustle of clothing, and knew that someone had definitely come through the corridor before it was destroyed. *It worked!* The thought gave her a thrill of satisfaction, and the comfort of knowing that at least she wouldn't be back in Balmark anytime soon. Even if she did get beaten for destroying her husband's precious Dark Way.

She heard the man groan and sensed his movement, her hand tightening reflexively about the orb and bringing it to her chest as the strange doglike whining continued. Then a rasping croon broke the silence. "Are you all right, my pet? Is my little one all right?"

Silence followed, then a whine and snuffle, and the voice spoke again. "See? He didn't get us after all. The master saved you." Another whine. "I don't know. Probably somewhere in the Highlands. But we will find him again, and by then you will be much stronger."

He's not one of Rennalf's! she thought, a wondrous joy flooding her.

Outside the latch rattled again as both guards called more urgently. "M' lord! Are ye all right?"

The voice beside her croaked an affirmative, then told them to open the door. There was a pause. The men explained they had no key. Her companion told them to hack it down. She thought they'd laugh, or question, but after only a few moments the ring of axes on wood echoed around her and shortly the door swung outward. An arc of ruddy torchlight swept into the room and over the man who had just come through the Dark Way—clearly not one of Rennalf's. The left half of his face had been seared into an inhuman mask, the scalp above it puckered and hairless, attached to a right half that appeared completely normal.

The guards took one look at him and erupted into protest. "Here, sir! Who're ye?! Where's Lord Rennalf?"

The wretch barked at them to be silent and back away, and they obeyed with eerie docility. A prickle crept up Carissa's spine as she realized he was using the power of Command. Not unexpected for a warlock. Which he must be, to have come through the malfunctioning corridor. *But you have no business here*, she thought at him. *So hurry up and walk away.* Rennalf's guards would surely follow him as soon as they were able, leaving her free to slip away unnoticed. He stepped out of view into the hallway and she waited, listening intently, imagining him striding away, down the stair and into the Great Room. Soon the guards would follow. So focused was she on this scenario that she nearly cried aloud when the rasping voice sounded again, still outside the opening. "If you want to find him again, my pet, we must go."

He pulled the door back farther, and for the first time Carissa saw the small doglike thing that must have come through the Shadow path with him. It stood in the midst of the room, staring at her like a spaniel on point. But it was no dog.

It reminded her of a small stoop-shouldered old man, its forequarters too large for its slender, almost withered hindquarters. A dark ruff bristled at its shoulders and head, framing front-set green eyes and a short snout filled with small, sharp teeth. A tab of hair tufted its lower jaw, and the dark bristle continued down its front legs, ending just above wide, long-toed . . . paws? The green eyes were fixed upon her, their stare kindling a new and nameless dread in her heart. This thing knew her somehow and meant her ill. The longer she lay locked in its gaze, the more certain she became of that, images of death and blood and unspeakable savagery leaking into her mind. Her own death. Elayne's. Cooper's. Her brother's . . .

Fear rolled through her in waves, shortening her breath, speeding her pulse, tightening the muscles in her belly. Slowly she sat up, seeking to gain some advantage over it. And failing.

"What is it now?" came the rasping voice. The scarred man stepped into the doorway, bringing a torch from one of the hall sconces. The sudden brightness forced Carissa to look away even as the man hissed with surprise. "YOU!" he croaked.

She blinked up at him, shielding her eyes from his light, surprised in her turn and now alarmed. *He knows me? How? Was I wrong about Rennalf sending him? Is he one of those waymakers they were talking about?*

The man seemed to grimace—or maybe smile—and his rough voice tried to wheedle, "I'm hurt you don't recognize me, Carissa. After all the time we spent in Esurh? All the times I saved you?"

She stared at him, bewildered, struggling to see past the scars and the scalp and the opposing half head of gray hair to something familiar. His words whirled through her mind like pieces of a carpenter's puzzle that refused to go together. *Esurh? Saved me? Was he some ship hand? Some minor servant I didn't notice?*

And then it hit her: "Danarin!" Or so was the name by which she'd known him all those months he'd used her to get himself close to Abramm. His real name, she'd learned at the last, was Rhiad, right-hand man to High Father Saeral, sent to kidnap her brother and bring him back to the Mataian leader for possession. The same Rhiad she'd shoved through that first etherworld corridor, come back to her now in the destruction of the second, like some sort of bizarre cursing.

He smiled at her. "You do remember. Good." And then to the beast as it slowly sank into a crouch at his feet: "Here, now! None of that!"

The creature's head swiveled from her up to Rhiad with a growling bleat. "No," Rhiad said again, stepping past it to seize Carissa by the arm and haul her upright. "I have another use for her. One you'll like much better. She's very important to him, you know."

The beast's green eyes returned to Carissa, the tip of its long tail flicking back and forth. She shuddered, having no idea what Rhiad was talking about, and not wishing to. She just wanted to get away from him, wanted to push him off her and flee. But somehow she knew the little beast, small as it was, would not allow that. Even if she could escape Rhiad's verbal powers of coercion.

Thus when he pressed her forward with his hard, pinching grip, she went unresisting, out the door, past the startled but immobile guards and down the stair to the empty kitchen to pilfer the supplies left by Rennalf's men. From there they went to the stable, where he made her saddle Heron and mount, then bound her hands with a leather cord, which he tied to a metal ring on the saddle's hump. He took for himself Cooper's horse, Arrow, who snorted and kicked and sidled away, until the strange little beast came round and caught the animal's gaze with his green eyes. Then the horse stood still and trembling while Rhiad loaded him up, climbed aboard, and invited his pet to ride in his lap. It made the six-foot standing leap as if it were nothing. Finally, covering the beast with his cloak and taking up Heron's knotted reins, Rhiad led them into the rainy afternoon and down to the main road. There he turned toward Aely and Old Woman's Well and the junction to Springerlan, and there Carissa dropped the first of her rings.

31

Upon his return to Springerlan, Abramm lingered in the stable, brushing Warbanner down as was his habit. The grooms had protested the first time he'd elected to do it, but by now had grown accustomed to his eccentricities and left him alone as he required. Today they left him alone even more than he required, having cleared the building shortly after he'd tied Banner outside his great, straw-filled box stall and begun to brush.

Now, except for Trap standing quietly on guard some distance off, he was alone, enwrapped in the comfortable silence of horses snorting and thumping and rustling in their straw. Outside, normal activity still bustled, but no riders entered this wing of the stable, and no groom or stableboy dared intrude upon its sanctity. Even when the last light of day faded and the lanterns were brought, they were hung surreptitiously only at the ends of the aisle. No one came in with one to light the middle.

Because they wished to honor his desire for privacy? Or because they were afraid of him? More likely the latter, for there was much to fear in the cloud of suspicion and heresy now boiling around Abramm.

He didn't know why he was down here dragging his feet. Hadn't he decided his course back at Graymeer's? He would confess at last all of who he was and trust Eidon to deliver him from what seemed certain disaster. But the closer he'd gotten to Springerlan, the greater had grown the burden of his fear, and the more tenuous his resolve. True, it seemed his use of the Light to destroy the corridor had also killed all the spawn that lived in Graymeer's and evaporated the mist to boot. But he'd already heard that the Mataio was claiming that for its own victory—the brotherhood had been conducting round-the-clock worship vigils since the ball last night—and Abramm had no proof of his work in it. And without the morwhol, no one had reason to believe he was not what all his enemies were saying: the cause of last night's disaster at Graymeer's and the deaths—already exaggerated fivefold from the truth—wrought by the monster. He was a Terstan heretic in league with the Shadow, a madman who had the audacity to claim he had actually been the White Pretender, a purveyor of evil and destruction who must be removed.

You should not have come . . . you bring only bloodshed and death . . .

He suspected emissaries awaited him in the anteroom of the royal apartments even now, messengers sent from the Table or the Mataio to call him into their presence. Or if not that, Blackwell would be there, pressuring him about the patch, providing all his reasons for why Abramm should wear it, why it wouldn't matter that much, why it would only be long enough to buy him the time he needed to corral Gillard and remove the threat of rebellion. . . .

It wasn't fear of death that disturbed him, he'd discovered, it was the fear of going to back to what he'd been. Little Abramm. Ignored, discounted, reviled. Cast out. It was losing the regard of men he had long wished to impress—though the man he most coveted was lost now regardless of what he did. Simon already knew what he was and had made his choice. His disgust would only increase should Abramm lie before all the Table and try to pretend he was something Simon knew very well he was not.

It was one thing to know all that. Another to face the men themselves and see the disgust and disappointment in their faces. He had come so far so fast, he supposed he should have expected this. Indeed, it was worse for all the early successes. When he'd stood on *Wanderer's* deck almost four weeks ago, contemplating his run for the Crown, he'd expected it to be impossible. He'd expected weeks, maybe months of waiting and preparing and political jockeying. He'd expected to fail and had been ready—he thought—to deal with that. Now, coming off so many successes, the prospect of failure was unbearably bitter.

And yet, was that not precisely what Tersius had done? Laid aside all his divine rights and privileges to endure the very things Abramm so feared—to be mistreated and ignored and despised? To go to that mount outside Xorofin and let the crowd impale him and the Shadow have him?

I'm not that strong, my Lord Eidon.

Not in your flesh, my son, but you know whatever I ask of you, I will give you the power to do. And to bear.

And is that what you wish me to bear, then, my Lord? To go back to being nothing and no one again? Scorned and ignored and helpless to do anything of consequence?

You will never be nothing or no one to me, my son. Nor helpless to do anything of consequence.

"Sire?"

The voice—not Trap's—spoke at the same time as Warbanner's head came up with a snort and he sidled away from the newcomer, the sleek plane of his side knocking Abramm back a step. He slid his hand down the stallion's muscular shoulder, murmuring words of reassurance as he looked over his back at Byron Blackwell approaching him down the stable aisle, enwrapped by the corona of light cast from the lantern in his hand.

Banner gave another snort and toss of his head, but Abramm shoved him back to his original spot and bid him settle down. Keeping a respectable distance, Blackwell hung his lantern on a hook between two stalls, then turned to face the king.

"Sir, I'm sorry to intrude—"

"Then why have you?"

Blackwell stopped several strides away and gaped at him. "I . . . I wasn't sure . . . well, I heard you'd returned from the headlands some time ago, and there are men waiting outside your chamber—"

"Now *there's* an unexpected development," Abramm said sourly, aware of his sarcastic tone, but not caring. He was king. And this day had not gone well. And he was not at all happy to see Blackwell here.

Blackwell bore it stoically, standing straight, hands at his sides. "Sir, the Mataio has officially accused you of being Terstan."

"As we knew they would."

"They've issued a proclamation and are demanding the Table denounce you. The Table's been arguing about it all day." He paused, and his hands came up to clasp each other in that annoying gesture he seemed to fall into when rattled. "The patch will need time to cure, sir, and there's no telling when they'll finally bring their demand to you."

Abramm swept the brush across Banner's back and down his flank. "I'm not using the patch, Byron."

He glimpsed the count's openmouthed stare out of the corner of his eye, just before he dropped out of sight as Abramm bent to brush the sweat-clumped hairs on Warbanner's hock. He ran a hand down the horse's leg, checking for swellings and tender spots, but there weren't any.

On the far side, Byron cleared his throat and tried again. "Sir, no one will be put off by a simple denial this time. And they are not going to let you refuse. . . ."

"They will receive neither denial nor refusal." He stepped back and dropped the brush into the wall-bolted bin beside the open stall door. "I suggest you distance yourself from me right now. You might want to prepare a declaration of denunciation, as well. Or perhaps it would be better to simply leave town." Unhooking the horse, Abramm led him into the stall, removed the lead, then stepped out again. The half door creaked as he shut it, then slammed the bolt home.

Byron was still standing there, hands clasped at his waist. "I would never denounce you, sir. I believe with all my heart you are just what Kiriath needs right now, and I know I am not alone in that."

"Then perhaps you should get your fellows to come forth and make their views public."

"Sir—"

"There comes a time when a man has to stand up for who he is and what he believes. I've had enough hiding."

"Sir, they'll arrest you for heresy. Bonafil's already talking about the need for you to be cloistered in one of the Mataio's far keeps so you may be delivered from the spell that has ensnared you. And once they take you, you know what'll happen to the rest of us. If you care nothing for yourself—"

"Why do you think I told you to leave town?"

"Please, sir . . . I'm as eager to have you reveal the truth as anyone, but it needs to be done on your own terms, not theirs. And certainly not Gillard's."

And that one pierced to Abramm's heart. Of all things, the worst was to have this matter forced upon him. To have to go before the Table like some misbehaving child and confess to something that not only wasn't a crime, wasn't heresy, but was the only true way to know who Eidon really was. The only true power that could protect the realm from all the dangers it faced.

"The idea of your being be dragged before those self-righteous sticks," Blackwell went on, "and questioned like some common criminal is—well, the idea infuriates me."

"As it does me. Which is precisely why I intend to go to them first."

Blackwell flinched, and his eyes, fixed upon something down the aisle, darted back to Abramm's. "Go to them, sir?"

Abramm glanced at Trap. "Captain, would you see that Erad is saddled?"

"Yes, sir."

As Trap wheeled away, Abramm returned his attention to Blackwell, still staring at him in horror. That sense of crazy bravado welled up in him, reminding him of the night he'd told the Dorsaddi he would awaken their Heart, not even knowing at the time what that Heart was. He had not done it, but the heart had awakened all the same. And nothing had turned out as he had expected. Or feared.

Perhaps it would be thus again, although he didn't think so. Indeed, he felt certain that disaster loomed ahead, and all he'd come back to accomplish would remain undone. He'd left Hur for naught. But if that was Eidon's will for him, so be it.

He jerked up his chin and, holding Blackwell's gaze with his own, pulled free the laces of his leather jerkin, folding under the front edges of his blouse's slitted neckline to reveal the golden shield glittering on his chest.

Byron didn't quite gasp, but his eyes grew wider still as they fixed upon it. His prominent Adam's apple bobbed against the white linen of his cravat as he swallowed. At Abramm's back came the clump and clack of Erad being led from his stall farther down the aisle, the lead's slide-hook clinking as Trap snapped it to the tie ring.

Abramm glanced over his shoulder. He hadn't really intended Trap to saddle the horse, but seeing as there were no grooms in the immediate vicinity, he realized there was no one else.

A sudden spate of footfalls, rustling, and low voices drew his attention back to the other end of the aisle behind Blackwell, where two cloaked figures had appeared out of the darkness to hurry toward them. One was very tall, the other very short—more boy-sized than man. Abramm's hand dropped to his sword as Byron whipped around with a cry, and the duo stopped in their tracks halfway from the stable door to where Abramm stood. Immediately they flung back their cowls, and a deep, familiar voice rumbled up the aisle. "My lord, it's only us."

"Haldon? Jared?" Blackwell cried almost indignantly as he stepped toward them. "What are you doing here?"

Haldon ignored him and continued on toward Abramm, bobbing his head in a half bow of greeting, his glance sticking briefly on Abramm's now exposed shieldmark. "Gadrielites burst into your quarters, sir. Front and back doors simultaneously. We barely escaped through the panel in the bedchamber."

"Panel in the bedchamber?" Blackwell demanded. "What panel?"

"So now they know of it?" Abramm asked, also ignoring Blackwell.

"Well, sir, we hope they think we went out the window and climbed down the trellis, but we can't be sure. They're all over the palace, but it doesn't look as if they've followed us."

"That you know of," Blackwell said.

"What about the armsmen?" This from Trap, having left Erad to join them.

"There weren't many, Lieutenant," Haldon said to him. "Most had disappeared for some reason. And those that remained—well, I'm sorry to say they were part of it." His gaze came back to Abramm. "Nor were they all Gadrielites. Some of them were Gillard's men. I recognized Matheson's voice for sure."

"So Gillard has joined forces with the Mataio." Given his brother's hatred for him, and the desperation he must be feeling right now after his failed attempt at assassination, it was his only option.

"Joined forces and taken over the palace it sounds like!" Blackwell said, turning to Abramm. "You've got to get out of here, sir."

Haldon glanced at the lantern burning brightly from its hook on the post and moved to turn down its flame. "The grooms have been ordered to report when you arrive, sir," he explained. "So far they haven't obeyed, but sooner or later they're going to have to say something. For now this stable is counted as unoccupied, and it's kept people away. No one's really sure where you are."

"What about Captain Channon?"

"I don't know, sir. He came by and warned us to be ready to move, then left."

Abramm turned to Trap. "They'll have the roads north blocked for sure."

"There is a way out through the King's Preserve."

"Which Gillard knows well. He'll have the docks covered, too."

"We could try Southdock. I know plenty of places to hide there."

"No, Southdock's going to have more than enough troubles shortly." Abramm exhaled sharply and paused as he thought. Then, "We'll cross the river, but not by any of the bridges. We'll have to use a barge. And we'll need someone on the bridge to distract the guards. Blackwell, do you think you could handle that?"

They all turned to Blackwell, who was staring hard down the stable aisle in the direction from which Haldon and the others had come, though he didn't appear to be looking so much as listening. His eyes were blank, almost glazed with the intensity of his concentration.

"Blackwell?"

The man didn't move. Didn't even blink.

"Blackwell?" Abramm stepped toward him. "Are you ill?"

The man started violently, as if all the life came rushing back into him at once. He looked around, dazed. "Sir?"

"What's the matter with you? Did you see something?"

"See?" He frowned, and then understanding dawned. "Oh. No. I thought I heard hooves or voices or something."

Abramm glanced at Trap who was already making for the end of the stable. He disappeared into the gloom, reappeared not long after and waved an all-clear. Abramm turned back to Blackwell and explained about the barge and Bunman Bridge.

"A barge, sir?" Blackwell said weakly.

"You have an aversion to barges?"

"To the water, sir. I can't swim. I nearly drowned as a boy."

Abramm cocked a brow at him. "Well, that makes you an even better choice for the role of distracter, since you'll be on the bridge. You'll have to disguise yourself. Perhaps an old woman with a cart. A heavily laden cart."

"Yes," Trap said, rejoining them. "They'll have to search all the crates. . . ."

"But how will I know when you wish me to move?"

"Let us take care of that."

"And what about after, sir?"

"Why, hopefully you'll be free to go your way, find a place upriver to stay the night, and see what your options are in the morning."

"So you're fleeing the realm altogether?"

"I'll let you know. If you're interested."

"I told you, sir, I am convinced it is you Eidon wants on the throne of Kiriath. And I will do whatever you ask of me to see that you regain it."

He stood there, hands working before him, eyes flicking from one to the other of them all standing around him. Then his gaze came back to Abramm, and abruptly he sank to one knee and bowed his head.

"Abramm Kalladorne, King of Kiriath, I give you my everlasting fealty, here before these witnesses. You are my king and ever will be. Whatever you ask, I will do, whatever I have, it is yours, whenever you call, I will come, so long as there is life in my flesh to do so."

It raised the hairs up the back of Abramm's neck every time he found himself looking down at the top of a man's bowed head and hearing those sacred binding words pledged to himself. It never seemed right, for what was he but a man like them? Perhaps much less of a man than some who had given him their liege. But once given, it could not be spurned, could not be disputed or protested. To do anything but accept made little of it and the man who gave it.

And so he swallowed down the squirming discomfort and touched his right hand to Blackwell's head as protocol demanded, his signet ring sparkling even in the dimmed light of the lantern. He said the age-old words of response with solemn dignity. "I receive this precious gift with gratitude and swear upon my name and my blood and my god that I will never abuse nor take lightly that which has been offered."

He pulled his hand away. Byron crouched there a moment, head bowed and motionless as if overcome with emotion. Abramm stepped back, and finally the other man took in a deep breath and raised his head and stood.

No one knew quite what to say at first. Then Trap murmured, "We have no time to waste, sir."

"Right." Abramm pivoted and stepped to Warbanner's stall door, slamming back the bolt and swinging the half door inward.

Blackwell protested at once. "You're not going to ride him, are you, sir?"

"I won't leave him here for Gillard to abuse."

"But everyone will know it's you."

"Only if they can tell it's him." He turned again to Trap, who already knew what he wanted and was already heading for the tack room at the end of the aisle. "I want him fully caparisoned. In as dark a color as you can find."

"Well, here, you'll need a light," Blackwell said, snatching the dimmed lantern from its hook. But as he moved to follow Trap, he stepped too close to Banner, who seized his chance and lunged, teeth snapping nastily just short of Blackwell's arm as the man jerked himself away. He crashed into the stall door, losing his grip on the lantern. It sailed into the stall, smashed into one of the few spaces where the straw was thinnest, and burst apart. Flames erupted as if from a firework, and Banner veered back with a snort and a squeal. The lead went taut; he tossed his head and it came free, slapping into the side of Abramm's face as the horse took off.

Releasing his frustration in a burst of unkingly epithets, Abramm grabbed a pail of grain and went after him, leaving the others to put out the fire. But as he reached the doorway, he found his way blocked by a curving wall of men, cloaked and cowled in gray, standing just at the edge of the arc of lantern light. Gadrielites.

Ten of them, all armed, though they had not yet drawn their swords. Momentum carried Abramm two strides into the yard before he stopped, already weighing options. Ten to one was not good odds, even for him. Trap could even it up, but he had an idea the doorway at the stable's far end was similarly guarded and Trap would have his hands full there.

He had no idea where Warbanner had gone, which was too bad, since he could really use the horse right now. The young stallion was far from trained to come on call. Worse, he'd already eaten his fill of grain while Abramm had been brushing him, so he was unlikely to come to it now, especially with all these strangers standing about. And once the fighting began, he'd get more spooked than he already was and run for the farthest corner of the yard. They'd be lucky if he didn't jump the fence and hie out into the wilds.

One of the Gadrielites at the center of the line cast back his cowl, flipped the right edge of his cloak over his shoulder, and stepped forward into brighter light, gloved hand resting on his sword hilt. Abramm recognized the hatchet face and tightly queued hair at once. "Prittleman. Your hubris knows no bounds, it seems. I have not given you leave to return to palace grounds."

"I do not need your leave, Abramm Kalladorne," Prittleman said, closing the gap between them. His eyes were fixed upon Abramm's chest, where the golden shield glittered faintly between the open neck-slits of jerkin and blouse. Even with the light at Abramm's back and his chest in shadow, the mark would be visible. Especially to a man so intent upon finding it as Prittleman.

The dark, too-close eyes climbed to meet Abramm's, a smile curving the hard lips. "I knew there was something wrong about you the moment I met you."

"The feeling was mutual, I assure you," Abramm said, shaking the grain pail in both hands, more out of habit than any real hope Banner would come.

"Rhiad was right, wasn't he? You came to us marked by the Shadow from the very start, and killed that sea beast with your evil power."

"I came to you marked, but not by Shadow. And it was Eidon's Light that killed the kraggin."

"Liar! Blasphemer!"

Abramm shrugged and shook the pail again.

"Your horse will not come. We seized him when he first came out of the barn."

Abramm laughed. "Now who's the liar, Prittleman?" That they'd done no such thing was obvious from the fact that none had been bitten, kicked, or trampled.

Prittleman stiffened, his thin face darkening, gloved hand curling round his sword hilt. "I've had enough of your insolence, heretic. You will come with us now."

"I'm afraid you'll have to catch me first." Abramm whirled and ran back into the barn. With ten opponents he would need the smaller space, since trying to maneuver them into each other's way out in the yard would be a feat greater than he could pull off. Behind him Prittleman shouted and, in a rasp of steel, thumped after him.

Only a few steps into the shadowed aisle Abramm turned back and flung the grain bucket hard into his pursuer's face. His blades sprang to hand, and in a heartbeat he'd slashed the thumb tendons on Prittleman's sword arm, the man's long rapier clanging to the stone floor from a suddenly useless hand. Prittleman's men had followed a few steps behind, not because they were afraid to engage, Abramm thought, so much as to grant their leader the honor of taking down their quarry alone. Prittleman, after all, had a reputation for having a fair hand with a blade. Not fair enough, though.

Now, as their leader swore and clutched his injured arm, the men behind him faltered, wide eyes darting up to Abramm in surprise. A moment they hesitated, then, urged on by Prittleman, surged around their leader's now hunched form. Abramm angled backward up the aisle, hoping to string the men out, so he could take them one or two at a time. As feared, he'd glimpsed Trap when he'd come in, faced off against another group of Gadrielites at the aisle's far end. There'd be no help from that quarter, nor from the other men clustered at the aisle's midpoint, before Warbanner's blackened, still-smoking stall. Neither Haldon nor Blackwell were swordsmen, and Jared was just a boy.

The first blade came slashing down, and Abramm caught it on his dagger, returning the strike with a lunge of his own that plunged his rapier into the shoulder of the man's sword arm. He gave the blade a quick twist and yanked it out, to block the slashing downswing of the next attacker. His first opponent now lurching backward into the path of an approaching third, Abramm slashed at the second Gadrielite's face, opening a cut on his brow. A second slash loosed the longsword from his hand, and for a moment Abramm had a barrier of staggering, howling men between himself and the other Gadrielites seeking to take him down.

Then all devolved into a flurry of flashing swords and rippling cloaks, of clinks and cracks and arm-jolting jars as he caught strike after strike and delivered thrust after thrust. There was no time or thought for such niceties as striking only nonlethal blows. He must incapacitate as many of his opponents as possible, and if some died in the process, so be it. They had started this fight, after all.

In the end, only two men remained standing and, having watched the fates of their fellows, they dropped their blades and fled, their gray cloaks sailing out behind them, breaking suddenly free, and floating to the ground in their wakes.

Abramm straightened and stood for a moment, catching his breath, eyes flicking across the fallen men, noting at once that Prittleman was not among them. He must have run away shortly after the contest had begun. At the far end of the aisle, Trap's battle appeared to have come to an end, as well, and—Abramm squinted in surprise—was that Channon and Philip and others of the royal guard with him? It was! How had they known to come and help?

Before he could answer that question, however, he turned back to the vanquished and, sheathing his dagger, walked among them to collect their weapons and see how many still lived. It was a distasteful, guilt-producing chore, for now that the threat was over, the men were only men again, rebels to be sure, but his own subjects nonetheless. And they were hurt—or dead—at his hand. Worse was knowing that some needed medical attention, yet he could not risk bringing down all Gillard's men upon him.

Thankfully, Channon and Trap joined him just as he tossed the last of the swords onto the pile of them he had made, and Channon took matters from there. Men were assigned to strip the cloaks off all of them, then separate the dead from the living and herd the latter into one of the empty stalls. Both upper and lower doors were then locked and barred as Channon pointed at the pile of confiscated cloaks.

"It appears we have our way out of the city, sir."

Abramm frowned at him. "As Gadrielites?"

"No one will dare to stop us. Not tonight."

"Then again, they might—Prittleman and a couple of others got away. They'll be back."

"But by then we'll be gone, sir. And they'd have to have wings to get word out ahead of us."

Abramm turned his frown to Trap, who shrugged. "The faster we move," he said, "the better our chances."

And then, as if to put the cap on the argument, here came Warbanner, walking back into the barn with a swish of his tail as if nothing had happened, stopping several strides in to lip the last of the grain from the fallen bucket.

32

Using soot from the burned-out stall, Abramm darkened Warbanner's face and neck, then swirled the deep blue caparison over him and set the saddle into place on his back. Less than twenty minutes after the attack had ended, he and Trap were ready to go.

Cloaked in Gadrielite gray, they no longer needed the Bunman Bridge gambit, deciding instead to make for a Terstan safe house Trap knew about on the Keharnen Rise. Using Haldon as a decoy—he was about Abramm's height—Channon and his men would head east across the preserve, hoping their own gray cloaks would get them through any guards already stationed at the one exit point in the eastern hedge. Once assured they were not being followed, they'd circle back to meet up with Abramm at the safe house.

As expected, their gray cloaks got Abramm and Trap through the palace gates without incident. From there they turned north onto the Keharnen road, congested now with carts, horses, and pedestrians as the citizens of Springerlan returned home for the night. The traffic forced them to keep the horses to a trot, hoping no one looked at them too closely. In fact, their cloaks turned out to serve another purpose. Not only did no one look at them closely, but people had a tendency to turn aside and move out of the way as if hoping *they* wouldn't be noticed. At the guard station that had been hastily established at the city's edge, they trotted past the line of carts and coaches waiting to be searched, and were waved on by harried guards who had more suspects than they could handle. After that, the lantern light and busy clatter swiftly gave way to shadows and starlight as the road wound up the side of the escarpment, and they found themselves eerily alone—few wanted to be out at night with the evils that roamed the land these days. Least of all now, with that new beast just come out of Graymeer's.

They cantered up the gentle incline, for once Warbanner's pace not outstripping that of his companion, thanks to the fact he'd been out all day. Nor was it in the horses' best interest to be riding fast up a road they could not see well. Even a canter was too fast, so once they were far enough from the city, they returned to a vigor-saving, ground-eating trot, which they maintained for over an hour, until the road grew too steep. As they climbed the switchbacks toward the top of the escarpment, Trap peered repeatedly into the darkness at the end of each north-side bending until he finally turned off onto what appeared to be a game trail.

It traversed the steep, rocky slope for a bit, then turned downward, entering a forest that echoed with the rush of running water. Abramm guessed it for the River Hennepen, which crossed the Keharnen Plateau from the east and cut through the rise here at the Springerlan's northernmost end, running down through the valley to join with the River Kalladorne. The trail they now rode wound through dense foliage to the cleft itself, and there ascended upstream along the chuckling froth of the Hennepen. The cleft narrowed as they climbed, until the trail was little more than a ledge running up the vine-cloaked wall.

Just below the top of the rise, Trap reined Erad sharply right and parted a curtain of vine to enter the good-sized tunnel beyond. The sound of the river faded swiftly behind them, and the darkness thickened to the point Abramm couldn't see his hand in front of his face. He was tempted to make a kelistar, but decided he'd better follow Trap's lead.

The horses' hooves thumped on soft ground, then clopped loudly over bare stone as they left the tunnel for a wider space reeking of horses and straw. Now Trap did make a light, revealing a dozen horses tied to a line on the left, and on the right, a jumble of boxes, rope, lumpish sacks, kegs, saddles, pack frames, and other assorted paraphernalia. Ahead, a smaller tunnel led off into darkness.

A whisper of movement behind drew Abramm's glance as three men emerged from the shadows framing the outside opening. Plainly dressed, with swords at their hips and Terstan shields exposed in the neck openings of their jerkins, they approached and offered to take the newcomers' horses. Abramm recognized none of them, and if they recognized him, they didn't show it. They did seem to know Trap, however.

"I'm surprised they let us in so easily," Abramm said as he and his liege-man walked down the second tunnel to the main room.

"The opening's cloaked," Trap said. "You can't get in unless you're Terstan and know exactly where it is. This canyon is riddled with caves just like this one. We passed numerous openings on the way up, though you couldn't see them in the dark. And it's so treacherous, if you don't go exactly the right way, you end up in places you don't want to be."

"Reminds me of the SaHal."

The main room was a cavern four times larger than the first, lit by keli-stars tucked in niches carved high into the walls. More gear and supplies had been stacked and dumped in the larger right side of the chamber, while the left served as a gathering/living space for the refugees. A long wooden table flanked by crudely made benches stood beside a raised stone fire pit, in which burned a small blaze. Rolled sleeping mats stood in a niche, and across from them, a large water cask lay on a stand, the ground wet beneath its spigot. Five men sat at the table, bent over a ragged map lit by kelistars clustered on a tarnished starstick. Others sat with their backs against the walls, looking worn and weary, women and children among them. They all looked up with interest at the arrival of the newcomers, and Abramm gave a start as he recognized first Seth Tarker, then Everitt Kesrin, among the men at the table.

"Kohal!" he cried, striding across the room to greet him. "I thought you were going to the Council Hall." And there was Yacopan, too, standing by the wall behind his employer.

"I did." Kesrin looked grim. "Watched them vote to summon you for an accounting. When Prittleman took the lead in making sure you appeared, I left."

"I took too long," Abramm confessed, still irritated with himself for his failing. "Let all my doubts get to me and dragged my feet until they came out looking."

Kesrin regarded him soberly. "I don't think it would have mattered. Not from what I saw at the Table. Prittleman was frothing at the mouth."

Abramm frowned at him. "How did you know I would come here?"

"I didn't. But I didn't want to stay in Southdock tonight. Many of us have fled. At least the city itself."

"So . . . what? You plan to wait it out here until things settle down?"

Kesrin glanced at his tablemates. "Well, Sire, that depends on what *you're* going to do."

Abramm noted that the moment Kesrin had let drop that "Sire," the idly curious regard of the others shifted to sharply focused attention. Now as he glanced around at them, every one scrambled to his or her feet, making various kinds of bows and nods and each pair of eyes darting from his shieldmark to his face and back. Each displayed a different reaction, too: wonder, chagrin, excitement, embarrassment, even anger. Seeing the direction of his gaze, Kesrin glanced round himself, then grimaced and said, "I believe we can find someplace more private to discuss this. Come with me, sir." He started toward the far side of the large chamber, then turned back. "Have you eaten?"

"Not since . . ." Abramm trailed off. He'd had a twistbread on his way out of the palace this morning, and nothing since. And yesterday he'd eaten little more.

Kesrin turned to one of the men. "Give us some of those apples and the cheese. I think we have a loaf of bread left, as well."

They took the food and retired to the far side of the chamber, where a battered square table stood among the boxes and casks. Kesrin bloomed four kelistars and set them on the wooden starstick at the table's midst, then pulled back one of the two chairs for Abramm. He would have stayed standing himself had not Abramm motioned him into the other chair, probably would have sliced the bread and cheese had Abramm not taken it from him and done the job himself.

Kesrin let him eat for a bit, during which Trap brought them a pitcher of water and two cups, then returned to the others at the long table. Once Abramm had eaten most of the cheese and bread, Kesrin returned to the subject. "So, my lord, what *are* you going to do? Stay and fight? Or run away?"

Abramm sliced off a wedge of apple and ate it. He didn't much like the term *run away*. But he didn't much like the idea of people dying because of him, either. "'There is a time to flee,'" he said softly, referencing a passage from the Second Word.

"And a time to stay and fight. I'm not judging you, Sire. None of us are. We just need to know what you're going to do."

Abramm sliced out another wedge, then sat staring at its crisp white meat and green skin. "I *want* to stay and fight," he said finally, feeling that desire with grim ferocity every time he thought of Prittleman and Gillard and the Mataio. "It's just that, since the day I set foot on Kiriathan shores, I've been haunted by visions of people dying because of me. And now it seems they're about to come true."

Kesrin leaned back in his chair as Yacopan brought him a cup of tea. He took it with thanks but waited until the man was gone before speaking again. "If people die, it won't be because of you; it will be because of what you represent. Freedom." His expression became grim again as he fixed his gaze on Abramm. "For make no mistake, sir. If you turn and run, there will be no freedom in this land. The Mataio will own it. And there are more than you know who would fight to see that stopped, both those who wear the shield and those who don't."

"But are there enough to win?"

Kesrin blew on his tea a few times before taking a sip. "Sometimes it's enough merely to fight."

This reminded Abramm too much of the conversations he'd had with Shettai. And yet . . . and yet Eidon had delivered him out of that. Superior numbers, superior forces had been defeated by inferior. It could happen again. Or not.

Over and over there was that vision, that sense that he'd come here to die, and that because of his choice and his presence and his intrusion, others would die, as well.

"'There is a time for war,' Abramm. 'And a time for peace.'" That was from the First Word. "Eidon has ordained both. And people die in war."

"I know. But it's different when your own decision is the one that sets it all in motion."

Kesrin met his eyes evenly. "I think that's part of what it is to be a king."

And then a man said from startlingly close, "Besides, you promised *me* you wouldn't back down."

Abramm jumped up at the sound of that familiar gravelly voice, a voice he had never expected to hear again, and certainly not in this place.

Simon Kalladorne stood in the wide aisle among the boxes, Ethan Laramor at his back, the men in the gathering area behind him all on their feet and watching. A blindfold dangled in Simon's gloved hand, and now his eyes darted to the shield gleaming in the neckline V of Abramm's jerkin, held there a moment, then flicked up to meet Abramm's gaze.

Kesrin, who had risen when Abramm did, murmured a quiet excuse for leaving and did so, taking his tea and Laramor with him. The two Kalladornes stood facing one another, Simon apparently as much at a loss for words now as Abramm was. Finally Abramm indicated the chair Kesrin had vacated and they sat, the starstick with its kelistars standing on the scarred table between them. Six green Wilshire apples lay scattered amid the crumbs, including the one Abramm had started to slice and eat.

Simon, with only a brief glance at the kelistars on their stand, had returned his gaze to Abramm. His weathered face was stern and unreadable, save for a remnant of the words he had just spoken, which continued to echo in Abramm's mind. *"You promised me you wouldn't back down."*

"Why are you here, Uncle? Gillard has won. I've been exposed for a heretic, and they tried to seize me on the grounds of my own palace."

"So I heard. Heard how you fought your way free, too. Ten against one."

Abramm had nothing to say to that.

"They say your skill is phenomenal."

"Of course they'd say that. Anything less and they look stupid and inept." He looked up sharply. "Is that why you're here? Because my skill is phenomenal?"

"No." The gray whiskers on his uncle's cheek rippled as he clenched his teeth. "I'm here because you asked me to decide who I thought was best for Kiriath." Again he fell silent, adding only when Abramm was about to speak, "I also find I have sorely misjudged you. And Gillard, it would seem." The voice was clipped, neutered by the pain from which it sprang.

It was an admission Abramm had spent most of his life longing to hear, yet now that he did, he felt none of the warm validation he had imagined, only the stark and bitter anguish of another man's failure. He had been to the valley where Simon stood right now, watching his own certainties crumble to dust. Too well did he know the shame of confronting one's own blindness and gullibility.

"Yet you met with him this morning," he said quietly.

Simon snorted again. "You know about that, do you? I suppose you would. As you also know, I am sure, that I did not go to your armsmen and give his position away." He paused, gloved finger tracing along a gouge in the tabletop. "Gillard's known your secret since he sent that assassin after you in your bedchamber, by the way. The assassin no one believed existed, because you couldn't possibly have disarmed him so easily." His tone turned ironic.

"That you met with him at all, though—"

"*He* was the one who wanted the meeting! I went solely in hopes of persuading him to abandon this mad course he has set for himself."

"He will never abandon it so long as I am on the throne," Abramm said.

"I know." Simon fell silent, caught up in unpleasant memories.

"So what did he want?"

His uncle released a resigned breath. "For me to join him, of course. He believed that once I had seen him move against you publicly, I would be forced to abandon my arguments on your behalf and declare for him."

"And having you, he expected the army to follow."

Simon smiled slightly, a dry irony in his eyes as he looked at Abramm. "You *are* quite the strategist, aren't you? Yes, that was his intent. Though I am not at all sure even had I gone with him it would have turned out so."

"You are our greatest hero, Uncle. The armsmen all revere you."

"I am an old man, my heroics twenty years and more in the past. And *I* did not kill the kraggin. Nor clean out Graymeer's in a day—if one can believe the rumors."

Feeling his face burn, Abramm returned his attention to his apple, picking up the knife to slice another wedge.

"Kiriath has a new hero now," Simon said softly.

Why did this suggestion always fill him with aversion and dismay? Why did it frighten him so, bring these words of denial to his lips? And why was it most discomfiting of all to hear it coming from this man?

His uncle went on. "I don't think you're aware of the reputation you have gained with the royal guard, sir. Are still gaining, in fact. After what you did at the ball last night—and again at the stable tonight—this tale of your being the White Pretender will no longer be doubted by anyone. Young Lady Madeleine's song will be sung far and wide, along with the one chronicling your exploits with the kraggin, and . . . well, as I said, we have a new hero in Kiriath."

"I did not come to be a hero!" Abramm muttered.

"Nor, I suspect, did you come to start a war. Yet a hero you are, and a war you have started."

And men will die because of you.

Abramm cut his wedge and popped it into his mouth, chewing slowly, tasting only uncertainty and dread. Simon picked up one of the apples, too, turning it in his large hands. "There is something else I must know, sir. Did your brother sell you into slavery?"

Abramm cut another wedge. "I have no proof of that."

His uncle's hands went still. "You're *sure* someone else wasn't behind it?"

Abramm snorted. "He came down to Southdock that night to laugh in my face, Uncle. Just so I *would* be sure."

Simon said nothing for a long moment, staring at the apple in his hands. "Yet you said nothing."

"Why could I have said? Without proof, who would have believed me? Anyway, it's over. And even if Gillard meant for me to die, Eidon meant for me to live. I never would have become the White Pretender if not for Gillard's treachery."

"And now you've come to pay him back."

Abramm looked up sharply. "Not at all!"

"No?" Simon's eyes narrowed. "Then why did you come?"

"Because . . . I believed it was my duty. That my people needed me." And here he was, blushing again at the hubris in his words, half expecting his uncle to laugh in his face.

But Simon did not laugh. Instead, he looked sadly sober. "They do," he murmured. "And that is why *I* have come to you." His jaw tightened and the blue eyes looked fiercely into Abramm's own. "To give you my fealty, here and now. In front of these witnesses." He tilted his head toward the men at the other end of the room. "If you will have it."

And so it was that Abramm stood, and his uncle, Simon Kalladorne, Duke of Waverlan, Grand Marshall of the Royal Armies, dropped stiffly to one knee before him, with all the men across the room now watching in startled attention, and for the second time that night, Abramm received a man's sacred oath of fealty.

This was far more discomfiting than receiving Blackwell's, however, because Abramm had always looked up to Simon. It didn't seem right to have the old man kneeling before him. And more than ever he felt the burden of something precious entrusted to him and the keen awareness that he was not remotely, in and of himself, worthy of receiving it.

After that they returned to where the others had gathered at the table by the fire and got down to business. Simon said Lords Foxton and Whitethorne and several others were firmly in Abramm's camp, waiting only for word from him to ride. "And there are many in the army who will side with you, as well, once they're sure what you're going to do. Right now no one knows. Gillard is already claiming you've fled, in fact."

Abramm sat at the head of the long table, Simon seated at his right, the rest of the men he knew best ranged along the benches, with the others standing behind them, faces lit by the pale light of the kelistars. "What do you suggest I do, Uncle?" Abramm asked.

"Set up a headquarters somewhere—north, maybe—but not too far, and put out a call for all who support the rightful king of our land to join you."

"But who would come? A few lords, perhaps. The armsmen have been trained to obey their superiors, not go hieing off every which direction. Besides, I doubt most of them even care who is king, so long as they get fed and paid."

Simon braced his forearms on the table, gloved hands folded. "I believe you'll be surprised, sir. I suggest the Valley of the Seven Peaks, south of the Snowsong."

"That's the one with all the ruins, isn't it?"

"The ancient city of Tuk-Rhaal, yes. More important, you have a holding there, Stormcroft. It's built on a promontory—virtually impregnable—with plenty of room inside for an encampment. A stream runs right by it, and the forests are filled with game. Not likely to see much snow, either, even once the storms get going. Not that I think you should wait that long."

He fell silent, waiting for Abramm's approval. And Abramm had no argument with his plans, it was just . . . hard to make the final decision. As easily as he had slipped into the mindset of waging war with the Dorsaddi, now that it was his own people, his own soldiers—men like Trap and Will Ames and Channon, boys like Philip and even Jared—how hard it all became. The thought of giving orders that could cost those men their lives, that would start the war he had never wanted to bring upon his land tormented him.

Simon read his mind. "Men will die regardless. Now or later. Fewer or more. That is why we are willing to give our lives as soldiers, Abramm, to defend this realm from those who would oppress her and steal her and defile her. Whether those come from within or without, the call to fight them remains."

"There is a time for war."

"You are Kiriath's rightful king," Simon went on. "And more, you are the right man for the job. You know I don't hold with your religious views, but if I believed Eidon existed, I would believe you are the man he has chosen."

Abramm sat back in his chair and let his gaze drift over the men around him, seated and standing, their faces grave but determined, all of them looking to him to lead them. He felt as he did that first day he stepped into Katahn's training compound, staring down at the sword being offered to him, knowing that, should he close his hand around its hilt, his life—and maybe even his soul—would change forever. Right now he was being offered another kind of sword. *But that's part of what it is to be a king.*

He released a low breath and nodded. "Very well. We stay and fight. For Kiriath. And for freedom."

33

Despite a cold and steady rain, Rhiad kept them moving throughout the night and most of the next day. Wet, exhausted, and numb with cold, Carissa followed in a half stupor. Around her, water pelted through the forest, dripping off leaves of red and gold and brown, and pocking the puddles on the muddy track they followed. The clouds hung so low they misted the treetops and all the world seemed dead and empty.

At first she could hardly believe what had happened, her struggle to comprehend and accept hampered by the speed at which events had transpired, and by the unrelenting and surreal nature of this ride through the dark and the rain. She hadn't spoken a word, nor had Rhiad, since they'd left the fortress at Breeton, though at times he muttered to himself. She thought at first he was talking to the creature he sheltered in his lap, but when at last she'd heard him clearly enough to catch the vitriol in his tone, she decided otherwise.

As to where he was going or why he'd come through that corridor, she had no idea. Nor did she know why he had taken her with him. Revenge, she could have understood, for she couldn't help wondering if his present scarred state was the result of her own actions four years ago in Esurh. But he'd said nothing about revenging himself on her, and had restrained his pet by telling it he had another use for her. *"She's very important to him,"* he'd added. Whoever "him" was.

Rennalf? Rhiad *had* come through Rennalf's corridor, though how he'd come to be in Rennalf's employ was a mystery that bordered on the inexplicable. Genuine or not, he was a known Mataian, and Rennalf would have no truck with a Mataian. Nor could she imagine Rhiad consenting to work for a border lord. In fact, she couldn't imagine *this* Rhiad consenting to work for anyone, for he seemed quite mad. Besides, if Rennalf had sent him, shouldn't they be heading north? Perhaps not, if he was taking her to another corridor. Heading north, they would find travel conditions increasingly difficult, so if another doorway lay to the south, that would surely be the direction to go.

"Eidon will make us a way," Elayne had told her at Owl Creek.

Well, if this was the "way" Eidon had made, Carissa was not impressed. Now, after almost twenty-four hours in the saddle, she was so tired she barely felt the pain of wrists rubbed raw in the attempt to free them and was all but falling from Heron's back every time the mare set a foot down awkwardly. She was beginning to wonder how much it would hurt just to let herself fall. Would Rhiad simply ride on unheeding? When he finally did stop, maybe she would be dead, and wouldn't that just fix his plans! Whatever they were.

Heron stumbled to a stop and Carissa looked up. Her captor had flung back his cowl to gaze skyward, where streaks of blue sky now showed between the rapidly shifting, orange-gilt edges of the breaking overcast. The rain was slacking off, too, though the forest still dripped vigorously. Suddenly the little beast sprang from under Rhiad's cloak to the ground and disappeared into the forest. After a moment Rhiad kicked Arrow forward again and Heron followed, their hooves sucking and squelching in the mud. Somewhere a jay squawked, and Carissa decided it was time to drop another ring.

In addition to her four rings, already minus one, she'd picked up a spoon, a hoof pick, a snarl of horsehair, and a handful of coins she'd found hidden at the bottom of one of Rennalf's supply packs which Rhiad had forced her to go through in the kitchen. These she had slipped surreptitiously into her belt hoping to leave Cooper a trail. She suspected now it was an exercise in futility. Even if Coop was still alive and had somehow managed to escape the prison Rennalf had confined him in, the idea that he'd find something as small as one of her rings in all the long stretch of muddy track they'd traveled was ludicrous. But it was better than doing nothing, and in this rain, he'd have little else to go on.

Guess I'll just have to trust Eidon to open his eyes, she thought sardonically.

She had just worked the ring free and dropped it, along with one of the coins, when the little beast returned and after yammering at Rhiad for a bit, led them off the track and through the forest to the hollow, hut-sized stump of a gigantic, lightning-felled tree. A long, dark mound of decomposed trunk marked the path of its fallen upper parts, some of which remained intact, propped on the logs against which they had fallen. The nearest lay ten feet away, swarming with bees in the waning light.

Rhiad dismounted, untied the tether that bound Carissa to her saddle, and pulled her off, leaving her clinging to the stirrup leathers while she waited for her numb and useless legs to work again. She was barely able to stand unsupported when he shoved a water bag into her hands, gestured at the nearby stream, then turned to the task of getting firewood, wielding his ax with surprising strength and agility.

She stood there, working slowly through her surprise, buffeted by thoughts of escape that were discarded as impossible. If she was no longer tied to the saddle, her hands were still bound. She'd be on foot, and even if she managed to elude her captors—unlikely with that beast around—how could she survive alone in this weather? All of which Rhiad had undoubtedly considered.

The beast brought them a rabbit for dinner. Or at least, it brought a rabbit to where they sat inside the massive stump. Rhiad immediately confiscated the animal and began to skin. For a while the creature sat in the stump's opening growling softly as it watched him. Then it whirled and vanished into the forest to return with another rabbit. This Rhiad also took, though he met greater resistance now, the little beast yammering its protest like a child. Afterward it paced before the opening, growling and hissing until Rhiad straightened from his work and sharply told it to be off.

The third rabbit Rhiad did not take, by now having spitted the other two and set them roasting over the fire. The beast whined at him for a bit, as if it wanted another confrontation, and when it was still ignored, it ran off again, leaving its latest kill where it had been dropped. The creature brought three more rabbits, and finally a porcupine. By then the rain had started up again, so it dragged its latest prize into the shelter of the stump, and lay down with it. Then, seemingly unfazed by having its face full of quills, the beast very deliberately tore open the porcupine's soft belly and began pulling out its organs—not to eat, but to play with. Carissa had never seen anything so disgusting in her life, and the creature seemed to know it, its great green eyes fixed upon her as it worked.

It had acquired quite an array of "toys" when Rhiad roused from his mutterings and noticed. Instantly furious, the man leaped up, seized the mutilated porcupine, and cast it out into the night, kicking the organs after it and screaming epithets all the while. When his pet snarled a protest, he seized it, as well, and hurled it out into the rain after its prize.

Shrieking as if it were being burned alive and heedless of Rhiad's ire, the creature returned to them in a heartbeat, throwing itself on the dry ground beside the fire where it rolled about frantically, shuddering and twitching. Its human companions watched in astonishment as gradually its cries subsided. At last it ceased to thrash and rolled to its feet, hunkering before its master with piteous cries and doleful looks. Rhiad stared at it a moment more, then fell to his knees, gathering his pet into his arms and nuzzling the wet, blood-smeared head as he croaked out a stream of apologies. The beast licked his face almost tenderly in return.

After a bit, when the rabbits were cooked, he let the creature go, and it settled quietly at the edge of the circle, licking the blood from its paws. Rhiad tossed Carissa's rabbit into her lap, heedless of the hot grease that immediately seeped into her skirt, or the fact her hands were still bound. She heard him mutter something about "he will pay" and "shouldn't have poked his nose where it didn't belong" as he settled tailor-style across the fire from her, tearing off strips of rabbit as if it were the "he" he referred to and stuffing them into his mouth. ". . . useless cripple, am I?"

Carissa's appetite had long-since vanished, but she forced herself to eat anyway, determined to keep up her strength should an opportunity for escape arise. And once she was warm, fed, beginning to dry out, and no longer over-whelmed with terror, she thought it wasn't an unreasonable hope. It occurred to her now that Rhiad had taken all the supplies they could find in the fortress kitchen, indicating he planned a journey of at least several days. The farther they went along the road, the greater the chance of running into someone who might help her. Or of Cooper catching up before Rhiad could take her through the corridor..

Outside, the rain had once more become a steady downpour. Rhiad broke off his muttering to stoke the fire, then laid on another of the branches he'd cut earlier. Taking advantage of what seemed to be a break in his angry internal ramblings, Carissa asked him if he'd loosen the bonds on her hands, since they were getting swollen. He straightened from his work over the fire and glared at her with his good eye. "You think I am so stupid I would let you free to stab me in the night?"

Carissa frowned at him. "*Stab* you, Master Rhiad?"

"No, you'd lack the courage, wouldn't you? But you would slip away if you could."

Carissa's eyes went to the beast, still licking itself beside the wall of the stump. "I doubt your friend would allow that, sir."

The madman considered his pet for a moment as it paused in its grooming to meet his gaze. "You're right. If you leave my protection, it *will* kill you— rip that pretty face right off your skull."

She stared at him in horrified astonishment, the gruesome images the beast had poured into her mind on first meeting resurfacing in all their bloody glory.

Rhiad chuckled. "I see it's shown you."

"What do you want with me?"

"What do I want with you?" The brow over his one eye arched. "I should think it obvious after what you and your brother did to me."

"That was an accident. I never intended that—"

"You intended to get rid of me, and this is what came of it. For that you will pay. You will both pay. He thinks he has won, sending me away from Springerlan as he did, getting you to help him destroy that corridor. Hoping to finish the job you started in Esurh."

"I haven't spoken to Abramm in four years. And I had no idea— You came from Springerlan?!"

But he didn't hear her, caught up in his own ravings again. "He took it all from me, just as I'll take it from him. So straight and strong and handsome. I'll take it all back, you'll see. I got his blood and hair. There'll be no mistake. It knows him already, just as he knows it."

He raved on, making little sense, his voice falling away to that vitriolic mutter that now filled her with an unspeakable sense of dread. For enough came through that she began to put the pieces together. There'd been a gate to the Dark Ways in Springerlan, now destroyed—at Abramm's hand, apparently—through which Rhiad had barely escaped with his pet. He had not intended to come to Breeton, at all, but to an exit in the sea village of Longstrand. She figured her own efforts to destroy the corridor to Balmark had somehow drawn him to her—along with the flash of Terstan Light Abramm had sent after him—transferring her from Rennalf's hands to those of Rhiad. Who was now on his way back to Springerlan to revenge himself upon her brother. The part she was to play in it all remained unclear and was not something she wished to pursue. So once she had the gist of things, she stopped really listening to the rest of what he was saying. It was hard to follow anyway, and she had no way of knowing how much of it was even real. Better to concentrate on the good part, which was that Springerlan was less than two weeks away, that they'd be traveling through populated areas to reach it, and that surely there'd be opportunities for escape. Besides which, she was fairly confident Abramm could handle this threat, seeing as he'd already chased both Rhiad and his pet out of Springerlan in the first place—and destroyed the etherworld corridor, as well. After Beltha'adi, surely Rhiad was nothing.

Except . . . Rhiad hadn't said where the gate to the corridor was in Springerlan. And its destruction had not been a subtle exercise of Terstan Light. It was very possible Abramm's secret was already out, that he'd already been deposed, Gillard put back in power. Or maybe those hideous Gadrielites had taken him, hoping to "restore" his lost purity. He might be on the run. He might be dead, for all she knew.

Across from her, Rhiad gradually wound down, his rough voice drifting away to inaudible mutterings. His head dropped forward repeatedly, a short lock of gray hair dangling loose against his temple. Finally, after nearly falling into the flames, he flashed a glare at her, then wrapped his cloak about himself and lay down beside the fire. In moments his breathing had slowed and deepened. Over by the stump's ragged-edged doorway, his pet stopped licking itself and looked up—first at Rhiad, then at Carissa. After a moment it crept over to where his master lay and crouched beside him to lick the cut that slashed across the palm of his gnarled left hand.

She watched it from the corner of her eye, uneasy being alone with it and unwilling to look at it directly. Rhiad had said it would kill her without his protection, and she believed him, despite the creature's small and spindly stature. She'd seen how high it jumped, how easily it killed, and she'd seen the light of cruel intelligence in its eyes.

As if it sensed her thoughts, the beast stopped licking and turned its head to look at her. When she did not return the glance, it stood and walked slowly over to stand in front of her, eye to eye. This close she noticed how oversized its strange, long-toed paws looked, and how big its short, upright tufted ears seemed. The green eyes sought to hold hers, but she refused to cooperate, studying the dark, leathery skin of its short snout, puckered and swollen beneath a forest of stiff black-and-white quills. She could smell the musky stench of porcupine guts on its breath and Eidon alone knew what else.

The beast stepped closer, triggering a sudden burst of warmth at the right side of her waist. Slowly the creature lowered its head to sniff her legs, running its quilled nose along the bent length of both, crossed tailor style before her and covered by her cloak. All the while those green eyes sought hers as the warmth at her side grew to a point of pain, like something pinching her. She wanted to ease back from the beast, but feared to anger it and figured it would only follow anyway. Its emerald eyes glowed in her peripheral vision, and the compulsion to shift her gaze the fraction it would take to focus upon them increased. Doggedly she fixed her attention on the dark night beyond the shelter's opening, where the firelight flickered off slashes of rain. Under her cloak her fingers sought the Terstan orb, which she had managed to slip under her belt unnoticed in the first few moments after Rhiad had captured her back in Breeton. It was the source of the heat at her side, downright painful now, probably only moments from starting her clothes on fire. She should take it off.

Her fingers were starting to unwrap the broken chain from her belt when she realized what she was doing and stopped. By then the creature was literally in her face, its nose but a hair from her cheek. The smell of it grew thick and stifling, and it was that which unleashed her revulsion. She erupted, striking the beast's face as fire seared her waist and ran up her arm. The thing yowled, leaping ten feet—much farther than the force of her blow could have thrown it—to land on all fours, hissing with fury, ruff bristling about a snout full of sharp white teeth. The fire continued to burn at her waist as she let go of the chain and found the orb itself. A strong and covering presence flowed out of it, which the beast seemed to sense, ears flattening and eyes blazing as they sought again to snare her own while the tip of its tail twitched rhythmically back and forth.

Then beside the fire Rhiad lurched up with a cry. He sat groggily, looking from one to the other of them, and finally grasping the situation, commanded the creature to leave her alone. It yammered an apparent reply, to which he responded, "You are not big enough yet. Nor strong enough. And *he* is not here."

The beast yowled sulkily, but returned to its place by the doorway nonetheless and promptly fell asleep. Soon afterward, Rhiad followed it, but it was a good while before exhaustion finally overwhelmed Carissa's fear.

In the morning, the rain had stopped again and the beast was gone, though its pile of carcasses had grown: Countless rabbits and mice, a raccoon, an owl, and a couple of jays now lay uneaten outside the stump's opening.

The creature came back as they were readying the horses, and Carissa was surprised by how much bigger it looked in daylight. The quills were gone, and golden honey glistened in their place. Seeing it, Carissa glanced to the log which had cradled the beehive and saw it was torn asunder, the honeycomb pulled out onto the ground, most of it eaten away. A handful of bees buzzed around it, seeming lost and bewildered.

She glanced at Rhiad's pet. *Surely* you *didn't pull that log apart.* It seemed to grin at her, licking the honey off its snout with a long black-mottled tongue, then vaulted again to Rhiad's lap as they prepared to move out. She heard it yammer softly at him. "I know there's not much," he replied. "It'll be better down in the valleys."

Another yammer, and Rhiad laughed. "Yes, there will be woolly ones. You will grow big and strong on them."

She had no idea what he was talking about, but it gave her a chill nonetheless. When they reached the road, she dropped the spoon she'd stolen from the fortress kitchen, praying if Cooper had managed somehow to follow, he'd get here before they found the "woolly ones."

34

Word had spread from the moment of its happening that Simon Kalla-dorne had given his fealty to Abramm as rightful king of Kiriath, and that all who chose likewise should muster at the Valley of the Seven Peaks, south of the Snowsong. Thus it was when the two Kalladornes reached the valley themselves, four days after leaving the cave along the Hennepen, they found themselves preceded. Tents, wagons, and makeshift shelters stood among the scattered ruins of Tuk-Rhaal in the bowl-shaped valley where, despite the rising wind, a wide column of men had come out to meet them. Their ranks stretched all the way to Stormcroft keep on the valley's far west side, and the moment Abramm rode out of the Eberline Gap into view, they started cheer-ing.

As the king pulled Warbanner to a stop, Simon drew up not quite abreast of him and glanced at him. A storm was blowing in from the north, a heavy bank of cloud lurking in the distant sky above the valley's jagged northern rim, and already the wind had grown strong and chill. It set the king's dark cloak billowing across the back of his mount, ruffled his blond hair and short beard, and tore at the blue-and-white banner draped over the dappled flanks of his young stallion—a banner stitched with the golden shield and red dragon rampant of his coat of arms. A banner Simon himself had brought to him.

Warbanner tossed his head and pranced with impatience, uneasy in the face of the crowd. Abramm held him steady, letting the reins slide through his gloved hands and absently taking up the slack again as he surveyed the gathering before him. His face was stern by nature, his expressions often hard to read, but just now there was no mistaking his astonishment.

"You didn't expect anyone to be here?" Simon asked.

Abramm glanced at him. "I didn't expect so many."

Simon returned his attention to the valley and didn't offer his own reaction—dismay the number wasn't greater. He comforted himself with the reminder that only four days had passed since Abramm had made his intentions clear. Many of his would-be supporters might only now be hearing the news, or else were still on their way. Some were, no doubt, still dithering. The nobles especially would be troubled, disinclined to declare support for either side. Going to war was not in their situational lexicon. It could take them days to accept the fact that the brothers really did intend to fight. Days more to build up the nerve to support one. Even then, the support was more likely to come as funds and supplies than men and arms.

Warbanner tossed his head again and sidled into Simon's mount, then hopped forward. This time, Abramm let him go, trotting slowly along the gauntlet of smiling, cheering men before him. Simon fell in at his right flank, while Shale Channon rode at his left. The remainder of his personal guard followed in their wake.

Warbanner ensured that the rank and file kept their distance, but all eyes were on the king as he rode by, the men's faces filled with admiration—and a rising hope. Simon had seen it before in armies. Those leaders who by their very person emboldened their men to new heights of courage and endurance. Maybe it was knowing the trials and horrors Abramm had endured—and emerged from unbeaten—that inspired them. Or the tales of his more recent exploits, spreading like wildfire even now across the countryside. Maybe it was just the way he carried himself, straight backed, sharp eyed, and unquestionably in command. Gillard, for all his size and ability and grandeur, had never achieved what Abramm did instinctively.

The crowd increased as they neared the looming walls of Stormcroft—a bastion dating back to the days of Eberline. It had been built to guard the pass here against barbarian hordes seeking to go through the Eberline Gap en route to Springerlan. Constructed on the smallest of the valley's seven peaks, it had two high guard walls, one inside the other, with the keep itself perched at the top. Men packed into the ward beyond the first wall and lined the wallwalks, cheering Abramm's entry. He rode a dog-legged path through them, ascending the steep hill to the second gate and on to the Keep's raised stoneworked porch. Stepping onto it straight from Warbanner's back, he tossed the horse's rein to young Philip Meridon and turned to face the men, his cloak tossing about him, his shieldmark—which he wore revealed as a matter of course now—glittering in the midday sun. When finally he had their silence, he spoke, his voice pitched to carry over the wind and the distance.

"I did not choose this battle, but I will not run from it, either. Yes, we have dire enemies to face and should not be pouring out our lives and substance in petty squabbles amongst ourselves. But if in order to face those enemies I must resolve this internal conflict first, then resolve it I will. I am your rightful king, the one chosen to lead you through the dark days that are coming.

"You are here today because you believe that, and I receive your loyalty with gratitude, regarding it a sacred trust. I will never take it for granted, nor will I spend your lives for no gain. But I will spend them if I must—for the good of the people who have been given into my charge. I believe Eidon is with us, and if that is so, then none can stand against us."

He paused, surveying the men before him, who seemed startled by his words.

"Let my brother come," he added. "Let him seek to do his worst. In the end, we will prevail!"

The men burst into cheers at that, and waving at them, Abramm went inside with his lords and his generals and advisors. A long trestle table had been set up in the Great Room for the midday meal, and as they were sorting themselves out to take their proper places, General Callums leaned against Simon's back and murmured, "He speaks well for a man untrained in such things."

"He's had a prince's training, Callums."

"But he was the sickly one. He may lack the backbone to carry this thing through."

Simon turned slightly to eye him. "Then what are you doing here, General?"

Callums gave him a wink. "I came because of you, sir Duke. Abramm might be good with words—and with a blade, I hear—but he can't know wools about running a war."

Simon cocked a dubious brow. "He may surprise you, friend."

"I hope he has the wit to recognize his lack and let wiser heads lead the way."

After they were all seated, the serving girls flocked into the room with bowls of savory venison stew, baked apples and raisins, and platters of fragrant, thick-sliced brown bread, warm out of the ovens. It was customary for men served thus to help themselves from the nearest bowl or platter and pass it on, but today they dined with the king himself—Gillard, ever careful to guard the "dignity of the office," always dined only with his exalted favorites—and so must follow the king's lead. As was his custom, Abramm waited until the food had been set out, and then, to the surprise of all save those who'd been traveling with him, offered up a prayer of thanks for both the food and the men who'd joined him in his struggle. It was a practice that had made Simon intensely uncomfortable at first, but to which, after four days, he was growing accustomed. While he still didn't understand the need for it, he sensed Abramm did it honestly and couldn't fault him for that.

The prayer completed, Abramm looked up with a grin and invited them all to dig in. They did so with gusto, some of them astonished all over again to see their king helping himself and passing on bowls and platters along with everyone else. The room soon filled with the clatter of utensils and the chatter of the men, and before long the serving vessels required replenishing. Simon, sitting to Abramm's right, happened to be looking round as one of the girls reached past the king to set a newly filled bowl of stew on the table in front of him. As she did, Abramm glanced at her and started visibly. She was already turning away from him, intent on hurrying back to the kitchen, and so was unaware that he watched her all the way, dark brows drawn together in an expression that could be either puzzlement or anger or both.

Looking at her more closely, Simon thought she did look familiar but was unable to place her, even after seeing her several times throughout the meal. She wore a serving girl's tunic and apron, her fawn-colored hair gathered into a single braid beneath her kerchief. Her plain, open face had seen more sun than was a noblewoman's wont, freckles spattering her small nose beneath a pair of gray-blue eyes that seemed to watch everything in the room—except Abramm. Who, after that first show of surprise, ignored her, his attention focused on the conversations around him as his newly acquired war generals spoke of how they had come to be here and what they expected Gillard would do. To a man they believed the younger Kalladorne was at least two weeks away from moving on them.

"He likes to take his time," Callums said. "And we all know how indecisive he can be. He may give us as much as three weeks to prepare, during which our numbers should continue to grow."

"By then the weather may well have turned foul, General," Abramm pointed out. "Gillard would be foolish to wait so long."

"Last I heard, he believes you've run away, sir, and don't intend to fight. Even when word comes to him you do—likely it already has—he'll balk at taking it seriously. Then there will be the question of who he can trust, how he should proceed, and whether he wants to attack you outright or wait for you to attack him. . . . As I said, I think we have at least two weeks and most likely three."

They went on to discuss possible scenarios for the coming conflict and, as was common in such gatherings, every man had his own ideas of what would happen and what would be best for them to do. Abramm listened to all of them, often questioning or disputing various points, but more, Simon thought, for the purpose of pressing the men to think about what they were saying than to persuade. Indeed, by the end of the meal even Simon was unsure where Abramm stood on the matter. Afterward, as most of them were dismissed and migrating toward the door, Callums suggested it was because Abramm didn't know what he meant to do. "You have to give him your input, Simon," he said. "You wait and see if he doesn't do exactly as you suggest."

He left Simon in conversation with Laramor, Kesrin, and Blackwell before the great hearth fire, not far from where Abramm spoke quietly with Lieutenant Merivale. Behind the king, the serving girls hurried to clear the table and were nearly finished when, to Simon's astonishment, Abramm turned abruptly from Merivale to step directly and deliberately into the path of one of them, stopping her in her tracks. It was the same girl who had caught his eye earlier, Simon noted, dismayed—even shocked—to realize the man who'd once taken vows of celibacy had a roving eye for the ladies. Worse was that he would even be thinking about such things when he had the campaign of his life to run.

The girl looked up at him in surprise, dirty platters stacked in her arms, a smudge of soot on one cheek. She certainly wasn't one of the prettier ones. It was then Simon realized he'd misperceived things, for Abramm wasn't flirting, he was glowering, and though the girl faced him bravely, her eyes were wide and her face pale.

"What the plague are you doing here?!" the king said quietly, his low voice almost lost in the crackle of the fire and the muffled clatter in the kitchen.

The girl's chin came up. "Trying to bring these platters back to the kitchen, sir," she said primly, showing far too much hubris for a serving maid.

"Put those blasted things down and come with me."

Before she could even start to obey, he took them from her, tossed them in a clatter onto the table, and pulled her none too gently to the deserted far side of the room, where they conversed privately. Whatever he was saying to her, he was clearly angry, looming over her in a way that would have intimidated most girls to tears. This one bore up under his displeasure sturdily, back straight, chin up, her gaze holding his almost defiantly as she answered him.

As another girl picked up the discarded platters, Simon glanced aside at Kesrin and found him watching the couple with interest. "She looks familiar," Simon said to him, "but I'm poxed if I can place her."

Kesrin flashed a dubious smile. "I don't doubt it, my lord, as out of context as she is."

"You know her?"

Kesrin turned again to the disputing couple. "That, sir, is Lady Madeleine, Second Daughter of the king of Chesedh."

Simon turned incredulous eyes upon the girl—Abramm was once more doing the talking—and saw at once that Kesrin's claim was true. "Lady Madeleine? What is *she* doing here? And dressed as a servant girl no less!"

"Researching her next song, she claims."

"*You* brought her?"

"Not knowingly." Kesrin turned back to him with a rueful smile. "You have to understand Lady Madeleine. She is very resourceful. And seemingly without . . ." He shrugged. "Well, she came disguised as one of my men-at-arms, if that tells you anything."

Abramm had finished his harangue, the two of them now seemingly engaged in a duel of angry gazes. Then he spoke a word and she flinched, turning away from him tight-mouthed and pale. As she fled to the kitchen, Simon fancied he glimpsed a shining tear track on her cheek. He had no time to contemplate, though, for at that moment, Abramm bore down upon them, his anger unabated.

"Were you part of this charade?" he demanded of Kesrin in a tight, low voice.

"Not willingly, sir."

"You let her come, though."

"Only after the fact of finding her disguised among my men. I couldn't very well send her back alone." He paused. "Not that she'd have gone anyway."

Abramm grunted, paced to the length of the rug laid out before the hearth, then returned. "You'll see that no harm comes to her, Master Kesrin. The responsibility lies with you."

"Of course, sir."

"And you'll see she stays away from me, as well."

Kesrin looked at him oddly. "I thought you were growing fond of her, sir."

"Fond of her?" Abramm's eyes rounded and he repeated himself, his voice rising a notch with incredulity. "*Fond* of her? How could I be fond of her? She's nosy, forward, headstrong, not very pretty, far too smart for someone with no sense of discretion—aye, no sense at all it seems—and she talks too much." He shook his head. "She has always been irritating, but this—" He broke off and shook his head again. "Just see she stays away from me. The cellar might be an appropriate place to lodge her."

"You're suggesting I lock her up?"

"If you think it would do any good, yes!"

He started to turn away, but Kesrin stopped him. "Sir, I know it's a surprise to find her here, but really, it's not as bad as all that. She can take care of herself quite well. And she can—"

"I know what she can do, kohal. But her skills will not be needed here. And if we lose—" His frown became a scowl. "Well, let's just pray we *don't* lose." With that he strode past them and jogged up the stair toward his private quarters, Jared scrambling after him.

Kesrin watched him go with a look of surprise. After a minute, a slow smile spread across his face. "Well." He glanced at Simon. "Looks like I was right, after all."

"Right about what?"

"Why, the two of them, of course."

A ghost of foreboding swept through Simon. "What do you mean, the two of them?"

But the Terstan did not answer him, for at that moment Ethan Laramor strode in with the news that another company of men had arrived, including, to the astonishment of everyone, Lord Temas Darnley, decked out in the most ridiculous of outfits and claiming he wished to fight with the rest of them.

Two hours later, the war council began. Abramm presided at the trestle table in the Great Room, with Simon seated at his right, Byron Blackwell to his left. Lords Laramor, Foxton, Whitethorne, and Darnley, General Callums, and the three other high-ranking officers among the company ranged down either side of the table. Everitt Kesrin had also been invited to sit in.

The king wasted no time getting down to business. "Gentlemen, I believe Gillard will come after me as soon as he can muster the forces," he declared in a tone that brooked no argument. "I know some of you don't believe that, but we'll just have to trust to time to prove who's right. Meanwhile, we'll prepare as if he'll be here within the week."

"Within the week, sir!" Callums burst out.

"Thus we haven't time for debate," Abramm said firmly. "First, I want an intelligence network in place as soon as possible, all the way from here to Springerlan."

"We have one already, sir," said Kesrin from his place at the table's far end. He leaned forward to see around the man at his side. "Through the Underground."

"The Terstan Underground?" Abramm asked, more for the others at the table, Simon thought, than for his own comprehension.

Kesrin nodded.

"I want someone in charge of that—a focal point for the information."

"Yes, sir. I'd suggest Seth Tarker, sir."

"Very good." From there Abramm moved directly to the matter of logistics, something they'd discussed much in recent days, for he understood well the importance of supplying the men and was adamant about not bleeding dry the people who lived in the immediate area. Normally the army had men in place to see to such details, but Abramm had only half an army, and that as yet unorganized. It was up to him to pull it together. To the surprise of everyone present, he assigned Darnley the responsibility of seeing the men were adequately provisioned.

And to their further surprise, Darnley protested. "Please do not think I am unwilling to fight, sir. In fact, I came out here expressly to do so."

Abramm regarded him soberly. "No one will fight at all if they lack sufficient weapons or food. It is not an insignificant position I give you. However, if you feel your skills would be better used in combat . . ."

Darnley frowned at him, clearly taken aback by Abramm's seriousness. After a moment, he nodded. "I see you are right, sir. I will be honored to see the men are fed."

"There is also the matter of the latrines. And water supply."

"Yes, sir."

Abramm continued to regard him with that sober, hawk-eyed gaze, then gave a clipped nod and went on. It soon became apparent that Abramm was running things, and more, that he knew what he was doing. Once he had all the details of logistics settled, he went on to his plans for the campaign itself.

"I want scouts along the road and groups of men already in place when he comes through. The first thing will be brief strikes—hit them and disappear. Or never let them see you at all. But this won't be about killing. I've said before, we have other enemies to contend with, and I don't wish to spill any more Kiriathan blood than we must. The first gambit will be to harass them. Let them know we're out there, that we know they're coming and we aren't afraid. The point is to strike them in petty ways and not get caught at it.

"Cut their cinches, loose the tether lines, and spook their animals. Foul their food, drain away their water, sabotage their supply wagons. Steal their weapons." He held up a finger. "That in particular! We'll use everything we can get our hands on. And any artillery he's bringing, I want disabled, the cartwheels broken, axles snapped. If they fix it, break it again." He had more: "Bridges destroyed, trees felled in the road, streams blocked so they back up and flood . . . whatever the situation lends itself to—all without letting ourselves be seen. Even things like cutting their tent ropes in the night work well."

Many of the men in his audience were frowning. "Sir," said Callums, "that will only delay, not stop."

"True. But when they do get here, they'll be ragged and disheartened, fearful that, if we can cut their tent and tether lines, we can also cut their throats, and wondering why we haven't. It wouldn't hurt to spread some rumors, too—particularly about how strong we are, how many men are joining us—that sort of thing. And any other way you can think to rattle them."

He fell silent, his gaze roving about the table, gauging the effects of his words on the men, and when he finally reached Simon, the latter couldn't contain himself, "Where did you learn to wage war like *this*, sir? It's . . ."

"Devious?" Abramm smiled. "I spent the last four years with the

Dorsaddi, Uncle. And before that was trained by the nephew of the great Beltha'adi himself."

"Esurhite," Simon said, scowling. "I should've guessed. And I'm not sure I hold with conducting battle on the sly. It walks the line of dishonor."

Abramm became grimly serious. "The best way to win a war, Uncle, is not to have to fight it at all. And I am not above using whatever means of subterfuge I can devise to accomplish that." He paused, frowning. "If we can strip Gillard's supporters from him, we won't have to kill them. And as I've said before, one of my highest priorities is to get this done without destroying the meager army we do have."

"The Gadrielites will not back off, sir."

"No. But their number is few, and I believe many of those who march against us do so more from compulsion than compunction." He paused again. "I've done this before and it works rather well."

The men stared back at him, processing the exchange and the startling new concepts he was bringing them.

Then Kesrin said into the ensuing silence, "At Jarnek. You did this at Jarnek before you faced Beltha'adi and his army."

And now Abramm grinned again. "Aye, and we rattled those men enough they wouldn't stand and fight when things went bad."

"When you defeated their leader in that trial by combat, you mean," Kesrin said. "Who wouldn't after something like that?"

Abramm shrugged, fingering the pewter goblet before him. "Well, perhaps we can arrange something like that again."

And at those words, all the men at the table froze, their eyes fixed upon him. He'd just virtually admitted the stories were true, that he really had been the White Pretender, really had slain Betha'adi in personal combat, and—

Simon's thoughts slammed into the second, greater shock hidden in the meaning of Abramm's cryptic words. *"Perhaps we can arrange something like that again."*

Nor was Simon the only one to make the connection.

"What do you mean, 'arrange something'?" Callums asked, recovering first. "You can't mean to challenge your brother one on one for the Crown."

The men chuckled uneasily, but Abramm, Simon noted with a chill of foreboding, remained stone serious. "It wouldn't be the first time a succession was decided thus in our history," he said quietly.

And that squelched all remaining levity. Men sat stiffly, exchanging startled, disbelieving glances, until Foxton finally said, "You would kill your own brother, Sire?"

"He's tried to kill me twice with his own hand, and three times has sent assassins." Abramm rotated his goblet with a series of tiny turns, then pushed it away with a sigh. "But no. I'd like to think if it came to that I would show him mercy. If life imprisonment can be considered a mercy." His gaze moved down the table now, catching and holding each man's eye in turn until he had confronted them all. "So what do you think, gentlemen? Will the soldiers abide such a contest? Will the lords? Will you?"

It was a perfect plan, Simon realized. Fair, economical, dramatic. And it would save the men Kiriath would need for future conflicts. But it would also mean one, if not both, of Simon's nephews could die. Silence closed around them, into which intruded the sounds from the kitchen, and the fire's crackle and the moaning of the wind against the keep walls. Outside, a horse whinnied, and there came the distant shouts of men working in the yard.

Finally, Laramor said firmly, "I will abide it."

"And I," echoed Foxton.

They went down the table, one after the other, the tally unanimous until it came to Simon himself, who could not seem to find his tongue as he grappled with the ramifications of Abramm's idea. The king's blue eyes fixed upon him flatly, as they had that day in the audience chamber. "You knew it had to come to this," Abramm said softly. "One way or the other."

Simon met his gaze for a long, silent moment, sick at heart, wishing he didn't have to choose, and knowing he already had. At length, he nodded, too. "I will abide it, sir."

Afterward, when the meeting had broken up and the others had left, Abramm turned to his uncle, whom he'd asked to stay behind. "Thank you," he said quietly.

"You don't have to thank me, sir."

"Oh, but I do. I am under no delusions as to why most of these men have come, Uncle. It is because of you."

They may have come because of me, Simon thought. *But they'll stay because of you. You are truly winning your crown the old-fashioned way—through the hearts of your people.*

"There is something else I would ask of you, Uncle. It would be a mighty blow struck in this battle of demoralization. But I will not force you."

"Whatever you ask, I will do."

"No. Do this only if you want to and it seems right to you." He paused and went back to fingering his goblet, as if he found his request difficult to utter. Then, "I would like you to be the bearer of my challenge to Gillard when he arrives."

Simon stared at him, his stomach seeming to drop all the way to his toes.

Abramm frowned slightly, forcing himself to meet the other man's gaze. "I know it will not be pleasant for you. On a number of counts. But it will make a powerful statement and might weaken Gillard's resolve, as well."

That it will do, my boy. He'll be devastated. Enraged. His ability to command rationally severely hampered. Simon felt his eyes narrow as he regarded his king. *And that's precisely why you're suggesting it, isn't it? Quite the strategist, indeed.* A lump of emotion suddenly lodged in his throat, born of sorrow and loss and an unexpected sense of admiration so keen it hurt.

"It'll be a few days before he arrives," Abramm went on. "Think about it and let me know when you decide. As I said, you'll suffer no penalty should you prefer not to do this. No one will even know I've asked."

But Simon shook his head. "I don't need to think about it, sir," he said. "It will be an honor to serve as your herald."

35

It had been almost two weeks since Carissa had been kidnapped by Rhiad. Yammer—as Carissa had named his beast—had increased dramatically in size, independence, and attitude. Grown to half the height of a horse, it no longer rode in Rhiad's lap. Its shoulders had swelled to massive proportions, muscles bulging beneath the bristly ruff, while its streamlined hindquarters had become a bundle of cablelike sinew that could propel it prodigious distances in a single bound. Able to outdistance a horse in moments and filled with restless energy, it couldn't abide their slow pace and was soon striking out on its own.

They traveled exclusively by night now, rising at dusk and settling into a cave or den or abandoned hut at dawn. Each evening as they saddled the horses, the creature would disappear into the gathering gloom, and rarely would they see it until it found them again just as the sky began to lighten. That it always returned testified of the bond that still existed between it and its master. Though they argued constantly now, they wouldn't leave each other for long. When rain had forced Yammer to huddle shivering in an abandoned bear den for several days, Rhiad stayed by it, though the creature could have easily caught up with him had he gone on. Likewise, though the beast could as easily strike out after Abramm on its own, it returned to Rhiad at the end of every night, the two of them passing the day pressed back to back, snoring in eerie unison.

Though its legs and face often bore the bloody evidence of its nightly killing sprees, Yammer no longer piled dead rodents and hares outside their camp. Instead, it brought them in alive to torture. Immobilizing them with gaze alone, it would slowly drag a claw through some portion of their anatomy. As the screams began, it would shudder and swell, whining with excitement, the tip of its tail twitching faster and faster. When its victim finally died, it would collapse beside the corpse with a great sigh, lie there a moment with something like a grin on its ugly face, then roll over and begin scratching its back.

Even if Carissa hadn't known what it was for—and as the days had passed, Rhiad had been increasingly specific about that—she would have hated it. It was ugly, smelly, and cruel. And always it watched her on the sly, as if waiting for its chance to do to her what it so enjoyed doing to smaller prey. She feared that chance would come soon, for Rhiad struggled increasingly to control it, and that only when it was with them.

Coming down the mountain into the more populous areas of the Goodsprings Valley, he had warned it specifically not to hurt the "hairless ones," though the "woolly ones" were fair game. The beast had no sooner taken its leave of them that night than it had killed three children near Aely, the first real town they'd encountered since leaving Breeton. Naturally it did not tell its master what it had done, and given their reclusive traveling habits, they heard nothing of that tragedy, nor the ones which followed it, for over a week. Meanwhile panic and terror spread throughout the valley, raising up mobs of monster hunters in every town. Not until one such group accosted them outside Old Woman's Well—an encounter from which they barely escaped—did they learn what had been happening.

That day, settled away in yet another cave, Rhiad had confronted his "pet," raging like the madman he was. *"You were made to kill Abramm and his kin!"* he'd shrieked. *"Not every living thing you happen upon! Keep this up and you'll have the whole land in an uproar. Abramm will be warned and flee before we can ever get to him!"* The beast had barely tolerated his outburst, growling and baring its teeth throughout, until finally it had faced him directly. For a few moments Carissa feared it would attack him. But tempers waned after that, and before long they were back to back, as usual, snoring away in unison.

Carissa had not been nearly as surprised as Rhiad by the revelation of Yammer's doings, but the news only increased the weight of her despair. Though shock and the rapidity of events had driven all thought of escape from her mind during their contact with the monster hunters, in retrospect she'd realized that even had she eluded Rhiad, she would've had to contend with Yammer—who would have killed her and anyone who helped her. Escape could only be accomplished in open sunlight or rain. She'd have to slip away while her enemies slept, an option more tenable now that there were people around to help, but one she was increasingly reluctant to consider, knowing others could be killed because of her, and quite possibly for nothing.

Thus it was that almost two weeks after she'd been kidnapped, she remained in her captor's clutches as they headed south toward Brackleford and the only bridge that crossed the River Snowsong. Though Rhiad would have preferred to cross by means of the less-traveled fordings upriver, his beast—which he called a morwhol—hated running water as much as it did rain, and refused to wade through even the shallowest stream. Which was odd, since it seemed not to mind the mud, and she'd seen it standing to its knees in stagnant puddles along the road. But moving water it could not abide. It wouldn't ride on a ferry, and even bridges were suspect. Crossing the span over the Ruk Ynnis, it could hardly even make itself step onto the planks, then fairly flew across the structure when it did, yowling all the way.

Assuming they weren't held up by rain again, Rhiad hoped to reach Brackleford an hour or so before dawn, when bridge traffic should be nonexistent. One advantage of the widespread panic was that, except for the patrols of monster hunters, no one traveled at night anymore, rarely emerging from the safety of their homes. Which was a good thing given the increasing population levels. They'd passed a sleeping farmhouse only moments ago and were now approaching a Mataian keep perched atop a nearby hill, the pyramid of thick glass panes that crowned its central dome glowing red from the Holy Flames within. Skirting the base of its hill, they spied a group of robed men with torches gathered in its open gateway. More monster hunters, Carissa judged. Probably returning after a night of fruitless searching and feeling lucky to be alive.

Hidden in the shadows along the road, she and Rhiad passed without being noticed, then started down a long, hilly incline toward Brackleford, the bright twinkle of its lights peeking now and then through breaks in the distant foliage. Soon they'd be across the bridge, nothing between them and Springerlan but time. Beneath her cloak she fingered the Terstan orb wistfully, wishing she had the courage to see if it could protect her from the morwhol as it had from the corridor.

"*Eidon will make us a way,*" Professor Laud had said. "*I am alive, am I not?*"

And so am I, she thought bitterly. *But unlike you, Professor, I am not free. And it doesn't look likely that I will be anytime soon.* She'd dropped the last of her trail-making booty days ago, and with it all hope anyone was following. Probably just as well, since they'd only be killed should they try to help. The only one who could help her now was Eidon. And, as always, he apparently had more important things to occupy his time.

It came as a bitter realization that, after all her fervent claims of never wanting to see Abramm again, she was about to get her wish. That they would die with so much unfinished business between them. She wanted to tell him it was never him she'd hated, wanted to explain as she wanted an explanation, wanted to understand as she wanted to be understood. Now she would get none of it.

The keep well behind them now, they were riding through dark, close walls of forest when a horrible screeching rent the night, driving a chill deep into her heart. Rhiad wrenched Arrow to a stop and sat up rod-straight in the saddle. Another scream tore at their ears, coming from somewhere east of the road down toward the river where it turned west through Brackleford. Was it a mountain cat? A dying pig? *No!* she realized. *It's Yammer!*

Simultaneously Rhiad reined Arrow off the road and urged him toward the sound, dragging Heron after him. They careened over hill and dale, skidding, slipping, leaping fallen tree trunks and small rock shelves, until, thankfully, the terrain flattened into a thickly grown forest. The scream came again, nearer now, men's shouts echoing after it. Rhiad cantered arrow, Heron following at a rapid, bone-jarring trot, and at last they burst into a cleared area on the bank of the dark, flat expanse of the Snowsong. A half circle of pig-tailed, pike-wielding Mataians in dirty white robes had backed the morwhol against the river's edge. At the midst of their curved line, two together bore a shallow bronze brazier of the scarlet Holy Flames and with this sought to intimidate their catch. It snarled and hissed at them, constantly shifting position in its attempt to face them all. Nearby lay the bloodied remains of several sheep amidst a ruined corral—bait for the trap now sprung.

Rhiad stopped Arrow just behind the men with the brazier and vaulted to the ground, yelling for the Mataians to stop. They ignored him, their attention on the beast.

"It is mine!" Rhiad cried, breaking through the line into their circle and turning to face them. "You will not harm it."

A Mataian with gray-streaked hair and numerous rank cords on his wrist finally looked at him, then frowned as if in consternation and exclaimed, "Master *Rhiad*?"

"Yes."

"The man with half a face!" someone cried.

"What are you doing here?" the first man demanded.

"Protecting Eidon's property, Brother—?"

"Laesl," said the man. "And this *property* has slain whole herds of sheep, as well as horses, cows, chickens, and people, too. Three at Aely, two at Lankster, and at Old Woman's Well, six of the town's most valiant men gone out to stop it. It is not Eidon's, brother, but a thing of evil."

"NO!" Rhiad cried, stepping toward the Mataian. "It is the judgment of Eidon upon the heretic who has stolen Kiriath's throne and upon all who support him."

A few more of the Mataians looked at him now, but only Brother Laesl spoke: "Abramm, you mean?"

"He is the son of darkness, who wears the shield of evil on his chest even as he pretends to be our Guardian-King!"

"But no longer, brother. He's been found out, doesn't even bother to hide his shield anymore. This beast is his creation, sent to intimidate us and slay Prince Gillard, who has driven him to the Valley of the Seven Peaks."

Rhiad stiffened. "Abramm is at Seven Peaks?"

"Yes," Laesl said. "Simon Kalladorne is with him and maybe a third of the royal army. As for Eidon's judgment, that's already playing out: they don't have a chance of survival against Prince Gillard."

Carissa reeled from this sudden onslaught of unexpected information. *Abramm is at Seven Peaks? That's only a day away! And* Simon *is with him?* If the morwhol truly was made to kill Abramm and all whom he held dear, as Rhiad claimed, Simon was at much at risk as Carissa, for Abramm had worshipped the man all his life. And with Gillard there, as well, the entire Kalladorne bloodline could be wiped out in two days' time!

Heron had come up beside Arrow, and now Carissa's eyes fell upon the mare's rein tied to the metal loop on the back of Arrow's saddle. She saw at once it was too tight to undo with her tied hands, but then she noted the knife Rhiad kept in the scabbard on his saddle, forgotten in his haste to save his pet. As she had been forgotten. He was turned half away from her now, his attention—and the morwhol's—fixed upon the man he argued with.

It's now or never, Riss! Heart pounding, she nudged Heron up against Arrow. Glancing again at Rhiad, she leaned to the side and closed two fingers on the knife's hilt. The men's voices rose. The morwhol yowled. Gingerly she drew the blade out far enough to get her palm around the hilt, then pulled it free and slid it quickly under the reins where they were tied to the ring. But with Heron up against Arrow's side now, the reins were slack and she had no free hand to pull them taut enough to use the knife effectively. All she could do was press them against the ring and saw.

On the riverbank, Rhiad's rising fury was only increasing his Mataian brothers' determination to kill the beast. She wasn't sure who moved first, but suddenly Rhiad was knocking the pike aside and pushing the man back. The other Mataians exclaimed in outrage, and then all their shouts were obliterated by the morwhol's mighty roar. Quicker than sight, it crashed into the two men holding the brazier of flames, sending both flying as it pounced upon the fallen brazier and sucked the scarlet flame into its throat. The green eyes glowed briefly red; the nostrils exhaled scarlet vapors as the beast expanded like a bellows. All around, holy men stood transfixed, horrified witnesses of what could not be happening—this monster of shadow should have run from the flames, not consumed them and found strength in them!

They should have run then, but everything was too far out of their ken. The nearest ones died before they'd even grasped what was happening, the beast ripping through them as it must've ripped through the sheep earlier. Rhiad stepped toward it, ordering it to stop. Perhaps he used the Command on it, but if so, it only worked to draw the beast's attention to Rhiad himself. The heavy snout came around, the green eyes blazed, and the tide of Command turned. With a low yowl, Yammer sprang at him. They went down in a tumble, light sparking from their union, green and red intermingled. Already Rhiad was screaming, writhing beneath the thing as his body flamed with scarlet light and melted into the great hunch-shouldered form, swelling it even larger than had the flames.

Panicked, Heron wheeled away, causing Carissa to drop the knife and almost lose her seat. Arrow fled now, too, lunging forward, the horses' opposing motion snapping the reins in two. Heron lurched away, racing through the trees as behind her men screamed and the morwhol roared and the chaos of Torments seemed to have blasted up from beneath the earth.

Carissa bent low over Heron's neck as the mare veered right, then left, stumbling and lurching through the darkness. Branches slapped Carissa's shoulders, clutched her arms, and snagged her cloak. She closed her eyes and hung on, praying as she had never prayed in her life—that Heron wouldn't fall, that the beast would tire or lose their trail—knowing it was useless. For she could feel it right behind her and see the green eyes in her mind. Then Heron tripped over some unseen obstacle, and Carissa went flying through the darkness alone.

———

A sudden gurgling snarl jerked Abramm's attention from the book lying open in his lap to the shuttered window on the wall to his right, his pulse accelerating wildly. He half expected a massive, hunch-shouldered beast with low-slung hindquarters to come crashing through it, claws flashing, green eyes boring into his own as it bowled him to the floor. The window remained closed and intact, however, the wind gusting nothing more threatening than a few raindrops against its shutters. But the prickle-warning of imminent attack remained upon him, and he had not imagined that snarl.

He looked around uneasily. The reading candle cast an eerie light across his spacious Stormcroft bedchamber. Piles of clothing and weapons and boots lay about the carpeted floor, slickers hung across the backs of chairs to dry, and cases of maps stood alongside a pile of books stacked on the table beside him. Trap lay blanketed on a pallet near the big bed, Jared just beyond him, both breathing deeply in undisturbed sleep. In fact, Trap was actually snoring intermittently.

That must have been what I heard, Abramm thought, feeling silly now as his pulse began to slow. *Serves me right for being up in the dead of night, filling my head with stories of bloodthirsty monsters.* The hearth fire having burned down to coals, it had to be some hours after midnight. *You should go to bed,* he told himself. *You have a battle to prepare for, remember? And it won't do to be half asleep should Gillard arrive tomorrow. And he very well could, you know.*

Besides, the Goodsprings bear was likely just a bear, the stories he'd heard this evening born of hysteria and ignorance more than truth. Such depredations were so common along with margin of civilization and wilderness, no one had thought the tale even worthy of reporting to him. He'd never have known about it had he not overheard two junior officers discussing it and stopped to question them himself. But wild as their tales were, they'd still clearly believed it was just a bear. So why shouldn't he?

Because if Laramor's right and the morwhol did go to the highlands, a reason-able route of return would be down the Goodsprings Valley? The tension that had lived in the pit of his stomach for days now, in anticipation of confronting his brother, wound itself a little tighter. *Surely, my Lord Eidon, you would not have me face both of them at the same time?*

That would be a disaster of unprecedented proportion. With both broth-ers' armies gathered here in the Valley of the Seven Peaks, there'd be a sea of victims for the morwhol to slaughter. And slaughter it would. In the weeks following Abramm's encounter with Rhiad and his beast in the bowels of Graymeer's, he had learned a good deal more about the little creature, which, as Madeleine had guessed, would not be little for long.

Morwhol. The beast of the night written of in the Words of Eidon's Rev-elation. The Ravager of Gilgan. The Demonwolf that smote the Egganites and killed two hundred armed men in a single night before it slew the one it sought. Spawned of the inner Shadow's deepest lusts—hatred, envy, bitter-ness, revenge—the morwhol, like all rhu'ema spawn, was a mixture of phys-ical and spiritual power, and thus was not subject to the rules of either world. Growing stronger with each life it took, the creature wreaked a path of destruction as it stalked the one for whom it was made, drawn especially strongly to those loved by him and who loved him.

Madeleine had been right, as well, that it would not be easily killed. Only its prey could kill it, she'd said, and then only by means of Eidon's Light. But in almost every such attempt on record, the morwhol had died last, and usu-ally of starvation. Because each was made with its target's own hair and blood, it was tied to that target mentally, able to know the man's thoughts as he knew them himself, and in so knowing, elude his attacks. Only one man in all the records was said to have killed one. But the wounds he'd received were so severe, he had died with the dawn. And he had been a man skilled in the use of the Light, shieldmarked since his youth.

In all likelihood, Abramm would simply be cut down, the monster turn-ing then to the soldiers who were with him. It was a prospect that gave omi-nous new meaning to his visions of dead men sprawled across field and lane, and made him question whether he should even bother to continue this con-test with his brother. Maybe he should just cancel the whole thing and send everyone home before it was too late.

Except . . . so far as he knew right now, the Goodsprings bear was just a bear. And, yes, he'd had nightmares in the last few weeks, but considering the pressures upon him, that was hardly surprising. That they'd all featured grisly rehashes of the vision Rhiad had inflicted upon him at Graymeer's was not surprising, either. Especially given the type of reading material he'd been choosing. And if the bear *did* turn out to be just a bear, he'd have thrown away everything he'd come back to Kiriath for—and ruined the lives of the men who'd sworn allegiance to him—for nothing.

No, he had to wait until the threat was real, and the fact was, Eidon still hadn't given him enough information to act upon. Unless he could figure out how to be in two places at once, he would just have to wait until something more developed. And in the meantime keep his focus on the one confrontation he did know was coming: the meeting with his brother.

Praying wouldn't hurt, either.

36

Carissa awoke to a pounding pain behind her eyes. At first it was so intense she thought she must have fallen on something and impaled herself. That horror swiftly gave way to the certainty that the morwhol really had ripped off half her face, as it had promised, for the pain spread from her eyes down through her left cheekbone and jaw. There were other pains, as well— her shoulder, her wrist, a terrible burning in her side.

She could hear the beast rustling in the forest nearby, its breath coming in short staccato bursts, as if it were digging, or scratching, or . . . talking to itself? The strange breathy whispers waxed and waned in volume—definitely talking, though she'd never known it to sound like this before. It reminded her of Rhiad. If she concentrated, would she be able to make out words? Trying made her head feel as if it would split, and she gave up at once. Then, before she could stop herself, a moan slid from her throat. The breathy whispering silenced. She went rigid with dismay and rising panic.

Something rustled through the foliage toward her, and she felt again its presence, looming over her.

"My lady, you must keep silent." That was a woman's voice, nearly inaudible.

"She's alive, then." Not a woman's whisper—a man's! A familiar one.

She cracked her eyelids, but all she saw was darkness. Nearby new whispering began, not the monster now, but a person. "Lord Eidon, deliver us. Enfold us in the walls of your Light and hide us from this evil thing that seeks us. You are our rock of refuge, Lord. . . ."

Suddenly Carissa could see again, just barely. A woman knelt to one side of her, a man to the other, their faces limned by a light so weak it almost wasn't there. Three others crouched beyond them, and arching around them all was what appeared to be a dome of ice crystals, shimmering with a pale, ethereal light so delicate that, were it not for the dark, she'd never have seen it. Even now she had to look at it just right to see it.

At first she worried the morwhol would see it, as well, but it seemed not to, crashing through the forest around them with little whines, which faded as the crashing moved off. . . . Then it roared, the sound deeper and heavier than anything she'd heard it make before. It roared again, frustration evident, and they held their breaths, listening as it ranged around them—slowing, sniffing, moving more carefully, coming closer then moving away . . . she struggled to track it.

It roared again, a deafening blast that echoed off the trees and raised gooseflesh all across Carissa's back and arms. The man's hand slid over hers and gripped it, drawing her eyes to his face, clearer now in what seemed a brighter light. She could make out his short gray hair, the crow's-feet that framed his dark eyes, the once-hated Thilosian goatee that had grown endearing over time. *Cooper!*

An incredulous joy flashed through her, and she squeezed his hand, drawing a quick warning flick of his eyes before he went back to watching the darkness beyond the gauzy barrier of Light. Her gaze switched to the woman—yes, it was Elayne!—whose eyes were closed, face set in concentration.

The beast roared again and again, the volume diminished somewhat by distance, while the cracking of branches came more frequently, accompanied by the loud and vigorous rustling of dead leaves, as though the morwhol were taking out its frustrations on the foliage. The next roar was even more distant. But just as they were beginning to relax, it came back, thrashing wildly through the forest around them, keening and yowling and roaring again, circling and circling around the glittering dome and sniffing both ground and air as if it couldn't figure out what had happened. Then its circles widened and the roars receded until again it would break off and return to the spot where the scent was strongest.

If only it would rain! Carissa thought. *Rain washes away scent. Then it would get confused and—* Her thought stopped as her ears picked up on a soft irregular pattering erupting in the forest all around them. She listened more intently, hardly believing what her ears were telling her. Yet as the drops slid through their ethereal dome and plopped upon her head and face, she could not deny the truth: it was raining. And not only would that wash away her scent, it would drive the morwhol to ground!

Eidon has made us a way!

Out in the forest the creature's roar had never been more powerful. It could not seem to keep silent as it traveled, marking its rapid movement away from them. The last roar was so far away they could barely hear it. And still they waited. The sprinkling turned to a light but steady rain, and before long they were drenched. Yet they did not move.

Finally, after an exceeding long time of silence, Elayne opened her eyes and turned to Carissa. Before she could speak, Carissa exclaimed, "You found my rings and coins!"

Elayne smiled. "We did. And the spoon and hoof pick, as well. That was very clever of you, my lady."

"I just wish we'd gotten you away sooner," Cooper added gruffly. "I think he must've conjured some sort of cloaking illusion over you while you slept, because even when we found where you'd left the road, we could never find *you*. We almost had you at Old Woman's Well, but then those hooligans showed up and we barely got away from them. Tonight was all Eidon's doing, for old Heron, bless her heart, ran straight for us, and when she fell, you practically flew into our arms."

A chill crept up Carissa's spine as Elayne said, "I just wonder why he waited so long."

"Maybe because we were all safer while I was with him," Carissa said. "We never could have escaped the beast at night anyway. Or—" She broke off, glancing at the gossamer dome around them. "This wouldn't have kept it out if it had known we were here, would it?"

"No, my lady," said Elayne. "But it didn't need to." She turned to Cooper. "Now, Felmen, we're getting wet, and the lady has taken a nasty hit to the head. We must bring her someplace dry and safe—"

"No," Carissa interrupted. "I must go to the Valley of the Seven Peaks. To warn Abramm. He's there, you know. Right now. Waiting to do battle with Gillard."

No one looked surprised by her revelations, and Cooper said, "I'm sure the king is already aware of that beast. The panic has spread far and wide, after all. And as you say, he's got Gillard to worry about—"

"That beast was made to find and kill him, Coop. And if he's up at Seven

Peaks, it can reach him in a day. Easily."

Cooper frowned at her. "Then I don't see how *we* can warn him, lass, since the beast would arrive long before we could."

"It hates the rain. It always finds a place to hole up until it stops. That's surely why it gave up looking for us just now. It doesn't like daylight, either. So between that and the rain, we have a window of opportunity."

Cooper frowned down at her, and she knew him well enough to guess the paths his thoughts were taking. He would want to go alone, claiming he could travel faster without them and that it would be better for Carissa to stay safe in the nearest village under Elayne's care. Yet he would be loathe to leave either of them with the beast still out there.

"It wants me, too," Carissa said softly, heading him off. "Likely you, as well. When it wakes it will come for me. Even if we are protected, the village will suffer. Plus, if you spend your time getting me safe, you will not get far enough yourself to elude it. And we have no idea on whose side the weather will be tomorrow." She hesitated. "The beast doesn't like pure daylight or rain, as I said, but if the rain stops and the clouds stay . . . the overcast will shield it enough to travel. And I think the closer it gets to Abramm, the more compelled it becomes."

Cooper continued to frown, Elayne regarding him soberly.

"Besides," Carissa added, averting her eyes to stare at her interlaced fingers, "Eidon has told me I have something Abramm needs." *And he has something I want.*

"Something *Abramm* needs? What?"

"I don't know. Perhaps my knowledge of the ways of this morwhol. I have lived with it for almost two weeks now, listened to its conversations with Rhiad. . . ." She paused, struck by that last horrible memory of the pair of them. "It absorbed him, Coop. Sucked him into its body as if he were nothing more than water. I think that's made it stronger still. We don't have time to waste."

Cooper glowered at her for a moment, but finally he relented. "Very well. I don't like it, but your arguments are persuasive. Unfortunately, Heron's gone lame. You'll have to ride double with me. It will be a miserable time for you, my lady."

"And you think misery is an unfamiliar companion to me?" Carissa asked wryly. "Whatever happens, it will be far better than what I've been through these last weeks, believe me."

Simon sat his horse at Abramm's side in the middle of the Valley of the Seven Peaks, the rain drumming on their oiled canvas slickers as they watched for the first sign of movement in the mist-cloaked mouth of the Eberline Gap. Scouts had come at the noon meal with the news that the first of Gillard's forces would arrive within two hours, so Abramm had mustered his men and ridden out to meet them.

He now sat atop Warbanner on a small rise, nothing but the horse and the coat of arms draped over the animal's rump to reveal him as the king. Even Warbanner stood quietly, subdued by the rain. Abramm's lords and generals ranged around him—Simon, Foxton, Whitethorne, Laramor, and even Everitt Kesrin—while below and before them stood a long front of archers. The rest of his soldiers were spread out in ranks at their backs. At first there'd been great excitement at the prospect of doing battle. If Gillard refused Abramm's challenge, Abramm meant to attack him then and there, while his forces were yet strung out and his men exhausted from their long march. But time and boredom and the steady, gray rain had transformed the wait into a dreary restless vigil. Many sat huddled now beneath their woolen cloaks, uncomfortable, to be sure, but warmed by their own inner tension.

Simon thought the not-knowing was worse than merely waiting for the inevitable, and thus in his own mind had nerved himself for fighting. Though the scouts and harassment parties were confident Abramm's plan to wear down the enemy had worked, no one could predict Gillard's actions when he was challenged. In fact, Abramm's lords were evenly divided as to whether he'd accept it or refuse.

At Simon's side, Abramm shifted in the saddle. "Here they come," he murmured, pulling his telescope from under the slicker and putting it to his eye. Below him, the commander of the bowmen called out his own alert. Up and down the line voices echoed the call as a great rustling stirred in the multitude behind them all.

In the gap ahead, across the puddled, ruin-dotted field, forms emerged from the mist. Simon brought up his own scope and fixed it on the men straggling into view. They walked wearily, their faces downcast, their clothing wet and mud-stained. The singles became clusters, and the clusters, bands as more and more of them arrived, devoid of all semblance of military order. They stopped along the field's margin where the slope flattened and the evergreens gave way to grassland, and there formed into groups, presumably the squadrons they belonged to. Gradually a frontline took shape and began to advance across the field toward Abramm's waiting army. Behind them several lopsided wagons trundled into view, their wheels mismatched and many of the spokes splinted and bound or missing altogether. Though the sight of the enemy before them and the shouts of their commanders roused some of the men to new vigor, straightening their shoulders, putting new energy in their strides, most looked grim and flat-eyed.

Abramm had earlier designated as a reference point a red-leaved bush growing up out of the crumbled remains of an ancient Tuk-Rhaalan wall. As the line of men neared it now, he nodded to the commander of his bowmen. The man bawled the order to "present and draw," and a hundred bows emerged from beneath their oiled slickers, each already nocked with an arrow. The longbows flipped to vertical and flexed back as strings were drawn to noses and a hundred arrow tips pointed at the sky above the oncoming army.

The commander had his eyes on Abramm as Abramm watched the advancing men. Past the red bush and on to the clump of withered holly. He nodded again, the command went out and a hundred arrows flashed through the air, silver streaks sailing through the rain. By design, they fell just short of the nearest of Gillard's men, for Abramm remained adamant about preserving the lives of a force he still considered his own. But it worked. As the arrows rained down upon the field, the line of men stopped, and Simon saw fear take them, borne on wings of exhaustion made worse by the constant harrying they'd endured getting here. Some were already shouting and turning away. Angry bellowing ordered them to hold the line. Men grabbed each other, struggled, broke free as more and more turned tail, and the line dissolved entirely.

"See," Abramm said with quiet satisfaction. "Already they fear us."

"It would be easy to take them now," Simon murmured.

"We'll wait."

The panicked flight didn't last long—the men had nowhere to go but back up the gap and into their fellows, who were not about to let them flee. Before long the crisis passed and the enemy troops spread out along their line.

"They're humiliated," Simon said. "They will be angry now."

Abramm smiled grimly. "More important—*Gillard* will be angry. Although I haven't seen him out there yet, have you?"

"No, sir." The scouts had said Gillard was riding with the first column, though, so he'd be here before long. Already his underlings—Harrady, Matheson, Prittleman, and several of Prittleman's Gadrielite lieutenants—had gathered front and center of the camp. And here came Moorcock to join them.

As another wave of men marched out of the gap, Abramm turned toward Simon. "It's time," he said quietly. "You may proceed."

Simon glanced back at the men who would accompany him, then gathered up the reins and led down the rise. Together they trotted slowly across the wide strip that served as buffer between the two armies, the rain finally letting up a bit. In the camp ahead, all the bustling activity had ceased near the front line, men turning to watch them, the small knot of their leaders pulling out telescopes and holding them to their eyes.

A surprising number of the rank and file were cloaked in Gadrielite gray—new converts, most likely, pressed into service by emotion or impulse, or the compulsion of others. Many more wore the standard wool and armor of the Kiriathan army, their tabards still bearing Gillard's coat of arms. A little over halfway between the two lines, Simon pulled his horse to a stop, cast back the hood of his slicker, and waited as his escort caught up, letting the men ahead get a good look at him. He could see the wave of startlement sweep through the camp as he was recognized and word spread. Head after head turned his way as each pair of eyes confirmed the truth. So far Simon's siding with Abramm had been only rumor for most of these men, discounted as one more lie come to dishearten them. Now, for the first time, they saw the rumor was true.

Simon could see with his bare eyes the open mouths of Harrady and Matheson and others—men he'd worked and served with for years, men of honor and determination who, convinced of the rightness of their cause, would not be deterred by hardship and fatigue. Nor even by the sight of their once-revered ally, Simon Kalladorne, publicly showing his allegiance to Abramm. The men they led, however, were another matter. Coming on top of all they had so far endured, seeing Simon serving as Abramm's herald struck a mighty blow to their morale. He saw it in the eyes of those closest, and in the shock that wilted the bodies of those farther. Hearing the challenge Simon was about to make would strike an even greater blow.

By now he had everyone's attention and the rain was hissing away to only a few errant sprinkles. Drawing a deep breath, he bawled out Abramm's challenge in his best battlefield roar: "I am Simon Kalladorne, son of Galbrath, brother of Meren, Uncle of Abramm, Grand Marshall of the royal armies of Kiriath, and I speak for His Majesty, King Abramm, rightful ruler of the land, to his brother, Gillard, Crown Prince and heir to the throne. Thus says the king:

"'This battle is between you and me, brother. Why spill other men's blood when we can settle it one on one, in the manner of our ancestors? I propose a meeting between us tomorrow at noon, on this very field, to decide in a trial by combat who shall wear the crown of Kiriath. What say you, Gillard, to this challenge? Will you accept?'"

Simon's words echoed into silence, broken only by the small movements of the men and horses around him, the jingle of tack, and dripping of the water off them. Harrady and Prittleman watched him like statues, paralyzed by the shock. Then Harrady spoke, and behind him, a runner dashed back through the camp, presumably to find Gillard, who still had not appeared.

Simon waited. Gradually the soldiers began to stir, their chatter rising on the silence as the news spread. Prittleman and Harrady seemed to be arguing, and Simon smiled to himself. No question the men Gillard had brought here would favor this turn of events. Not only would they not have to risk their own lives, but many were no doubt convinced their leader could easily best "Little Abramm" in a one-on-one confrontation, Abramm's demonstrations at the ball and the royal stables notwithstanding. Prittleman, of course, had felt the touch of Abramm's blade on his own flesh, but Simon suspected that had only made the man more desirous of seeing Gillard best him.

And finally here was Gillard himself, mounted on the intractable Nightsprol. His white-blond hair frothed about his shoulders, gleaming as bright as his gold and silver breastplate. He rode his fidgeting mount to the edge of the gathering and stopped there, staring at Simon and army ranged behind him. After a moment he signaled the horseman at his side, who advanced a few lengths into the field and shouted back Gillard's answer.

"His Majesty, King Gillard of Kiriath, accepts the challenge of the Pretender who seeks to steal his crown. He will be here on this field tomorrow at midday, where he looks forward to driving his blade through the Usurper's heart and so ending this question of who will wear the crown of Kiriath."

As Simon's had before him, his words echoed into silence. They sat regarding one another for a long moment, then Simon nodded, and simultaneously the two parties reined their mounts around and returned each to their own side of the field.

As he returned, Simon saw that Abramm had pushed back the hood of his slicker, sitting Warbanner bareheaded and wearing the simple circlet of rule on his brow, so that all might see and know his presence. He was looking at something beyond the returning party of his herald, and when Simon glanced back he was not surprised to find Gillard still there, returning Abramm's gaze grimly. Abramm broke it off as Simon drew up to him, favored him with a nod and a quiet thank-you, and then they all turned to head back to Stormcroft for the night.

As they did, Simon noted the rank and file of Abramm's forces had spontaneously formed themselves into a long gauntlet through the camp. A gauntlet not of curiosity, but of honor and respect. For they all knew what Abramm would risk for their sakes on this field tomorrow. Simon stole a glance at his nephew, riding tall beside him, the slicker still cast back. He did not look at the men as he passed them, his thoughts seemingly elsewhere, fixed perhaps on the task that lay before him, but Simon knew the transfer of loyalties had been completed. His own presence no longer mattered. Abramm had won the hearts of his men with his courage and willingness to sacrifice. More importantly, he'd won the hearts of many who were encamped on Gillard's side of the field, as well.

It had been long indeed since Kiriath had had a king like this.

37

Everything was going precisely as Abramm had planned, yet the sense of oppression remained. He had returned from giving his challenge to Gillard, changed into dry clothing, eaten at the long table with his generals, and then attended the Terstmeet Kesrin had conducted in the Great Hall. He had been doing so every night since they'd arrived, and the room was more packed tonight than ever. While he supposed he should give thanks that so many were being exposed to the truth of the Words, he knew many of them came for reasons other than their interest in Eidon: fear, curiosity, the desire to please their king, the desire to be seen as united with their king. . . . Kesrin told him not to worry about it, that it would eventually sort itself out. But it only brought into the light one more complication of being king.

After the meeting, the room more or less cleared, and Abramm's generals gathered by the fire to discuss today's events and predict tomorrow's. Weary of all the speculation and fighting a deep, unrelenting dread, Abramm donned his woolen cloak again and sought the solitude of the keep's eastern tower. Trap went with him and stayed on guard at the bottom of the steep spiral stair—even here he feared assassins and spies, and given Gillard's history, rightly so.

Abramm conjured a kelistar and held it before him as he climbed the narrow stair, musty walls brushing his shoulders as he spiraled to the right. The sound of rain drumming on a wooden roof increased as he climbed, becoming a loud rush as he emerged onto the stone-floored turret at the top. Flicking out the orb, he strode to one of the narrow embrasures opening in the turret wall and leaned against the stone ledge. The valley stretched before him, cluttered with tents and picket lines and glowing campfires around the occasional angular forms of a wall, or a gateway, or a portion of the old aqueduct.

He had given Gillard the Eberline Gap, and he wondered if his brother had discovered yet that the only other out for him and his men—northeastward up and over the Pass of the Old Ones—was guarded by men who carried the banner of the shield and dragon. His eyes were drawn now toward that pass, hidden in the cloud cover, and anxiety rippled through him, clenching his gut again, worse now that darkness had fallen. More stories had come in about the Goodsprings Valley bear. It had killed a family at Aely, they said, and the men at Old Woman's Well had mustered a group to hunt it down. All rumor. Nothing solid to tell him he must go. Except this dread gathering in his middle.

If it's at Old Woman's Well, it won't be here for days. I'll be done with Gillard long before then. . . . But what's the point of facing him, possibly even killing him only to die myself the next day? Maybe I should call this whole thing off.

The thought sickened him. *But if I'm going to die, anyway . . . Fire and Torment! I should never have come back. All I've brought is trouble.*

He clenched one hand into a fist where it rested against the stone ledge. *My Lord, I am dust and I know it. And if I ever thought I was not, you have brought me yet again to the place where it has become abundantly clear. What am I to do? Stay here and face my brother, or try to find this monster before it kills again? You have promised in your Words to guide us if we ask, and I am asking. Show me the way I should go. . . .*

A prickle of warning washed up his spine as his thoughts broke off, all his attention fixed upon the sound he had just heard. The rain had lessened, allowing him to hear what he had not been able to before. Maybe a sniff or the grit of a leather sole on the stone. That sixth sense of awareness, dulled and ignored by his inner turmoil, now bloomed into active seeking. His nape hairs lifted as he realized he was not alone.

Beneath his cloak, his right hand slid to the hilt of his rapier, and he turned his head just slightly. The rain cooperated, dying away almost entirely, until only a chorus of the water dripping off the turret roof remained. There—if not a sniff, then someone with breathing troubles.

He turned, flicking back his cloak with his left hand as he drew the blade free with his right and a kelistar bloomed into being. A woman huddled in the embrasure across from him, cloaked and cowled in dark blue, her blue-gray eyes wide in a pale face dusted with freckles.

Abramm frowned at her, suddenly befuddled. "Madeleine? What are you doing here?"

Her eyes left the tip of his sword and focused on his own. Their rims were red and her cheeks were shiny with tears. "I'm sorry, sir. I did not know you meant to come here. I'll take my leave at once." She started to move.

"No." He slid the rapier back into its scabbard, then looked up at her. "You have not answered my question. Why are you up here? And—" He stepped toward her, conjuring another kelistar, since the first had drifted to the floor. "Are you *weeping*?"

She gave a start, then brushed her cheeks with a hand. "No! Why would I be?" But she could no longer meet his gaze and wiped at the tears again, turning partway back to her window. "I . . . I get homesick sometimes."

She contemplated the floor, glanced at the view out her window, then made herself look at him again, a smile straining her lips. "Kiriath can be a lonely place for an outsider."

He believed that was true, yet somehow he knew she was troubled by more than homesickness. Something warned him off pressing her, though—a light in her eyes that made his heart catch and a new anxiety stir in him.

"I know what you mean," he said, turning back to his own window.

"But you are not an outsider. You are king."

"Which may be the loneliest place of all."

He stared at the camp and the clouds and the darkness. After a moment she came up beside him and for once said nothing, gazing out at the scene below. Her presence gave him an inexplicable comfort, for somehow he could feel the Light in her, buoying him against the dark weight that sought to press him down.

The rain started again, drumming lightly on the roof, and after a time he spoke. "The Words say all who bear the shield have a destiny, unique to each of us. A place prepared for us, in which we are privileged to serve. I thought being king of Kiriath was mine. Now I'm not so sure."

"Not sure?" Astonishment raised the pitch of her voice. "How could you not be sure, my lord?"

"I may have forced it. I fear my own arrogance—"

"From the very start, has not Eidon made a way for you? Opened all the doors?"

"Eidon is not the only one who can open doors. And as for a way, a way to where? Where am I, my lady? The morwhol is killing people out there because of me." He nodded toward the dark window. "And even if I can take it down with me, I'll still be dead. What's the point in facing my brother tomorrow, knowing that? Yet if I abandon everyone now, I know Gillard will not be merciful to those who have stood with me. If I had not come back, none of this—"

"No." She cut him off. "Stop there, sir. If you had not come back, the kraggin would still be prowling Kalladorne Bay. Kiriathan Terstans would still be hiding from the Gadrielites, fearful of declaring the truth, as if it were something shameful instead of something glorious. *You* have made it glorious. And those people you see in your dreams? They are not dying because of you."

"How do you know about the people in my dreams?"

She turned her gaze toward the opening. "Because I have seen them, too." Tears glittered upon her eyelashes as she pressed her lips together to keep them from trembling.

"You share my dreams?"

"Echoes of them, I think. I'm sure they are not as vivid as yours."

How much does she see? Does she know how they always end? Is that why she's weeping? "So you know it is coming."

"I do not *know* anything. It was feeding you images of people dying back in Springerlan before it had done anything. It may be doing that still, for all you know." She paused. "For it to be the Goodsprings Valley bear, it would have to have grown awfully fast."

"Mushrooms sprout from the ground overnight. And who knows what 'fast' is when it comes to shadowspawn."

"Well, even if it is, *Rhiad* made it, not you. Out of his own hatred and jealousy. And your brother is ready to spill the blood of hundreds here for the same reasons. Their sins are not your fault. All you've done is stand for what is right." She laid a hand on his arm, her eyes bright with fervor. "I do not know how it will turn out. But I do not believe you will fail in what you have been called to do."

Her gaze seized his own and held it, the Light flowing out of her touch on his arm, electrifying him with the force of what she had said—and something more. Something rising in her—and in himself—that he desperately did not want to acknowledge.

Footsteps pounding up the spiral stair behind them delivered him, bringing them both around as Trap, a kelistar in one hand, burst out of the stairwell into the turret room. He stopped in surprise, eyes tracking from one to the other of them, as Abramm realized he'd had no idea Madeleine was up here. Then, as always, he put his personal questions away and attended to the business at hand.

"Sire, a woman claiming to be your sister is at the northwest edge of camp. In the company of two Terstans—commoners, apparently."

"My *sister*? How could she be here?" The last he knew, Carissa was living a life of freedom and adventure traveling the world, planning never to return to Kiriath.

"Lord Simon has gone to see if it's really her. He'll bring her back if it is, though the messenger said she looks too bedraggled to be a proper lady of any sort." He paused. "She's also claiming to have information about this bear that's been marauding up north."

Abramm felt a frisson of dread. "She specifically said it was a bear?"

"I only know what the messenger told me." Trap paused. "Surely if she were living in Kiriath, though, you would have known. I mean, wouldn't she have contacted you?"

"She's a Kalladorne, Lieutenant," Abramm said resignedly. "And as angry as she was with me, I could very well see her avoiding me. But let's go see for ourselves. Whoever she is, if she has news of the beast, I'll want to talk to her."

————

Carissa sat on a bench in the squadron captain's tent at the northwest edge of Abramm's camp, Elayne and Cooper seated beside her. She was shaking from cold, exhaustion, and bitter frustration. These men were just doing their jobs, but after all she'd endured to get here, their attitudes of unconcern and disbelief were as hard to tolerate as their slow, bureaucratic ways. And the more she'd let her urgency out, the more they'd dug in their heels. Thus she was forced again to sit and wait.

She and her companions had reached Brackleford shortly before dawn to find the Snowsong had flooded and taken out the bridge, leaving the old fording barge as the only means of crossing. As they had waited to board in the predawn light, the rain had stopped, and fear was reborn. No one else seemed inclined to hurry, and by some perverse fate an extraordinary number of travelers had turned out that morning to ride the first fording. The crowded barge had barely pushed away from the shore when the morwhol bounded up.

It stopped at the water's edge, its green eyes gone strangely dark. Even so, she'd felt the compulsion of its Command, willing her to throw herself into the water and come back to it. Cooper had held her fast even as the orb flared in opposition at her waist, and so, abandoning its efforts with her, the beast turned to the men pulling the ropes. Their action had almost stopped when Cooper sprang to take the place of one, and Elayne went to stand at the back of the barge, blocking them from the beast's line of sight. Roaring mightily, it had wheeled away, attacked a nearby cart, savaged a gold-leafed sapling, and finally bounded into the darkness heading east.

"*It'll go upstream to find a narrow place to cross,*" she'd told her companions. Which might just give them time to reach Abramm first. Especially if the rain started again. It had fallen intermittently, then more steadily as they neared the Valley of the Seven Peaks. By the time they were climbing the final stretch of switchbacks, they were soaked, their horses drenched, and the trail submerged under a glistening stream. But at least they were assured the morwhol had not beaten them.

When at last they'd reached the top, she'd all but crowed her joy—only to run into these uncooperative soldiers who seemed to think that noble blood somehow conferred upon one a resistance to rain and mud and exhaustion. That a princess would never, by some impossibility of constitution, show up at the edge of a military camp in the middle of the night, and certainly not as ill clad and disheveled as she. At least they had brought her to their lieutenant, who brought her to his captain, who was finally persuaded to send someone to the keep with her message, though it was her mention of the Goodsprings sheep-killer that swayed him more than anything.

Thus she sat with her companions in this tent, the rain drumming on the canvas and trickling to the ground all round them, while the captain sat behind his camp table and regarded them narrowly. Carissa had learned from the guards that Gillard and his army had arrived this afternoon, and that he had accepted Abramm's challenge to a trial by combat for the crown. A perfectly reasonable solution for the man who had been the White Pretender, she thought. Amusement flickered at the notion, then died before the sudden, gut-clenching realization that this would be no simple who's-best match. One or both of them could die tomorrow.

Assuming either lived long enough to even face each other.

It felt like an eternity before she heard the sound of hoofbeats and the

jingle of tack, a snort or two, then the wet, smacking footfalls of riders dismounting into the mud. Two men pushed through the tent's hanging flaps
and stopped.

Carissa leaped to her feet, astonished, delighted, overwhelmed. "Uncle
Simon! Lord Ethan! Surely Eidon does live!"

Simon was staring at her as if he could not believe his eyes. "Fire and
Torment, lass!" he said finally. "What horrors have befallen you? And how is
it you can be here and none of us have any word?"

"It is a long story, Uncle." She stepped toward him. "I must talk to
Abramm. He cannot stay here. Nor can we."

"They said you have news of the renegade bear?"

"Bear?! It is no bear! It is a beast of the Shadow, made for Abramm, to
hunt him down and kill him. And all his kin besides."

She expected her words to surprise, expected to have to explain and
defend them. And though her uncle was surprised, she didn't think it was
because he did not know what she was talking about. He glanced uneasily at
Laramor, who murmured, "Perhaps we should discuss this up at the keep,
Simon."

Simon agreed they should, and soon were all trotting upward through the
camp, passing innumerable tents and awnings stretched from carts, all gleaming wetly in the lamplight. Carissa was amazed at the number that had gathered here. Through Stormcroft's outer gate they went, then the inner one,
finally stopping at the keep itself, where they dismounted.

The first thing she saw when she emerged into the Great Room was the
silk banner hanging from the rafters—white background beneath a golden
shield surmounted by a red dragon. The sight gave her a start, for while she
knew at once that it must be Abramm's device, she also knew a man's coat
of arms was designed before he was born. That these matched so perfectly
the very symbols Abramm bore on his body could hardly be coincidence.

A great blaze had been built up on the hearth, and the room had been
cleared of servants and all armsmen except Abramm's personal guard.
Abramm himself stood with several lords, bent over a pile of curling maps on
the long table. He straightened as she entered, and the sight of him made her
breath catch, for there was no failure to recognize him this time. And they
were right, he did look like Great-grandfather Ravelin.

Standing there, dressed in fine leather and wool, cloaked in dark blue
embroidered with gold, and flanked by some of the highest lords and generals

in the land, there was no question he was in charge. Not even the shieldmark, glittering defiantly between the open neck edges of his jerkin, could diminish him. If anything, it added to his charisma.

He has become all I ever hoped he would be, she thought as she crossed the room toward him. *Wearing that kingly authority as if it were the most natural thing in the world. And I'll bet he doesn't even realize it.*

He came around the table to face her, but this time she did not throw herself upon him, did not weep tears of joy and relief, though after all the struggle of getting here, all the dreadful fears, it seemed she should have. She'd gone from wanting never to see him again, to wishing for nothing else, to right now complete deadness. Which was not at all how she expected to feel in this moment.

When she said nothing, he took the initiative. "So you've come back."

Pain laced the edges of his voice, springing from the old hurt she had inflicted and was, by her stoicism, continuing to inflict. Except, she had no desire to hurt him anymore, did not hate that shield on his chest at all . . . she simply couldn't seem to make anything work. As if the whole situation was more than she was equipped to handle. *As with everything else, it seems.*

A crease formed between his level brows. "They tell me you have news of this bear marauding in the Goodsprings Valley."

"It's not a bear," she said, finally breaking free of her silence.

He waited.

"It is a morwhol. At least that's what Rhiad said—"

"Rhiad is with you!" Alarm and surprise opened his face. Like Simon, he did not ask her what a morwhol was.

"I think he's dead," she said. "The last time I saw them, the beast appeared to be . . . *absorbing* him."

Abramm glanced at one of the men standing across the table from him, an older man with sharp eyes and short gray hair whom she did not recognize. "I think we'd better sit down, and you can begin at the beginning."

And so she told of her time with Rhiad—how he'd come through the corridor with the little beast, kidnapped her, made her ride with him, and finally how she'd escaped, racing to reach Abramm in time to warn him. Except when she reached this part, she was certain he had already known it was coming.

"You say it cannot travel in the rain nor open daylight?" he asked her. They sat at the long table now—Abramm and herself, Uncle Simon, Ethan

Laramor, and the other men, most of whom she did not recognize. There was also a young woman she did not know, and two armsmen, the latter standing back from the table, one of whom looked an awful lot like Trap Meridon.

"That's right," she replied in answer to Abramm's question. "Nor will it touch running water. It will only jump over it or use a bridge."

"So with the Brackleford bridge out," said Ethan, "it'll have to go upstream to cross. And with the flooding it won't be a short trip. If the rain forces it to ground we'll have an even bigger window. I doubt it will get here before tomorrow night, sir."

"We'll have time to find it, then," said Abramm.

"Find it?!" Carissa squeaked, staring at him in horror.

He looked up from the map and cocked a brow. "You think I should leave it free to kill whomever it encounters as it pursues me?"

"Abramm, you cannot stop it."

"No, I am the only one who *can* stop it."

Her eyes dropped reflexively to the mark on his chest, the old anger rising. "Why does it always have to be *you*?"

"Because it was made for me. You said it yourself." He leaned over the map again, running a finger along the blue line that represented the Snowsong. "Assuming Ethan's right, we have a day to find it. Once we figure out where it might cross, we'll have an idea of its route."

Absorbed in his plans, he did not see his men exchange uneasy glances, but Carissa did and gave thanks that someone here had sense. Until Simon opened his mouth and made things even worse.

"My lord, we can't possibly find it before noon tomorrow."

Abramm's head came up and he regarded his uncle gravely. *Noon tomorrow,* Carissa thought, suddenly sick again. *That's when he's supposed to face Gillard! Fire and Torment! Eidon, he is* your *servant! Why are you letting all these enemies come against him?*

"You're saying I should wait," Abramm said quietly.

"I am."

"And how many innocents will die because I've tarried?"

"How many more will die if you don't?"

"If I'm dead at its hand, though, there won't be a—" He broke off, glanced at Carissa, then said, "You must be exhausted, Riss. We'll not keep you any longer. Lieutenant Merivale, will you escort the princess to her chambers?"

"Yes, my lord." The man who looked like Captain Meridon stepped to her side and pulled back her chair as she arose.

As they ascended the stair, the conversation resumed, Simon quietly continuing with his point. "Sire, you're set to win the crown for good tomorrow and end this war before it starts. Don't throw that chance away. You know where this creature is right now, and that it is driven to seek you out. Let it come to you, then. The north banks of the upper Snowsong are mountainous and unpopulated. . . ."

Despite Carissa's pretense of being too fatigued to climb the stairs quickly, his words fell out of earshot before he'd finished, and Lieutenant Merivale was there to ensure she didn't go back and eavesdrop. He led her to her third-floor chambers without comment, where Elayne awaited her, having agreed to serve as her maidservant, while Cooper had been quartered in the barracks with the royal guard off the first floor.

Carissa was glad for someone to whom she could pour out her frustration at being cut off and dismissed, her warnings virtually ignored. "It's just like when I found him in Esurh," she railed. "He has his own plans and I'm not part of them."

"My lady," Elayne said when she'd finally run down, "Eidon's hand is on him. Did you not see the banner of his coat of arms? Felmen says he wears both those devices on his body."

Carissa looked up at her from where she sat in the chair by the fire. "So what are you saying? That Eidon will protect him? The way he protected Professor Laud? And Brenlan Throckmorton, while he was being tortured to death at the hands of the Gadrielites? Elayne, no one for whom a morwhol was made has ever survived the encounter."

"I know. But you have done what you can do. And it is out of your hands."

Carissa threw up her hands and turned away. "So what am I supposed to do? Just forget about it?"

"For now. And trust him. Know that he is worthy of that trust." She smiled. "You'll see."

But Carissa only snorted and thought she'd seen quite enough to know just how worthy Eidon was of being trusted. But later, bathed, fed, and wearing the nightgown Elayne had brought down from Breeton, Carissa lay on the straw-mattressed bed in her chambers and stared at the ceiling. The fire flickered erratically, casting strange lights across the planking and rafters. Elayne, exhausted, had long since fallen asleep on her pallet by the hearth. No less exhausted, Carissa could not find slumber. Everything that had happened, everything that was set to happen, ran through her mind like an endless waking dream. After all her fears and struggles to get here, she'd changed nothing, and it left her feeling empty and confused. *Why did I have to come at all? Just to have my nose rubbed in the fact that I've been wrong about Abramm and that precious shield?*

Certainly she had been wrong. Seeing him in the Great Room with his lords, seeing their deference to him, their admiration for him—*even Uncle Simon!*—was a memory that surfaced over and over, often swiftly overlaid by more fearful images, but always returning. The quiet way he was determined to do whatever he had to do, regardless of what it cost him. She had hated that part of him in Jarnek. That sense of duty that had driven him back to face Beltha'adi when he could have fled with her to safety. Although in retrospect she'd come to realize that had they fled, neither of them would've left the SaHal alive, even apart from Rhiad's treachery. It had been his courage and willingness to risk his life facing Beltha'adi that had saved not only the two of them but all the Dorsaddi, as well. And so it was here.

She rolled onto her side, straw crackling beneath her, pieces of it poking through the linen cover, and her gaze caught on the Terstan orb left on the bed table when her clothing was sent off to be cleaned. It glowed softly against the stained and pitted wood, its white light a stark contrast to the hearth fire's reddish illumination. After a moment, she pushed up on one elbow and picked it up, remembering how upset she'd been in that cistern when she'd first seen the shieldmark on his chest. Shock, fury, grief. She had not understood how he could have done such a hateful thing to himself, for she had believed it would cripple him and drive him mad. If he ever returned to Kiriath, he would be ridiculed and humiliated. Instead, here he was at the head of an army determined to fight for him, revered by men who had given him their fealty. The shield she'd been so sure would ruin him had only made him stronger. Had, in fact, made him what he was.

Yes, she'd been wrong about it. Completely and utterly wrong. And it was humbling to have to admit it. Perhaps that was part of the reason she hadn't wanted to confront him. Seeing him strong and whole and successful would not have reminded her so much of the gulf that lay between them as it would the fact that his new faith had not destroyed him. And if it had not done all the things she had said it would, what did she have to hold against it?

She rolled the orb between her fingers, studying its bright, clear light, and thinking about the recent events in her own life. Even though she couldn't see the purpose in it, yet she saw the way it had been orchestrated. Was it just luck that Cooper and Elayne had seen her trail and followed? Happenstance that Heron had bolted straight toward them instead of a compass-full of points elsewhere? Was the rain that had chased away the morwhol last night a coincidence? Or the washed-out bridge that had forced it north up the Snowsong, or the Brackleford ferry pushing off just in time? Or was Someone's hand behind it all?

She stared into the orb, recalling how it had stopped Rennalf from taking her to Balmark, how it had destroyed that horrid corridor, protected her from the morhol's Command and maybe even from its claws. She'd thought it was Rhiad protecting her, but maybe there'd been someone else. Maybe she'd not been as alone as she'd believed.

"Go to your brother. I will make you a way."

I only half obeyed that command, she thought. And everything went wrong and it was miserable and horrible, and yet . . . here I am. Can you hear my thoughts? Did you make me a way? But if you did, why? I don't seem to have anything to give to Abramm. And what does he have that I want?

Well, the last one was easily answered. He had purpose. He had a place in the world. People who loved and admired him. He had right now almost everything he'd ever wanted in life. And he had a relationship with the one whose Light lived in this orb.

Is that what I want?

The question hung in her mind, as bright as the orb itself, and she remembered the scar-faced man who had stood between her and the north gate at Highmount, barring her way as the ells had urged her on. "I will let you go," he had said, "if that is truly your wish." But it was not her wish at all.

The orblight beat against her face in a warm and soft caress, drawing her sight down into it. She frowned, peering closer. Is that him? Her heart began to thump. Yes!

Light flared around her, clean and bright and clear, after all the darkness she'd endured. He stood before her, his dark eyes gentle and full of understanding. He knew what she had felt and feared and longed for. He knew. His orb burned against her palm, his power reaching out to her. And suddenly she saw. He was real and with her now, as he had been all along. Ignored, discounted, railed at, yet he had not abandoned her. Emotion welled in her—remorse, desire, wonder that he should care when she had not, wonder at what he offered her: a chance, finally, to belong. To be wanted and protected and loved, even when she had been so thoroughly unlovable.

Her fingers closed around the talisman. The stone pressed hard against her hand, blazing hot, as if it were melting into her palm. Her heart fluttered. Voices rose in chorus around her, too beautiful for words. He smiled at her with eyes both young and impossibly ancient, and warmth flowed into the hole in her soul—warmth and light of purest gold. A vast presence enfolded her and she rode on wings of joy, transported for a moment beyond time, and flesh, and all the hurt and terror she'd endured to a place where none of that mattered, all the cursing turned to indescribable blessing.

She returned slowly to herself, the parting gentle but firm, the sense of presence withdrawing until she was only herself again, sitting on her mattress in a room gone dim with the dying fire. Elayne still lay on her side before it, snoring softly. Carissa looked down at her hand, the chain still looped around her palm. The orb had vanished.

38

Tonight, my Golden Prince. We come tonight, and we will have our due from you. The voice was dry, inhuman, tauntingly familiar.

Abramm jerked awake with a gasp. Darkness enveloped him, tainted with the scent of musty age and a hint of woodsmoke. It took him a moment to remember where he was: in bed in his chambers on the second floor of the keep at Stormcroft, the night before he was to fight Gillard for the crown. The night candle must have gone out, but Trap and Jared slept nearby. He could hear the whisper of their breathing in the silence now that the rain had stopped outside.

It was only another dream.

Tonight . . . tonight we come. . . . The voice rasped again in his mind, as sharp and as clear as if he'd heard it with his ears. His breath caught and his nape hairs rose as he felt the sudden conviction that it was here in the room with him, creeping along the floor in the darkness, stalking him, drawing nearer and nearer. . . .

He sat up in horrified realization. This was no dream. The morwhol was close. He felt it now on the fringes of his awareness, somewhere to the north-east—

Loping up a long shallow ravine toward a dark gash in the pale cliffs ahead, beside which stood the clustered roofless pillars of the first of the many ancient shrines that lined the Pass of the Old Ones. Heavy cloud cover swallowed the cliff-tops and moisture hung in the air, condensing in a plume of white off his tongue, rising up in front of his face—

Abramm wrenched free of the vision, and panic seized him, demanding he rouse Trap and Channon and Kesrin and send them to face it, delay it, divert it while he fled. Or he could leave right now, steal away in the darkness without anyone's knowledge.

Yes. Steal away. And then it would follow him and rip a bloody path through the armies encamped in this valley. It would like that. It would gain much power from that.

He didn't care. His whole life was going to pieces around him, and he knew—absolutely *knew*—that if he tried to face that beast he would fail and die. Or worse, be left crippled and disfigured. Carissa had sat at that long table in the Great Room earlier and told him that was, in fact, Rhiad's preferred end for him. *"He'd rather see you ruined and abandoned than dead."*

But he'd already known that weeks before Carissa had ever come: *"You will lose it all, Abramm Kalladorne,"* Rhiad had promised him in Graymeer's the day of the picnic. *"Crown and people and station. Face and skill and body. I will take it all and no one can stop me!"*

He sat there for some time, seriously considering treachery and an unspeakable act of cowardice, bile burning the back of his throat, his heart hammering against his chest. Then finally, grimly, he forced himself to breathe again and cast the craven notion aside, even as he cast aside the shadow-spawned fear that birthed it. Then he turned to the Light, recalling that the One he served had lived in the ultimate courage of becoming a man whom other men could seize and do unspeakable things to. Had, in fact, let them do those things, because it was Eidon's will for him, and because it was the only way to bring the Light to all of them. Tersius had not run from that, so Abramm would not run from this. If it was Eidon's will that he be crippled and disfigured for the rest of his life, so be it. But he had to believe it was not.

Gradually he began to feel himself again. Not calm, exactly, but in command of himself, at least, and ready now to act. Drawing a deep breath, he flung off the blanket and swung his legs over the side of the bed. As he reached for his breeches, Trap rose from his own pallet near the door with an alertness that said he had not been asleep. "Sire?"

"It's coming." Abramm pulled on the soft wool. "It'll be in the valley by dawn. I'm going to meet it."

"Here? Now?" Trap sprang from his pallet—he was fully dressed—and groped for his boots.

Abramm slid his leather jerkin over his head. "You're not coming with me."

"Abramm—"

"No." The king regarded his liegeman soberly. "We both have responsibilities. Mine is to meet the morwhol. Yours is to serve me as I will."

Trap stared at him, his face so white every freckle stood out in sharp relief. But he said nothing.

Abramm sat again and began to pull on his boots. "Wake my sister and Lady Madeleine," he went on in a voice whose evenness belied his inner turmoil. "Get them mounted and out of here. Take Haldon and Jared with you. Go by the south route through Bright Falls Canyon as fast as you can. Jared—" he turned to the boy who had just now begun to rouse sleepily from his pallet—"see that Warbanner's saddled and brought round to me."

The boy stared at him blankly.

"NOW!" he barked. And Jared was gone like a flash.

"If you won't take me, take Shale," said Trap.

"No." Abramm stood and reached for his weapons. "If it can't get to me, it will only go after the others until it can." The belt and scabbard jingled as he settled them into place on his hips. "Besides, there's nothing any of you can do. I'm the only one who can kill it."

"You don't know that for sure, sir."

Abramm paused and looked round at him. "Perhaps not for sure, but I'll not gamble other men's lives on the chance the records are wrong." He pushed the end of the sword belt through its brass loop, attached the scabbarded dagger, and grabbed his mantle. "Oh, and send someone to find me a broadsword. Maybe a pike, as well."

He started for the door, then turned back to rummage through his saddlebags for his sling and pouch of stones. Probably none of the weapons he carried would do any good against the thing he faced, but he could think of nothing else to do.

He ran into Madeleine in the hall, apparently having awakened already on her own, for she wore a nightgown of white gauzy material, her tawny hair, softly kinked from the braids, flowing in a long loose curtain about her shoulders. Her face was pale, her blue eyes very wide. "It's here, isn't it?" she said.

"Not quite, but coming fast."

"And you're going out to meet it."

"I am."

She nodded, hesitated a moment, then her mouth firmed and her chin came up. He cut her off before she could speak: "No."

"Why not? It will only be after you and those you love."

"Which is why it attacked that little girl on the headland? And why it's ripping up every peasant it comes across?"

"Those are your people, whom you care about deeply. I am just the Second Daughter of Chesedh. And as clear as you've been about your feelings toward me, I know I'll be perfectly safe."

He stared down at her, recalling those moments in the Great Room last week when he'd said those unkind things about her. All of them true in one way or another, and yet . . . here was that strange catching of his heart again, a ghost of a feeling he'd thought lost to him forever, a quick flash of Shettai, and then a terrible, gut-wrenching fear that, as in the Great Room that day, transmuted instantly to anger.

"What is *wrong* with you that you want to have anything to do with this?" he demanded fiercely. "That thing is going to rip me to pieces, and if I don't find a way to kill it in the process—Eidon alone knows *how*—who knows how many others it will get, as well. That's something you want to sing about? Something you think people will want to hear?" He started to push past her.

"I will sing of sacrifice and devotion and courage," she said softly, her voice gone husky and trembling. It stopped him in his tracks and drew his eye down to her, standing so close in the narrow corridor her shoulder almost brushed his chest. Her eyes glistened with tears as she added, "But I don't believe it will end as you say."

Another flash of memory hit him—Shettai on the balcony of that tiny room they'd shared the night before he fought in the Val'Orda. How Madeleine could remind him of Shettai, he did not know, for they were not at all alike. But she did, and it only squeezed his terror tighter. "You're not going!" he said firmly and continued on down the corridor.

But at the corner of the stair, he glanced back. She stood where he had left her, looking after him, a fairy princess in the white gauzy bedgown and the mantle of long silken hair, her face shining with tears. It made his heart ache to leave her on such a harsh note, but he feared anything less would encourage her. Still, he could not help himself:

"This will be hard for my sister. She could use a friend. Will you stay with her until it's over?"

She stared at him mutely, then wiped the tears from her face and nodded.

After that he knew he had to go or he would undo all that his harshness had achieved.

Downstairs he rousted Blackwell from his couch and, with him, Haldon, and Lord Laramor serving as witnesses, signed and sealed the document that declared who was to succeed him—it wouldn't be Gillard. Then he was ready to go—and here was Carissa, dressed to ride with Cooper, his wife and young Philip Meridon attending her. No longer the reserved, stone-faced beauty, she flew into his arms, weeping openly.

"I'm so sorry," she said. "I have been such a fool, too blind and stubborn to see the truth." She drew back from him and dropped her eyes to the shieldmark glittering in the V of his jerkin, then touched it almost reverently. "I see it now, though. Finally." The Light stirred within him, and his breath hissed as her gaze came up to meet his.

He gaped at her. "Carissa, have you—"

She nodded, smiling ruefully as she laid her hand flat against his chest. "Just a few hours ago, in fact. I was going to tell you in the morning, but . . ." The smile gave way to trembling lips and more tears and she buried her face against him, hugging him fiercely. "Come back to us," she murmured. "Eidon was with you in Jarnek. I am sure he will be with you now."

And then, before he could say a word, she pushed away, gathering her reserve about her like a cloak and wiping the tears from her face, and headed for the door. Haldon and Cooper both gave him grim-faced nods and followed her.

By then Simon had arrived with Foxton and Whitethorne, armored and dressed to ride, and though Abramm had given no such order, he wasn't surprised. Taking Simon aside, he told him of his arrangements for the women. "About an hour after I leave I want you to get the men up. Pull those on the northeast lines back to the center of the valley."

"But—it's nearly dawn. I thought the thing went to ground during the daylight."

"Not when there's clouds like these. And I don't think it's going to rain anymore."

Simon looked gray. "Well, then, I will go with you."

"No one's coming with me. The men will need your command now more than any host has ever needed it. If I fail to kill this thing, it will continue to live on in the area of my death, and I do not know how far that area extends."

He paused, then added, "I know you've never believed me about this thing, and I fear you don't even now. Do not take it lightly, Uncle. It will carve a path of devastation through this army such as you have never seen. Don't try to stop it, just get the men out." He paused, considering, then sighed. "And you'd better send word to Gillard's commanders, as well. Tell them to move their men back from around the mouth of the Pass of the Old Ones."

"Pass of the Old Ones?" Simon's brows drew down. "You're not going there, are you?"

"That's the way it's coming."

"How do you know that?"

Abramm turned his eyes to the east. "I can feel it, Uncle. And sometimes, I see things through its eyes. . . ." *A dark forest, dripping with moisture, a narrow rutted trail, leading upward* . . . He shook it off. "If all goes sour, get to Carissa as fast as you can. Blackwell is with her, and he has the documents you'll need."

"Documents?"

"I've made her my heir."

"What?!"

"I know the succession usually passes to the man—but this is not without precedent. Queen Arielle ruled well and wisely. And I will not leave my people to Gillard, especially now that he's allied with the Mataio."

"And Carissa has agreed to this?" Simon demanded incredulously.

"She doesn't know. But she understands more about all this than you know. She has done much in these last years, and she has seen the Esurhites." *And taken the Star, as well. Not fair, my Lord! To take me away from her even as we're reunited.*

Simon was scowling at him. "I do not like this talk of succession, sir."

"Just promise me you will do these things."

It was slow in coming, but it came. His uncle exhaled deeply, then said, "I will see to her, sir."

Abramm held his gaze a moment, struck by the sudden incredible realization that the commitment he saw there was real. That the old revulsion and disdain had given way to admiration and even affection. His uncle had given him his liege almost two weeks ago in the cave beside the Hennepen. But he was giving it now by the look in his eye and the tone of his voice. For a moment it was hard to speak, and when Abramm did, his voice was low and husky. "Thank you."

He started for the door, and behind him, Simon said softly. "May your Eidon protect you, boy. Do the job and come back to us whole."

Abramm glanced back at him, startled. But there was no mockery in Simon's face, only grim resolution. After a moment Abramm gave him a nod, "I'll try, sir."

Then he turned to the other men—Laramor, Whitethorn, Foxton, and Kesrin, just having arrived—telling them that he would not be taking an escort and that until he returned they were to treat Simon's commands as if they were Abramm's own. With that he bid them all good-bye and strode for the door.

Warbanner awaited him outside, prancing restlessly, his pale coat gleaming in the night. Everything shimmered with moisture in the lantern light, and the scent of wet stock pens rose up in a great blanket of aroma. Water still dripped from tent edges and outbuilding roofs, ran down the spouts off the castle walls, but beyond that, the camp lay silent and still, most of the men asleep in accordance with his orders. Only after he was well away were they to be wakened—he didn't want some half-cocked commander taking it into his head to go with him. It had been hard enough to convince Trap and the others to let him alone.

He jogged down the high porch's steps, sword harness jingling, then slowed as a cloaked figure emerged from the shadows at the foot of the stairway. It was Madeleine again, dressed to ride, her hair pulled back from her face and hidden by the cowl of her cloak.

She was still pale, but calm now, her eyes dry as she looked up at him. "I am not here to try to change your mind," she said quickly, diverting the protest that had come to his lips. "And I will do all that you have asked of me. I only came because—" She glanced at the white folds of gauzy fabric he saw she held in her gloved hands. "Because in Chesedh it is traditional to send our men to war with a token of home—a glove, a necklet, a scarf." Her gaze came back to his. "For luck."

He frowned at her. "I don't believe in luck," he said. "I didn't think you did, either."

She bit her lip and looked down again, her face flushing. A moment she hesitated, then thrust the soft folds into his hands. "So take it for love, then."

And with that she fled, leaving him standing there, staring after her in astonishment, the white scarf dangling from his fingers.

"Take it for love?" Surely he'd not heard that right. And yet the memory

of her words sent a warm rush of emotion tingling through him. It lasted but an instant, overtaken by that chilling sense of being watched and stalked. He didn't have much time.

He looked down at the scarf, not knowing what to do with it. Should he stuff it in his sack? Tie it about his waist, where it might get in his way? Finally he gave up and stuffed it into his jerkin, aware of a faint scent of sage and lemongrass as he did.

Then he was striding for his horse and his destiny.

An armorer awaited at Warbanner's side with the broadsword and pike Abramm had asked for. The man helped him fasten the sword harness over his chest and shoulders, adjusting it so he could easily reach back and pull it free of its scabbard. The pike was secured in a sheath tucked out of the way under his right stirrup leather.

"You know how to use these, sir?" the man asked after Abramm had swung into the saddle.

"The sword, yes. The pike. . . ?" Abramm gave him a grin. "I'm sure I can figure it out." And then he was off, trotting through the sleeping camp, down the steepening slope to the gate in the inner wall and on across the larger outer yard to the main gate. He was surprised not to have seen Trap again, and a little disappointed not to have the chance to say good-bye. But it was all happening too fast. He had given the man quite a list of tasks to complete, and no doubt he'd had to argue Shale Channon into complying. At least he appeared to have been successful. Although Abramm wouldn't be entirely confident of that until he cleared the camp without seeing them.

He came out of the barbican and continued down one of the long lanes that radiated through the host encamped outside the castle, still at a trot, unwilling to rouse the men with the noise of Warbanner's gallop or risk running someone down in the dark. Thus by the time he'd reached the edge of camp, he felt almost as impatient as his horse and was relieved to nudge the animal into a gallop.

Flying across the dark, ruin-littered fields, it wasn't long before he realized he was being followed and glanced back to find a veritable troop riding in his wake. Now he knew why he'd not seen Trap nor Channon nor any other of his personal guardsmen in the moments before he'd left. Irritated, he pulled Banner to a stop and turned him to face his pursuers, now pulling up likewise, scattering about him in a rough semicircle. Small kelistars flared into existence, balanced on palms and saddle humps, and he stared around at a group of familiar, and by now beloved, faces: Trap, of course, Shale Channon, Ethan Laramor, Everitt Kesrin, Will Ames, and several other of his personal guard, in addition to Lords Foxton and Whitethorne.

"What is this?" Abramm demanded, Warbanner tossing his head and prancing impatiently at the delay. "I told you I wanted no escort."

"Nevertheless you have one, sir," said Captain Channon.

"You have jobs back in the camp. The men will need you. The people will need you. And you'll be no help to me, anyway."

"We can be witnesses of your courage, sir."

"I don't *need* any witnesses of my courage." *Plagues! There probably won't be any courage to witness!* "And you'll just provide more targets for it to strike at."

"They say it will be focused on you, sir," said Foxton.

"Yes, and after it kills me, it will go for all of you. Especially for you, since it will know you are men that I care about."

"Yes, Sire," Trap said. "But Kohal Kesrin says that in killing you, it will have killed that part of itself that is most alive and thus become vulnerable to the blades and power of other men. Especially if it's already been weakened in battle."

Abramm scowled at Kesrin. "You know this for fact?"

"It is what I believe the Words teach, sir," Kesrin said with a respectful nod. "Though, admittedly, I know of no instance in which my theory has been tested."

"Then it could all end in ruin."

"Yes, sir."

"It's a risk we are willing to take," Trap interjected. He paused as Abramm's gaze came back to him. "We might well be able to see it's slain, my lord. If you cannot."

Abramm stared hard at him, shocked to discover he had no argument for that. He let his gaze slide over them again, one by one, angry that Trap should have thought of this and that he himself could think of no rebuttal. How could he turn them down now, realizing that if he should fail—an all too likely possibility—hundreds of lives could be saved by their presence?

"Very well," he relented. "But keep your distance until it's obvious I'm finished. There'll be no leaping in to help me—you all know there's nothing you can do until I'm dead."

"We know, sir," said Trap.

A moment more he regarded them, then wheeled Warbanner and launched him up the slope onto the remains of the ancient road that skirted the northern edge of the valley. Still in fairly good shape, the road was grass-grown and wet with rain but smooth enough. They kept the horses to a canter, and the clash of stone and hoof thundered up around them. While a slower pace would have been less likely to attract the attention of enemy patrols, time was running out. More and more Abramm saw the night through the morwhol's eyes as the beast came up the pass from the other side. It ran with an eagerness he had not sensed before, like a hound hot on the scent of its prey, for it knew he was coming to meet it and already was filling his mind with visions of what it would do to him.

He clung to the Light and turned them aside, one after the other. Madeleine's words held like a shield before them. *"I don't believe it will end as you say."*

Gradually the morning dawned around them. Gnarled, black tree-shapes emerged from the murk. The clouds hung low overhead and drifted through the trees. To their left, the land ascended sharply and disappeared into the clouds. To the right lay the valley floor, the camps of the two opposing armies mostly hidden in mist. Both sides were already stirring, but Gillard's was much more active than Abramm's.

They entered a stand of spruce and emerged at the mouth of the steep-walled canyon that led up to the pass from this side. A rush of brown water tumbled out of it in a boulder-strewn channel that crossed under the road here, spanned by the crumbling stonework of a Tuk-Rhaalan bridge, still sufficiently intact to be serviceable. They clattered across it and circled the base of the long flat-topped knoll that extended into the valley. Crumbling walls and pillars crowned its terraced top, their heads cloaked in clouds that were once more spitting rain.

This was the Temple of Dragons, if he recalled the map correctly. The road wound around this knoll, then switchbacked up the slope beyond it into the canyon itself. He had no idea what he would find there—the road might be impassable. Regarded as a place of Shadow ruled by ells, people had long avoided it, so the maps showed nothing.

Then, as if triggered by his thoughts, he saw again through the eyes of the beast, now racing up the opposite side of this pass to meet him—

Rock walls soared closely around a steeply ascending road, lined with stone shrines. Each held a robed statue, wreathed in individual hues of light. Lavender, blue, red, amber—they flashed past as the beast galloped upward. Its bloodlust burned so hotly now, it could not keep itself quiet, its triumphal yowls echoing back and forth up the canyon and down the other side.

Abramm blinked free of the link as he rounded the base of the temple knoll, the beast's cries coming down as a distant echo in his ear. Warbanner flung up his head with a snort, but Abramm kept him on track. Setting his jaw against his own rising fear, he rode on, his men thundering after him. The clouds hung lower here, new veils rising from the moisture-soaked ground.

He was slowing Banner to adjust to the reduced visibility, when directly ahead he spied horsemen behind the parting mists, ranged ahead of him to block the road. A command rang sharply through the morning quiet, and more riders rode out of the mist into position along the road, closing off any avenue of escape to the valley on the right. As Abramm hauled Banner to a stop, he noted a good number of them were cloaked in gray. Regular foot soldiers stood both behind them, and across the road to Abramm's left, the men ranged across the temple knoll's steep slope. Together with the horsemen they formed a long funnel drawing down to the riders who waited at its apex. Of those, one wore the pale robes and gray mantle of a Mataian, another, Gadrielite gray. Between them, mounted on a tall black horse, sat a big man in a golden breastplate and purple cloak, his shoulder-length, white-blond hair secured by the circlet of kingship upon his brow.

39

It was the circlet that caught Abramm's eye as he walked Banner toward them, for it was not the original. Thanks to Simon, Abramm had that in his own possession, though he wasn't wearing it. He hadn't even considered it. *Yet here's Gillard, audacious enough to make his own circlet and wear it out here as if he were already king.*

The mist swirled and shifted around the men, alternately obscuring and revealing them as Abramm approached. To Gillard's left sat Prittleman, holding his bandaged right hand close to his middle as he glowered at Abramm in self-righteous triumph. Belmir rode on Gillard's right, his face closed and hard, with a flinty look in his eyes Abramm had seen only rarely, and never before directed at himself. Gillard wore his usual sneering disdain.

"I know you got my warning," Abramm said as he drew up before them, "or you wouldn't be here. I can only conclude you didn't take it seriously, else you'd not have brought these men with you." He gestured at the soldiers surrounding them.

Gillard smirked. "I'm told this beast is only after you and those you care about, brother. These men have nothing to fear."

"These men are my subjects, whom I am duty bound to protect. They have everything to fear. Even you might not be completely safe."

Gillard's face went dark. "I know what you're trying to do, *little* brother, and you'll not wiggle out of our contest that easily. Did you think all the nonsense about you being the White Pretender would really scare me out of accepting? Far from it! I'm eager now to test your mettle."

Abramm opened his mouth to respond, then reality shifted—

A huge, long-faced stone man peered down from a narrow alcove on the left, heavy browed, eyes flickering red-orange in the shadows. The ancient road wound upward, clinging to sheer walls, the air heavy with the scent of damp stone. Mist swirled overhead, shredding in a brief window to frame a rocky crag gilt by the sun, bright against blue sky— "Aaug! Look away! Look to the velvet shadows and the dark, damp rock. Feel the fire inside. We are close now. Very close. Friends will make more clouds to shield."

The creature crowed its victory as again Abramm pulled free of it.

His brother affected a high-pitched, mocking voice, "'The monster is coming, brother Gillard. Best take your men and flee while I go out to meet it, for I alone can do so.'" He reverted to his natural, deeper tone. "You thought I would heed that?" He spat on the ground between them. "That's not the way *this* tale will end. You got the kraggin. I'm taking this one."

Abramm gaped at him. "*I'm* the one it's after!"

"If that's true, we'll just hold you here until it comes. That way *we* can choose the battlefield."

When Abramm had told Simon to send word the morwhol was coming and for the men to be moved away from the pass, the last thing he expected was that his brother would seek to face the monster himself.

"Gillard, you can't—" He broke off in frustration, realizing anything he said would be discounted as another attempt to seek his own glory.

Gillard smirked at him, savoring his victory as he'd done that night in Southdock six years ago. Gritting his teeth, Abramm gestured at the soldiers surrounding them. "At least get your men out of here."

His brother rocked back in the saddle. "But then we would have no one to witness what we do."

"All we're going to do is *die*. You and I, seeing as you're so intent on taking my place. I see no reason to drag them along with us."

He loped up the narrow winding road, looking to the deep shadows instead of the painful brightness above, savoring the sharp smell of stone and the growing scent of horses and men—one man in particular. A roofed shrine slid by on the right, cut out of the sheer stone walls sheltering the Lady within. Her eyes pulsed amber. "Yes, she will make us a covering."

Abramm shook away the vision, and fire turned to a ball of ice resting in the pit of his stomach as he realized who the "friends" were—rhu'ema.

Gillard gestured grandly at Belmir. "Have you not noted my companions, Abramm? Your once esteemed Discipler, now a master among the Holy

Brethren? The venerable and righteous Lord Prittleman? We ride under the protection of Eidon's Sacred Flames." He glanced over his shoulder at the group of Guardians Abramm now saw standing up the road, half hidden in the mist, holding the flattened bronze orb of their traveling brazier aloft. "What need have *we* of fearing monsters of the Shadow?"

"You're trusting in *them* to keep you safe? Plagues, Gillard! They'll just make it stronger."

Belmir's face slackened with astonishment, then drew down into a thunderous frown as Prittleman sputtered about Terstan heretics and blasphemy.

I don't have time *for this!*

Abramm glanced at the line of archers hemming him in on the left. Gillard must've thought the steepness of the hill behind them would be enough of a deterrent not to warrant another line of horsemen. Or maybe it would've been too hard to hide them. In any case, Abramm could probably charge Warbanner straight up the hill through their ranks to the top of the knoll before they knew what had happened. According to the map, a narrow track led from the back of the temple complex to the main road up the pass, joining it well beyond Gillard's line of men.

Prittleman was still raving when an ear-piercing yowl cut him off and brought every man to horror-stricken attention. It came again, a black arrow of sound that froze the body as it impaled the heart with the knowledge that something evil and brutally violent was at hand. Dying echoes rolled over the knoll and the road and the lines of men made suddenly aware of their own mortality.

Like the rest of them, Abramm sat transfixed, stunned by the realization that the visions that had long tormented him were about to become reality. Then Warbanner reared up, screaming an angry challenge. The moment he came down, Abramm wrenched his head around and kicked him hard. They flew up the hillside and through the line of archers as easily as Abramm had predicted, had topped the misty knoll by the time he heard Gillard bellowing orders behind him, then Trap's voice, swiftly swallowed by a rising tide of shouts and screams and the muffled thunder of hoofbeats.

Abramm never looked back, guiding Banner up a wide bank of grass-grown steps, across a plaza, up another bank of steps, and finally racing him for all he was worth up a long promenade flanked by mist-hung pillars and low crumbling walls. At its end they clattered up the stepped sides of the temple's wide porch, through the arched opening of its freestanding façade and across the flat beyond, wet grass intermingled with the irregular remains of the stones that had once formed the temple's main floor.

Then the mist parted and the knoll ran out. Warbanner skidded to a stop at the edge of a steep-walled, boulder-strewn canyon, churning with runoff. The passage Abramm sought was not here after all. Perhaps there'd been a bridge once, but today they faced a deep cleft, too wide for Warbanner to jump, the other side too steep to offer purchase even if he could.

They returned to the temple porch to find Trap, Channon, and the rest of Abramm's men having taken a stand at the midpoint of the promenade Abramm had crossed only minutes ago. Gillard's men had closed with them, and the two groups struggled fiercely. Banner was fast enough, Abramm knew, that by the time anyone saw him he could easily evade them—but to what purpose? The horse wasn't faster than the morwhol, and it would only be a matter of time before the beast hunted them down. Besides, Abramm wanted Banner as far away as possible when he was finally forced to face off with it. Better to take his stand here.

Knotting the reins to keep them on the horse's neck, he sprang from the saddle and—

Cresting the top of the pass, he flung himself down the now-descending trail, shrines looking on with bright benevolence, swirling shreds of mist rising up around them. The man-scent was growing stronger, swelling his head and chest with bloodlust till it felt as if they would burst.

The jolt of his landing pulled Abramm back to himself. Warbanner had stopped and was looking round at him in puzzlement. With a shout, Abramm swatted his pale hindquarters, and the stallion wheeled with an indignant snort. He trotted a few paces along the top of the stair, glanced at Abramm again, then plunged down the steps and raced away. Too late Abramm realized he'd taken the pike with him.

The battle on the promenade had shifted, and a few horsemen had broken through the line, racing headlong now toward Abramm's position on the temple porch. Leading them was a big man in a golden breastplate. Abramm jogged down the porch stairs to meet him, unwinding the sling from his wrist as he went. He pulled a stone from his pouch and slid it into the sling's leather cradle just as he reached the bottom. Praying for more of the uncanny accuracy he'd enjoyed outside Graymeer's the day of the picnic, he dropped it back and let fly. Gillard's eyes widened as he spotted Abramm for the first time, shifted his weight backward to stop his horse—

The stone struck dead center of that gleaming breastplate with enough force to knock Gillard out of the saddle and reeling on his horse's rump. The morwhol screamed again, closer now than ever. Gillard's horse, already flustered by his rider's erratic weight shifts, spied Abramm now, too, and shied violently, as if Abramm himself had been the source of the scream. Gillard hit the ground rolling and came up with his rapier in hand.

But then he staggered and leaned forward, coughing and gasping back the breath that had been driven out of him when the stone hit him midchest. By the time the three gray-cloaked men who'd accompanied him pulled up to flank the royals, though, he'd recovered, advancing toward Abramm with a sneer. "You just gonna throw rocks at me, little brother, or will you finally show me you really do know how to use those blades you wear?"

The taunt stung, as always, rousing the familiar, almost instant anger. And better to save the stones for later, anyway. Swiftly Abramm rewrapped the sling about his wrist and pulled out his blades, rapier and dagger both. One of the Gadrielites tossed Gillard a buckler, and the brothers closed, circling.

As soon as Gillard's back was to the steps, Abramm attacked, forcing him to retreat awkwardly upward. Halfway to the top, he broke it off and danced out of the line of attack, ascending even with his brother. Gillard remained condescending.

"Well, apparently you do know something of the sword, after all."

"The stories are true, Gillard. I really was the White Pretender." And again Abramm attacked, forcing Gillard back on the diagonal this time, not letting up until they'd reached the porch itself. By then Trap and Channon had left the main battle on the promenade to engage the three who'd come with Gillard, a contest Abramm was aware of only peripherally.

The bloodlust was overwhelming. Eagerness made his great limbs shake as he loped down the trail, the scent of his prey strong now, and close. He came around a bend in the canyon walls, the road curling across the face of the steep grassy slope below. And finally, there they were: gray-cloaked men ranged across the hillside, their backs to him as they looked down into the mist-filled valley below them, the slopes of the temple knoll rising to their right. Blind, deaf, ignorant as the woolly ones. He laughed and slowed to savor the moment. They had no idea they were about to die. . . . Then he was among them, biting and slashing and tearing.

Abramm wrenched free of the other's mind, trying to master the trembling in his own limbs, and the shadows of fear and guilt that sought to overwhelm his soul. "Gillard, this is stupid. That thing is killing your own men! Let me face it."

"I thought they were *your* men." Gillard bared his teeth, circling the tip of his rapier in Abramm's face. "It'll be here in good time, little brother."

"And then it will kill you, too."

"No, it will kill *you*. And once you're dead and it's vulnerable, then *I* will kill it—avenging the loss of my brother as I rid the realm of yet another dangerous enemy." He paused. "It's close now. Can you feel it?"

He leaped onto an outcropping, his powerful hindquarters launching him from there onto the back of a fleeing man. His fangs sank deeply into his prey's flesh, and he sucked up the scarlet flame of his life energy even as he sucked up the blood.

Of course Abramm could feel it! Breathing down upon his neck, a dark oppressive presence filling his mind with visions of carnage that were no longer portents but reality. But how did *Gillard* know—

As Abramm grasped the implication of his brother's words, Gillard capitalized on the shock they produced to launch a combination of thrusts and feints that nearly relieved Abramm of his dagger. Then Abramm's sword tip caught the top of Gillard's breastplate, a hair's breadth from jumping the edge, and stopped his momentum. They returned to circling, moving slowly across the porch.

"So you're part of it, too, then," Abramm said. That day at Graymeer's when Gillard's palm had been slashed just like Abramm's: Rhiad had needed *his* blood, too. The morwhol had been birthed by the hatred not of one man, but two. Gillard must be linked in the same way Abramm was. He had known all along that it was coming and what it intended to do.

Gillard laughed. "Surprised you, did I?"

No wonder he let that left line of the funnel be so weak. He meant to draw me up here, away from the others. And now through that mutual link with the morwhol, Abramm grasped the rest of the plan, as well: Gillard's alliance with the Mataio had never been sincere. He was only using them, knowing the morwhol would go after them and that many of them would be killed. When it became evident they had not aided him in his battle against the beast, he would not be beholden to them in the aftermath, the alliance dissolved, all obligations nullified.

"Everything Rhiad promised me is coming true," Gillard went on, flashing that feral grin again. "I can feel your shock, Abramm. I can feel your fear,

your helpless fury. Soon it will get even better. Soon I will feel your pain."
The grin turned to a snarl as he drove in with his rapier, aiming for Abramm's
throat.

Abramm brushed the lunge off. "If you can sense it, you must know it's
already killed your partner. Two nights ago, north of Brackleford."

"Rhiad's not dead, brother. He's simply been transformed."

"Absorbed, is how Carissa described it. Screaming all the way."

"Yet he is alive, and no longer the crippled ruin you made of him. In fact,
he's more powerful than ever."

"Powerful, indeed, since he must know you mean to kill him, yet that has
not stopped him. Why is that do you suppose?"

With a snarl, Gillard went after him, too confident, too fast. Abramm
caught the blade between dagger and sword and flicked it from his brother's
fingers. Gillard staggered back, eyes wide, his hand opening and closing as if
he could not believe the blade was gone.

"Now get out of here, Gillard. While you still can."

Gillard staggered forward a step, looking dazed. Then anger hardened his
face. "No! I told you—this one's *mine!*"

*On the misty hillside above the knoll, he flung a lifeless body aside and lunged
for another victim. He was delirious now from the screams and the blood and the
terror—and all the scarlet life flowing into him. "They're so stupid! Just like the
woolly ones, running all together, making it so easy."*

Gillard dove at him. Caught still in the morwhol's perception, Abramm
was bulled to the ground, where the force of his fall slammed his hand into a
stone paver and he nearly lost his rapier. His grip tightened, the stars faded
from his vision, and as Gillard started to pull himself off him, Abramm
slammed the butt of the rapier hilt into the side of his head, then shoved his
brother away and rolled free, gaining his feet and backing away. Gillard arose
likewise, only to charge again, and this time Abramm was ready. His rapier
slid over the edge of the breastplate and just under the collarbone, while his
dagger sank into Gillard's left thigh. The blades slid out again instantly,
Abramm already leaping out of range. But Gillard launched no counterattack,
staggering back with a howl as his left leg collapsed and he dropped to one
knee, gripping his shoulder.

And then a throaty breath and the click of toenails on stone somewhere
in the mist to his right told him the morwhol was here. He turned from Gillard, backing farther to keep his brother in his line of sight while he sought

to find the beast. The temple façade appeared through the mist, the doorway flanked by a pair of pillars. Portions of a low curved wall extended concavely from the outward sides of those pillars, perhaps having once encircled the area in front of the opening. Beyond the walls stretched the flat of the porch, littered with fallen pillars, the fragments of the once great stone sculptures that had sat atop them and a scattering of small dark-leafed bushes. From around the back of the façade, the beast slunk into view, prowling beyond the opposite wall, its ugly, blood-covered snout aimed toward them as it watched them with eyes no longer green, but dark against white, and eerily human.

Abramm was horrified by its size, for it was vastly bigger than when he'd last seen it, bigger even than the description Carissa had just given him. Its hunched and hairy shoulders were massive as a bull's, and the sleek, brindled hindquarters rippled with powerful muscles as it prowled, the tip of its tufted tail flicking back and forth. It was *far* too big to face with only a rapier, and seeing it now, Abramm realized it would be considerably more formidable than the kraggin. It had a man's mind, like the veren, but linked as it was, it also knew Abramm's own thoughts as he had them. Worst of all, like Gillard, it knew his weaknesses. All the ways to provoke and intimidate him, so as to give the Shadow within him ascendance.

Even as he realized this, he saw Gillard laughing at him, enjoying his dismay.

And just seeing that laughter kindled Abramm's anger. It flared briefly, before it was overwhelmed by a barrage of horrific images and sensations and rising fear as the Shadow within him took control. He put them down, barely, clinging to the Light, reminding himself that none of the awful ends he'd just been shown could happen without Eidon's permission.

The beast continued its circuit around the outside of the wall, Abramm turning to follow it, careful to keep aware of Gillard. Behind the façade it went, and he sensed its presence without seeing it, tracking its estimated position with his eyes. It passed briefly behind the opening and was gone, only to emerge a moment later on the other side, leaping onto the low wall and seeking to engage him again. Failing that, it turned its gaze upon his brother.

A shiver of fear, not Abramm's own, went through him, and it struck him suddenly that if the beast absorbed Gillard, it would be stronger still, physically and otherwise. No sooner had he thought it than he jammed dagger and rapier into their sheaths, then released the sling from around his wrist as he fingered three stones from his pouch. He barely had the first loaded when the morwhol sprang, clearing the twenty feet between it and Gillard as if it were nothing. It bowled the big man over as if he were a child, sinking its teeth into his shoulder. Abramm heard his screams two ways, felt his terror only one. But he did not let it disrupt his concentration, seeking the Light and letting fly with the stone. Already Gillard's body glowed faintly with scarlet light. The stone flew true, turning to a white fireball in the air and hitting the beast square in the side of its head—without effect. The second one hit, as well, and in its wake came a narrow, jagged bolt of Light that crawled over the beast in a netlike flash the moment it hit. The morwhol convulsed, released its victim with a yowl, and bounded away into the mist, leaving Gillard sprawled unmoving on the stonework.

Abramm's own shock kept it from fleeing far, for he had not expected to throw the Light at all, had not even tried, and had no idea how he had accomplished it. Which, of course, the morwhol now knew. Worse, he'd apparently done no more damage than to break off its attack upon Gillard, which may or may not have saved his brother's life.

Grimly, he slid another stone into the sling, had just grasped the end of its leather strap, when the morwhol burst out of the mist in front of him, a great snarling shadow bearing down so fast he hardly had time to fling his stone. White fire slammed into the morwhol's head, right between the eyes, a killing blow for a lesser creature. This one only recoiled with a snarl and returned to its circling. But at least it had recoiled. Maybe his spindly burst of Light *had* done something, after all.

Back around the broken pillars and freestanding portions of wall it went. He readied another stone, then stiffened as voices hissed in his ears, soft as the sighing of a breeze. *You should not have come here, Abramm Kalladorne . . . your people will die because of you.*

Glancing up, he saw a ribbon of red light sidling through the mist near what must have been the top of the Temple façade. Rhu'ema. The morwhol's "friends" come to watch. And help? *You should not have come,* the voices hissed. *They'll die, and their blood will be upon your hands.*

Toenails clicking on stone made him turn. The morwhol stood in the opening of a low wall, and the dark man-eyes snared his own the moment he looked at them, drawing him into them like a snake striking from its hole. Again the horrific visions poured into him. Again the Shadow within him rose in response, and terror claimed him. The thing stepped toward him, its jaws gaping. He couldn't move. Could hardly breathe. It took another step.

This is the end. . . .

And somewhere deep within him a Presence stirred, a Light flickered, and he remembered he was not helpless after all. Shaking off the fear and the binding of the silent Command, he slung—and hit. Likewise a fourth time. Then a fifth, the accuracy of his aim filling him with awe. But at the same time he knew he was only delaying the inevitable. The stones were doing little damage, and soon he would run out.

He let it get closer the next time, only to see his seventh stone miss entirely. Shocked, he dropped the sling, whipped out the broadsword, and dove over the wall, the morwhol right behind him. It must have expected him to scramble away rather than dive for the ground, for it sailed clean over him, stumbling on a fragment of stony wing as it came down. Abramm, meanwhile, had landed on his side, sword clutched in both hands. He rolled back to brace against wall just as the creature pounced upon him, impaling itself on his blade. With the steel plunged deep into the rough-maned chest, he sent the Light flooding into it. The monster's shriek of shock and pain nearly shattered his eardrums. Stinging spittle flew across his face as the beast scrambled to free itself, dark blood gushing down the hilt, eating through his leather gloves on contact. The Light pulsed again, burning away the tainted blood in a wild, hissing sizzle. Screaming and frantic, the creature wrenched itself off his sword, stumbled across the pavement, then collapsed, panting in rough deep grunts.

Abramm shoved himself up, knowing he must seize the moment while it lasted—too late. At his first movement, the beast rose on three legs and trotted away, leaving dark blood pooled on the pale stone. Yowling piteously, glaring at him all the while, it went back to circling, limping heavily at first, but, as with the veren, healing all too soon. Abramm began to feel truly afraid.

How am I supposed to kill this thing, Eidon?

But the only answer he got came from the voices whispering in his ears, feeding the fear at the back of his mind. *You're going to die . . . you should not have come . . . it will end as you have seen.*

Around behind the façade it went, and Abramm glanced up again toward the rhu'ema. The mist had risen and thickened overhead, revealing the top of the façade, squared off above the rounded summit of its entry arch, and flanked by a pair of stone dragons rearing up from the stone pedestals beside it. The sight of them transfixed him with a stunning chill of portents, the shock so great he had to look away and then back again, to be sure he hadn't imagined them—nor the way their eyes glowed with red fire.

The dragon and the shield. They lifted the hairs on the back of his neck, and he knew it was no accident he was here, knew there was far more going on here than him simply meeting this morwhol.

The broadsword kept it away for a time, but that, too, only delayed the inevitable, wearing him down as the creature played with him, feinting and dodging to draw him after it, only to turn and attack. It fed the fear and the reckless angry frustration that kept him swinging and missing until the sweat ran off his brow and his arms shook. His fear rose in choking waves and made him swing the sword wildly as he kept reaching for the Light, the blade before him firing and fading, firing and fading. He did not understand it. He had fought the fear off here already. Had fought it off even in his fleshly strength in the Esurhite arenas. Now he carried the Light within, had served Eidon with a whole heart these last four years, had come in obedience and at least a measure of trust. Why wasn't it working? Why was it so hard now?

Because you have more to lose than you ever did in Esurh, my son. Because you are much too attached to the man you have become and the blessings you have been given. Because you will not trust me.

But I am trusting you! I would never have come if I didn't trust you.

Then cast your blades aside!

Cast them aside? It will kill me for sure.

The beast attacked, snarling and spitting, and he swung the blazing sword yet again, saw it evaded almost lazily. *You're going to die,* the rhu'ema whispered. *And all your people, too.*

Another lunge. Another swing. He didn't see the column until the broadsword collided with it in a great ringing clang, the force of impact jarring into palm and wrist and shivering the hilt loose in his fingers. He tightened them frantically, just managed to keep from dropping it.

Cast your blades aside. To throw the Light, he knew he had to trust only it. To become vulnerable, *knowing* Eidon would do the work through him. Even with something so small as the staffid that had been hard, and right now it would be easier to fling himself off the cliff beyond the temple and trust Eidon to catch him than to cast aside this blade with the morwhol slavering in his face.

You have to be willing to lose it all, Abramm. To give it all to me and trust me to treat you fairly, to do you good. Have I ever let you down?

No, my Lord. But . . .

It is the Shadow within you that fears. Trust the Light.

The beast circled round the low wall, past the tiered benches, dark eyes upon him, tail flicking.

Very well, my Lord Eidon, I will trust you. It's obvious I'll get nowhere otherwise. And setting his jaw, he flung the broadsword away, the blade clanging as it hit the stone pavement and slid to a stop.

The morwhol attacked at once. And here were Abramm's rapier and dagger, leaping to his hands as if they had life of their own. And if they were feeble, silly weapons for the beast he faced, at least he could maneuver them quickly and skillfully, tired as he was. *I should have used these at the start*, he thought.

But it didn't take him long to realize he was again delaying the inevitable. He would never kill the beast this way, for while he was growing more and more tired, it was growing stronger, almost as if it were sucking the energy out of him. *Cast your blades aside.*

It was harder now, because he knew he had nothing to replace them with. *Trust me.*

His throat was raw from his panting. Sweat ran off his brow, stinging his eyes. Rivulets coursed down his side, and his arms shook all the time now. His back and shoulders were starting to cramp as stars flashed at the edge of his vision. He had used up all he had, had come to the very end of himself. Just as he had in that cistern four years ago when he'd finally come to Eidon in the first place. With nothing.

And that is the only way you'll walk through the door of your destiny, my son. You must trust me completely, no matter what sight tells you. Put aside your own ideas and plans and let me do as I wish with you.

He glanced up again, the undulating ribbons of light coiling and uncoiling as they strained toward him, driven back by flares of white and silver and gold. As in Jarnek he felt their hatred. Even more than the crowds in Esurh had, they despised him, lusting to watch him fail and die, would have fallen upon him themselves were it not for the power of Eidon, stopping them.

Trust him.

And so for the second time, he made himself stop and stand straight and fling both weapons away, the ring of their blades on the stone making him cringe. *I will trust you, Lord.*

The morwhol emerged from the doorway of the temple gateway, Rhiad-eyes fixed upon him, jaws split as if it were laughing. Abramm waited for the Light to roar through him and blast it away, but nothing happened. Then, in the blink of an eye, the creature lunged, swiping his chest with its claws, the force of the blow knocking him ten feet. He landed on his back, the breath driven out of him, his leather jerkin slashed to flapping strips that let the folds of the scarf he'd tucked within come billowing out.

Flat on his back, stunned and struggling to regain his breath, he stared up at the rhu'ema-wreathed dragons on their pedestals, heard their laughter in his head. *So much for your destiny—loser!* A dark shape loomed over him, blotting them out. Hot, stinking breath rushed over his face and the eyes that looked into his own were a man's eyes, brown irises on a white orb, long lashed, familiar. Rhiad's voice rasped in his ears. *And now, my Golden Prince, you will know what I have known. First we will take that handsome face . . .*

The beast's claws hovered above his right eye. *My Lord, I cast my blades away, as you asked. Where is the Light? Why aren't you stopping this?*

The claws drew nearer, and he couldn't stop his instinctive flinch away, nor the horrible mewling that slid out of his throat. *Oh, Eidon, please!* Yet on they came. Something sharp pressed into his brow. *Surely now the Light will come.* But it did not. The claw pressed harder. He scrunched his eyes shut just as it slashed downward, tracking fire across brow and cheek, all the way to his jaw. Blood trickled hotly down his temple and he gasped, as much in shock as in pain.

Oh, Lord! What are you doing to me? Where are you? I'm trusting, and you promised. You promised.

A sharp cackling intruded on his pleas. And then Rhiad's voice again. *You will lose it all, Abramm Kalladorne. Crown and people and station. Face and skill and body. I will take it all and no one can stop me! Even if you live, you will never wield a blade again. Women will shrink in horror at the sight of you, while men will shake their heads in pity.*

It went to work, then, cackling and babbling and shrilling with glee as it shredded his sword arm into blood-soaked ribbons. The pain, both physical and mental, was so great he thought sure he'd fallen through some hole that had taken him to Torments. Voices called him. Rhu'ema voices. Rhiad's voice . . . those of his men, yelling and screaming. Was he already dead and the beast at work on his friends now? He couldn't tell what was real and what was not.

And then somehow it all drifted away, as if he had become cut off from his body. A white froth had erupted from his chest. He reached up with his good arm to touch it—marveling that he could move anything at all—and found it not to be froth, but soft, gauzy folds of fabric spilling out of his split jerkin. He clutched it, stirring up the scent of sage and lemongrass. Madeleine.

She was here . . . but not in body, linked somehow to his soul. He felt her horror at what was happening to him, her anguish at his pain, her deep, unacknowledged love for him. And she was praying. *"Eidon, please! Remind him how the Shadow blinds him, remind him who he is and whom he serves. What it is that really matters in this life. I know you hold him in your hands and that you will never let him go. Let him know it, too. . . ."*

Remind him of whom he serves. Who did he serve? *Eidon, Lord of Light, Creator of All, the Just and Righteous and True . . .* The one who promised to guide him, to bless him and prosper him, and never to forsake him. The one who always kept his promises because he alone was unable to break them. The one who had seen Abramm through his years of slavery in Esurh and from that made him something he had never dreamed he could be. The one who delivered him from Beltha'adi and brought him to Kiriath. Whose Light had slain the kraggin, who had given Abramm the crown when he should have been mocked and turned away, who had given him the favor of his people and an army of men sworn to follow him. Who'd given him Simon's affection, long yearned for, and Carissa's return. From the other side, all that had looked as impossible as the situation he now faced.

And then there was the greatest impossibility of all—that the creator of all life and light had found a way to reach past the Shadow that tainted Abramm, as it did all men, and make him his own. If he could do that, surely he could handle this morwhol. If he had not done so, if he truly meant to take away all he had given, then he had a reason.

You must be willing to give it all up.

I'm willing, my Lord. Take it all, for none of it matters without you. I don't know what you're doing, but I know in the end it will make sense. And I know you will not forsake me, even though I fail and insult you and disobey you, again and again. Yet you remain faithful.

And in that, Abramm Kalladorne, King of Kiriath, finally found his rest.

40

The light blew through him in a mighty torrent, as if the sun itself had entered his flesh and was burning its way out in a single purifying blast. He had an instant of realization, of dismay and terror, then a sweeping fire of agony overtook him, so intense it made his other hurts seem inconsequential. In a heartbeat it was gone and he floated in some place apart from earth and flesh and time, a place of laughter and delight and a glorious light that washed warmly about him like the waters of a gentle sea. He swam in it, floated on it, rolled and wriggled and reveled in it, and felt, with a deep unshakable certainty, his sovereign's pleasure.

Gradually it drifted him downward, back to the cold, hard ground, its brilliance fading into a cocoon of sparkling effervescence through which he began to see dark shapes and lighter ones moving around him, hear voices speaking without understanding what they said. Only at the last minute did he realize he was going back.

I want to stay here, Eidon. In you.

You are in me, Abramm. No matter where you are. As I am in you.

But . . . it is so hard.

You thought it would be easy to walk into your destiny? That all would just be handed to you?

No, my Lord. I knew it would be a battle. I just did not expect to have to fight myself so much.

And so this trial has made you stronger, and that much closer to becoming the man I wish to make of you.

I thought you had already done that.

Oh no. I have only just begun. But do not fear. Along with the trials I will bless you beyond your wildest dreams.

It faded then, and Abramm came back to himself, lying on the stone plaza, clutching Madeleine's scarf to his chest. The dragons loomed over him, dead-eyed and naked of their cloaks of mist. The sun had dawned, washing the sky with the brightness of a new day and driving the shadows back into their canyon.

The last of the Light washed out of him and pain returned, especially in his left arm. Not his right arm, but his left. Perplexed, he lifted the right one, held it before his face, turning his hand this way and that. It was cut and scraped and blood-spattered but it worked just fine. His left, however, would not move, and the pain was increasing by the moment. He lifted his head finally to look past the blood-stained scarf billowing on his chest and found his left arm a bloody mess, ribboned with lacerations, strips of flesh mingled with the shredded sleeve of his jerkin, and here and there the sickening white gleam of bone. Nausea lurched in his middle and he dropped his head back, blotting out the image as he blotted out the panicked thoughts that whirled up from the floor of his mind and focused on the fact that it was his *left* arm, not his right! Despite the way it had seemed while the beast was attacking him. Rhiad had wanted to take from Abramm what he had lost himself. And Rhiad had lost his left arm. Though he'd crowed about destroying Abramm's sword arm, in his frenzy at the end, he must've gotten confused.

Suddenly there were men hovering around him and one of them began doing something to his injured arm. Familiar faces peered down at him, etched with concern: Trap, Channon, Kesrin, Laramor. He looked from one to the other and finally asked, "Why the plague are you all staring at me?"

"Because you're alive," Trap said, squeezing Abramm's right shoulder. And now his face burst into a smile. "You're *alive.*"

Alive, but with only one arm. I'm going to be a one-armed man for the rest of my life! Again he stopped the panicked thoughts, bemused that after everything he'd been through, everything he'd just learned, he could still be such an idiot. *Eidon lives within me. He has called me to the privilege of serving him and left me alive to do so. Who cares if I only have one arm?* It was the Shadow within him that birthed all this panic. And he would never be free of it—not so long as he lived in this body—so he might as well get used to that fact and not be so surprised when it revealed itself.

He swallowed on a dry mouth. "What about the morwhol?"

"Dead." Trap glanced up across Abramm's body as the men on his left side shifted to form a opening through which he could see. His adversary lay sprawled at the base of one of the dragon pedestals ten yards away, the dark bristly hump of its massive shoulders unmoving, the long, lithe hindquarters tangled limply beneath it.

He frowned. "How did it get so far away?"

"There was an explosion. . . . You don't remember?"

"I remember the Light . . . rushing through me." He dropped his head back. The man was binding up his injured arm with linen strips, the pain coming in ever stronger waves.

"Somehow you pulled the Light from us again," Kesrin said at Trap's side, "drawing it into yourself, then flinging it out toward the beast. It was as if lightning had struck. The force of the blast knocked us flat on our backs, and I swear they must've heard the boom all the way to Springerlan." He smiled now, too. "I would very much like to know how you did that, sir."

Abramm laughed weakly. "Just gave up trying to fight the thing myself and let Eidon do it." *And trusted him with all the things I feared to lose. As I have to trust him now about my arm.* He swallowed again and turned his gaze back to Trap. "It's really dead, though? You're sure?"

Trap grinned at him. "We're sure."

Besides his arm, the cut on his face was starting to hurt now, as well, and there were slashes on chest and hip, all burning with a fierce hot fire. He heard Channon ask the man working on his arm how it was going. "I've got it bound good enough to get him back to the keep," he said. "It'll need to be cleaned and stitched up, though I'm afraid—" Channon must've stopped him, for he said no more and turned to the other wounds on Abramm's body, surprised to find that the bleeding had largely stopped. "And the cuts on your face are already closed."

"Must've been the Light," Abramm said.

"Can it do that, sir?"

"The morwhol was shadow-spawned," Abramm replied. "And the Light can heal the wounds of the Shadow."

"Though not always entirely," Kesrin said.

"No, not entirely."

Here was Channon again. "We've got a stretcher here, sir. We'd like to move you onto it—"

"No." Abramm pushed up onto his right elbow, struggling not to let the pain show. "I already left my last encounter with my brother on a stretcher. I'm not doing it again."

"But, sir—"

"Where is Gillard anyway? Is he still alive?"

"Yes, sir. They're seeing to him now. He's not regained consciousness."

Abramm nodded. "Very well, then. Get me up. I'll ride. I don't suppose anyone's seen Warbanner?"

"Just his tail, waving good-bye," Trap quipped.

Abramm sat upright so they could bind his injured arm to his torso. Then they helped him stand, a feat he accomplished with gritted teeth and a minimum of reflexive hissing. In the process he learned the slash to his hip was worse than he'd thought. Still he *could* walk. He had taken a few tentative steps to prove it when a thunderous cheer erupted from every side. He stopped and blinked around, seeing for the first time the multitude that encircled him. Soldiers from both armies crowded the plaza, perched on ancient walls and fallen pillars and each other's shoulders, all of them grinning and cheering and waving their fists in the air. And there was Simon, holding the horse they'd brought for Abramm to ride, looking as overcome with emotion as Abramm had ever seen him.

Abramm stopped before him, half irritated, half bemused. "Uncle, what are all these men doing here? I told you to keep them away."

"I know, sir, but when I learned what Gillard was planning for you—and that Laramor and the others had gone with you—"

"Without my consent."

Simon nodded. "Nevertheless, you made me leader in your stead, and I made the decision. I do not regret having made it. The mists lifted right after Gillard fell, and we all came up to watch you fight the beast."

"So much for my hopes of keeping you safe."

His uncle grinned wryly. "We're soldiers, my lord. We're not accustomed to keeping safe. Besides, you can hardly ask us to flee, when you yourself refused." He paused, sobering. "You have made yourself a great army here today, sir. Men who will follow you through anything."

Abramm glanced again at the throng around him and, realizing he was right, relented. "I suppose I owe you my thanks, then, Uncle," he said finally, and let the older man help him into the saddle. Once settled, he looked around at the men Simon said would follow him through anything and lifted a hand in acknowledgment, which set them cheering even louder. He rode